Zyla
&
Kai

KRISTINA FOREST

ATOM

First published in the United States in 2022 by Kokila,
an imprint of Penguin Random House LLC
First published in the United Kingdom in 2022 by Atom

1 3 5 7 9 10 8 6 4 2

Design by Jasmin Rubero
Text set in Haarlemmer MT Pro

A CIP catalogue record for this book
is available from the British Library.

ISBN: 978-0-3490-0379-5

Printed and bound in Great Britain by Clays Ltd, Elcograf S.p.A.

Papers used by Atom are from well-managed forests
and other responsible sources.

MIX
Paper from
responsible sources
FSC® C104740

Atom
An imprint of
Little, Brown Book Group
Carmelite House
50 Victoria Embankment
London EC4Y 0DZ

An Hachette UK Company
www.hachette.co.uk

www.littlebrown.co.uk

For my sister-friends.

♡

This is a story about a boy and a girl ~~who fall in love~~.
This is a story about a boy and a girl ~~who run away~~.
This is a story about a boy and a girl.

Part One:
Boy Meets Girl

It is a Friday afternoon in late May at Roaring Rapids Water Park and Ski Resort in the Poconos, Pennsylvania. But it's not an *ordinary* Friday at Roaring Rapids. Today happens to be the Senior Day trip for three high schools from southern New Jersey. There is St. Catherine's Catholic School, Hopkins Preparatory School, and Cedar Regional High School. It's been overcast most of the day, with light showers erupting every hour or so, but the weather hasn't stopped the students' fun. If anything, they splash and swim in the wave pool with even more fervor. They dash to and from waterslides, dodging raindrops as if it's a game.

Overall, morale among the students is high. The school year is almost finished, and freedom is on the horizon.

Unfortunately, a big thunderstorm is on its way. And soon the park employees and school chaperones will have to herd the students back into the lodge, where they will be encouraged to participate in movie night or play board games and foosball in the lounge.

But before the storm and everything that will come after, we will focus on the activity at the ski lift. This is where we find Reggie Hodges. Reggie has been an employee at Roaring

Rapids for approximately eighteen months. He graduated high school two years ago, and he is "trying to figure things out," much to the chagrin of his parents, who think he is simply slacking and avoiding college. Is Reggie lazy? Yes, he will admit this. But he also genuinely enjoys working at Roaring Rapids, specifically operating the ski lift. Up here, it's quiet and peaceful, especially during summer, as most people stick to the water rides down below. Except on Senior Day, when groups of teens dressed in bikinis and swimming trunks wrap themselves in towels and ride the ski lift over and over again. And even though Reggie warns everyone to keep their hands and items inside of the lift at all times, occasionally someone will drop their phone, and inevitably someone will lose a flip-flop.

Still, Senior Day is usually a piece of cake for Reggie. But not this year. You see, Reggie is having a pretty bad day. A bad week, really. Nicole, his latest ex-girlfriend, dumped him four days ago because he forgot her birthday. She sees this as further evidence of his slacking nature. In the days since, Reggie has failed to win Nicole back. His stomach tightens and twists at the thought of not being with her again, so much so that he's spent most of the day feeling extremely nauseous.

So when a boy and a girl approach the ski lift at 4:17 p.m., Reggie is not in the best mood, his mind not quite as sharp. He doesn't notice that, unlike the other students, the boy and girl aren't dressed in swimwear, but normal clothes. Reggie will later learn that the boy is Kai Johnson of Cedar Regional High

School, and the girl is Zyla Matthews of St. Catherine's.

Kai is tall and stocky, and Zyla is petite and quiet. Later, Reggie will hardly remember her bright red, circular glasses. He will not remember how Kai repeatedly cleared his throat or snuck nervous glances at the girl beside him. Or how Zyla's eyes were red, as if she had been crying.

In the moment, Reggie glances at his watch, noting that it's close to 4:30 p.m., when the ski lift officially shuts down during summer.

"This is the last ride of the day," he mumbles to the pair of teens. "Please keep your hands and items inside of the lift. Please do not purposely drop anything into the woods below. There are animals who dwell on the grounds, and they would not appreciate it. Once the lift reaches the top of the mountain, stay seated. It will bring you around so that you will come back in this direction, where you will dismount on this same platform."

Reggie takes a step to escort them onto the lift, but the boy interrupts him.

"Actually, is it possible to only ride the ski lift up?" Kai asks. "Isn't there a trail you can take down the mountain back to the resort?"

Reggie blinks at Kai. No Senior Day teen has asked this question today. "Yes, there's a trail," Reggie says. "You can walk it if you want, I guess. Takes about forty-five minutes or so."

Kai nods. "Cool. That's what we'll do."

Zyla, who has been silent, glances up at the sky. "It's really cloudy," she says. Her voice is soft, low.

5

"We'll be fine," Kai responds. He reaches out and squeezes her hand. She bites her lip, but she squeezes his hand in return.

Watching them, Reggie feels a twinge of jealousy. Nicole often harped about how he didn't show her any affection. How he didn't hold her hand in public or kiss her on the cheek while standing in the grocery store checkout line. It wasn't that he didn't *want* to do those things. Participating in PDA made him feel awkward because his gangly limbs lacked the ability to move gracefully. Once, while he and Nicole were at the Laundromat, he went to put his arm around her shoulders, and he accidentally knocked her in the side of the head. She winced, he profusely apologized, and an old woman folding clothes a few feet away snickered. Reggie's face burned with embarrassment.

When Reggie looks at Kai (not yet knowing that his name is Kai or that his companion is named Zyla), he bets this kid hasn't shied away from PDA a day in his life. He moves with ease as he reaches over to zip up Zyla's backpack, letting his hand linger on her shoulder. These two probably go everywhere holding hands and stealing kisses, deeply in love. They'll see how hard things get once they're Reggie's age in a couple years, and one of them suddenly wants to break up, leaving the other gutted and alone.

Reggie continues to analyze how Kai leaves his hand placed on Zyla's shoulder, wondering why the simplicity of performing this act evades him. Then he notices they're *both* carrying backpacks. Odd. Before he can give this any more thought, his phone vibrates in his back pocket. It's Nicole. She is finally call-

6

ing him back, and suddenly that's the only thing that matters.

Reggie quickly helps Zyla and Kai onto the lift. "Be careful on the trail," he says absentmindedly as they rise higher and higher. He answers the phone and hears the reassuring sound of Nicole's voice.

After Reggie and Nicole spend an hour on the phone, crying, arguing, and deciding to meet later for dinner, Reggie goes down to the lodge to clock out and is pulled into his boss's office, where he learns that the two students who rode the ski lift, Kai and Zyla, have not returned. And somehow, this is Reggie's fault.

"I told you during your lunch break that you weren't supposed to allow anyone to walk the trail this afternoon due to the storm," his boss says, raising his bushy eyebrows. "Didn't you listen to a thing I said?"

"Uh," Reggie says. He vaguely remembers his boss approaching him while he ate his ham-and-cheese sandwich in the breakroom, but he'd been staring at his phone the whole time, willing Nicole to text him back. No, he hadn't heard a thing his boss said.

"You've got to be kidding me. Do you know what kind of trouble we can get into here, letting two kids disappear on our watch? No. *Your* watch." His boss closes his eyes and rubs his temples. "Reggie, I can't possibly keep you on after something like this."

"What?" Reggie gulps.

Suddenly, his impending reunion with Nicole doesn't seem

so sweet. Imagine what she will say once she finds out that in addition to being lazy and forgetful, Reggie is now jobless too? On cue, the nausea returns. He'll never have a chance at getting her back now.

And that is why he blurts, "Wait, I did tell them not to take the trail."

His boss pauses in the act of retrieving termination papers from his desk. He looks up at Reggie. "You told them, and they didn't listen?"

Reggie nods, and the lie rolls off his tongue. "I said they'd have to stay on the lift as it circled around, that they weren't allowed on the trail. When they didn't immediately come back, I thought maybe they stayed up on the mountain to take pictures or something. People do that sometimes before climbing back on. I waited for almost an hour. That's why I came directly to the office. To tell you that they hadn't returned. And . . . and they were wearing backpacks, which I thought was weird."

"Backpacks," his boss repeats. "Why would they need backpacks?"

Reggie shrugs, trying to come up with a possible explanation. "Maybe they were planning to run away or something. I don't know."

His boss's eyes widen. "This is not good. Not good at all. Why didn't you just say that right away? You sat here and let me go on about firing you, for goodness sake!"

Reggie smarts at being reprimanded, but there is also relief. Because his boss no longer blames him. He won't lose his job or mess up his chance at winning back Nicole. And anyway, why *did* Zyla and Kai have backpacks? It is a valid question. Maybe them running away isn't completely implausible.

Soon, the office is filled with the students' teachers and park rangers, and they want Reggie to recall every possible detail from his interaction with Zyla and Kai. What time did he see them? What was the last thing they said to him before getting on the lift? Were they behaving strangely?

Reggie squirms nervously under their scrutiny.

"It seems they went onto the trail even though they were instructed otherwise, and they were wearing backpacks," his boss interjects. "We think they might have been planning to run away."

Reggie waits for someone to ask where, exactly, they'd run away *to* if they went up a mountain. But this question never comes up. There is too much hysteria.

One of the teachers, a short white woman named Mrs. Deaver, sighs deeply. She turns to another teacher and says, "I wouldn't put it past them. Given what they've done before."

What does *that* mean? Reggie and his boss share a confused look. The entire cluster of teachers begins chattering, and the park rangers join in, asking more questions, which Reggie's boss answers. Reggie bets that the teens are okay. He thinks back to the one moment of their encounter that he can clearly recall, when Kai gently placed his hand on Zyla's shoulder. They probably just wanted some alone time without adult supervision. They'll turn up sooner or later. But Reggie would rather not wait around until that happens. It will not look good if he shows up late to his and Nicole's reunion dinner.

As he stands off to the side, waiting for his boss to dismiss him, Reggie can't help but overhear as the teachers struggle to understand what's happening or, more importantly, why. Zyla and Kai have been broken up for months. Why, exactly, would they decide to run away together now?

Reggie blinks, puzzled. Those two teens, the ones he assumed were deeply in love, are really broken up? He, too, begins to wonder what happened between them.

You see, Reggie is not alone in his assumptions about Zyla and Kai. Those closest to them have their own opinions and preconceptions about their relationship as well. And these ideas can sometimes obscure the truth.

To understand Zyla and Kai, it would be best to see what happens through their own eyes.

This is where our story begins.

THEN: Last July
Chapter One

Girls. They were going to be the death of Kai.

His girl problems always snuck up on him when he least expected them. He was standing at the Tilt-A-Whirl, working, minding his business. It was the middle of July and he was sweating so much, his silly bright orange Sailor Joe's Amusement Park polo was sticking to his back. The park was filled with kids from, like, ten different summer camps or something wild, and they wanted to ride the Tilt-A-Whirl until they made themselves sick.

Still, he had reason to be in a good mood. A *real* good mood. Tomorrow was Friday, and Kai had finally saved enough money to buy a new pair of Air Maxes, and his best friend, Jamal, had been flirting heavy with the girl who worked at the water ice stand, and she'd promised them free cups after their shift. Kai was even starting to feel a little less disappointed over the stuff that had happened with Camille last week. She'd been so cold in the way she'd dumped him *over text*, claiming that he didn't pay her enough attention. Which was bullshit. Camille was the one who'd become increasingly hard to please over the last couple months, requesting that Kai jump through hoop after hoop, and he'd done it. When had he ever failed to pay her attention?

Their three-month-long relationship had been rocky for some time, so the breakup didn't come as much of a surprise, but it sucked to be dumped nonetheless. Now it was best to just move on.

Then he heard it. The sound of someone screeching his name like a banshee.

"Hezekiah Johnson!"

His *government* name.

He turned, pulling his attention away from the spinning Tilt-A-Whirl. Kids ran through the park, swarming his vision, but somehow, he was able to spot Camille right away. She stormed toward him, scowling, with clenched fists.

The hairs rose on the back of his neck. He wasn't sure what he'd done, but he knew he must be in deep shit if Camille had bothered to abandon her ice cream stand on the other side of the park to come and find him. Her long, curly hair blew in the wind, and her golden-brown skin glowed in the summer sun. Distantly, Kai wondered why girls looked the prettiest when they were pissed.

Camille ignored the line of people waiting to ride the Tilt-A-Whirl, and she advanced toward Kai until she was crowding him, causing him to back into the operating booth.

Kai balked and eased away, attempting to put space between them. "Yo, what's good with—"

She didn't even give him a chance to finish before she poked him in the chest. "*You* flirted with Sharee Wilson in *broad day-*

light for everyone to see three days ago. Oh no, Kai, don't even try to deny it, because Tyesha was there, and she told me how you and Sharee had lunch together and you were all in her face. I bet you thought that I wouldn't find out even though I work at this park too, but I guess you forgot about that."

Camille was wrong, but Kai wasn't sure if telling her so would defuse the situation. Sharee Wilson had been more than interested in chilling the other day when they were both waiting in line to get hot dogs during their lunch break, but he hadn't really paid her any mind. He could barely remember anything that she'd said to him.

"I just have one question for you, Kai," Camille continued. "Do you know who I am?"

"What?"

"I said, do you know who I am?" she snapped.

Kai shook his head, and Camille sucked in a furious breath. "I mean, yeah, I know who you are," he said quickly. "It's just that you're wrong."

"I'm wrong?" Steam was practically coming out of her ears at this point. "How so, Kai?"

"One, I didn't flirt with Sharee Wilson. We just talked, barely. That's it. And two, why does it matter who I flirt with if we aren't together?"

"Of course we're together!"

Kai winced and cast a glance at his surroundings. The little kids waiting in line were definitely ear hustling on their conversation, staring at them with wide, intrigued eyes. Nosy as hell.

Kai needed to deescalate this situation, and fast. Camille had a temper, and she loved a scene. She was the type of person who snapped on servers at restaurants when they gave her Pepsi instead of Coke, and demanded to speak to the manager.

"Camille," he said slowly, "you broke up with me. Do you want me to pull out the text for proof?"

"What are you talking about? I didn't break up with you." She stared at him, incredulous. "I said we should *take a break*."

Kai blinked and squinted. He felt like the meme of that white lady who's confused by a math equation. "What's the difference . . . ?"

"The difference is that you can't go talking to other girls!" She was back to shrieking.

But she wasn't the only one. Behind him on the Tilt-A-Whirl, kids were shouting, "Stop the ride! Stop the ride!" A boy was puking up his lunch, and it was flying onto the kids seated beside him as the ride spun around and around.

It was the grossest shit Kai had ever seen. So gross that he stared for a stunned moment and watched in silence before he jumped into action and stopped the ride.

Suddenly, a frowning white woman with long French braids was standing right in front of Kai. Her tie-dye T-shirt read CAMP BEETLE BUZZ in bright green letters.

"You let the ride go on for too long!" she hissed. "Do you want the kids to get a concussion on this thing?"

"I'm really sorry, ma'am," Kai said, watching as the kids wobbled dizzily off the ride. Some clutched their stomachs.

The puking kid was pale in the face, like he might pass out. Kai bit his lip. "I'll walk him to the infirmary for you."

"What you need to do is worry about your job," the woman said. "Instead of flirting when a child's safety is in your hands. You clearly can't handle the responsibility."

That's when he felt it. The first prickling sensation deep in his gut. Something he hadn't experienced in a long time. He took a deep breath and willed it away.

"Ma'am—"

"Well, he doesn't have to worry about flirting with me anymore," Camille said over his shoulder, cutting him off. "Because we are done. For real this time, Kai. I should have listened to everyone when they warned me about you. Now you can add my name to your long list of exes. I'm sure you'll forget about me when you have a new girl by next week."

Kai rubbed his temples. The feeling in his gut was expanding now, traveling up his through his stomach, spreading to his neck with a heavy pulse. "Come on, Camille. Can we talk about this later, please?"

"He tried to kill us!" a little girl shouted, pointing a finger at Kai. She was a victim of the flying puke. It speckled her T-shirt.

"Look!" the camp counselor said. "You've terrified them!"

Camille sneered. "No, we definitely *cannot* talk about this later."

"Everybody, shut the fuck up!"

Kai's explosion created a shock wave of silence. Camille's eyes widened, and she stepped away from him. The woman with the French braids gasped and held a hand to her chest. Even the kids waiting in line stared, mouths gaped open.

But Kai was the most shocked of everyone. He was breathing deeply, slowly realizing that he'd lost control of the situation, of himself. Ironic that he'd been worried about Camille's temper when he should have been concerned for his own.

Damn. He hadn't messed up in so, so long. How did he let this happen?

He squeezed his eyes closed. Quietly, he said, "I'm sorry. I didn't mean to say that."

The woman shook her head, disgusted. "Oh, your boss is going to hear about this, buddy."

His boss? If she was going to tell his boss, this could get back to Aunt Brenda and Uncle Steve.

"Ma'am, wait," Kai said, his stomach sinking. The camp counselor stormed away, and Camille had the nerve to turn to Kai and smirk.

"Good luck not getting fired," she said before spinning on her heels and sauntering back toward the other side of the park.

Kai stood there, feeling stupid as hell. He should have listened to Jamal when he'd said that Camille would be trouble. Everyone had expected that Kai and Camille would get together, simply because he was the football captain and she was captain of the dance team. It was completely superficial, but the idea had intrigued Kai anyway. Camille was beautiful and intelligent. Plus, she flirted with him every chance she got. When they both found themselves single in the spring of junior year, it had seemed kind of like fate. She could be mean, true, but he'd figured there was something deeper underneath, a softer side that she only showed to people she trusted. He'd even glimpsed that side for a fleeting moment before it all ended. He never would have guessed that they'd be so wrong for each other. That she'd lead to his downfall.

It only took about five minutes for Kai's boss, Antonio, to summon him to his tiny office on the edge of the park.

"I told you about dating your coworkers, didn't I? It's nasty business. Nasty business for sure. You've gotta be smarter than that."

Kai sat on the other side of Antonio's desk, eyes on his sneakers. He knew better than to interrupt Antonio midscold. The office trailer smelled like cigarettes, even though smoking wasn't allowed on the park premises, and Antonio's desk was covered in unopened envelopes and sandwich wrappers left over from his lunch. Antonio's father had opened Sailor Joe's Amusement Park in the sixties. Apparently, at the time it had been South Jersey's biggest attraction. That is, until the Six Flags opened up in Jackson an hour away, and people found out you could take a bus to Dorney Park over in Allentown. Now Sailor Joe's was like a forgotten relic. Local summer camps brought their kids here because it was cheap, and every teen in the surrounding area applied for a summer job because they knew Antonio barely paid attention to what went on in his own park. It was why the paint on the rides was peeling, and the Sailor Joe mascot costume smelled like mold, and whoever was unlucky enough to wear it had to be prepared to make children cry all day. Sailor Joe with his chipped, dark beard and piercing, kooky eyes looked more like a terrifying pirate than your local friendly seaman. Antonio didn't care to purchase a new costume.

An employee at Sailor Joe's could get away with almost anything. Unless a customer complained to management. Then Antonio was on you like white on rice.

"Look at me, son," he said to Kai now.

Kai did as he was told. Antonio stared back at him. He scratched his overgrown beard. "You're a good kid, Hezekiah. I expect this type of behavior from the other knuckleheads I hire, but not from you. No, not from you at all."

"I'm *sorry*." Kai leaned forward, pleading. He felt sweat gathering at his armpits. He hated to disappoint people, especially any figures of authority. "Camille got under my skin, and I shouldn't have let her. I should have been paying attention to the ride. It won't happen again. I swear."

"I know it won't. Because I'm taking you off Rides."

"What?" Kai's mouth went dry. *Shit. Shit. Shit.* "Are you . . . Am I being fired?"

Antonio laughed. *Laughed.* Slapped his thighs, and his stomach heaved with every deep breath. And he wasn't letting up. He kept laughing until there were literal tears sliding down his cheeks.

Hopeless and confused, Kai could only stare. What the hell was so funny about being fired? Immediately he thought of his Morehouse College application. Would getting fired from his summer job lower his chances of acceptance? Getting into Morehouse was his number-one goal and had been for years. He couldn't let anything stand in the way of that. But more importantly, what would Aunt Brenda and Uncle Steve have to say if he lost his job today over arguing with Camille and some camp counselor?

"No, son, you aren't being fired," Antonio finally said, still chuckling. "You'd have to do a lot worse, yes, you would. Just ask Xavier Black, who got caught shoving three hundred dollars from the food court cash register into his socks last summer. No, no, you aren't being fired. I'm moving you to Games."

"Oh." Kai let out a sigh of relief. The Games section was boring, mostly because the games were corny and rigged and nobody wanted to waste their time or money, but whatever, that was cool. Kai could deal with boring. He'd be the king of boring. He'd be the best boring Games attendant in the whole freaking park. As long as he wasn't being fired, it was all good.

He relaxed. "When will I start?"

"Now. I'll walk you over to your new station, and you can stay there for the rest of your shift." Antonio stood up. "But I have to tell you that I've already spoken to your uncle Steve."

Kai froze halfway out of his seat. "Come on, Antonio. For real?"

"I hired you as a favor to your uncle, and he's a good friend of mine. He asked me to let him know if anything ever happened, so I kept my promise." Antonio walked around his desk and clapped Kai on his shoulder. "I'm going to assume this is the first and last time I'll have to call him." He motioned for Kai to follow him out of his office. "Let's take this walk. I'll bet you'll find that you prefer Games, son."

Kai nodded, his stomach twisting. He was in deep shit after all.

Chapter Two

Antonio had a slight limp and moved at a slower pace, so as he and Kai passed the food court and the entrance to the water park, Kai felt the eyes of each orange-polo-clad employee staring at him. Half of his coworkers had probably already heard about what went down earlier with Camille. No doubt the story had evolved to include some elements that weren't true. By now people were probably saying that Kai was the one who threw up and that he'd cursed at a child, not an adult. The rumor mill game at Sailor Joe's was strong.

Kai avoided making eye contact and kept his gaze forward. He was embarrassed, and that was annoying. But being annoyed was nothing compared to how he'd feel after the talk he'd have with his aunt and uncle later. He wished he could go home now and get it over with.

They finally reached the Games section and walked by the Ring Toss stand, Whac-A-Mole, and Shooting Baskets before they finally stopped at Balloon Darts. A girl was already sitting at the booth with her head down, flipping through a magazine. She was petite and brown-skinned. Her hair was parted down the middle and slicked back into a curly ponytail. She glanced up as they approached, and Kai vaguely recognized her. He'd seen her around the park wearing those same bright red, circular glasses once or twice. He couldn't remember her name, though. Zoe or Zena . . . something like that.

"Zyla," Antonio said. "What have I told you about reading those magazines while on the clock? This is a job, not leisure time, young lady."

"Sorry," she replied, sighing. She pushed her magazine aside. Kai noticed that the pages were marked with sticky notes. "It's schoolwork, and I don't have any customers."

"That's because you're too busy reading your magazine. You need to smile and look welcoming!"

She nodded, very serious. "Oh, yes, my lack of customers definitely has something to do with my smile and nothing to do with the fact that people think the games are rigged."

Kai snorted, and Zyla turned in his direction. She gave him a quick once-over, pausing on his red-and-black Retro J's before returning her gaze to his face. Something about her direct and unflinching stare made Kai stand up a little straighter. She had big hazel eyes and a thin silver septum nose ring. Her lip gloss shimmered in the sun.

Wait . . . why was he staring at her lips? Look at him, losing focus already. He glanced away, feigning fascination with the unpopped balloons on the wall behind her.

"And we agreed you wouldn't wear pins to work either," Antonio said, pointing at the cluster of small enamel pins on the collar of Zyla's polo. A tiny pair of scissors, a baby elephant, and some type of bird with its wings spread wide. "They aren't part of your uniform, Zyla."

"Sorry," she repeated. Slowly, she began removing the pins from her collar, placing them down in front of her.

"Thank you," Antonio said once she was finished. "Now, Zyla, this is Hezekiah—"

"Kai is good," Kai interrupted.

Antonio nodded and started over. "Zyla, this is Kai. He'll be working with you at this booth for the rest of summer."

"Ah," she said, sparing Kai another glance.

That was it. Just *ah*. A good *ah* or a bad *ah*? Kai had no idea. Her flat expression gave nothing away.

"Zyla will show you the ropes, son," Antonio said, patting Kai on his shoulder. "Any questions, come find me later. And Zyla, please keep that magazine out of sight."

Then Antonio ambled away (most likely itching for a cigarette break, Kai figured), and Kai and Zyla were left alone. Zyla didn't look exactly thrilled to be sharing her space with Kai, but she did remove her black mini backpack from the seat beside her in order to make room for him.

"Thanks," he said, gracefully hopping over the counter and sliding into his seat.

Zyla raised an eyebrow at his sudden display of athleticism but remained silent. She reached for her magazine and reopened it to a page of a girl wearing a fur leopard-print coat and black jeans with rips in the knees, standing on a busy city street. She grabbed a Post-it and stuck it right on the girl's jeans.

Kai wanted to ask what that was about, but he didn't want her to think he was trying to be in her business.

Instead, he leaned forward, propped his chin in the palm of his hand, and tried not to replay the scene with Camille and the camp counselor on a loop in his mind. He winced thinking about the way he'd cursed at them. Camille had been dead wrong rolling up on him in the middle of his shift with her drama, but he should have known better than to let her get him so riled up.

What would his aunt and uncle say once he got home? Sitting around anxiously for the next hour and a half was gonna kill him. At least over here, in the ghost town of the Games section, he was far away from majority of his gossiping coworkers. He half expected a tumbleweed to roll through, like in those black-and-white westerns his uncle Steve watched. The silence was broken by a group of little kids running and screaming at the top of their lungs on their way to the Ferris wheel. Soon they were followed by three boys around his age, who didn't even consider stopping to play a game. Although one boy did slow his walk as he noticed Zyla. She didn't look at him. Not even when he called out, "Yo, girl, what's up?" only to move on, frustrated, when she failed to respond.

Kai glanced at his coworker, who continued to flip through her magazine, scrutinizing each page. Was it gonna be like this for the rest of summer? Her ignoring him and basically the world while he stared at people who avoided Games like they'd catch scabies if they came any closer?

Wasn't Zyla supposed to be showing him the ropes? For real

for real, he didn't care to learn the rules of Balloon Darts. But it wasn't in his nature to sit *right next to* someone and not talk at all.

"So . . ." he started.

Zyla looked up and waited for him to finish his sentence. Problem was he didn't really know what else to say, especially not with the way she stared at him. Like she was expecting him to say Something Important. He cleared this throat. "What's with the Post-it notes?"

Suddenly, she shifted to block her magazine from his view and squinted at him. "Why?"

"Why?" he repeated. "I don't know. Just was curious. You don't have to tell me."

"I know I don't have to tell you."

O-kay. So now he knew not to ask Zyla any questions. *That's exactly what you get for bothering her.*

He turned away and sat with his eyes closed, willing the time to move quickly.

"I flag any outfits that I find interesting," Zyla said after a long pause. Kai looked at her out of the corner of his eye, hesitant to turn completely in her direction in case she shut him down again. "It really is schoolwork. I wasn't lying."

Kai turned fully, taking in the enamel pins that she'd refastened onto her collar and the wide-legged tan pants she wore instead of the standard khaki shorts. The white Stan Smiths on her feet.

"You like fashion?" he asked.

"Something like that." She returned her attention to her magazine.

And the conversation ended that fast. Well, at least he'd tried. It was going to be a *long* summer.

"So what did you do?" Zyla suddenly asked. She was looking at him again.

Kai blinked. "Huh?"

"Antonio put you in Rides because that's the most popular area and you're a popular person. You must have done something bad if he put you back here in Games. It's the designated area for antisocial people like me. Less customer interaction."

So the rumor mill hadn't reached her yet. Kai weighed what to share. They'd just met, and he didn't want her thinking poorly of him. That he was a player or some disrespectful kid who yelled at adults and made children puke, and—wait a minute...

"You already knew who I was before Antonio introduced us?" Kai asked.

"Of course I know who you are," she said, shrugging as she closed her magazine and stuffed it in her backpack. "Kai Johnson, star athlete of the county with a public Instagram account. Who doesn't know you?"

Kai couldn't help but smile. This girl, who seemingly couldn't be bothered in the slightest, knew who he was.

"Do you go to Cedar High?" he asked. He didn't think she did. Cedar High was a big school, but Kai liked to think that he'd be smart enough to remember someone like her.

"No. I go to St. Catherine's."

"Oh, right." The girls' school. Three of Kai's exes went to St. Catherine's. He'd dated Gianna during the spring of his freshman year. Then the winter of sophomore year brought Desiree and Corinne, whom he'd dated back to back. He'd actually met Corinne at Desiree's birthday party . . .

"I'm not rich," Zyla said.

Kai blinked again. "What?"

"Whenever I tell people I go to St. Catherine's, they assume I'm rich. But I'm not. My great-aunt has money, and she pays for me to go to St. Catherine's because she feels bad for me."

"Oh." He wasn't sure what he was supposed to do with this information. Zyla had a pinched look on her face, like she regretted revealing so much. She swiveled in her seat and stared pointedly at the bottle stand game across the way.

"Well, how much money does your aunt have?" Kai asked. "Because I've been trying to transfer to St. Catherine's for years, but they won't take me for some reason. You think she'll pay for me?"

Zyla laughed then. It was really more like a glorified snort, but her whole face lit up, and when she turned to Kai and smiled, displaying the small gap between her two front teeth, he realized that Zyla was strikingly beautiful. And he was relieved that he'd managed to make her laugh. He wanted to know what he had to do to keep her smiling at him this way.

He nodded at her backpack. "Can I take a look at your

magazine? I'm into fashion too. Might be able to give you some pointers."

She rolled her eyes and laughed again. Kai felt like Super Mario collecting gold coins.

"You don't look like you're into fashion, Kai Johnson," she said, sizing him up.

"Come on, this is my work uniform. You don't know how I dress in real life." He pointed at his sneakers. "These are proof."

"Those are nice J's," she conceded. "I'm not a sneakerhead, but I can appreciate the dedication."

"Your sneakers are fresh too, though, so I guess you know a little something."

"Oh, wonderful. Thanks, Kai Johnson. All I've ever wanted in life is your approval."

Kai grinned. "Why do you keep saying my full name like that?"

"I don't know. I just do. Rolls off the tongue. *Kai Johnson*."

Something bloomed in Kai's chest at the slow way she said his name. He stared at her and she stared back. He felt himself leaning forward, needing to be physically closer to her, which made no sense because he was literally *just* reamed out by his now ex-girlfriend to the point that he almost got himself fired, and Antonio *just* lectured him on cooling it with dating coworkers. Yet here he was moving closer to this girl because he could not freaking help it.

He lowered his voice and looked right into Zyla's hazel eyes. "What's *your* last name?"

28

Zyla paused and blinked, taking in the sudden lack of space between them. Then she smirked a little and leaned closer too, conspiratorially, like her last name was top-secret information that could only be shared if whispered. Kai waited, staring at her mouth. She cleared her throat.

"'Sup, kids?" Kai's best friend, Jamal, appeared out of fuck-knows-where and smacked his hand down onto the booth, causing both Kai and Zyla to jump back. He smiled at Zyla and brought out his hairbrush, smoothing it over his waves. "How you like your new coworker here, Matthews?"

Matthews. Zyla Matthews. Kai smiled triumphantly. Super Mario almost had all his coins and was seconds away from rescuing Princess Peach.

Zyla leaned away from Kai to turn in Jamal's direction. "He's okay, I guess," she said.

"He's silly is what he is." Jamal sighed. Unlike the rest of the Sailor Joe's employees, he wore a white polo and a name tag that said JAMAL SMITH: INTERN. It was bullshit, of course. Antonio didn't need an intern, but Jamal, who basically had *finesse* tattooed on his forehead, somehow managed to convince Antonio to not only hire him but give him the title of intern so that he could say he spent the summer managing a group of his peers. In reality, he walked through the park trying to talk to girls all day. Occasionally, he did help Antonio with his accounting. Despite his overall dislike for school, Jamal was really good at math.

To Kai, he said, "Didn't I tell you Camille wasn't worth it? But nah, you just *had* to have her. Now look at the shit she caused.

You know she's going around telling people she got you fired?"

Kai shot Jamal a look as Zyla shifted farther away. "Yeah, well, we're broken up now, and have been for almost a week, so . . ."

He raised an eyebrow, signaling to Jamal that he was ruining his game, but Jamal didn't catch it. He just kept on going.

"I mean, you should have seen this coming after that time she convinced you to buy those Jhené Aiko tickets and then bailed on you at the last minute. I hope you don't think she's the perfect girl now, Loverboy."

At this, Zyla pivoted completely forward so that Kai could only see her side profile. Those last few coins slipped right through Super Mario's fingers.

But Kai was wrong anyway, now that he thought about it. Zyla was no Princess Peach. She definitely did not give off damsel in distress vibes.

"Come on, bro," Kai said quietly to Jamal. It wasn't just that his game was completely blown. Jamal knew how much Kai hated the nickname Loverboy. He'd come up with it back in middle school when Kai got his first girlfriend. Loverboy sounded like the name of a corny eighties soft rock band that no one listened to anymore. And anyway, deep down, Kai knew he wasn't a lover boy, but a hopeless romantic. At least that's what his aunt Brenda had told him. He wouldn't admit any shit like that out loud, though.

"What?" Jamal shrugged, confused by Kai's frustration. Then Kai discreetly nodded his head at Zyla, and Jamal said, "Oh."

Zyla wasn't paying either of them any attention at this point. She had her phone out, scrolling.

"Anyway," Jamal said, "I came here to let you know that business is slow today and Antonio needs to make cuts, so you both can go home early."

Zyla suddenly rejoined the conversation and smiled. "Seriously? *Yes.*"

"Really?" Jamal said, surprised. "I thought you'd be mad about losing hours."

"Usually I would. But not today. I have stuff to work on."

She hopped up and swung on her backpack, lifting the latch on the booth door. Kai hastened to follow behind her. Maybe if they walked to the parking lot together, he'd have a chance to do some damage control for the things Jamal had said about Camille. He didn't know why, but he cared about how Zyla saw him.

And yeah, he was gonna walk her to her car and then ask for her number.

Jamal smiled at Kai and shook his head a little. "Bet you're happy to be going home now, Matthews. How's Jade liking math camp? You think she's smarter than me yet?"

Zyla snorted. "She's been smarter than you."

"Damn, that's cold. She's what, twelve?"

"Eleven."

"Wow, wow, wow. Ice-cold, Matthews."

Zyla laughed, and Kai watched them, raising an eyebrow. They knew each other. And that made him jealous. Not because they were clearly friends and Jamal had made her laugh. Jamal was friends with everyone and made everyone laugh. Kai was jealous because Jamal had known Zyla the whole summer, and Kai had really just become aware of her today.

"Well, I've gotta go be professional and whatnot, so I'll see you around," Jamal said, backing away. "Kai, I'll hit you up later."

The two of them were left alone again. Kai gestured for Zyla to walk ahead of him. "Ready to clock out?"

She nodded, eyeing him in that curious way. They walked without speaking. Zyla was short and curvy. She didn't even reach his shoulder. Kai was pretty built thanks to football, and he felt slightly massive walking beside her. He kept trying to think of something to say. He was good at small talk, but he got the feeling that Zyla was comfortable with silence. He usually wasn't, but he could be.

Antonio was MIA when they walked into the office to clock out, and Kai was glad that he'd avoided another lecture. When he and Zyla reached the parking lot, she paused on the sidewalk.

"I don't have a car," she explained.

This was low-key perfect. "Oh, do you need a ride?"

"No, my mom will be here soon. But thank you."

Damn. "Sure, no problem." He stuffed his hands in his pockets. "It was nice to meet you today. I think I might like Games better than Rides thanks to you."

She smirked. "It was nice to meet you too."

"Random, but do you like that actress Evie Jones? She's in a new movie that comes out tomorrow. I forget what it's called."

"Every Time We Meet," Zyla said. "It's a remake."

"Right, right. I was thinking about going." He watched her face. Was she picking up what he was putting down?

"Cool. I've heard good things."

Apparently not. He'd have to try harder.

"Hey," he said, "I don't know if you have plans tomorrow night, but I think it might be dope if—"

"I'm going to stop you right there, Kai Johnson," Zyla said, holding up her hand. "It *was* nice to meet you today, and I think you and I will get along just fine at our deserted Balloon Darts booth, but I want to save you some time and tell you that nothing is going to happen between us."

Kai blinked. Wow. Shut down in five seconds flat. A record.

It sucked to be rejected, and he'd probably agonize over it later, but for now he had to save face. Plus, he respected her straightforwardness. He took a deep breath and stuck out his hand. "Fair enough. Friends?"

"Friends." Zyla shook his hand in two quick pumps and then let go. "See you tomorrow."

He walked to his black Jeep, which had been passed down from his uncle, and glanced over his shoulder once to wave goodbye. Zyla stood on the sidewalk and lifted her hand. Friends. He could do that. He had extra room in his life for new friends. Maybe it wasn't such a bad thing that she'd turned him down. Maybe it was just the universe's way of telling him to chill the fuck out on the girls front.

He blasted 21 Savage on the way home, and when he turned

onto his street, dread sprouted in his stomach and spread throughout his body. Aunt Brenda's and Uncle Steve's cars were both in the driveway. Today's earlier events came rushing back to him. He'd have to talk to his aunt and uncle about what had happened at work as soon as he walked in the house.

But then Kai got closer and realized the situation was even worse. Uncle Steve was sitting on the front porch, reading his newspaper. He lowered it and noticed Kai crawling down the street, and he folded the paper and put it aside. He'd been waiting for Kai. *Shit.*

His stomach dropped as he pulled into the driveway and watched Uncle Steve rise from his chair. Uncle Steve had the same look on his face that he'd worn in those early days when Kai couldn't stay out of the principal's office or when he'd been pulled off the field in the middle of a game for starting a fight. The look that said, *You're in trouble again?* That look was his biggest fear. These were the moments when Kai felt the most alone and misunderstood.

After everything his aunt and uncle had done for him, Kai's only desire was to make them proud. He *needed* to make them proud so that the sacrifices they'd made for him weren't wasted. It was all he'd been trying to do since he'd turned himself around.

He slowly got out of his car and made his way to the porch steps to meet his doom. He heard his mother's voice in his ear then. *It's gonna be okay, Hezekiah, baby.* He clung to that as Uncle Steve clapped him on the shoulder and led him inside.

Chapter Three

If you would have told Zyla this morning that not only would she have a full-blown conversation with Kai Johnson, but that he'd flirt with her *and* ask her out within a sixty-minute time span, she would have told you to lay off the bath salts.

But he *did* flirt with her, at least that was what it seemed like with the way he'd stared so deeply into her eyes, like he'd been trying to solve the puzzle that was her mind. And he'd definitely been gearing up to ask her out before she'd cut him off.

She watched as his Jeep pulled out of the parking lot, and she held her backpack to her chest, mystified. Like . . . it was *Kai Johnson*. He'd dated at least a quarter of the girls in her year at St. Catherine's, and on Cedar High's game days, girls showed up with his number painted on their cheeks even though he didn't even go to their school! Okay, so a quarter of the girls was a bit of an exaggeration. But nevertheless, it was absolutely bonkers, and Zyla had thought her classmates were delusional. But she had to be honest, she understood it now. Kai Johnson was disarming. It wasn't just that he was handsome with his smooth brown skin and bright white teeth (what, was he like a model or something in a former life?) but from the way Kai strutted around Sailor Joe's all summer, and from the stories she'd heard from her classmates and coworkers, Zyla had expected him to be a bit of a jerk or stuck up. The kind of boy who commanded attention and was annoyed when he didn't receive it. But he seemed . . . normal? Whatever that meant. He was chill. More than that, he was kind of funny. And flirtatious, but that wasn't surprising.

She'd completely embarrassed herself, blabbering on about how Aunt Ida paid for her to go to St. Catherine's. She didn't want Kai thinking she was a spoiled and rich private-school girl like so many of her classmates. She'd felt a buzz in her gut when he'd looked at her so closely and asked for her last name. There'd been some kind of gravitational pull that had made her move closer to him, but thankfully Jamal had appeared and broken the spell. Zyla meant what she said. Nothing was going to happen between her and Kai. It wasn't because he'd recently been dumped by Camille Vaughn—the most popular, most beautiful, and meanest girl at Sailor Joe's—and it was kind of sketchy that he was moving on so quickly. It wasn't that he and Camille had a big blow-up scene that eventually landed him in Games (yeah, she'd heard about that incident even though she'd pretended otherwise). And it wasn't that Kai had dated way too many of her mutuals or was a known player. Zyla just didn't date, period.

Now she and Kai would be working together, and they'd agreed to be *friends*. Go figure. At least it would make the rest of her summer more interesting. She couldn't wait to call her best friend, Beatrice, and tell her about this later. She would have preferred to tell her in person, but Beatrice was spending the summer in Paris with her dad.

The whole Kai Johnson thing had Zyla in a daze for a good fifteen minutes before a school bus pulled up directly in front of her and she was almost trampled by a summer camp stampede. She darted aside, almost tripping over a kid in the process, and pulled out her phone. No response from her mom, who should have been here to pick her up by now. Typical.

Antonio wasn't surprised to see Zyla when she walked into his office unannounced. He was sitting at his desk, working on a Sudoku puzzle, an unlit cigarette hanging out the side of his mouth. He glanced up at Zyla and raised an eyebrow.

"She's late," Zyla explained, pulling out the chair across from him and plopping down.

"Ah." He held up his puzzle book. "You finished yesterday's in almost ten minutes. Want to try a harder one?"

"No thanks." Instead, she retrieved her magazine and flipped through the pages she'd marked today, the editorials that she'd return to for inspiration when necessary. She was itching to get home and work on her portfolio. Or maybe finish the black denim jumper she'd started two weeks ago. Her free time was already limited as it was, between her job, and looking after Jade, and taking care of Aunt Ida, and doing things most seventeen-year-olds didn't have to be bothered with. She wished for a few spare minutes to look over her designs before she had to help with dinner. Why couldn't her mom just be on time for once?

It wouldn't be like this forever, though. By this time next year, she'd be gone. *Gone*, gone. Like in a different country, on a different continent, completely separate from everyone in her life, and able to live on her own terms. It was the only thing she wanted.

"How did Hezekiah do today?"

Zyla pulled her attention away from the Gap ad she'd marked earlier of a Black girl with cornrows wearing an oversized bomber jacket and looked up at Antonio. "Who?"

"Sorry, I mean Kai. I've known him since he was a kid, you see. When he first moved in his with uncle. That's why I call him Hezekiah."

"Oh." She pictured Kai's warm brown eyes and the way he'd smiled at her right before he almost invited her to the movies. *Ugh, get ahold of yourself.* She cleared her throat. "He was fine, I guess. Not much action happens at Balloon Darts, you know. It's not like he had to talk to any customers."

"I placed him with you for a reason, Zyla. I did. It was *strategic*, it was." Antonio moved his hands around as if he were speaking about particles in the atmosphere. "I believe that you're an exceptional young lady, Zyla, and I see lots of potential in you. I see potential in Hezekiah too. He's just so easily distracted. My hope is that maybe some of your ability to be focused, with the exception of your magazine reading, will rub off on him."

"Oh," she said again. Kai was easily distracted? By what?

The second she began to ask, her phone vibrated loudly on

Antonio's desk. It was a text from her mom. I'm here.

She sighed and stood up. "My mom's outside. Thanks for letting me hang out here. Again."

Antonio nodded at her. "Tell your aunt Ida I said hello. And remember to leave the magazine at home tomorrow, please."

Zyla smiled and saluted Antonio, who only shook his head. They both knew she'd return with a new magazine, or possibly her sketchbook.

"Got it, boss," she said.

Zyla's mom was in the middle of wiping her eyes when Zyla opened the door and sat in the passenger seat.

"I'm sorry, baby," her mom said, using the review mirror to fix her eyeliner, which had smeared. "Keith and I got into a big argument." *Sniffle, cough, sniffle.* "I got a little caught up."

"Okay." Zyla buckled her seat belt as her mom pulled out of the parking lot and into traffic. Zyla stared at the license plate of the car in front of them and waited. Her mom didn't need much prompting to continue talking. She rarely did.

"He broke up with me," her mom said. "Can you believe that? After three months, all he had to say was, 'It's just not working.' Apparently, he didn't see himself getting married to me."

Zyla sighed inwardly and remained silent. Her mom reached forward and turned up the radio. Whitney Houston's "Heartbreak Hotel" blared through the speakers, and her mom began to sing along, loudly and off key. Through it all, Zyla continued to stare straight ahead. She'd read once that dolphins stopped behaving badly when their trainers ignored said bad behavior. Her mom wasn't a dolphin, but Zyla was desperate enough to try anything.

They reached a stoplight, and the song changed to "Back at One," by Brian McKnight.

"Keith loves this song," her mom mumbled, lips trembling.

Then she finally lost it. In a loud whimper, she began crying. Ugly crying. Snot dripping, mascara running, blotchy-cheeks-type crying. All while Brian McKnight sang about his girl who was a dream come true.

Zyla's resolve began to waver. Her heart squeezed watching her mom like this. "Mommy . . ."

"I just don't get it." Her mom leaned her forehead against the steering wheel, and her shoulders shook as she sobbed. "What's wrong with me?"

"Nothing. They're idiots. You know that." Zyla reached forward and rubbed her mom's back in small circles. "Forget Keith. He doesn't deserve you."

"But I love him. I really, really do."

Zyla closed her eyes and tried not to think of the other times her mom had said these same words to her about previous partners. "You'll get over him, Mom. You're strong and you can do better."

The car behind them honked as the light turned green. Zyla's mom didn't make a move to put her foot on the gas. Her head remained leaning against the wheel. The car honked even longer.

"Mom, it's a green light."

"I can't drive like this," she groaned. "I can't."

The drivers around them were becoming more insistent with their honking. Zyla was pretty sure she'd heard someone shout at them just now.

Calmly, she said, "Mom, just pull over and we'll switch, okay? I'll drive home, and you can sit in the passenger seat and relax. How's that sound?"

Her mom sniffled. "That sounds good."

"I think it sounds good too. Just pull over up ahead."

Zyla coaxed her mom to sit up and drive until she was able to pull off to the side of the road. Then she got out of the car and walked around the front while her mom crawled across the center console until she was curled up in a ball in the passenger seat. Her orange sundress pooled around her feet.

As Zyla drove the rest of the way, her mom continued to cry quietly. Her cheeks and nose were bright red now. Zyla's mom was Black, but she was so fair-skinned that people thought she was white when she wore her auburn hair straight. "Your mom's a white lady?" was a question that kids frequently had asked Zyla when she was younger. That was back when they'd lived in Kissimmee, Florida, mere miles from Disney World, the happiest place on earth. Ironic that those had been the saddest years of Zyla's life.

She kept shooting glances at her mom to make sure she was holding herself intact. And she went back and forth between pity and anger. Pity that her mom's heart was broken once again. And anger at her mom and on her mom's behalf for that same reason.

She pulled into their driveway and cut the engine. She stared at their house—Aunt Ida's house. It still didn't feel like a space that belonged to them, even though Aunt Ida tried to say otherwise.

"Mom, we're home," Zyla said, gently rubbing her mom's shoulder.

Her mom looked up and glanced at the house in confusion. Then she blinked. "Oh. That was fast." She turned to Zyla. "Thanks, babe."

Zyla shrugged, feigning nonchalance, pulled the keys out of the ignition, and grabbed her bag. Before she could open her door, her mom reached for her and hugged her close to her chest. Zyla wanted to resist, to tell her mom that she wouldn't be around forever to pick up the pieces. That the pieces fell apart too often. But she inhaled her mom's familiar scent: burnt hair and cosmetic spray from the salon where she worked. She looked into her mom's hazel eyes and couldn't bring herself to say the things that she felt.

Finally, her mom pulled away and held her hand to Zyla's cheek. "I'm blessed to have you for a daughter."

Suddenly desperate to hold on to this moment, Zyla said, "Mom, promise me you won't call Keith again. You always talk about how you should take a break and focus on yourself. Maybe you should try that this time."

Her mom frowned slowly. "Don't involve yourself in grown

folks' business, Zy." She pushed open her car door and got out, not even giving Zyla a chance to respond.

By the time Zyla stepped inside the house, her mom was already rushing upstairs to her bedroom, shutting the door behind her.

Zyla sighed. *Great.* She was handling dinner by herself tonight, then.

"Leanne?" Aunt Ida called after Zyla's mom. She was sitting in her La-Z-Boy, wrapped in her fuzzy light pink robe and matching slippers, watching *Wheel of Fortune.* Her old Boston terrier, Bartholomew, who was blind in one eye, barked at the sudden ruckus. Aunt Ida nudged him with her foot until he quieted. "Stop with that noise, boy." She looked at Zyla. "What's wrong with Leanne?"

"Keith broke up with her," Zyla explained, sliding off her sneakers.

"Hmph. And which one was he?"

"Doesn't matter. I'm gonna start dinner. Chicken Alfredo okay with you?"

Aunt Ida nodded. "But make sure you add oil to the water while it's boiling, otherwise the noodles will stick together. Matter of fact, just give me a second. I'll help you." She started to stand but quickly winced. She had arthritis in her knees.

"It's fine, I can take care of it," Zyla quickly said, rushing toward Aunt Ida and helping her ease back into her chair. "Oil in the water. I'll remember."

Before Aunt Ida could try to protest, Zyla hurried away into

43

the kitchen. Her little sister, Jade, was already sitting at the table, a math workbook open in front of her.

"Is Mommy okay?" Jade asked, turning around to face Zyla. Their mom had cornrowed Jade's hair and added bright pink and purple beads to the ends that rattled with each movement of her head.

"She's fine. Just had a bad day." Zyla walked over and hugged Jade sideways. She glanced down at the equation Jade was working on and felt her eyes blur for a second. Was she embarrassed that her eleven-year-old sister was exponentially smarter than her when it came to math? No. She was extremely proud, really. Jade had qualified for a scholarship for a special program for students gifted in mathematics. It was one of the hardest summer programs to get into in New Jersey. Her baby sister would make history one day. She'd probably help send people to the moon. "How was camp?"

"Good. I don't want it to end."

All good things come to an end. Zyla wanted to say this. She often felt torn between being realistic with Jade and letting her believe that the world was a simple and easy place. But Jade was eleven. She deserved the freedom to be ignorant. The freedom Zyla never had.

"There's three more weeks left of camp, kiddo," Zyla said. "That's basically a lifetime."

Their mom didn't join them for dinner. After Zyla, Jade, and Aunt Ida finished eating, Zyla sent Jade upstairs to shower, and she stayed behind to wash dishes. Aunt Ida refused to buy a dishwasher when there were people in the house with working hands and arms.

While Zyla scrubbed the pasta bowl, Aunt Ida sat at the kitchen table, chewing sunflower seeds with her dentures. Bartholomew snored at her feet.

"Don't be like her," Aunt Ida suddenly said.

Zyla didn't need to ask which *her* Aunt Ida was referring to.

"I gave Leanne everything that I'm giving to you right now, and she threw it away," Aunt Ida continued. "She's been up there crying all night over another fool. Don't be like her."

Zyla kept her back to her great-aunt. She *knew* she didn't want to be like her mom. But it was only okay when *she* said it.

"Men are good for nothing, and they'll run you into the ground. Your uncle Herald left me his money and this house, but he was good for nothing. A liar and a cheat. Your father is the same way. Steer clear of men like that. You hear?"

This was a speech that Zyla heard often. She could almost recite it word for word. Her favorite part was the way Aunt Ida said *your father*, like she wouldn't ever demean herself to say Zyla's dad's actual name.

"You hear what I'm saying to you, Zyla?"

Zyla finished drying her last dish and placed it on the rack. She turned around to face Aunt Ida, who stared at her expectantly. Aunt Ida's brown skin was wrinkled, and her hair was coily and white. She was much older now, but Zyla saw traces of the nineteen-year-old who'd eagerly married the boy she'd met in the youth group choir. The proof was in their wedding photo, which hung on the kitchen wall right behind Aunt Ida's head. Zyla stared at it, wondering if Aunt Ida had any idea at that time just how much of a liar and a cheat her husband would eventually become.

"I hear you," she finally said. "I'm going up to my room. Let me know if you need anything." She felt Aunt Ida's eyes on her as she left the kitchen.

Zyla's mom was locked away in her bedroom. Zyla was tempted to lean her ear against the door to make sure her mom was okay, but she was still mad at her and didn't feel ready to talk yet, so she continued down the hall and peeked in on Jade, who was lying on her bed, working on more math problems. Zyla smiled at her sister and finally made it to her own room, which was an organized mess. It was the first room she'd ever had to herself. Before they moved in with Aunt Ida, Zyla had to share a room, and sometimes a bed, with Jade.

Her shoes, which she'd carefully thrifted or bargain bought, with the exception of her new Stan Smiths, lined the floor in rows. Yards of fabric were thrown over her desk chair and desk beside her sewing machine, and the denim jumper she was currently working on was draped over her mannequin torso. Magazines filled with her Post-it notes were stacked in piles by her bed.

She turned on some Jorja Smith, pulled today's magazine out of her bag, and sat down on her floor, flipping to the Gap ad of the girl with cornrows. She grabbed her scissors and carefully cut out the ad image, adding it to the binder where she kept her mood board photos for her portfolio. She hadn't settled on her portfolio theme yet, but it was going to have something to do with the beauty and versatility of Black women and how that played into fashion. She'd figure it out by the time she needed to send her portfolio to Parsons Paris and the London College of Fashion. Going to school abroad would be expensive, of course, but Zyla had been saving up with the money she made at Sailor Joe's, and part-time during the school year, she earned extra cash answering the phone and scheduling appointments at the salon where her mom worked. In addition to the loans and scholarships she planned to apply for, the biggest help would come from Aunt Ida, who'd promised to pay a large chunk of her tuition with some of Uncle Herald's money. He might not have been a good husband, but he'd made a lot of smart investments while he was alive, and now Zyla could reap the benefits.

She paused and closed her eyes, imagining her future life in Europe. In between her classes, she'd have lunch outside at fancy cafés and . . . wait a minute, was that Kai Johnson smiling and sitting directly across from her in her imaginary Parisian café? *No, no, no.* He had no place in her European fashion school daydreams. *What the heck?*

It was stupid anyway. Kai had probably already forgotten about her by now. She bet he was out at a party, most likely making up with Camille Vaughn.

A knock at her door broke her treacherous train of thought.

It was her mom. She poked her head inside. "Hey, baby, you busy?"

Zyla looked down at the binder in her lap. Yes, she was busy. Clearly. She looked back up at her mom and said nothing.

Her mom gingerly stepped inside the room. Her hair was wrapped in a silk scarf, and she was already dressed in her pajamas even though it was only 8:00 p.m.

"I wanted to apologize for earlier," she said quietly. "For how I behaved in the car. The crying, getting mad at you. All of it."

"Okay."

"And thank you for taking care of dinner."

Zyla nodded, feeling both sympathetic and frustrated. She wanted to ask if her mom had called Keith, but she was afraid to know the answer. Her mom lingered in her doorway and looked around the room. She pointed at the denim jumper on the mannequin. "Hey, how's that coming along? Want me to try it on?"

No, go away. It was on the tip of her tongue. But Zyla had created the jumper with her mom in mind. Her mom was her first-ever model, back when she was in middle school and they'd had to make their own clothes because they didn't have enough money to go shopping. Many things had changed since then, but Zyla still thought her mom was the epitome of beauty.

"Yes," Zyla said, standing up. She helped her mom into the jumper, and she knelt down in front her, pinning the fabric on either side of her waist. It needed to be taken in a few inches.

Her mom ran her hand over Zyla's head. "Have you thought

about how you want me to do your hair for back-to-school?"

Zyla shrugged and tried to talk around the pins in her mouth. "Box braids, I guess. Something easy."

"We can do that," her mom replied.

She began to hum softly. "The Sweetest Taboo," by Sade. Sitting in front of her mom as she hummed and rubbed her head made Zyla feel like a kid again. Even though she was only seventeen years old, Zyla hadn't felt like a kid in a very long time. This was because three things happened to her in quick succession at the young age of eight.

The first thing: Her parents got divorced. They were living in Miami at the time, and Zyla hadn't really understood what had happened. Just that her dad was moving out, and she wouldn't see him every day anymore. He'd kissed her on the cheek in the courthouse hallway and promised he'd come visit that weekend. Then he'd kissed a crying and fussy two-year-old Jade and promptly left. On his way out, Zyla heard him say, clear as day, that he wouldn't bother with this "marriage crap" ever again.

Zyla's mom had decided that ice cream would cure everything, so she drove them to a parlor near the courthouse. And after her mom ordered three cones of rocky road and sat herself down on the bench with her two daughters, she burst into tears and let her ice cream cone fall right out of her hands. Alarmed, Zyla watched as her mom's sobs became deeper, how her body began to shake. Soon Jade was crying too, and she dropped her cone and it smeared her pretty little dress and landed in a heap on the ground, melting into the sidewalk.

Completely out of her depth, Zyla tried her best to console her mom and her baby sister. She was so overwhelmed that she felt like crying too, but somehow, she knew that would only make things worse.

After a few moments, her mom finally got herself together and began bouncing Jade on her knee.

"I swear I'm never doing this again," she promised. "I need to focus on me. And you girls."

Zyla nodded, trying to offer what little encouragement she could. "You'll be okay, Mommy." Her mom smiled at her then and pulled her close. Holding both of her girls to her body.

The second thing: Her mom broke that promise to herself. Three weeks later, she was dating one of her coworkers from Pete's Groceries, a younger guy named Allen or Albert. And when they inevitably broke up, Zyla's mom was sobbing once again, curled up in a ball on the couch, as if the world were ending. She went on like that for a week. It was then that Zyla learned how to boil noodles and heat up frozen dinners. She also learned how to properly coax her mom to eat, take showers, and remind her when she needed to be dropped off at school.

Then there was the third thing: Only a few months after his divorce from her mother, Zyla's dad was engaged. Zyla and Jade were forced to sit at Applebee's with him and his new fiancée, Renee, as they broke the news. Zyla tried her best to keep Jade entertained while her dad and Renee argued about what appetizers to order. Zyla watched them fiercely bicker over something so small. She wasn't surprised when they were divorced after only five months.

She wondered why they even got married in the first place. And she wondered why her mom willingly set herself up for failure and heartbreak time and time again.

What was wrong with these people? Her parents. The people who had made her.

She thought of this now as she looked up at her mom's face, swollen from crying over Keith earlier tonight. She thought of Aunt Ida downstairs in the kitchen, so bitter even years after her husband had died. And please. Don't even get her started on her dad.

Zyla wasn't going to be like them. She'd known better since she was eight years old. She wasn't going to make the mistake of falling in love.

Chapter Four

Kai was suspicious. Last night when he got home from work, his uncle Steve and aunt Brenda didn't lecture him like he'd expected. He wasn't grounded. His car privileges weren't revoked. There were no long talks about his blowup at work, and Aunt Brenda didn't end the night in tears, begging Kai to try harder, like back in the old days. No one suggested calling Dr. Rueben, who Kai would already have to see in a few days for his weekly appointment anyway, so, really, what would be the point of that?

Instead, Uncle Steve led Kai inside. He simply asked, "Bad day?" Kai nodded, waiting for retribution that didn't come.

What was happening? It made no sense, and he didn't trust it.

He continued not to trust it the next morning as he sat at the kitchen table, dressed in his Sailor Joe's polo, a bowl of Froot Loops in front of him.

Aunt Brenda sat across from Kai and sipped gingerly from her coffee mug. Her thick, dark hair was pulled back in a tight bun at the nape of her neck. She wore a sleeveless white button-up and blue jeans. She was an English professor at UPenn during the school year, and she spent her summers teaching classes at the local community college. Soon she'd be out the door, on her way to work.

Kai bounced his knee and watched her as he scooped another spoonful of cereal. When he first moved here almost nine years ago after his parents died, seeing Aunt Brenda's large brown eyes and friendly smile reminded him so much of his mom, he'd lock himself in his room just so that he wouldn't have to look at her. It made him too sad. They'd been fraternal twins. Were still fraternal twins? Kai didn't know the right way to phrase it. Was his aunt considered a twin now that her twin was dead? Sometimes, he wondered if being an orphan meant he was no longer someone's son. Maybe that was a question for Dr. Rueben.

Aunt Brenda looked up and caught Kai's eye. She smirked. "Are you going to keep bouncing that knee of yours or are you going to tell me what's on your mind?"

Kai stilled, his spoon halfway to his mouth. Despite his nervousness, he felt himself smile. Nowadays, his aunt read him so easily.

"You and Uncle Steve didn't bring up what happened at work yesterday," he said slowly. He paused, not wanting to shoot himself in the foot. But they'd agreed long ago to speak to each other with complete honesty, so he pressed on. "I guess I'm just surprised that you guys don't care about it."

"Who says we don't care?"

Well, there went that bullet going right through his foot. "Oh."

"Your uncle and I are going to have a talk with you once he gets downstairs."

"Cool." Kai took a deep breath and nodded.

Shit. They were probably taking something away. That's what they used to do when he misbehaved in middle school. He'd go two days without his comic books and NBA 2K, and that would straighten him right out. But what could they take now? His car? He fingered the keys in his pocket. He should probably look up the bus schedule. He might have already missed the one that went toward Sailor Joe's this morning, which meant he was probably gonna be late to work. He was already on thin ice with Antonio. He might take him out of Games and put him on janitorial duty. Or worse, make him wear the Sailor Joe's costume. Nah, he wouldn't do that, right? It would be a new level of cruel.

Or maybe it would be the TV in his room. That was cool, he could live with that. Plus, he'd be away at football camp in a few weeks anyway. Wait, maybe they'd take his phone. Now *that* would suck. He wouldn't be able to talk to anybody, but the real issue was that he wouldn't be able to listen to any music while he ran. He would just be stuck with his thoughts and the sound of his feet hitting the pavement. Some runners liked that, but Kai didn't. Maybe one of his old phones was lying around here, stored with his iTunes history. Probably somewhere under his bed. Damn, if his room were more organized, he'd know exactly where they were. Or maybe—

"Hey." Aunt Brenda reached across the table and gently covered Kai's hand with her own. "You've got that spiraling look in your eyes. It's not as bad as you think, I promise."

"Okay." Kai took another deep breath and tried to ground himself. *I am in the kitchen with my aunt, eating a bowl of cereal. Nothing bad has happened yet.* He took another deep breath and let it go, feeling his pulse return to normal second by second.

"Finish your breakfast," Aunt Brenda said, pointing at his bowl. She stood up and placed her coffee mug in the sink.

"Morning," Uncle Steve said as he entered the kitchen. He was an accountant at a firm over in Philly, and he wore a long-sleeve button-up and slacks every day, regardless of the weather. His bald head was shiny with whatever product he used to make it shiny. Usually Kai cracked a joke about it, but not today.

"Good morning," Kai mumbled, watching Uncle Steve kiss Aunt Brenda on the cheek as he passed her on his way to the fridge. He grabbed the orange juice and poured himself a glass, then turned around to face Kai.

"So," he said. "About yesterday."

Kai sat up straight. Something he respected about Uncle Steve was that he usually got right to it.

"A bit of a mess, wasn't it?"

Kai nodded. "Yeah. I just . . . I didn't mean for that to happen. I'm really sorry."

"We know you are," Aunt Brenda said, resuming her seat across from him. "We know you've been working really hard on yourself, and we think you've been doing such a great job."

"Thanks." Kai glanced at Uncle Steve, waiting for him to weigh in. Sometimes he felt like his aunt and uncle played good cop, bad cop. Or in his case, loving guardian and also-loving-but-sterner guardian.

"It's true," Uncle Steve said, nodding. "We're proud of you. But your aunt and I have talked it over, and we think maybe you could do with some restrictions."

Ah, here it was. Kai waited for them to lay down the law. *Please not the phone, please not the phone.*

"Honey," Aunt Brenda said gently, "we think you need to cool it with the girls for now."

Kai blinked. "Wait . . . what?"

The girls? The *girls*? That's what they wanted him to get rid of? But why?

"Dating has been a distraction for you for a while now," Uncle Steve said, walking over to the table, sitting down next to his wife. "And yesterday proved that the distraction is only getting worse. We can't have you and Camille putting your jobs in jeopardy over whatever relationship spats you're having."

"But Camille and I already broke up," Kai said.

"Right, and we think that's the best choice," Aunt Brenda said, encouragingly. She paused, as if she were weighing her words. "Kai, honey, the girls you date aren't the problem, necessarily. They've seemed pleasant when we've had the chance to meet them in passing. It's just that this isn't the first time that one of your relationships has gotten you off course. Remember when you were so upset after your breakup with Deja Foster freshman year that you failed your algebra midterm?"

"Or that time when you talked on the phone all night with

Whitney Brown and then woke up late for basketball tryouts," Uncle Steve added. "Coach Franklin almost didn't let you on the court, but he knew how valuable you were to the team, so he made an exception."

"And now this situation yesterday with Camille," Aunt Brenda said. "Those are just a few examples. We can't remember the last time that you didn't have a girlfriend, and you put so much of yourself into your relationships, you know? They become all-consuming for you. We just think it might be best if you take the rest of the summer and your senior year to focus on school."

"And sports and your extracurriculars," Uncle Steve said.

Kai leaned back and stared at them. He was in disbelief, to be honest. "So . . . what you're saying is that you don't want me to date from now until graduation?"

They nodded.

Sheesh. Had he really dated so many girls that they felt the need to come to this decision? He thought back and counted each girlfriend from middle school to Camille.

Nine. Nine girlfriends. Damn.

But why did the number matter? If Kai had a connection with someone, he had to act on it. Was he just supposed to ignore that now? Wouldn't that be like messing with fate or something? Being someone's boyfriend gave him this sense of purpose that he didn't find anywhere else. As a boyfriend, it was his job to make someone happy, and he liked that. Not to mention that being single was hella lonely. He'd tried to explain this once to Jamal, and he'd laughed and said, "Yeah, well, I call you Loverboy for a reason."

Because the right person was out there waiting for him, somewhere. Kai wanted to have a real love like the one his parents had.

"I don't know," he said, apprehensive. This was too much. Honestly, he'd rather be forced to give up the phone. "Not dating until after graduation? That's so far away. What about until after I take the SATs or once midterms are over?"

Uncle Steve gave him a firm look. "Morehouse is the goal, isn't it?"

Kai nodded. He wanted to go to Morehouse College in Atlanta, just like his dad and Uncle Steve had, and he wanted to be a history major too.

"If you take your love life out of the situation, that gives you a lot of time to focus on other things," Aunt Brenda said. "Like your application. We know how important getting into Morehouse is to you."

"You have your whole life to find a girl and fall in love, Hezekiah." Uncle Steve reached across the table and patted Kai on the shoulder. "You don't need to worry about that now."

"How about this, we can revisit dating after you get your decision letters," Aunt Brenda said.

Kai glanced back and forth between his aunt and uncle, biting his lip. Maybe Uncle Steve was right. Kai had his whole life to fall in love with the right girl. And after what happened with

Camille yesterday, maybe it was best that he didn't deal with anybody on a romantic level for a while.

That's a lie. You literally just tried to bag Zyla Matthews yesterday.

He shook that thought away.

More than anything, he wanted to make his aunt and uncle happy. The least he could do was give this a try.

Aunt Brenda smiled at him. "You're just too cute for your own good, honey."

She said this often, and Kai never really understood how someone could be too cute for their own good. What was wrong with being cute? But in this moment, he kind of got what she meant. At least he thought he did.

"Okay," he said. "No dating."

They both smiled at him then, proud and content. Kai knew he was making the right decision.

No dating. It couldn't be *that* hard.

"Damnnn, bro. No dating at all?" Jamal shook his head and laughed. "You're not gonna survive that."

Kai snorted. "Wow. Thanks for your support."

"What?" Jamal shrugged and clipped on his intern name tag. They were standing in the small locker area outside of Antonio's office. In a few minutes, Jamal would have to give morning announcements before everyone started their shifts. "I'm just saying. You basically have to change your whole lifestyle now. Are you prepared for that?"

"I don't think it's that deep."

"You say that now. So, wait, does this mean you can't be my wingman anymore?"

Kai laughed. Jamal and his priorities. "Pretty sure I can be your wingman. I just can't do much more than talk."

"Then that's cool with me. I wish you luck on your journey, bro."

Kai shook his head and followed Jamal outside toward the food court area, where everyone was waiting. It was already hot as hell, and it was only a little after 9:00 a.m. They'd be melting pretty soon. Then he remembered he wasn't stuck on Rides anymore. He'd have shade at the Balloon Darts booth, which made him think of Zyla and their agreement to be friends. But how good of friends would they be? Would she spend most of their shift ignoring him, or would they talk? If it was the former, he came prepared. He pulled his old copy of *The Autobiography of Malcolm X* out of his cargo shorts pocket.

"You reading that again?" Jamal asked, nodding at Kai's book.

"Just trying to pass the time today. The Games section is hella boring."

Jamal smiled knowingly, picking up on what Kai wasn't saying. "Let me guess, you tried to bag Matthews and she turned you down, so now you're gonna read while she does whatever it is that she does with those magazines."

Kai couldn't help but laugh. "Pretty much."

"Wow, Loverboy, she could resist *your* charms? She's on a whole different level."

Kai shrugged. It didn't matter what level Zyla was on. He couldn't date anymore, and she didn't like him like that.

The morning-shift employees were congregated at the wooden tables. When they noticed Jamal and Kai approaching, some sat down, but others kept talking anyway. Camille and her friends were perched at the front table on the left. They whispered to each other and snuck glances at Kai, giggling like children on the playground. It took all of Kai's energy not to roll his eyes. Kai knew Camille was petty, but he hoped she'd relax and not act this way for the rest of summer. She sat up straight and stared at him, narrowing her eyes, like she dared him to come over and talk to her. It almost seemed as if that's what she wanted, just so she could embarrass him again, but this time in front of their coworkers. Not today.

As Jamal walked to the front so that everyone could see him, Kai pivoted and walked to the back and found a seat at an empty table. He kept his gaze forward and ignored everyone's stares, trying his best to appear nonchalant. He might have gotten in trouble yesterday, but today, he wanted everyone to know he was just fine, even if that wasn't exactly true. Out the corner of his eye, he saw Camille glare at him and turn around in a huff. Kai smirked, feeling triumphant.

Halfheartedly, Jamal began giving morning announcements. Eight summer camps were arriving today. Remember to wear sunblock. Hydrate. Blah, blah, blah. He said that verbatim. Half listening, Kai's eyes roamed the crowd of employees. He didn't realize what, or *who*, he was looking for until he spotted Zyla a few rows ahead of him. Her head was down, and she was sketching in a notebook, once again ignoring everything around her. Today she wore thick gold hoop earrings, and her hair was brushed up into a curly ponytail at the top of her head. Her hair looked soft. He wondered what it would feel like to touch it.

Give it up, my guy. It's not gonna happen with the two of you.

Right. He needed to stay focused.

Kai sighed then, louder than he meant to, and at that moment, Zyla turned around and saw him. Her eyes widened in surprise when she realized that Kai had already been looking at her. Before he could even lift a hand to wave, she whipped back around so quickly that it almost made him laugh.

He'd definitely made the right choice by bringing his book today.

Chapter Five

Zyla was confused. Kai Johnson had been looking at her. Why? Was he looking now? Should she peek and see? *No.* She would definitely not do that. Plus, he probably had been looking past her at Jamal, like everyone else. She didn't need to embarrass herself by catching eyes with him twice in a row.

It would get easier soon, this feeling of being overwhelmed when it came to Kai Johnson. She wouldn't get this annoying sensation, like butterflies were swarming around her esophagus. They were friends now, and she was going to have to work with him almost every day. Eventually, she'd be able to look at his cute face and it wouldn't affect her in the slightest.

Yes. That's exactly what would happen. Her logic made perfect sense.

She pushed her glasses farther up her nose and returned her focus to her sketchbook. Last night, she stayed up late, going through pictures Beatrice had sent her of Paris street fashion, and she was trying to incorporate those looks into a new outfit she wanted to create for her portfolio. Would making her own beret from scratch be too basic? Darn, maybe. Or maybe not? She could barely hear herself think over the sound of Jamal's voice. She didn't understand his whole intern arrangement with Antonio. What did Jamal do, exactly? None of the employees, herself included, ever took him seriously as an authority figure.

When Jamal dismissed them, everyone stood up and reluctantly walked to their stations. She felt like they were a herd of cows. Oh! Cow print. She could make a beret with a cow-print pattern! Now *that* wouldn't be basic at all. She froze in the middle of walking and whipped out her sketchbook again, ignoring her grumbling coworkers as she held up traffic. Sorry, but they would have to walk around her. Sometimes she got an idea and just had to get it down right away. Otherwise it would be gone in an instant.

She sketched the pattern feverishly. Cow-print berets! Absolutely brilliant. Finding the fabric might be tricky, though. She'd probably have to go to Philly soon, which meant she'd need a ride from her mom, which then meant she'd have to work around her mom's current dating schedule. She and Keith were back together again as of this morning. Ugh. If only Zyla were allowed to take the train to Philly by herself. Her mom wasn't strict about most things, but Zyla going to Philly alone was a big no-no. If only Beatrice were home and she and Zyla could go to Philly together. Sometimes having only one best friend had its downsides.

"Hey."

Zyla looked up, and Kai Johnson was suddenly standing beside her, smiling politely. He was almost a foot taller than her. She struggled to hide her surprise as she stared into his handsome face. His eyes were a deep chocolate brown, and his features were perfectly symmetrical, with full lips and thick eyebrows. And his eyelashes were long for no reason at all, being that he didn't even wear mascara. It wasn't fair that he just walked around with this perfect face.

She forced herself to look away and glanced down, noticing the all-white Adidas shell-tops he wore on his feet. Between these sneakers and his Jordans from yesterday, she was intrigued to know what his entire collection looked like. She respected anyone who paid attention to aesthetics as much as she did. She looked up at him and cleared her throat.

"Good morning." *Good morning?* Since when was she so formal?

"You looked deep in thought," he said. "I didn't want to bother you, but I thought I should ask if you wanted to walk together."

She raised an eyebrow, confused. "Walk together where?"

"Oh, um, the Balloon Darts booth?"

"Oh." *Duh, the place where you both work.*

He started to back away, his smile turning apologetic. "But I mean, completely understand if you want to walk alone. You did look busy. Sorry for interrupting."

"No, no," she hastened to say. "It's okay. Sure, let's walk together."

She tried to force herself to relax. She didn't enjoy feeling like a perpetually besotted deer in headlights with no control over her emotions. Kai was making a friendly gesture because they were friends now. If she wanted to become immune to him, she'd have to fully immerse herself in this so that she could finally be at ease.

It would be kind of like how her dad taught her and Jade to swim by throwing them into the pool as toddlers, waiting for their instincts to kick in, and hoping for the best. Sink, *then* swim.

They began to walk side by side in silence. Kai stared straight ahead, looking relaxed, his gait measured and calm. It was either he didn't care that half of their coworkers were watching him and whispering to each other, or he genuinely didn't notice.

When they reached the Balloon Darts booth, Kai lifted the latch for Zyla, and she walked around to claim her seat behind the booth. He sat beside her and looked around at the customers trickling through the park, dressed in swimwear or cutoffs and T-shirts, heading directly to the water park or rides. He sighed deeply, longingly, as if he'd signed his life away to the god of monotony and was just now coming to terms with his decision.

"You'll get used to it," Zyla said. "How boring it is."

Kai looked at her and laughed. "Are you a mind reader, Zyla Matthews?"

"No, Kai Johnson. But I am a seasoned Games attendant."

"Ah." He nodded slowly. The corner of his mouth turned up in a smirk. "And as a seasoned Games attendant, what more can you tell me? Being that I'm so inexperienced and in need of guidance."

66

"Well—" Wait. Was he flirting? She couldn't tell. She bet this was just his *way*. Old women probably thought he was flirting when he passed them on the street, politely said hello, and commented on what great weather they were having. She didn't need to keep reading so deeply into it. "The only real advice I can offer is that you should bring something with you to keep busy."

"Oh, yeah?"

"Yes." She tapped her sketchbook with her pencil. "Like so."

"Well, in that case." He dug in his pocket and whipped out a book. *A book?* How messed up was it that she just assumed Kai didn't read because he was a jock or a pretty boy or whatever?

Very messed up, she decided.

Kai pushed his book toward her. *The Autobiography of Malcolm X.* She hadn't read it, although she'd meant to. She picked up the book and turned it over in her hands. It was old and worn, and some of the pages were bent at the corners. She imagined Kai staying up late at night, carefully reading each page and dog-earing whatever passages spoke to him.

"How many times have you read this?" she asked, sliding his book back over.

"This'll be my fourth time."

"Fourth?"

He snorted. "Don't look so surprised."

How could she possibly hide her surprise when he refused to stop surprising her?

"Really?" she said.

"Yeah. My dad was a history professor. This was his copy, actually."

Was . . . past tense.

Should she ask about that?

No, she definitely shouldn't. If he wanted to tell her more, he would. She should stop being nosy and just mind her own business.

"I'll have to read it for myself one day," she said.

"And once you do, you'll have to tell me what you think." He smiled at her, and she wondered if she imagined the way that his eyes sparkled. Probably a trick of the light. Or maybe he exuded so much charm that his eyes legitimately sparkled.

God. This sink-then-swim approach with Kai Johnson was hard. At this point, she'd waded in waist deep. She figured that was enough for today.

"Um, I'm just gonna . . ." She trailed off, pointing at her sketchbook.

Kai nodded. "Right, cool."

He leaned back, opened his book, and began reading. Zyla put her head down and went back to sketching.

They went on like this for a good hour. Just as Zyla was about to comment on the fact that they were basically getting paid to read and draw, she looked up, and, what do you know, they had their first customers.

A couple in their twenties stood in front of the booth, staring at Zyla and Kai expectantly. The woman wore a denim high-waist miniskirt, a pale yellow crop top, and espadrille wedges. Zyla wasn't a fan of wedges herself, but she had to admit that this woman was wearing a quintessential summer outfit. Her boyfriend was super buff. His tight, bright orange T-shirt hugged his muscles, and he wore loose basketball shorts as if he'd come to Sailor Joe's straight from the gym. From his disinterested yet annoyed expression, he looked as if he'd been pulled away while in the middle of his favorite workout.

Zyla nudged Kai, who finally glanced up from his book. "Oh," he mumbled, slightly surprised. He looked at Zyla and waited for direction. She suddenly realized she hadn't had the chance to show him what to do when they had a customer. She would have to take the lead. She stood up and pushed her sketchbook aside.

"Hello, welcome to the Balloon Darts," she said with false cheeriness. "For five dollars, you get three tries to pop a balloon. Eight dollars for six tries. If you win, you get to pick one of our prizes." She pointed to the assortment of large teddy bears perched to the left of the balloon wall.

"Five dollars?" the guy said, frowning. "Seems like a rip-off. What about three tries for two dollars?"

"Um, no. Sorry." Zyla held in a sigh. She thought the prices were a little high too, but this wasn't her park. She just worked here. "It's five dollars."

"Come on, babe. Just pay the girl," his girlfriend said, pulling on his arm. She leaned into him. "I want you to win me one of those cute teddy bears."

"Fine." The guy pulled out his wallet and smacked a five-dollar bill onto the counter.

Zyla picked up the bill and stuffed it in the fanny pack behind the booth, designated for holding whatever money they made during their shift. It was probably the only cash this fanny pack was going to see today.

"Can you hold on to this for me?" she asked Kai.

"Sure." He reached for the fanny pack and watched her, slightly amused. "I should probably write this down so that I know what to do next time."

"Oh, don't worry," she said, smirking. "It's very easy to remember."

Zyla heard him chuckle as she grabbed three darts from a container behind the booth and handed them to the customer. She and Kai then stood to the side as the man proceeded to throw the darts without managing to pop any balloons. The third time, he actually hit one, but the dart bounced off and fell on the ground.

"What the hell?" he said, throwing up his hands. He glared back and forth between Zyla and Kai, like he thought they were playing a trick on him.

Here was the thing: The darts weren't sharp enough to puncture the balloons. Earlier this summer, after she'd spent weeks watching people try and fail to win at this game, Zyla played herself, but from a closer distance, figuring maybe people just weren't throwing fast enough from far away. But the balloons didn't pop when she threw them from a few feet's distance. And they didn't pop when she gently prodded them with the edge of the dart, which she realized was extremely dull upon examination. The balloons didn't pop until she deliberately stabbed them with force. When she'd pointed this out to Antonio, he'd waved her away and said, "It takes special skills to win at Balloon Darts."

Zyla had no idea what those skills were. But apparently this guy today didn't have them.

"I want another try," he said, digging into his wallet.

"That'll be three more dollars," Zyla said. "Because it's eight dollars for six total tries."

"Yeah, I got it. Whatever." He slapped three dollars onto the booth, and Zyla noticed Kai holding in a snicker as he stuffed the money inside the fanny pack.

The guy threw three more darts to no avail.

"What the fuck?" he said, once again pulling out his wallet. "I need three more."

His girlfriend frowned, apprehensive. "Babe, maybe—"

"You gonna give me some more darts or what?" the guy said to Zyla, shrugging his girlfriend off.

"Of course," Zyla said. "That'll be five dollars."

"What? Not three?"

Zyla shook her head. "No, you see, it's five dollars for three total tries, and eight dollars for six total tries. If you want to play again, you'll have to start back over with three tries at five dollars."

"That makes no sense!"

Zyla started at his sudden outburst. She was pretty sure a

vein just popped in his forehead. Adopting her best Placate the Customer attitude, she took a deep breath. "Well, it does make sense. As I just explained, the system goes five dollars for—"

"I'll give you three dollars for three more tries." He slammed the handful of dollars onto the booth counter with way more force than before. "Just give me the darts."

"It's five dollars for three," Kai said calmly, moving around Zyla and stepping closer to the booth counter. "If you want to play again, we'll need two more dollars. If not, there are plenty more games here to play at Sailor Joe's. We'd be happy to recommend some to you."

The guy narrowed his eyes and sized Kai up. Kai stood there waiting, quiet and patient.

"Fine." The man tossed out two extra dollars.

Kai scooped them up and zipped them inside the fanny pack. Zyla handed the man three more darts, and she and Kai stood off to the side again and watched silently as the man threw three more times, hitting a balloon with each throw, yet not managing to pop a single one.

Zyla looked at Kai, and he smiled at her in that amused way again. Instead of feeling nervous at the sight of his smile like before, she felt herself relax. Like they were in this together. Ridiculous customers did that to you.

The man started cursing under his breath, and his girlfriend tried to intervene again.

"Babe, seriously. I don't really need the teddy bear. Let's play another game. Or get on some rides."

She looped her arm around his waist, but he disentangled himself. "No, I'm gonna win you that teddy bear like I said. I'm good enough to win this game. You don't think I can win?"

Zyla couldn't help it. She burst out laughing. She quickly covered her mouth when she realized her faux pas, but what else was she supposed to do? This guy was wasting his money in the name of toxic masculinity. How could she *not* laugh?

Kai turned to her, wide-eyed, trying to fight his own smile. He moved a little closer and leaned down to whisper something, but then they were interrupted.

"What the hell is so funny?" the man asked, staring at Zyla. "You think it's funny that I can't win your little rigged game?"

Zyla shook her head. "Sorry, I wasn't laughing at you. I was laughing at something else." She then added, "And the game isn't rigged." That was a lie, but she was obligated to say it.

He narrowed his eyes and balled his hands into fists. "I want my money back. All of it."

"I'm sorry, sir, but I can't do that." She pointed at the sign above her head. NO REFUNDS.

"I said, give me my damn money!"

To Zyla's astonishment, the man leaped over the booth and tried to swipe the fanny pack out of Kai's hands. His girlfriend screamed for him to stop, and Zyla stumbled backward as Kai pushed her out of the way. Kai remained still as he held the fanny pack close to his chest. The man stood in front of him, panting like an enraged bull.

"Give me my money," he demanded, advancing on Kai.

"There are no refunds," Kai said, his voice low and measured. "It's only thirteen dollars. Don't make it bigger than what it is."

"It's *my* thirteen dollars, and I want them back."

He shoved Kai hard in the chest, and Zyla gasped, although Kai barely even lost his footing. Meanwhile, the dude's girlfriend was screaming at him, as if that was going to help anything. Frantically, Zyla took in their surroundings. The other employees working the games across the way were staring at them, and so were the few customers passing by.

"Sir, let's think about this logically," Kai said, taking a deep breath. "I'm sure we can come up with a solution here."

"What I want is my money, and if I don't get it, I'm gonna logically kick your ass."

He shoved Kai again, even harder this time, and Kai almost fell, refusing to lose his grip on the fanny pack. Something flashed in Kai's eyes then. He was quick to check it, but Zyla didn't think he could be pushed much further, literally or figuratively. When the guy moved toward Kai again, Zyla suddenly found herself jumping in between them.

"If you want to fight him, you'll have to fight me too," she said. "You think you can beat both of us up at once? Because I doubt it."

"*Zyla,*" Kai hissed, trying to move her aside, but she planted her feet firmly. Her heart was beating so fast. She had no idea what she was doing. This guy could likely break her in two and then move on to fight Kai, but she wasn't going to sit there and do nothing or watch him assault Kai because he was sour over losing some stupid game!

The man stared down at her, nostrils flaring, and Zyla waited for what he would do next.

Twenty minutes later, they walked out of Antonio's office into the bright sunlight. Before the situation with the customer could escalate any further, Jamal had showed up and used his walkie-talkie to call security. The good news was that calling security was enough to scare the customer and his poor girlfriend into leaving. The bad news was that Antonio heard the walkie-talkie exchange between Jamal and security, so he told Jamal to send Zyla and Kai to his office. Zyla was terrified that Antonio was going to fire her. Losing her job would be the *worst*. Not only would it put a huge dent in her fashion-school savings plans, but Aunt Ida would be pissed. Antonio hired Zyla as a favor to Aunt Ida. Thankfully, Antonio had barely even talked to them before his mom called, saying her fridge was leaking. Antonio was so frazzled, he simply told Zyla and Kai to go home for the day and come back tomorrow ready to work.

Zyla had the strange feeling that she'd lived to see another day. And Kai wasn't in trouble either. He stood beside her, grinning. She could feel the relief wafting off him in waves.

"What were you thinking getting in that guy's face like that?" Kai asked, turning to her. He shook his head. "He could have seriously hurt you."

75

Zyla shrugged. "I-I don't know. I just wasn't going to let you get beat up, I guess."

Kai paused, staring at her in wonder. Quietly, he said, "Thanks. For the record, I wouldn't have let him beat you up either."

Zyla felt herself smile, and Kai grinned in return. It was the most ridiculous yet endearing exchange she'd ever had.

"I can't believe you stayed so calm the whole time," she said.

"I used to get into a lot of fights when I was younger," he admitted. "Not really interested in that anymore."

"Oh, yeah? Same."

"Really?" He turned to her in disbelief. *"You?"*

"Yeah." She shrugged, not really wanting to get into how she'd been bullied when she was younger, basically for being poor. "What's so surprising about that?"

"I don't know. You're so chill. And little." He hooked his index finger and thumb around her slight wrist for emphasis.

"I'm five foot three," she said, swatting him away. "That's basically average height. Just because I'm not as big as you doesn't mean I don't know how to use my hands."

She curled her hands into small fists and pretended to jab at him like a boxer. Kai dodged her and laughed.

"Wow," he said. "I'm terrified."

They began walking in the direction of their booth to get their things.

"Ayo, Bonnie and Clyde!" someone called.

Zyla looked in the direction of the voice. It belonged to

a boy who was working the Twister, the one wooden roller coaster at the park. Zyla knew that his name was Matt, but she hadn't spoken to him before. He waved at her and Kai enthusiastically.

"Heard about what you did today!" he shouted. "Wild shit!"

"Is he calling *us* Bonnie and Clyde?" she asked, turning to Kai.

"I think so," Kai mumbled, suddenly looking exhausted. But he smiled and nodded at Matt. "I guess Jamal's nickname has spread."

Right. After witnessing their exchange with the customer, Jamal had jokingly coined them Bonnie and Clyde. Apparently, he thought their behavior was very "ride or die." Zyla hadn't thought it was very funny because the nickname was inaccurate. She and Kai weren't a couple. Or bank robbers. They were simply two amusement park workers who had tried their best not to get assaulted.

She looked around and finally noticed that their coworkers were watching them as they walked to the Games section, just like they'd watched Kai this morning.

Like a domino effect, the nickname followed them to the Balloon Darts booth. Coworkers who hadn't even so much as glanced at Zyla were suddenly calling her Bonnie. It freaked her out, this misconception that she and Kai were now considered a pair of some sort. But Kai didn't seem the least bit disturbed. It was as if he barely heard anyone calling out to him.

"Doesn't this bother you?" Zyla hissed once they reached their booth and grabbed their things.

Kai shrugged. "It'll die down soon, and they'll move on. It's just how it works."

"How *what* works?"

"The Sailor Joe's rumor mill. We'll be old news by next week."

She thought about the way people gossiped in clusters while clocking in or during their lunch breaks. No one ever gossiped with her directly, but she overheard things. That was how she'd found out about Kai and Camille's big argument yesterday. Apparently, everyone had moved on from that to focus on her and Kai's new Bonnie and Clyde status.

They finally reached the parking lot, and just like yesterday, they stood and faced each other.

Kai shoved his hands in his pockets and rocked back on his heels. "So, um, is your mom coming to get you?"

"Oh. No." Zyla said, just realizing she had no way to get home. "It's too early. She's at work."

Kai nodded. Hesitantly, he asked, "Do you . . . want a ride?"

Did she?

"That would be great," she said. "Thank you."

As luck would have it, they were neighbors.

"I can't believe you live in Cedar too," Kai said as he turned onto her street and pulled up in front of her house.

Aunt Ida sat outside on the porch in her old rocking chair. Bartholomew was napping in her lap. She paused her rocking and sat up, squinting at Zyla and Kai. Then she frowned.

"Yeah, we've lived here for almost three years," Zyla responded, looking at Aunt Ida, who continued to frown at her and Kai. She had a feeling another "men are good for nothing" lecture was in her future.

"How is it possible that I haven't seen you around?" Kai asked.

"I don't know. Probably because I just go to school and come home." She added, "Or I'm in Hamilton Heights. That's where my best friend lives."

"Hamilton Heights? Whoa, fancy," he said. "I live like a ten-minute walk away from you, over on Charleston Avenue. I run by your house all the time."

"Really?" She finally pulled her attention away from Aunt Ida. "I've never seen you run by before."

"I run late at night. Really late. You're probably already asleep."

"I'm a night owl," she said. "Next time, shout my name from the street and I'll come to my window and wave."

He grinned. "Which window is yours?"

"That one right there," she said, turning and pointing. "All the way to the left."

"Got it. Make sure you're on the lookout. I'll pass by around midnight."

She smiled. "I'll be up."

"Good." His grin widened. Then he caught sight of Aunt Ida on the porch. "She doesn't look too happy to see me. I guess you'd better go."

Zyla sighed. "Don't take it personally. She's never happy to see anyone who identifies as a male." She finally opened her door and got out. "Thanks for the ride, Kai Johnson."

"You're welcome, Zyla Matthews."

She stepped back, and Kai honked his horn as he pulled off. Zyla once again found herself hugging her backpack to her chest, watching his Jeep drive away.

Sink, then swim. It had worked after all. Just not in the way she'd expected.

She started for the porch and sighed inwardly as she took in Aunt Ida's pinched expression.

"Who was that?" Aunt Ida asked as Zyla walked up the porch steps.

"Nobody. A friend from work."

"Mm-hmm," Aunt Ida mumbled, eyeing her.

Zyla hurried inside so that Aunt Ida wouldn't hear her laugh.

Later that night, at exactly 11:57 p.m., Zyla was texting with Beatrice, who was on Paris time. Beatrice woke up at an ungodly hour every morning to do hot yoga, and she and Zyla were sending funny selfies back and forth when Zyla heard someone shout her name outside. Immediately, she dropped her phone and went to the window.

There was Kai Johnson, jogging in place on the sidewalk under the streetlight. He almost looked like he was glowing. He wore a sleeveless white T-shirt, basketball shorts, and running sneakers. He gazed up at Zyla with a huge smile on his face.

"Hey!" he called.

She almost shouted "Hey!" back, but she didn't want to wake her mom, whose room also faced the street. So instead, she leaned out of her window and waved with gusto.

"See you tomorrow," Kai called as he jogged away.

She watched him go, and the esophagus butterflies took flight.

In that moment, she knew being friends with Kai Johnson was probably going to change her life. And she wasn't sure if that was a good or bad thing.

When news of Zyla and Kai's disappearance reaches Jamal Smith, he is standing by one of Roaring Rapids' waterslides, holding his crush, Alanna Thomas's, flip-flops, towel, and sunglasses, and the flip-flops, towels, and sunglasses that belong to Alanna's friends. The girls are currently standing in line for the waterslide. Jamal suggested that they get lockers to store their belongings, and that way he could get on the rides too, but they said they didn't trust the lockers, and that it would be better if he watched their things instead. Disappointment doesn't even begin to explain how Jamal feels.

You see, he and Alanna had an agreement that they'd spend Senior Day together. They've been circling each other since last summer, and Jamal thought this would be an opportunity to Define the Relationship, but Alanna has spent most of the day running from ride to ride with her friends. Whenever Jamal tries to leave, she promises him that very soon they'll have their alone time. Five waterslides and one quick break for lunch later, that hasn't happened.

He feels like a towel boy, following her around this way. His backup plan had been to sit in the outdoor hot tub until midnight with her, but now that won't happen because the teachers said there is going to be a torrential downpour tonight. The students will be stuck inside the lodge. It's already beginning to drizzle.

Jamal wonders what happened to his ability to finesse. When did he become such a sucker? He used to tease his best friend, Kai, about being a Loverboy, but now look at him, basically following in Kai's footsteps. Honestly, Jamal blames Kai for his current sucker behavior. Jamal wasn't someone who *wanted* to be in a relationship. Keeping things casual was definitely the way to go. Then there was that day at Sailor Joe's last summer when he saw Kai and Zyla squaring off against that bodybuilder dude. Zyla stood in front of Kai with her arms out, a fierce and determined look on her face, as if she could protect him. And Kai kept trying to move her out of the way because his desire was to her protect *her*. It made Jamal think of Bonnie and Clyde, people who were so ride or die.

Later, after Jamal had intervened and the guy and his hysterical girlfriend finally left the park, Zyla and Kai burst into laughter and stared at each other, wide-eyed. Jamal can't seem to put his finger on exactly what kind of look they shared, but it was a look that people exchanged in movies. Like they were seeing who the other person was for the first time. Watching them, a light bulb flashed in Jamal's mind. *I want that.* It was so odd, because he hadn't had that thought before, and Zyla and Kai weren't even dating at the time. Kai had the whole girlfriend ban and Zyla never seemed to be interested in anyone.

Jamal wasn't surprised when they finally got together. What surprised him was that they eventually broke up.

Speaking of Kai, Jamal wonders where he is. He hasn't seen him since they got off the bus this morning, before he went with Alanna. That was hours ago. It's almost 5:30 p.m. now. Kai's been moody and weirdly introverted since he and Zyla broke up. Jamal wants to talk to Kai about it, but Kai refuses to discuss Zyla. The few times that Jamal has even mentioned her name, Kai practically winced. After two and a half months, the heartbreak is still that fresh.

Jamal knows that Zyla is here at the water park today too, just like the other senior girls from St. Catherine's. He just hopes that Kai doesn't accidentally run into her, because that could be disastrous. Just like what happened on St. Patty's Day.

He is thinking about all of these things when he hears someone call his name.

"Yo, Jamal!"

Jamal looks up to find his basketball teammate Brandon Davis jogging over to him.

"What's up, B?" Jamal asks. Then he remembers he's holding a bunch of towels and flip-flops. He places them down and daps Brandon up.

"You hear about what just happened to Bonnie and Clyde?" Brandon asks.

Jamal hasn't heard anyone call Zyla and Kai that name in

months. He gets an uneasy feeling in his stomach. "No, what happened?"

"It was wild, yo," Brandon says. "Kai saw Zyla kissing some Hopkins Prep boy, so then he walked up and stole him in the face! Then two other Hopkins Prep boys jumped in and Kai beat them up too! Then Kai ran off and nobody has seen him since!"

"What?" Jamal grabs his phone and calls Kai, but it goes straight to voicemail. He then sends Kai a quick text, **Yo bro you good?**

"Your girl was there too," Brandon adds. "That Beatrice chick. The rich one."

Jamal looks up from his phone and scowls. Zyla's best friend, Beatrice, is not his girl. In fact, she's probably his least favorite person. It's funny to think that months ago, momentarily, he considered trying to pursue her instead of Alanna. "Not my girl," he mumbles, glancing down at his unanswered text.

What the hell, Kai? Jamal should have known not to leave him alone. Not today, when there was a chance he'd see Zyla again.

Just then, Alanna and her friends return, giddy and exhilarated from riding the waterslide.

"Hey," she says, smiling and taking her towel to wipe her face. "The ride was so much fun, Jamal."

She is so beautiful that Jamal simply blinks at her in response, barely registering as her friends reach to grab their things and Brandon begins to fill them in on the recent drama with Kai and Zyla.

"We're going to get on one more ride, and then you and I can get ice cream," Alanna says to him. "I promise."

"I—" Jamal starts, then stops. Because he knows that he and Alanna aren't going to get ice cream. Despite his best efforts, Alanna isn't really going to give him the time of day. It doesn't matter anyway. Kai and Zyla, his once gold-standard couple, have already proved that nothing really lasts. There's no point in trying this girlfriend thing. "I can't."

"What?" Alanna says, blinking in surprise.

"Sorry."

He has to go. Kai needs him. As it begins to rain harder, Jamal abandons what might have been his chance at a ride-or-die relationship and goes off to search for his best friend.

Chapter Six

"I've been meaning to tell you that I made a new friend," Kai said to Dr. Rueben as soon as he walked into his office.

Dr. Rueben smiled and closed the door behind Kai, waiting for him to get settled on the couch before he spoke.

"Did you?" he replied, sitting in his chair across from Kai. "What's their name?"

"It's Zyla," Kai said. "The girl I told you about. I feel like I can officially say we're friends now."

"The one who works at the Balloon Darts with you?" Dr. Rueben folded his hands across his stomach and leaned back in his chair. "I thought you decided on the first day you met that you'd be friends."

"We did," Kai said, resisting the urge to wince at the memory of Zyla turning him down when he'd asked her out. "But now we're, like, legit friends because we have a routine. We've been carpooling for the past couple weeks because we have the same shifts. When I pick her up, she shares whatever snack she's eating with me, and then we sit at our booth and read and talk, and I don't know. It's nice, I guess."

Dr. Rueben nodded. "Would you say that you enjoy her company?"

Kai pictured Zyla's smile and the small gap between her front teeth, the way she'd waved at him when he showed up outside of her window that night last month.

"I do," he said.

"Why do you think that is?" Dr. Rueben asked. "What is it about her company that you enjoy?"

Kai paused and stared down at his cargo shorts. He had an evening shift at Sailor Joe's later today after he left Dr. Rueben's office.

He hadn't really analyzed *why* he liked being around Zyla. Dr. Rueben had a way of asking simple questions that managed to stump him.

Dr. Rueben wasn't really a doctor. Rueben Choi, LSCW-R, was a youth social worker with a private practice for psychotherapy on the side. Kai had been seeing him since he was nine years old, about a year after he moved in with Aunt Brenda and Uncle Steve.

On the morning that Aunt Brenda and Uncle Steve took Kai for his consultation meeting, they told him he was going to see a doctor who would help with his behavior. Kai pictured a white man with white hair, wearing one of those white doctor gowns. Kai would be led into a room with white walls, and maybe the doctor would stick something in his ear or give him a shot that would magically fix him. Make it so that he wouldn't be so sad anymore. Or anxious. So that being sad and anxious wouldn't eventually turn into anger when combined.

Instead, when they showed up at Rueben Choi's office, Kai was surprised to see that Rueben was Asian and fairly young. He had a gentle-looking face, and his long black hair was tied into a low ponytail. He wore a green polo with jeans and sneakers. Kai hadn't met a doctor before who wore jeans and sneakers. His office was filled with toys and picture books, even some graphic novels and comic books that Kai liked to read. And instead of giving Kai a shot or attempting to poke around in his brain, Rueben let Kai peruse his library. He didn't say anything when Kai sat on the floor pretzel style and flipped through a copy of *Captain Underpants and the Attack of the Talking Toilets*. In fact, Rueben sat across from Kai and asked him very non-doctor-like questions. What else did Kai like to read? What were his favorite subjects in school? What were his favorite sports? Games? TV shows?

Rueben listened patiently as Kai explained the plot of *The Legend of Korra*, which then meant he had to explain the plot of *Avatar: The Last Airbender*.

"Those sound very interesting," Rueben said. "I'll have to give them a try."

Kai looked at Rueben and squinted. There was no way he could really be interested in the shows Kai watched, was there? "What kind of doctor are you?"

"I'm not a doctor, actually," Rueben said. "I'm a therapist."

"A therapist," Kai repeated slowly. He didn't know what that meant, but he'd look it up later. "So what am I supposed to call you?"

"You can call me Rueben if you'd like."

Kai shook his head. It felt disrespectful to call an adult by their first name. "Can I just call you Dr. Rueben even though you're not really a doctor?"

Rueben smiled and nodded. "Sure. Dr. Rueben works."

And that's what Kai had called him ever since.

Now, Kai looked around Dr. Rueben's office, which was the same, more or less: filled with toys and books. Dr. Rueben had gotten married and had two kids since Kai first started seeing him. He was older, of course, and he'd cut his hair, but he still wore jeans and sneakers.

Kai thought back to Dr. Rueben's question. Why did he enjoy Zyla's company?

"I like her personality," he said. "She's cool. I mean . . . to be honest, I still kind of have a crush on her. But it's not like my crush even matters. She doesn't want to be more than friends, and I can't date anymore. It's not like we're going to end up together."

"Does that disappoint you?"

Kai shrugged. "No. Yes . . . I don't know. On one hand, yeah, it would be cool if she were into me and we dated. On the other hand, I do like being her friend. It's less complicated. Being around her is so easy. Unlike—" He stopped abruptly.

Dr. Rueben tilted his head and waited. "Unlike . . ."

Kai sighed. "Unlike how it was with Camille."

"Ah."

"She gives me the stink eye *every* time I see her. We've been broken up for weeks. I wish she'd just let it go. It's not like she even really wanted me around when we were together. I kept failing her little tests and making her unhappy. Like when she'd randomly go the whole day ignoring my calls and texts for no reason, and if I stopped texting her at a certain point, she'd call me and say I didn't try hard enough to get in touch with her, that she could have been legitimately mad at me, and I didn't care enough to find out why."

"You also mentioned that she would literally test you. For example, you once said she randomly quizzed you on her favorite color and got upset when you said pink, because her favorite color is technically magenta."

"Right!" Kai leaned forward, placing his elbows on his knees, propping his chin in his hands. On television shows and movies, therapists were always taking notes during conversations with their clients, but Dr. Rueben didn't do that. He had a great memory. Sometimes, he repeated entire conversations back to Kai verbatim, like just now.

"And then there was that time we went to the movies and she got pissed because I didn't ask for extra butter on the popcorn," Kai continued. "She didn't even tell me she wanted extra butter. She just expected me to know. Like, why would I know something like that without being told beforehand? She was so mad, she got up and left before the movie even started. I wasted twenty bucks on tickets, and she didn't even care."

Dr. Rueben nodded. "Yes, I remember we talked about the importance of good communication after that incident."

"Yeah. I mean, at that point, we were already a lost cause. Camille had this reputation for being mean, and a lot of the other girls at school hate her and stuff, but in the beginning, she was nice to me. She was considerate, and when we talked, she had this way of looking at me like I was the only person in the room. Then after a couple weeks, it changed, just like that, out of nowhere. I kept hoping to see that softer side of her again. It only briefly reappeared that time I told you about, when I came to her house right after she'd had some big fight with her older sister, which wasn't new because they were constantly fighting, but when Camille answered the door, she hugged me and started crying. For a minute, she just let me hold her. She wasn't criticizing me or pointing out something I'd done wrong. She looked at me and told me she was happy I'd come over. It was the first time I'd heard her say that to me the whole time we'd been together. I thought we finally reached a turning point. Then the next day she texted me and said she wanted to break up—or take a break. Whatever the hell she said. I was confused but relieved, to be honest. We weren't right for each other."

Kai was damn near out of the breath by the time he finished talking. It felt good to get this off his chest.

"You say you felt relieved. Were there any other feelings? Is there any part of you that is disappointed your relationship with Camille didn't last?" Dr. Rueben asked.

"Maybe a little," Kai mumbled, mulling this over. "When

we first got together, I had this idea that we'd be a good match, happy. That we'd have a fun summer working together, and when school started up again in the fall, she'd come to my games, and I'd go to her dance competitions or whatever. That maybe we'd stay together throughout college and maybe we'd even get married. That sounds stupid now, but I wanted something that would last. Instead I just have another failed relationship. And it's annoying that thanks to her, people think I'm some cheating player. Meanwhile, I'm still a freaking virgin."

Kai sank deeper into the couch. It was soft and smooth. He loved how it enveloped him and his feelings.

"Not every romantic relationship will work out, and it's okay to accept defeat," Dr. Rueben said. "Do you think maybe this is why your aunt and uncle asked you not to date? They wanted you to focus more on your studies. But maybe they were trying to spare you from feeling heartbreak again."

"Maybe," Kai repeated. "No, I know that's one of the reasons. My aunt Brenda said my relationships could get *all-consuming*. I don't want to disappoint them. I need to focus on other things, like getting into Morehouse. That's the most important goal."

"Yes, Morehouse," Dr. Rueben said. "And football camp, which you'll go to in a few weeks."

"Yeah, exactly." Kai sat up, regaining some sense of vigor.

"And your platonic relationships. Like developing a new friendship with your coworker Zyla."

"Right, that too." Kai nodded. Although he'd have to be a little more careful on that one and dial back on his crush.

"This is a great approach to have." Dr. Rueben glanced at his clock on the wall. "Kai, we're nearing the end of our session, so we'll have to continue our conversation next week. Before we finish, I'd really like for you to think about being more open to accepting defeat sometimes. In some cases, it means we can move on to better things. Taking our wins with our losses."

Kai nodded. "I'll think about it. Thanks, Dr. Rueben. See you next week."

Back in his Jeep, Kai pondered what Dr. Rueben said. Taking wins with losses. As someone who played sports, Kai could understand that concept. His forty-five-minute session with Dr. Rueben had flown by. There were some weeks when he couldn't wait to get to therapy and unload his thoughts. Then there were other days when he either didn't feel like talking or had no idea what to talk about. Whenever that happened, Dr. Rueben referred back to the approach he took when they first met, and he'd ask Kai about what he was watching and reading. And Kai found sometimes it was nice just to spend almost an hour telling someone why *Atlanta* was one of the best shows on TV. He felt slightly lighter after every session—even if he'd spent most of it crying, because sometimes that happened too.

He didn't really know who he would be without therapy, and he was happy that he went, although it wasn't something he talked about with many people. Jamal knew, and so did Camille, and he'd told one other ex-girlfriend, Desiree, once because she'd wanted to hang out and Kai didn't want to lie about why he couldn't see her at the specific time she'd asked.

But otherwise he kept the fact that he had a therapist to himself. He wasn't embarrassed about it. He just didn't want his friends to act weirdly around him. He didn't know many other seventeen-year olds who had a therapist, especially not many Black seventeen-year-olds. But then again, he didn't know many seventeen-year-olds with dead parents, regardless of race.

He knew that lots of people struggled with anxiety. He wasn't the only one who had panic attacks every so often, where he felt like he couldn't breathe and his lungs were working overtime. But he didn't know if many people had stress dreams like he did, where they walked through a completely empty house. No furniture, no people, no cars in the driveway. A clear sign that he'd been left behind, abruptly, without notice.

However, he'd learned from Dr. Rueben that the different facets of his anxiety were manageable. His anxiety liked to make him feel like the world was ending, but the more logical part of his brain knew that wasn't true.

Because at the end of the day, he'd already faced the worst day of his life nine years ago. He remembered it so very clearly. He could instantly recall the smell of the grass on the football field, feel the sweat running down his neck and torso during his Pop Warner game. He'd been staring down the field at Gregory Vogel, their quarterback, who was supposed to launch the ball across the field to Kai so that he could catch it and hopefully complete a touchdown. Kai's body had been tensed, ready to run for the ball at any moment, and then the referee had blown his whistle. Suddenly, Coach Peterson was jogging toward Kai, his expression riddled with worry. He waved for Kai to come off the field, and Kai wondered if he'd done something wrong. But he'd gone over the play a million times, so how could that be? Then he saw his aunt Brenda right behind Coach Peterson, and her eyes were red. Kai searched the bleachers, looking for his parents, and he couldn't find them. He knew they were going to be late to his game because they were training for another bike marathon, and the only time they had to do that was on Saturdays. Kai had gotten a ride with one of his teammates, and his parents promised they'd be there before the first quarter ended. But it was almost halftime and they weren't here yet. In that moment, he knew something was wrong.

When he reached his aunt Brenda and she wrapped him up in her arms, smearing her tears over his cheeks, he was already beginning to feel numb. Then she told him about his parents' accident. How they were hit by a driver who fell asleep at the wheel and swerved into the bike lane. That neither one of them had made it.

He held Aunt Brenda's hand as they walked to her car. She told him she was bringing him to her house, that his uncle Steve would be home soon. She'd started the engine, and something about the loud, unexpected noise it made startled Kai. Suddenly, he burst into tears, and he couldn't stop crying, and he couldn't catch his breath. He bent over and wrapped his arms around himself, rocking, as he struggled to breathe. The tears kept flowing, and he was moaning, heaving deep sobs. He was scaring himself, but he couldn't stop.

Dr. Rueben later explained that what he'd experienced was a panic attack.

This was what he was thinking about as he pulled in front of Zyla's house to pick her up for their evening shift. She was standing on the sidewalk, waiting, clutching her mini backpack to her chest. The sight of her smiling face loosened the knot in his stomach that grew whenever he recalled the worst day of his life.

"Hey, Kai Johnson," she said as she approached the car, holding a pack of Chips Ahoy! cookies.

"Hey," he said, leaning over to open the door. He could feel the smile on his face mirroring hers. He tried to tell himself that the warm feeling in his chest at the sight of her was a completely platonic reaction.

Chapter Seven

About thirty minutes into their shift, Zyla looked up from her sketchbook to find Camille Vaughn walking by, glaring at her and Kai. Kai, nose deep in his book, ignored Camille. Zyla, however, couldn't help but stare back. Before Kai got moved to the Balloon Darts booth, Camille hardly set foot in the Games section, at least as far as Zyla noticed. Yet this was the fourth time in three weeks that Camille had performed her stink-eye drive-by. It would be one thing if Camille were simply glaring at Kai. They were exes who went through a bad breakup. But she was giving the stink eye to Zyla too, as if Zyla were somehow involved in their drama, which she most definitely was not!

She hadn't felt this kind of dislike directed at her since the days of her middle school bully, Amanda Preston. That was when they'd lived in Oakland with her mom's best friend, Paul, who owned a beauty salon. She and Jade shared Paul's guest room, while her mom slept on his living room couch every night. Zyla's mom only had enough money to buy Zyla and Jade the essentials, so they mostly shopped at secondhand stores, which Zyla didn't mind. Every time they went to the Goodwill, she felt like she was unearthing small treasures. Items like old scarves and vintage T-shirts that had once been discarded by other people took on new meaning for Zyla. Amanda Preston, another girl in her seventh-grade class, who looked pristine with the newest sneakers and backpacks, her long hair braided and twisted with shiny new clips, teased Zyla mercilessly about her clothes.

One day during lunch, Amanda taunted Zyla about her mustard-yellow corduroy knee-length skirt and an Earth, Wind & Fire concert tee. She tripped Zyla as she walked by their table, and Zyla's lunch went flying as she fell hard on the ground. The kids around her laughed and pointed. She was fed up with them, especially Amanda. She reached for her milk carton, which had remained intact, and she stood slowly, approaching Amanda in measured steps. Amanda and her friends were busy laughing when Zyla dumped the entire carton of milk onto Amanda's head. When Amanda screamed in horror and pushed Zyla in retaliation, Zyla pulled her from her seat by her beautiful long braids, and they had a full-out brawl right there in the middle of the lunchroom.

Zyla had been the victor. But she was the only one who took pride in that. The principal suspended her, and her mom was absolutely furious when she picked her up from school. She'd had to leave work early and cancel an appointment with one of her few clients.

Her mom hadn't been surprised, necessarily. Zyla seemed to get into fights wherever they moved to for one reason or another. Always being the new kid was hard. Especially if you were the poor new kid. Maybe Zyla's mom knew that, because instead of taking Zyla straight home and putting her on punishment, she drove to the Goodwill. She ordered Zyla to stay in the car while she went inside, and a few minutes later, she returned holding a newly purchased used sewing machine.

"Here," she said, placing the heavy thing in Zyla's lap. "Don't fight with people over your school clothes. Make your own that look better than theirs."

Now it wasn't like Zyla thought she'd ever come to physical blows with Camille. But she couldn't help noticing the similarities between Camille and Amanda Preston. They were both beautiful and walked around with a sense of superiority. In the two years that Zyla had lived in Oakland, she couldn't remember Amanda Preston having a kind word for anyone. Similarly, Zyla had heard Camille say some really nasty things to her friends about other coworkers when she thought no one else was listening.

Did gaining a new friend in Kai mean gaining an enemy in Camille Vaughn? It didn't help that people were still calling her and Kai Bonnie and Clyde. Some people even thought they were hooking up, which was ridiculous. Honestly, she'd kind of expected that Kai and Camille would have patched things up by now. They had been the couple that everyone talked about. Picture perfect, at least from the outside. Camille had no reason to be jealous of Zyla because Zyla wasn't her competition. She'd see that soon enough.

Zyla watched as Camille continued on, throwing one last

glare over her shoulder. All the while, Kai kept reading. He had a concentrated look on his face, furrowed brows. He paused in the act of turning a page and glanced up at Zyla. That was when she realized she'd been staring. She felt her face get hot and she cleared her throat, fumbling for something to say.

"I've got to be honest, I'm surprised you and Camille aren't back together already," she blurted.

Kai snorted. "Nah, that's not gonna happen."

"Well, you should tell that to Camille. I've had enough of her weekly stink-eye drive-bys. She's obviously doing it to get your attention."

"Stink-eye drive-bys? Is that you what you call them?" He laughed, closing his book. "I see what she's doing. I just ignore her. You should too. Eventually, she'll stop."

"So you have no plans to get back with her at all?" Zyla asked, surprised.

"Nope." He leaned back in his chair and shrugged. "Even if I wanted to, which I don't, I can't."

Zyla waited for him to elaborate, and when he didn't, she said, "Okay, and why can't you?"

He slid her a glance and bit his lip, almost like he was deciding whether or not he wanted to share more. "My aunt and uncle basically said that they don't want me to date until after graduation."

"After graduation?" Zyla felt her eyes grow to the size of golf balls. *"You?"*

Kai smirked and shook his head. "You sound just like Jamal."

"I'm surprised, is all," she said. What would the girls at St. Catherine's think once they found this out? "Wow. What are you going to do?"

He laughed again and shrugged. "Not date? That's the only option."

"Wow." She paused. Then, "How many exes do you have, exactly?"

"Nine."

"Nine?" she repeated. Kai winced at her tone, and she immediately felt bad. "Sorry, I'm not trying to sound judgmental or anything. I'm not judging you. I hope that's not what you think. Because I'm not judging you."

Blabbering. That was what she was doing. She clamped her mouth closed. She *wasn't* being judgmental, and she'd known that Kai had dated a lot. It's just, the number was surprising to someone like her. Someone who hadn't even kissed another person before.

"I mean, I was surprised when I finally counted them too," he said. He held up his fingers and began listing their names. "Taylor White, Iris Cho, Deja Foster, Gianna Rossi, Whitney Brown, Desiree Truman, Corinne Campbell, Ashley West, and Camille Vaughn."

She looked at his fingers. Whoever he dated next would hold the spot of the tenth girlfriend. The last pinky finger. After graduation, according to his aunt and uncle's wishes.

In the weeks that they'd been carpooling and getting to know each other, his aunt and uncle had come up a few times. But he hadn't mentioned his parents. There could be various reasons for this. Zyla didn't really talk about her dad unless someone asked outright.

Curiosity got the best of her. "Why do you live with your aunt and uncle?"

"Oh, um, I've lived with them for a while now." He stared at his hands, his fingers spread out over his kneecaps. "My parents died when I was younger, so . . . yeah." She must have looked surprised, because he hastened to say, "I know I haven't said anything about it before. Didn't really know how to bring it up. It's not something you can easily slip into conversation."

His lips quirked up into something that wasn't quite a smirk, and he shrugged. Meanwhile, Zyla felt like the world's nosiest jerk.

"Oh my God, Kai. I'm so sorry, I had no idea." *Of course* she had no idea. What was she even saying? That explained why he'd said his dad *was* a history professor. She felt terrible for even asking about his aunt and uncle. And she felt even worse because she had more questions. How did his parents die? How old was he at the time? This was why it was important to mind your own business!

"It's cool," Kai said. "It happened a long time ago."

Zyla nodded. "Still. I'm sorry."

It grew quiet between them. Zyla stared down at her sketchbook, and Kai watched the kids running by toward the water park. She wanted to get rid of the awkward silence, to see his smile again.

"I have an idea," she said. Kai glanced at her and raised an eyebrow. "If I can name your exes in order the way you did just now, you have to buy me a slushie. If I mess up, I'll buy you a slushie."

"No," he said, and her heart sank a little. "I don't want a slushie. I want curly fries."

She laughed, overwhelmed with relief. She took a deep breath and held up her fingers, just like he'd done. "Okay. Taylor, Iris . . . Gianna?"

"Nope. It was Iris, then Deja." Kai shook his head, smiling. "Damn, you didn't even make it past two! I'll give you one more try. That's it."

Zyla squinted, thinking hard. She'd only heard the names once, but asking him to repeat them again felt like cheating, and she wanted to win fair and square. "Taylor, Iris, Deja, *Gianna*, Ashley, then Corinne—"

"No, you skipped over Whitney and Desiree." He was laughing harder now. "You owe me those curly fries, Zyla Matthews. Better luck next time."

He reached out and patted her lightly on the arm. His palm was warm, and she felt a tingle spread over her skin at his touch. Before either of them could react, he pulled his hand away. She stared down at her arm and warned the esophagus butterflies that they'd better remain calm.

"It's dead here," Kai said, regaining her attention. "We aren't getting any more customers. We might as well walk and get those fries now."

"I don't know." Zyla looked around, apprehensive. "What if Antonio comes by and we aren't here?"

"It's Thursday night. Antonio is in his office watching *Superstore* on his tablet."

"Oh yeah." She stood up, and he stood too. "Okay, let's go."

Kai bought Zyla a slushie anyway, even though she lost. He wasn't just going to sit there and stuff his face while she ate nothing. That wasn't his style. They sat at a table in the deserted food court, and he felt her watching him as he smothered his curly fries with almost every condiment imaginable and began to eat them with a fork. She laughed and took a long sip of her slushie. It was like they were playing hooky while being at work.

Kai glanced around and noticed that Tyesha, who worked the hot dog and fries stand, was smirking at them as she texted on her phone. When Tyesha took their order, she'd called them Bonnie and Clyde, which apparently was a thing that was still happening. According to Jamal, who kept his ear to the Sailor Joe's rumor mill, people thought Zyla and Kai were hooking up. Kai hoped it was because people were incapable of thinking that a boy and a girl could be strictly platonic, not because he was unable to hide the hearts in his eyes whenever he was around Zyla.

"Why do you have so many exes?" she suddenly asked. She looked down at her slushie and quickly shook her head. "Never mind. You don't have to answer that if you don't want to."

"It's okay." He shrugged. After he'd admitted he'd dated nine people, it wasn't a strange question. "I guess I've just liked a lot of people."

Zyla laughed. "I think what I meant to ask is, why haven't any of your relationships lasted?"

"Oh. Um, well, different reasons. Sometimes we find out we're not really that compatible, or we're too busy with sports and clubs, or we realized it was just the kind of thing that was only meant for summer or winter break. I don't know. I haven't had any bad breakups, really. They just kind of dissolved . . . Well, except for Camille."

"Hmm." Zyla squinted. "Interesting."

He didn't like that he was the only one under a microscope. "How many exes do *you* have?"

"None."

Kai blinked. "What?"

"I don't have any exes." She fingered one of the pins on her collar. "I've never dated anyone."

Kai stared at her, doing a terrible job at hiding his shock. He didn't get it. She was so beautiful. And smart and funny. He'd asked her out the first day he met her, like an infatuated fool. He kind of assumed lots of people did the same. Maybe she was aromantic. Or just very selective. Not everyone had to date their way through the tri-county area like he did.

"Um, can I ask why not?" Kai said. Then he backtracked. "You don't have to answer if you don't want to."

Zyla glanced down at her hands in her lap. Today, she wore a thick silver ring on the middle finger of her right hand.

"My parents—" she started, then stopped and cleared her throat. She looked up at Kai. "My parents divorced when I was younger, and my mom got full custody of me and my sister, while my dad only got visitation. We lived in Florida at the time, and after my dad moved and remarried, my mom wanted to move too, and we kept moving around for years. Maybe I don't get into relationships because I don't know when I'll end up leaving again."

Something about her answer gave Kai pause. It was the way she said it, almost robotically, as if it were rehearsed. He felt like he wasn't getting the full story as to why she hadn't dated before. But he wouldn't push. Everybody was entitled to keep their business to themselves. He knew that better than anyone.

"Where have you lived before?" he asked.

"Oh, everywhere. I was born in Miami. Then we moved to Kissimmee. After that, we moved to St. Louis, then Oakland, and then Baltimore. In the middle of eighth grade, we moved to Philly, and then we came over the bridge to Cedar to live with my aunt Ida so that I could start freshman year at St. Catherine's."

"*Damn.* You've lived in almost as many cities as I have ex-girlfriends."

Zyla smirked. "Maybe I should quiz you next time."

"What kind of quiz? I like quizzes."

Kai and Zyla both jumped as Tyesha suddenly materialized at their table. She held a rag in her hand.

"Sorry, didn't mean to interrupt y'all," she said, grinning, showing off her braces. "I just need to wipe down the table before the food court closes for the night."

Kai looked at Tyesha and frowned. She was part of Camille's crew, and Kai wouldn't have been surprised if she'd been eavesdropping on their conversation this whole time.

Zyla seemed to share the same thought, because she stood up and said, "We were just leaving."

Tyesha continued to grin at them. "See you later, Bonnie and Clyde."

Kai shook his head as they walked away. "People here are nosy as hell. Damn."

Zyla nodded in agreement and turned around to eye Tyesha, who was texting once again. She was probably texting Camille lord knows what.

Kai brushed it off and checked the time on his phone. "Thirty minutes until the park closes," he said. "Wanna get on some rides?"

She smiled. "Yeah. Why not."

When they finally reached the Balloon Darts booth, Zyla realized they only had five minutes left in their shift. They'd screamed as they'd ridden the Twister and laughed as they ran through the janky fun house. They'd even ridden the Tilt-A-Whirl, and after the ride ended, Kai had kissed his index and middle fingers and held up a peace sign in parting. Zyla had snorted and shaken her head. All the while, she'd noticed their coworkers watching them with special interest, probably thinking that she was Kai's newest girlfriend. How nosy. And incorrect.

Now, Zyla watched Kai as he stuffed his Malcolm X book in his pants pocket. She felt guilty that she'd accidentally made him share that his parents died. She didn't want to bring it up again, though, so how could she apologize? Maybe she could offer a truth of her own instead.

"I lied to you earlier," she said.

Kai turned to her and raised an eyebrow. "About what?"

"When I said I don't date because I moved around a lot. That wasn't true." She took a deep breath and wanted to look away, but she refused to break eye contact. "My parents make really bad decisions when it comes to love, and they're both really unhappy. I don't want to be like them, so I just avoid falling in love, or dating, altogether."

Kai stared at her closely. He was quiet as he mulled over her words. Finally, after she felt as though the silence was stretching on a little too long, Kai said, "I see where you're coming from. But love is a beautiful thing to witness when it's real. My parents were crazy in love with each other. That's what I remember most about them. My aunt and uncle really love each other too. When it's right, I think it makes all the difference in someone's life."

A warm feeling spread through Zyla's body as she listened to Kai sincerely and openly talk about love, the one thing she couldn't really understand. It was mesmerizing. He held open the door, giving her a glimpse into this romantic emotion that she'd purposely evaded. She could step through the threshold if she wanted to see what it was about.

But she wouldn't.

"Ehh, maybe you're right," she said. "But probably not."

Kai laughed and shook his head. "We'll have to agree to disagree, then."

He looked past her and nodded his head at Jamal, who was walking toward them.

"If it isn't my favorite crime couple," Jamal said, smirking as he leaned down on the booth counter.

Zyla rolled her eyes. "This is your fault, you know," she said. "People won't stop calling us Bonnie and Clyde now."

"I actually think it's my best nickname yet," Jamal said. "Even better than Loverboy."

Kai sighed. "What's up, bro?"

"Alanna Thomas is having a party at her house tonight, and we're going." Jamal smiled dreamily. "You know how I feel about her."

Kai snorted. "Okay, cool. I just need to drop Zyla off at home first." He turned to her and grinned. "Wait, you should come with us."

"No, thanks." The answer was automatic. It's not that she didn't like parties. She went to parties with Beatrice a lot. Granted, they were mostly parties that Beatrice threw at her house or parties thrown by Hopkins Prep boys, but Zyla couldn't go out tonight. She'd promised Aunt Ida that she'd clean the downstairs bathroom after work. "I don't even know Alanna Thomas. I don't want to just show up at her house."

"That doesn't matter," Kai said. "Alanna's cool. She wouldn't care if you came."

"Alanna is sweet. And she's *bad*," Jamal said. "Like the baddest girl on the planet."

Zyla raised an eyebrow. "So that's why you like her? Because she's bad? What about her personality? Or the way she treats other people?" Why were boys so brainless when it came to stuff like this?

Jamal shrugged. "I said she was sweet."

Zyla sighed, and Kai laughed.

"What?" Jamal said. "You think I'm shallow, Matthews? I'm really not. I'm nothing but a gentleman to the girls I like. How about this, do you have a smart, funny, and cultured friend you can introduce me to? I promise she'd find me absolutely charming."

Zyla smiled, thinking of Beatrice. "I do have one friend. But she'd probably eat you alive."

Jamal smiled too. "Now I'm intrigued."

They walked together to clock out, and before she knew it, the three were driving home and pulling up in front of her house.

"You sure you don't wanna come with us to Alanna's?" Kai asked as she slid out of the passenger seat and Jamal walked around the front of the Jeep to take her spot.

"I'm sure," she said. "Have fun."

"I'll get you to hang out with me outside of work one day," Kai said, holding up a finger in declaration. "One day."

Zyla laughed. "Maybe."

They pulled off, and Kai beeped his horn twice. Jamal leaned out the window and waved.

Maybe it was because she was starving for companionship without Beatrice. Or maybe it was because she really didn't feel like cleaning the bathroom. Either way, she kind of wished she'd taken them up on their offer to go to Alanna's party. There was something so easy about spending time with Kai, and now she knew that she could hang out with him without worrying that their budding friendship might threaten to turn into something more. Kai couldn't date, and now he knew why she didn't date.

She hoped they'd have a chance to hang out for real. By then, she'd definitely be over the little crush she'd formed.

Chapter Eight

Per usual on a Saturday morning, Zyla woke to the sound of gospel music playing downstairs in the living room. Today it was Kirk Franklin's "Brighter Day." This was Aunt Ida's way of telling everyone that it was time to get up and do their chores.

Zyla dragged herself out of bed and across the hall to clean the upstairs bathroom. She'd been smart to clean the downstairs bathroom yesterday and get it out of the way. As she scrubbed the tub, her mom walked by holding a basket of laundry.

"Morning, Zy," she mumbled sleepily.

"Morning, Mom."

Downstairs, Zyla heard Aunt Ida instructing Jade on the correct way to shake out the carpet powder, and when Jade turned on the vacuum, Bartholomew started barking like he was under attack. A typical Saturday morning in Aunt Ida's house.

Except for one thing: Today, once their chores were done, Zyla's mom was going to take Zyla to Philly to get fabric. She was finally going to make that cow-print beret for her portfolio. One step closer to submitting her fashion school applications.

That put some pep in Zyla's step, and she almost threw her

113

shoulder out as she rushed to wipe down the bathroom sink. She barreled downstairs and practically wrestled Bartholomew to put on his leash so that she could take him for a walk. Other dogs would have jumped at the chance to go outside, but not Bartholomew. He was the world's laziest canine.

She hustled him down the street, and he made grumpy little noises the entire time, pausing to sit and scratch his butt every few feet.

"Will you hurry up and go to the bathroom, please?" Zyla asked.

Bartholomew glared at her and turned to sniff a bush. *No, I will do my business on my own time. Not yours.*

Zyla groaned. "You are so annoying."

She swore that Bartholomew almost grinned at her then. She sighed and looked down the street. Some of the neighbors were outside, cleaning their cars or working in their gardens. They shouted to each other across the street and waved with friendly smiles. Cedar was definitely the most suburban place she'd ever lived. She used to think towns like this only existed in movies.

She wondered what Kai was doing right now in his part of Cedar, which was only a ten-minute walk away. She hated to admit that sometimes she stayed up past midnight, waiting to hear the sound of his feet pounding on the pavement, to hear him call her name. It hadn't happened again after the first day they'd met. On those nights, she fell asleep feeling foolish. What was she thinking? He hadn't said he'd stand under her window *every* night. It's not like they were Romeo and Juliet or something.

Bartholomew barked at her, and she turned, realizing that he finally decided to do his business by a streetlight pole. He stared at her indignantly. *Clean up my mess, human. I'm ready to return home.*

Once they were back at Aunt Ida's, Zyla ran to get showered. Her mom usually finished her chores first, and chances were she was already dressed and almost done with hair and makeup by now. Zyla needed to hurry. They had to be over the bridge and into Philly soon if they wanted to beat Saturday-afternoon traffic.

After she showered, Zyla undid her flat twists and left her hair out, thick and curly. Even though it was going to be ninety-two degrees later today, she wore her white Doc Martens and paired them with a sleeveless sunflower-print baby-doll dress and a black leather cross-body bag. She wore thin silver hoop earrings the size of tea saucers and applied her shimmery lip balm. She cleaned her glasses, gave herself one final quick approving glance in the mirror, and went down the hall.

Her mom's door was slightly ajar, and she heard a Toni Braxton song playing softly in the background. Zyla poked her head inside. "Hey, Mom. You ready?"

Then she paused, taking in the sight before her.

Her mom was sitting on her bedroom floor, painting her toenails bright red. She was fresh faced, and her hair was in the curlers she set last night. She was wearing an old sundress that was only meant to be worn around the house. She looked up at Zyla and smiled. "Ready for what, babe? Your dad called me, by the way. He said he's having a hard time getting ahold of you."

For a moment, Zyla was speechless. She was so surprised to find her mom this way, when she should have been fully dressed, that her mind went completely blank.

Slowly, she said, "We're going to Philly today. You said you'd take me after we finished our chores." She didn't even bother to address how she'd been ignoring her dad's calls because she didn't feel like talking to him.

Her mom blinked, eyes wide. "Oh, shoot. I thought we agreed to go next Saturday."

"No." Disappointment crept through Zyla's bones and made a heavy nest in her chest. "I have to work next Saturday, and Jade has her camp ceremony."

"Shoot, shoot, shoot." Her mom held her hands to her mouth. "Babe, I got my dates mixed up. I made plans with Keith this afternoon. He's leaving tomorrow for two weeks for some work thing. I won't see him again until the end of summer."

Zyla suddenly felt like she might start crying. Quickly, she said, "Okay, I won't take that long. I already know what kind of fabric I want, and I called Genie ahead of time to let her know I was coming. If we leave now, we'll be back before dinnertime, and you can see Keith before he goes."

"We're supposed to go to some outdoor festival in an hour. He already bought the tickets." Her mom shook her head and bit her lip. "Babe, I'm so sorry. What days are you off next week? I'll try to work something out with my boss so that I can take you then."

Zyla stared at her, dumfounded. It was no longer about their mutual lack of availability, or even that Zyla had been looking forward to escaping suburbia to visit her favorite city for the afternoon.

No, the issue here was that she and her mom had made plans together, and those plans went out the window as soon as her mom's boyfriend called.

Zyla knew this was a battle she couldn't win, but she was too angry to care. She'd absolutely go down swinging.

"Mom, you promised that you'd take me just the other day. This isn't a Philly trip I'm taking for fun. It's for my portfolio. How could you forget that quickly?"

"I don't know. I'm really sorry, Zy." She shrugged helplessly and then froze. "Oh! How about this, I'll ask Keith if he can get a refund on the tickets, and he can just come with us to Philly. That way, you can get your fabric, and I can see Keith before he leaves." She reached for her phone and started texting. "I'll tell him right now."

"*What?*" Zyla's mouth fell open. "No! Mom, I don't want Keith to come too."

Her mom looked up at her, confused. "Why not? Don't you want your fabric? I know how important finishing your portfolio is. We're killing two birds with one stone here. Plus, you're hardly around when Keith comes over. It would be nice if you got to know him better."

"For what? He'll just break up with you again once he gets back from his *work trip*."

She put *work trip* in air quotes, and her mom narrowed her eyes.

"Young lady, if you don't want to go to Philly with Keith, that's fine. But what you're not going to do is sit here and disrespect me."

"I'm not disrespecting you," Zyla said, even though she felt her tone purposely toeing the edge of nasty. She needed to check herself, and quick, but her anger was taking over that logical part of her brain.

Her mom leveled her with a gaze. "Lose the 'tude, Zy, or you won't be going anywhere, anytime, ever. You got that?"

Zyla balled her hands into fists and sucked in a deep breath. She wanted to scream at her mom. *Choose me for once in your life. God!*

If Zyla ever had kids, which was unlikely, she would not have to decide between a partner and her children. She wouldn't put herself in a situation where she'd have to choose. She would not sit around looking foolish, waiting for some no-account person to take her out on a date before they fell off the face of the earth for a "work trip."

She spun on her heels and stormed downstairs.

"What did I tell you about stomping around my house?" Aunt Ida yelled as Zyla pushed her way outside.

She paced back and forth on the front porch. She didn't need her mom. She could take the bus to the train station and go to

118

Philly alone. She knew how to get to Genie's Fabrics. She didn't need to have someone with her.

But if she left without any word, she'd give both her mom and Aunt Ida heart attacks, and then she'd really be grounded for sure.

Why, why, why couldn't she be allowed to just go by herself? Oh, she couldn't wait until she was away at college, where she could do whatever she wanted. But she needed the new fabric in order to create the portfolio piece to include in her college applications!

Maybe if she weren't so freaking antisocial she'd have tons of friends that she could ask to join her. But she only had Beatrice, who wouldn't be home for another two weeks.

Zyla's stomach sank. She had no one else.

She felt tears burning the back of her eyes, and she wiped her cheeks when she realized they were wet.

Then she heard the sound of feet pounding on the pavement. She looked up, and to her surprise, Kai Johnson was jogging right toward her house.

Chapter Nine

Kai didn't usually like to run during the daytime. There were too many noises that his headphones couldn't drown out: lawn mowers, people playing the radio as they barbecued, car horns honking, other joggers breathing heavily as he passed by them. But at night, when it was quiet and everyone else was inside the safety of their houses, Kai felt like Cedar belonged to him.

He'd missed last night's run because he'd stayed over at Jamal's after they got back from a party in Hamilton Heights. Kai didn't know the kid whose party it was, some boy named Mike who went to Hopkins Prep. Kai and Jamal usually avoided that crowd. Hopkins Prep boys acted hella entitled, and they got into sketchy shit and took drugs with weird acronyms that Kai hadn't heard of. They lived in small mansions, and their parents *never* seemed to be home. Majority of them were white, and last Halloween, a group of them dressed up in blackface and posted a video rapping A$AP Ferg lyrics with aluminum foil over their teeth for grills. After the video blew up online and the media caught wind of it, the students weren't even suspended. They just got a slap on their wrists from their headmaster.

Kai and Jamal only wound up at last night's party because

their basketball teammate Brandon Davis played in a summer league with that Mike kid. Brandon kept saying he didn't want to go to the party alone. The whole time, Kai wished he'd just stayed home and gone for a run instead.

But if he'd done that, he wouldn't have been forced to run this morning. And then he wouldn't have turned down Zyla's street and spotted her standing on her front porch.

He'd be lying if he said he wasn't hoping to see her, even though he shouldn't have been hoping for that because it wouldn't help his crush go away. What he didn't expect was to find her crying.

"Hey," he said tentatively, slowing down as he stopped at the bottom of her porch steps. "What's wrong?"

"Nothing. It's stupid." She shook her head and forced a smile, descending a step so that she was closer. "So you run during the day too?"

"Not really. Just today. I was busy last night." He ascended a step so that he was closer.

She nodded and looked out onto the street behind him. Her eyes were red, and she stood with slumped shoulders. This was the first time he'd ever seen her wearing something other than her work uniform. In her sundress and white boots, she looked even prettier, if that was possible. In his ideal world, where she was into him and he was allowed to date and he wasn't sweaty from running, he'd be picking her up for a Saturday-afternoon date.

He wondered what her real plans were for the day.

"I was supposed to go to Philly with my mom," she suddenly

said as if she'd read his mind. "I need fabric for this project. But we're not going anymore because she has plans with her boyfriend."

"Oh." This was why she was upset? It didn't seem like a big deal to him. "Why don't you just go without her?"

"I'm not allowed to go to Philly by myself." She crossed her arms and frowned, looking slightly childish. Kai almost laughed and pointed this out to her, but he had a feeling she wouldn't find it as funny.

"I mean, I can go with you," he heard himself say. He didn't have shit to do today. Why not? "Your mom doesn't know me, though, so I don't know if she'd be into that."

Zyla's whole face lit up like a light bulb flashed inside her brain.

"Kai," she said, grinning. "That is a *great* idea. Come inside with me."

Before he knew what was happening, Zyla reached down, grabbed his arm, and pulled him up the steps and through the front door. Immediately, a little old dog ran up to him and started barking. Zyla shooed the dog aside and led Kai into the living room. The same old woman who watched him and Zyla from the front porch whenever he dropped her off sat in her reclining chair, drinking a glass of water. Kai looked around and decided if he had to use one word to describe this house, he'd say "cozy."

The old woman eyed Kai suspiciously as Zyla said, "Aunt Ida, this is my friend Kai. He's going with me to Philly today since Mom can't come."

"Good afternoon, ma'am." Kai smiled, remembering his manners.

Aunt Ida's eyes widened. "Y'all are doing what now?"

"Auntie, is Zy outside?"

Kai turned, and standing on the staircase was a woman who looked a lot like Zyla, but a few shades lighter. Her long reddish-brownish hair fell in waves over her shoulders, and she wore bright red lipstick and a white tank top with black jeans.

"Oh," she said, pausing when she realized they had company. She walked toward them, shooting a quick glance at Zyla. "Hello, I'm Zyla's mom."

"I'm Kai," he replied, noticing that she and Zyla had the same hazel eyes. "It's nice to meet you."

"Nice to meet you too." She glanced at Zyla again and tilted her head, waiting for further explanation.

"Kai's going with me to Philly," Zyla said. "We're going to catch the train and go to Genie's. Maybe get food, do some exploring."

"Oh, well that sounds fun." Her mom smiled at both of them. "Philly is such a great city to explore."

"Yeah," Zyla said, nodding slowly. "I should be home by the time you get back from your date."

Her mom paused then, and she and Zyla stared at each other. Kai suddenly felt like he was in the middle of a standoff, that Zyla and her mom would reach for their pistols at any moment, Old West style.

"Leanne, you're gonna let Zyla go to a strange city with some boy we don't even know? What's wrong with you?"

Everyone turned to look at Aunt Ida, who held her skittish little dog in her lap.

Zyla's mom rolled her eyes. "It's not a strange city, Auntie. It's Philly, and we used to live there." She paused and looked at Zyla. "Zy knows her way around. And she has a friend with her. I don't mind if she goes, just not alone. It's okay."

"Yeah, I'll be fine," Zyla said, staring at her mom. She finally turned away to look at Kai. "We'd better get going if we want to make the afternoon train."

"Right," Kai said. "Let me run home and get my wallet. I'll pick you up and drive to the train station."

"Okay." Zyla smiled, and in her eyes, he saw deep relief.

Knowing that he was helping her made him feel empowered, like a better person. Aunt Brenda and Uncle Steve wouldn't be mad at him for helping a friend, right? This didn't have anything to do with his crush at all. He strolled out of her house and ran home with purpose.

And he smiled the whole way. He was getting that afternoon date after all. Platonically speaking, of course.

Kai followed Zyla as they walked through South Philly toward the fabric store. When they turned onto South Street, it was packed with people doing weekend shopping and day drinking at Wet Willie's. And he smelled cheesesteaks. He *always* got a cheesesteak when he came to Philly. Damn, he was hungry. He was in such a rush to get dressed, he didn't have time to eat after his run like usual. He held a hand to his stomach as it grumbled.

All the while, Zyla walked beside him, a pinched expression on her face. He figured she and her mom must have gotten into it again after he left her house, because her mood had worsened by the time he picked her up. He asked once if she was okay, and she nodded tightly. Then she thanked him again for coming with her, and she sounded a little guilty, as if she'd managed to rope him into doing something he didn't want to do, which couldn't be further from the truth. He was happy to be here and help her when she needed it. He was even okay with walking beside her in silence.

Suddenly, she reached out and placed her hand on his forearm. He froze and looked at her. She was smiling.

"We're here." She pointed up at a sign that said GENIE'S FABRICS & THRIFTS.

He followed her inside, and he felt as though he'd walked into a time machine. An old Prince song was playing loudly overhead, and every inch of the tiny store was covered in racks of clothes from the eighties and nineties. That was where a handful of customers were browsing. To the left of the store up against the wall were reams of different fabric patterns. A tall white woman with red hair stood behind the counter, wearing a leather choker necklace, square-framed sunglasses, and a sleeveless plaid red flannel. When she spotted Zyla, she smiled and waved.

"Hey there, Zy. Haven't seen you in a while."

Zyla ran toward her. *Ran.* Kai hadn't seen her look so excited before.

"I've missed you," Zyla said, reaching across the counter and throwing her arms around the woman. "It's been forever."

"I know," the woman said, squeezing Zyla back. "The burbs treating you well?"

Zyla shrugged. "I guess. Speaking of suburbia." She turned around and looked at Kai. "This is my friend Kai. Kai, this is Genie. She owns the store."

Kai walked forward and shook Genie's hand, which was covered in a spiderweb tattoo. A black widow stared back up at him.

"It's nice to meet you," he said. "Cool store."

Genie beamed. "Thank you. Just for that, you get thirty percent off any vintage tee of your choice."

"Vintage tees are always thirty percent off," Zyla said.

"Well, he can have a *thirty-five* percent discount."

Zyla laughed and rolled her eyes. "Do you have the cow-print fabric we talked about?"

"Yep, it's in the back. Give me a few minutes and I'll bring it out for you."

Genie disappeared behind a wall of beaded strings into the area where she must have kept her fabric.

"She's nice," Kai said to Zyla.

"Yeah." Zyla nodded. "She was, like, my only friend when I lived here."

Kai frowned. "Weren't you in middle school then?"

126

She nodded again.

"And your only friend was an adult who owned a thrift store?" Something about that made him so sad.

"A thrift *and* fabric store." Zyla shrugged. "Genie's cool. I didn't really think about her age or my own." She laughed quietly to herself. "I guess that makes me sound like a huge loser, huh?"

Kai shook his head. "I would never think of you as a loser. You're probably the dopest person I've ever met."

Once the words were out of his mouth, he winced.

Whoa there. Slow down on the honesty, buddy. You'll scare her off. Do you want her to think you're trying to date her?

Avoiding eye contact in case she was looking at him in horror, he focused his attention on the tub of pins by the register. "Hey," he said attempting to change the subject. "Is this where you get your pins?"

"Yeah." Her voice was soft. When he finally looked up, she was smiling at him. Gently, she looped her fingers around his wrist. "Want to check out some fabric with me?"

"Sure."

He followed her to the wall of fabric. She began rolling out the reams to test the texture and took a few pictures of the ones she liked. She chewed the inside of her mouth and squinted one eye. Kai smiled. She had a cute focused face.

"I need rose-gold satin," she said. "I promised my best friend that I'd make her winter formal gown this year."

"What about your own?"

She glanced at him. "My own what?"

"Winter formal gown. Do you make your own dresses too?"

"Oh." She shook her head and laughed. "St. Catherine's dances are terrible, so none of us ever go. Beatrice goes to the Hopkins Prep winter formal every year. Someone always asks her."

Of course. Fucking Hopkins Prep boys. "Has anyone ever asked you?"

"Once or twice. I said no."

"Why?" He bet it had something to do with her reluctance to date or fall in love.

"Because Hopkins Prep boys are high-key annoying."

"Aren't they?" He felt immense relief to hear her say this. "Jamal and I went to one of their parties last night, and it was trash."

"Sounds about right. Beatrice drags me to them sometimes." She laughed as she inched down the line of fabrics, pausing in front of dark blue denim. "I need to make another pair of overalls."

Kai blinked. "You can make overalls?"

"Yeah. It was tricky the first few times I tried, but it's not so hard anymore. Just time consuming."

"Wow. You're really into fashion. Like . . . really into it." He knew she sketched all the time and put sticky notes in her magazines, and that she dressed nice, but he was finally putting it together now. "You're basically a designer."

"The plan is to be a *world-famous* designer," she said. "I'm

128

working on my fashion school portfolio right now—it's why I need the cow print. By this time next year, if I'm lucky, I'll be in Paris or London." She turned to him and smiled. "Years from now, you'll be able to say you knew me way back when."

"Wow. I can picture you walking through the streets of Paris, all cool and stylish or whatever. You'll fit right in."

"Thank you." She beamed, and a warm feeling spread throughout his chest. "It's expensive, but I've been saving up, and I'm going to apply for scholarships and grants. My aunt Ida put aside some money for me too, so if I do get in, we're going to make it work."

"Nice," he said. Then he had a realization. "There'd be an entire ocean between us."

"That's kind of the point."

Kai blinked, taken aback, and she quickly backtracked. "I don't mean from you, of course. Just here in general. And, you know, my family and stuff."

"You want to get away from your family?"

Kai simply wanted to go to Morehouse, which was only a two-hour flight away in Georgia. But the idea of being even that far from Aunt Brenda and Uncle Steve, truly on his own, made him nervous.

"I'm applying to schools in New York and LA too." Zyla had that slightly guilty look on her face again. "My whole life has been dictated by my mom's whims. Where she wants to move. Who she's dating. Whether or not she likes her job. I've had control over so little for so many years. And I have so many responsibilities all the time. If I'm far away, I'll finally be able to live the way I want, without fearing that my mom will somehow find a way to make me come back home and help her take care of things."

"It almost sounds like you'd be escaping her."

"I guess I would be in a way." She smirked, then suddenly became very serious. "I feel so stupid and ungrateful saying this to you."

"Why?" Kai asked, confused.

She bit her lip. Softly, she said, "Because your parents died."

"Oh." He blinked.

"And my mom is alive, and I'm sitting here complaining about her. That's really insensitive, and I'm sorry."

"I appreciate you saying that," Kai said. "But you don't have to apologize. My parents aren't here anymore, but that doesn't change the relationship you have with your mom."

"I know," she said quietly. "She isn't a bad mom. Not really. I don't want you to think that. She supports my dreams and everything. It's just, sometimes being her daughter isn't very easy."

Kai wondered again if being an orphan meant that he was no longer someone's son.

To Zyla, he said, "I get that."

They were quiet as she ran her fingers over the denim fabric. "Is it hard being without your parents?" she asked, then winced. "Sorry, that was a really, really stupid question."

"It's not stupid," he said. He didn't want her to feel like she had to walk on eggshells around him. He talked openly about this stuff with Jamal, so maybe he could do the same with Zyla too. "It is hard. Some days are better than others. I've been in therapy for a long time . . . so that helps."

"Really?" She turned to him, eyes wide. He waited for her to start acting weird now that she knew this about him, but she just said, "That's really cool. I probably need a therapist too, honestly."

"I mean, I personally think everyone could benefit from therapy."

Zyla smiled at him. He was thankful when she changed the subject and asked, "Where are you thinking of going to college?"

"Morehouse. My dad went there."

"An HBCU. Nice." She continued walking down the line of fabrics, and he followed behind.

"My uncle went there too. He and my dad played football together. And that's where he met my mom. She went to Spelman." He watched as Zyla ran her fingers over some silk. "They locked eyes at a party, and apparently it was love at first sight."

"Really?" She glanced back at him and smiled. "That's sweet."

Kai felt himself smile too. "Yeah, my uncle took me there a couple years ago, and when I stepped foot on the campus, I just felt this presence, like a connection to my parents. Like I knew that's where I was supposed to be. I know it probably sounds weird."

"It doesn't," Zyla said, turning to him again. "I bet you'll be the big man on campus there like you are here."

Kai laughed. "Is that how you think of me?"

"Isn't that how everyone thinks of you?"

"I don't know. I haven't heard that one before." He paused, intrigued. "What do people say?"

"Mostly they just talk about how hot you are," she blurted, then literally clamped her hand down over her mouth. "Oh God," she said through her fingers. "Did I just say that out loud?"

"You did." Kai grinned so wide, he thought his cheeks might split. Zyla thought he was hot. It gave him the sensation of a runner's high.

She covered her face with her hands, and she'd never looked more adorable to him. "I'm just going to let the floor swallow me whole right here," she said. "Please feel free to leave and let my mom know you couldn't save me."

"I can't do that. Your aunt Ida will beat my ass."

Zyla snorted. Kai reached forward and gently pulled her fingers away from her face. She stared at him bashfully. Some eighties love ballad was playing overhead, and it caused his heart to expand in his chest.

"You don't have to be embarrassed," he said. "I already know I'm hot."

She swatted at him. "Oh, of course you do."

They stood there smiling at each other. Then suddenly, Genie called from the register, "Here's your cow print, Zy."

Zyla blinked, mumbling, "Oh yeah."

Kai was a little sour that their moment had been ruined, but he followed Zyla to the front of the store. She ran her fingers over the cow-print fabric, mesmerized. "I'm going to make a beret," she explained. "And maybe a matching clutch."

"Cool." Kai wasn't sure what else to say about making clothes. "I bet it will look nice."

A burst of thunder crackled overheard. Kai glanced outside, and the sky, which had been blue and clear, was now an ominous gray. People on the street were covering their heads from the light drizzle.

Genie wrapped Zyla's fabric in an extra-large trash bag for protection against the rain. "You two had better get back to the train station before it really starts coming down."

Zyla thanked Genie, promising she'd be back to shop soon once she got paid again.

"Damn, I'm hungry," Kai said as they stood by the door.

"Me too." Zyla frowned. "And I don't want to go home yet. I told my mom we'd get food and explore."

"I don't see why we have to let the rain stop us."

Zyla pointed to her hair. "This is reason enough."

Kai stared at her thick curls. Then he got an idea. "Wait here."

He walked back to the fabric wall and called Genie over. By the time he returned to Zyla, he had a yard of black cotton fabric. He held it out to her.

"To cover your hair," he explained.

She stared at him. "You bought fabric just so that my hair wouldn't get wet?"

"Um, well, yeah." Maybe that was extra. He felt a little stupid now. "I can return it, though. I mean—"

"No, no." She quickly took the fabric from him and wrapped it around her head. "Thank you so much, Kai. This is very sweet."

"No problem." His runner's high was back.

They stepped outside. In a matter of seconds, the drizzle turned into an outright downpour.

Kai pointed at Ishkabibble's across the street. "Cheesesteaks?"

Zyla nodded. "Cheesesteaks."

Then, just as Kai took a deep breath and prepared to dart into the street and get drenched, he felt Zyla's hand close around his.

"So we don't get separated," she said. She looked down at their hands and up at him again, a little nervously.

He didn't care why she was holding his hand. Only that she was doing it at all.

"Okay," he said.

With fingers interlocked, they made a run for it.

Chapter Ten

The rain had officially addled Zyla's brain. That was the only explanation for why she would impulsively grab Kai's hand before they ran across the street into Ishkabibble's.

And it would explain why she was sitting here with Kai, eating a cheesesteak when she didn't even like cheesesteaks that much. This one was good, though, if she ate around the onions.

Kai smiled at her across the table. His cheesesteak was already halfway gone. His clothes were rain soaked, just like hers. But her hair was dry thanks to the fabric he'd bought for her. It lay folded beside her bag now, and she was careful not to get any crumbs on it. She had the absurd thought that it needed to be preserved in order to keep the smell and memories from today. Who knows, maybe she could start building a small shrine to Kai in her closet, Helga Pataki from *Hey Arnold!* style.

Stop that right now.

She chided herself and focused on the present. Here she was in Philly with Kai Johnson, who was her *friend*. Her only friend, it seemed, until Beatrice came home.

She did have to admit that strolling through Philly, running hand and hand in the rain, and sharing a meal felt very much like things people did on dates. This was the first time she'd ever hung out one-on-one with a boy without it having to do with a school project. She wondered if this felt natural to Kai, given his dating history.

"Can I ask you something?" she said.

Kai paused midchew. "Go ahead."

"Have you ever loved any of your ex-girlfriends?"

The question had been on Zyla's mind since Kai revealed his total number of exes. In a way, he was like her mom: often in and out of relationships. She wondered how her mom was able to go through a breakup, have her heart decimated, then pick back up and start over again. She didn't feel comfortable asking her mom those questions, but maybe she'd gain some intel from Kai.

"I've been in deep like with girls," he said. "But I don't think I've ever loved any of them."

"You don't think? Isn't that something you should know?"

He smirked. "Okay, let me answer that again. No, I haven't loved any of them."

"Did you ever tell a girl you loved her even though you didn't?"

"No." He frowned. "Why would I do that?"

She shrugged. "It happens."

So at least now she knew he wasn't like her dad, who wrapped women into his web with false declarations and promises. It was what he'd done to his girlfriends and fiancées since her mom divorced him.

"Which ex did you like the most?" she asked. Here she was being too nosy again. She stared at Kai, expecting him to finally tell her to mind her business. Instead, he rested his chin in his palm and squinted off into the distance.

"I don't know. There was one ex I had pretty high hopes for in the beginning, when things seemed promising. Then her whole attitude changed. She could be petty, and she got annoyed easily, but I didn't know just how mean she could be until she showed me. I guess I liked the side of her that she wanted me to see in the beginning, when it was good."

"Are you talking about Camille?"

He leaned back and grinned. "I thought you said you weren't a mind reader, Zyla Matthews?"

"I'm not, Kai Johnson. It's just pretty obvious. You're probably the only person at Sailor Joe's who thinks Camille is capable of being a nice person."

He laughed. "I mean, yeah. Maybe she's not everyone's favorite."

"That's putting it mildly."

Zyla decided to leave it at that. She might overhear gossip here and there, but she didn't like to gossip herself, even about Camille, queen of the stink eye. Plus, Zyla felt like Camille had eyes everywhere, especially when it came to Kai. She wouldn't have been surprised if Tyesha or one of Camille's other friends had trailed them from Cedar and were here now, eavesdropping on their conversation.

She wondered what Camille would do if word got back to

her that Zyla had basically said she was the meanest girl at Sailor Joe's. Would she straight up want to fight? Maybe she'd do something diabolical like glue Balloon Darts to Zyla's seat at the booth, so that when Zyla sat down, she'd feel shooting pain. Honestly, that would be kind of hilarious and brilliant, like something an evil cartoon character would do.

"I guess I can be willfully oblivious sometimes," Kai admitted.

She was gearing up to ask how long it usually took him to get over a breakup when he suddenly turned the conversation to her.

"You've never dated," he said, "but have you ever had a crush on anyone?"

She felt her face get hot. She didn't know why. It was a perfectly normal question.

"Yes," she said.

"And has a crush ever expressed mutual interest in you?"

She thought about Jerrod Foster in the sixth grade, who wrote her a note asking if she wanted to be his girlfriend after she'd admired him from afar for weeks. And then there was Erin, who worked at Genie's last year for a few months. Zyla seized up every time she saw Erin standing at the register and made awkward statements that could barely pass as attempts at conversation. When Erin asked Zyla if she wanted to see a show together, Zyla gave some silly excuse about needing to watch Bartholomew that weekend. Eventually, Erin moved away for college, and Zyla had been relieved that she could shop at Genie's in peace without feeling like her heart was going to explode.

And, of course, there was Kai. Her crush on him had just been beginning to form when he asked her out to the movies after their first shift. She'd shut both him and the crush down pretty quickly.

At least that's what she'd been trying to convince herself of lately.

"Yes," she finally answered.

Kai tilted his head, looking at her closely. She could tell from his curious expression that more questions were coming, and she didn't want him poking around in her brain any longer. She might end up blurting more things she didn't mean to say aloud, like earlier when she'd told him that everyone thought he was hot.

She pointed at her cheesesteak. "This was really good."

"Right?" he said, smiling.

Zyla smiled too and glanced behind him, noticing that the rain had stopped.

"Maybe we should go back to the train station now, while we have a chance," she said, and Kai nodded in agreement.

Once they reached the train platform, Kai stood in front of the Eighth and Market sign and held up his phone to take a picture. Then he paused and waved Zyla over. "Want to take a selfie with me?"

"Oh," she said, surprised yet thrilled. "Yeah, sure."

She stood beside him and leaned closer. From the camera angle, it almost looked as though she was leaning her head on his shoulder. They both smiled wide as he snapped the photo.

She watched as he posted on his Instagram with the caption, "Quick Philly trip. Cheesesteaks were had."

Kai posting her on his Instagram meant something, didn't it? No, no. She swatted that thought away. People posted selfies with their friends on social media all the time. And that's what everyone else would think once they saw the picture too, right? It was no big deal.

Anyway, she didn't want to focus on that. She wanted to focus on Kai and how much she enjoyed his company. Her day had started off so terribly with the chores and Bartholomew being difficult, and that whole mess with her mom. Other than Beatrice, she didn't talk to anyone about her desire to get space from her family. And Kai had listened so attentively.

She felt light and warm. It had nothing to do with the August heat.

"Hey," he said, "so next weekend one of my friends is having a party at his family's beach house in Wildwood. I'm driving down with Jamal and Alanna and another friend. Do you want to come too?"

His voice was soft, and his eyes kept shifting from her face to the ground. If she didn't know any better, she'd say that Kai was nervous. Her stomach did a little flip.

"Yes," she said, smiling. "That sounds fun."

"Okay," he said, also smiling. "Cool."

Her silly esophagus butterflies swarmed in delight as the train pulled into the station.

Chapter Eleven

Kai didn't know why the hell he thought inviting Zyla to Brandon's beach house party tonight would be a good idea. For starters, he forgot that sometimes his friends lived to embarrass him.

"Kai, do you not believe in cleaning your car or what?" Darius, Jamal's cousin, asked.

Kai sighed and glanced at Darius in his rearview mirror before returning his gaze to the highway traffic in front of him. They were about twenty minutes away from the Wildwood exit.

"I just cleaned my car, like, two weeks ago," Kai answered.

"Nah, that was like a month ago," Jamal said, grinning beside Kai in the passenger seat with the window rolled halfway down. "I was with you, remember? Wait, now that I think about it, bro, it might have been two months ago."

"It's mad McDonald's wrappers back here," Darius said. "Just straight disgusting. Right, Zyla?"

Zyla, who was sandwiched in the back seat between Darius and Alanna, smiled. "I think it's pretty clean."

"Thank you, Zyla," Kai said, catching her eye in the rearview mirror.

She smiled at him, and he felt that runner's high again. After their shift ended earlier that evening, she'd changed into denim shorts and some kind of braided tank top. A gold necklace dangled down the center of her chest, and she wore gold shimmer on her cheeks. She looked beautiful. He was glad she'd sat in the back and not in the passenger seat, because he wouldn't have been able to stop staring at her.

"Zyla's just being polite," Darius said. "She's a *St. Catherine's* girl, of course."

Zyla laughed and swatted at Darius. "Stop it."

Through the rearview mirror, Kai watched Darius put his arm around Zyla and squeeze her shoulder. His fingernails were painted a shiny bright blue.

"Darius, why don't you be quiet and pass me some of those Doritos?" Jamal asked, turning around. He winked dramatically at Alanna. "How you doing back there, sweet thing?"

Alanna giggled. "I'm fine, thanks." To Zyla she said, "I can't wait to introduce you to my friends. You'll love them."

And this was the second reason Kai didn't know why he'd invited Zyla tonight. At least three of his exes were going to be at this party. *At least.* And each of them were friends with Alanna, who was student council president and essentially friends with everyone. Kai didn't know why he was tripping. It wasn't like Zyla was his girl or that he had to worry about her getting into it with any of his exes. She was just his friend.

His friend who he couldn't stop staring at.

He pulled off the highway exit and drove through the North

Wildwood beach town until they pulled up in front of Brandon's house. Brandon somehow convinced his parents to let him throw a party as one last summer hurrah. On Monday they'd be shipped off to football camp for two weeks. Once camp ended, Kai and his teammates would only have a few days before they started senior year.

Kai cut the engine, and Jamal quickly hopped out of the passenger seat and ran around the car to open Alanna's door. He offered his hand and kissed her knuckles as he helped her out of the car. Kai, Zyla, and Darius stood off to the side and watched this unfold. Zyla snorted, and Darius rolled his eyes, mumbling to Zyla that Jamal tried too hard.

Kai heard someone call his name, and he turned around, recognizing some of his classmates lingering on the front porch. He nodded at them and waved. Zyla leaned toward Kai and whispered, "Big man on campus."

Kai looked down at her and grinned, enjoying her nearness. She smelled like flowers, or something sweet and fresh. "Not really," he said.

"Okay, I'm outta here," Darius announced, throwing up the peace sign and walking toward the backyard. "Text me when y'all are ready to go."

Alanna and Jamal started for the porch, and Kai and Zyla fell into step behind them. Zyla bounced her shoulders up and down. "I haven't been to a Cedar High party before," she said. "I'm excited."

"It's nothing special," Kai assured her. The air smelled salty, and the breeze whipped Zyla's curly hair around her face. *Stop staring.* "Should be fun, though."

"Is this going to be one of those things where we walk inside and you're suddenly pulled away by, like, a million people and I'll end up standing alone in a corner the whole night?"

"No, of course not. I wouldn't—" Kai stopped when he noticed her smirk. "You're messing with me."

She smiled. "Only because it's so easy. I'll be fine. Even if I don't see you for the rest of the night."

They were inches away from the porch. Kai was suddenly overcome with the need to make up for whatever might happen once they entered the party.

"Hey, listen," he said, lowering his voice. He settled his hand on her arm, and she stilled beside him on the front lawn. "So, um, there's a chance a few of my exes are going to be here."

Zyla's eyes widened, intrigued. "Really? Which ones?"

"I don't know. Just don't believe everything you hear, okay? They might say stuff to you about me."

"Stuff like what?"

"I don't know." He was starting to sweat a little. He was overreacting. He needed to chill. But he kept talking anyway. "Most of them are cool. They probably won't say anything. I don't even know why I'm telling you this."

Zyla laughed, searching his face. "I can't wait to meet them."

No—wait. This was the opposite effect he wanted his words to have. But his time was up.

"Zyla, come with me," Alanna said, running over and grabbing Zyla's hand. "You don't want to be stuck with the boys all night."

She led Zyla up the porch steps, away from Kai. The dudes stared at the two of them, especially Zyla, the new girl no one had seen before. Kai fought the urge to run up and place his arm around her. To let them know she was off-limits, that she'd come there with him. But he had no claim to her in that way.

When Kai reached the porch, the boys turned to him, eyeing him with interest.

"That's you?" Raheem Poole, Kai's classmate, asked, nodding his head at Zyla as she and Alanna disappeared inside.

"Nah," Kai replied, stuffing his hands in his pockets. He narrowed his eyes at Raheem and quickly shook himself out of it.

Raheem and the rest of the boys burst into laughter. "Don't worry," Raheem said, holding his hands up. "We don't want no problems. She's with you. Message received."

Kai sighed and waved them away.

"Damn," Jamal hissed, coming to stand beside him. "I swore I was gonna get some one-on-one time with Alanna tonight."

"I feel you," Kai said as he watched Zyla and Alanna walk through the party. Right toward his exes.

Welp, it was out of his hands now.

"My best friend, Whit, is somewhere in here," Alanna said, her hand tightly clasped around Zyla's. She smoothly maneuvered her way through the thick throng of people. "Ugh, Brandon's parties are always so crowded."

145

Zyla kept her eyes on the back of Alanna's long burgundy Senegalese twists, careful not to lose sight of her in the crowd. Alanna was tiny, with light brown skin and a huge smile. Upon meeting her earlier tonight, Zyla understood immediately why Jamal was so enamored with her. Alanna was really sweet, just like he'd said.

A Flo Milli song was blasting from somewhere in the house, and everyone seemed to be drinking from red Solo cups. Lots of people knew Alanna, and they kept stopping her to say hello.

"Oh, there's Whit," Alanna said, leading Zyla into the crowded living room. "Whit! Hey, girl!"

A girl with dark brown skin and waist-length box braids sat on the arm of a chair and immediately hopped up when she spotted Alanna. "About time you got here! What took y'all so long?"

"You know Kai doesn't go above the speed limit," Alanna said. "This is Zyla."

"It's nice to meet you," Zyla said. "I love your skirt."

Whit smiled and glanced down at her high-waist black denim skirt. "Thanks, girl."

"Zyla works at Sailor Joe's with Jamal and Kai," Alanna said.

"Oh yeah?" Whit said to Zyla. "You live in Cedar?"

Zyla nodded. "Yeah, but I go to St. Catherine's, so that's why I don't really know anybody."

Zyla held her breath and waited for Whit to size her up or to stereotype her as a privileged private-school girl. But Whit only smiled.

"Nice," she said. "I used to do all-star cheer with a girl who goes to St. Catherine's." She paused, her eyes suddenly widening. "Wait. You're Kai's girlfriend, the one he posted on his Instagram the other day."

"I'm not his girlfriend," Zyla said, taken off guard. Then she thought of the way she and Kai held hands as they ran in the rain last weekend. "We're just friends."

"Really?" Whit seemed surprised. She glanced at Alanna, who looked equally confused.

"You and Kai aren't together?" Alanna asked, and Zyla shook her head. "Weird. Could have sworn you were. Especially given how you both were acting in the car ride here."

"*What?* How were we acting?"

But Whit cut Alanna off before she could answer. "Well, you *are* the one they're calling Bonnie, right?" she asked.

Zyla cringed. Had their godforsaken nickname somehow found its way outside of Sailor Joe's? "How'd you know that?"

"I'm on the dance team with Camille Vaughn," Whit said. "We had tryouts last weekend, and she wouldn't stop talking about you and Kai and how everyone was calling you Bonnie and Clyde, and that y'all jumped a customer. And she wouldn't shut up about that Instagram post. She was mad that Kai had moved on so quickly. But you're saying y'all aren't even boyfriend and girlfriend?"

"We're not," Zyla said weakly. Great. She was pretty sure this meant she was officially on Camille's hit list if the stink-eye behavior wasn't enough proof. "And we didn't jump a customer! He tried to fight us."

Whit waved her hand in dismissal. "It's whatever. Don't pay Camille any mind."

"Yeah," Alanna said, busy texting. "She's not nearly as intimidating as she pretends to be. Camille used to act weird around Whit too, since she's Kai's ex and all."

"Wait. *You're* Whitney Brown?" Zyla asked.

"Yeah," Whit said. "And oh my gosh, Alanna, we dated forever ago."

"Girl, please," Alanna said, glancing up from her phone. "It was sophomore year."

Whit gave Alanna a look. "I said forever ago, didn't I? It's weird to even think that he was my boyfriend at one point." She looked at Zyla. "Don't worry, Kai and I are cool now. I won't be weird around you since you're his . . . friend."

Zyla sighed as Whit and Alanna both giggled. Clearly, no one wanted to believe that she and Kai were simply friends. She glanced around at the strangers in the room. Well, strangers to her, but they probably knew Kai. Did everyone here think she was his girlfriend?

"Let's go in the backyard," Alanna said, regaining Zyla's attention. "Ash just texted and said she and Deja are out there."

Zyla followed Alanna and Whit until they were standing outside in the backyard.

Alanna shouted, "Ashley! Deja! We're over here!"

Zyla turned, and a tall, lithe girl with faux locs and a short girl wearing a striped maxi dress were making their way toward them.

"Is that Ashley West and Deja Foster, by any chance?" Zyla asked.

Whit nodded and laughed. "Did Kai give you a list of his exes or something?"

"Basically." Zyla smiled a little in response to Whit's laughter.

Chapter Twelve

Kai stood in the kitchen, surrounded by a handful of his teammates as they played flip cup, and he tried his best to pay attention to their conversation. Something about football camp and the end of summer. He couldn't focus, though, because he was officially in the twilight zone. He looked out the kitchen window into the backyard at Zyla, who was standing with Alanna, Whit Brown, Ashley West, *and* Deja Foster. He blinked and rubbed his eyes to make sure he was seeing correctly.

Whit, Ashley, *and* Deja? For real?

What were they talking about? It had to be him. No, never mind. That was really vain. He wasn't stupid enough to assume girls spent all their time sitting around talking about boys. And why would he be the topic of conversation, anyway? Zyla wasn't his girlfriend. He had no reason to be discussed. But still, if his name did come up, he hoped Whit, Ashley, and Deja only had nice things to say.

Then Zyla turned her head and glanced at her surroundings. Was she looking for him? He willed her to look in his direction. But then Alanna said something to her and Zyla faced forward again, laughing.

"Yo," Brandon said, waving his hand in front of Kai's face. "You hear what I said, bro?"

"Um, yeah," Kai mumbled, turning away from the window. He leaned against the sink. "Camp is gonna be cool. I'm looking forward to it."

He felt a little guilty for not fully paying attention, especially since they were talking about the upcoming season. This was probably what Aunt Brenda and Uncle Steve meant when they said he could stand to focus more. Kai was captain this year, and he should act like one. On Monday they'd leave for camp and be there for two weeks straight. Damn. Two weeks. He'd miss the end of summer. He kinda wished he and Zyla would spend at least *a little bit* of time together tonight. He groaned at his own thirsty thoughts. He felt like Jamal pining after Alanna.

"The senior trip is at the Poconos again this year," Brandon was saying. His mom worked in the school's administration office, so he got the scoop before everyone else.

"I already started saving up," Will Peterson said, trying and failing to flip his cup over.

"Damn, Will, come on!" Jamal groaned. "Hate having you on my team, bro. You always make me lose."

On the other side of the table, Chris Webb flipped his cup over perfectly, and so did Brandon. They gave each other a high five in triumph, and Jamal rolled his eyes.

"Will, you gotta go," he said. "Kai, come sub for him."

Kai lifted his keys. "Can't. I'm DD."

Aside from the fact that he was tonight's designated driver,

Kai didn't like to drink that much. His thoughts tended to spiral sometimes. And it wasn't like he needed to get a DUI in the car his aunt and uncle gave to him.

"We're gonna stay overnight in a lodge." Brandon continued with details of the senior trip. "Some place called Roaring Rapids."

"That's dope," Jamal said. "Too bad it just can't be us and St. Catherine's. It's annoying as hell that Hopkins Prep is going too."

Kai nodded in agreement. Each year in May, Cedar High, St. Catherine's, and Hopkins Prep went on a tri-school senior trip. It was supposed to foster comradery between the three schools, since they were so close in proximity. One last celebration before graduation. Kai hadn't given the trip much thought, to be honest.

"Let's go outside. It's getting hot in here," Jamal said.

The group made their way onto the back porch. People milled around in the sand near the bonfire. Ocean waves crashed loudly against the beach in the distance. Kai heard a cacophony of laughter and immediately spotted the source. Darius was now standing with Zyla, Alanna, Whit, Ashley, and Deja, and they were giggling at whatever he was saying.

Kai groaned. Darius was close friends with Camille. You would think that because Kai and Jamal had been best friends since middle school, and Darius, who lived with Jamal and was thereby one of Kai's best friends by extension, would choose Kai's side in the breakup. He hadn't. He was fiercely loyal to Camille. They were dance team cocaptains, and they spent hella time together. Darius taking Camille's side hurt a little. Kai tried not to take it personally. But still.

Jamal followed Kai's line of sight and grinned. "What do you think they're over there talking about?"

"No idea." Kai shrugged, hoping he looked nonchalant.

"Yo, so what's up with you and her?" Brandon asked, jerking his chin toward Zyla. "I've been meaning to ask since you posted that picture."

"Nothing," Kai said. "We're friends."

He should have known that picture would cause a stir. At the time, he was just so happy to be chilling with Zyla that he wanted everyone to know. Now he wondered if that was the best choice.

"That's it?" Chris asked. "Because Raheem said that you told him and his boys nobody could talk to her."

"What?" Kai shook his head. "I didn't say that."

"He said you were mad they were looking at her," Will added.

Well, that part wasn't false. But he'd tried his best to hide his annoyance with Raheem and his crew.

"So if someone here tried to talk to her and she gave them play, you wouldn't get mad?" Brandon asked.

Kai took a deep breath and considered his response. *Mad* wouldn't necessarily be the right term. More like disappointed. Gutted. Crestfallen. Given how Zyla didn't want to date, it was unlikely she'd be interested in anybody here. But it would be some shit if he brought his crush to a party and she ended up falling for someone else.

"She can do whatever she wants," he finally said. Because that was the truth, no matter how much he hated to admit it.

Brandon laughed. "Yeah, okay."

Jamal clapped him on the shoulder. "You don't have to stunt for us, you know. If you like her, you like her."

"We're *friends*," Kai repeated.

And then, almost as if he'd willed it, Zyla turned around, saw Kai, and smiled.

———

Zyla was starting to feel a little buzzed. As soon as Ashley and Deja joined their group, Ashley produced a bottle of red wine that she'd taken from her dad's vast collection, and she kept refilling everyone's cups. The wine was dry and tart, and it made Zyla feel warmer with each sip.

Darius had recently migrated over, and he and Whit were talking about their recent dance team tryouts and how Camille had made the incoming freshmen cower in fear. Darius kept calling Camille "Cami." Zyla figured he and Camille must be pretty close, because she hadn't heard anyone refer to Camille by that nickname before. Earlier when Whit brought up Camille, Zyla had cringed a little. But thanks to the wine, she was breezy and cool.

She glanced around at the people surrounding her. Ashley was on Cedar High's girls' basketball team. When Whit jokingly mentioned that Zyla knew Kai's exes by name, Ashley just laughed and asked if Kai ever told Zyla how she once beat him in a game of one-on-one. Deja had assumed that Kai and

Zyla were dating. Along with the Instagram post that was seen by apparently everyone in the world, she'd also spotted them talking on the front lawn earlier. When Zyla told her they were just friends, Deja looked surprised and said, "Oh! You look cute together, though."

She wondered what Kai was up to. She hadn't seen him all night. She kept hoping he'd find his way to her in the backyard, but he was probably preoccupied, as big men on campus often were. She laughed to herself, wondering what he'd think seeing her with Whit, Ashley, and Deja. Between the three of them and Camille, his exes seemed impressive in one way or another, and they were gorgeous. Maybe it was a good thing that nothing would come of the crush she had on Kai, the crush she refused to acknowledge. Because these girls left some pretty big shoes to fill.

"Let's go grab those chairs by the fire pit before someone takes them," Alanna said. And the group began to move.

Zyla felt wobbly, like she was walking in slow motion as she followed closely behind, and—oh, look! She spotted Kai! On the back porch with Jamal and some other boys she didn't know. Her heart leaped at the sight of him. He was so beautiful, standing there in his simple black V-neck and denim shorts. He always looked so *calm*. She wanted to run over and wrap him in a hug, to soak in his beauty and stillness.

He caught eyes with her immediately and smiled, raising an eyebrow. She knew him well enough now to know that he was silently asking if she was okay. His gaze quickly landed on the girls with her, and she saw him wince. Ha. He didn't look exactly thrilled that she'd found her way to three of his exes.

She gave him a thumbs-up and he nodded, flashing another one of those devastatingly beautiful smiles. Maybe she could just go over there with him now . . .

"Come on, girl," Alanna said, wrapping her hand around Zyla's. "Don't get left behind."

She reluctantly let Alanna pull her away, and they plopped beside each other, sharing a large beach chair.

"So, what's up with you and Jamal?" Deja asked Alanna, her words slurring slightly. "Y'all together now or what?"

"No," Alanna said coyly. "Not yet."

Whit rolled her eyes. "She's playing hard to get. I don't know why. She already knows Jamal would chase her to the end of the earth."

"He thinks you're sweet," Zyla heard herself say. Everyone turned to look at her. "I mean, that's what he told me a couple weeks ago. That he thought you were sweet."

Alanna grinned, and Whit leaned over and wrapped Alanna in a tight hug. "She is sweet. Our little sugarplum fairy student council president."

Zyla watched them and felt a little chasm form in her chest. She missed Beatrice.

Then she felt Alanna throw her arm around her shoulder. "Don't look now," she whispered in Zyla's ear, "but Kai is staring at you."

"Really?" Zyla whipped her head around and spotted Kai

on the back porch. His eyes were on her, just like Alanna said. Zyla's lips spread into a grin.

"I said don't look now," Alanna hissed, laughing. "You gotta learn to play it cool, Zyla."

Zyla turned back to Alanna and wrinkled her eyebrows, confused. "What do you mean?"

"Nothing." Alanna shook her head and smiled, like she knew something Zyla didn't, which only confused Zyla further. She blamed the wine.

"I'm just gonna go say hi to him," she mumbled, breaking away from the group. "See if he's okay."

Alanna continued to smile at her. "Okay."

Zyla walked toward Kai and felt like the sand was trying to slow her down again. Or maybe she was just being too eager. Either way, once she reached Kai, she felt like she'd climbed a mountain. He was leaning against the porch rail, and she didn't even bother to cast a glance around at his friends before she squeezed her way into the space between him and Jamal, stumbling in her haste.

"Whoa," Kai said, reaching out to steady her. "Careful."

Ugh, what a gentleman. She snuggled up against his arm and laid her head on his shoulder, soaking in his beauty and calm, just like she wanted to do earlier.

She heard a snicker and opened her eyes. Three boys she didn't know were staring at her.

"This is Zyla," Kai said simply, by way of explanation. "Zyla, this is Brandon, Chris, and Will."

"Nice to meet you," Zyla murmured. She could barely keep her eyes open now that she was so comfortable leaning against Kai. "You feel so nice."

She felt Kai's chest rumble as he laughed softly. "Thank you."

Tomorrow she might cringe recalling this moment. But right now, she could not care less.

Distantly, she heard Alanna call Jamal's name, and quick as lighting, Jamal said, "Gotta go," and dashed down the steps. Then the other three boys dispersed, and she and Kai were left alone in their corner of the porch.

"I see you made some new friends," Kai said.

Zyla opened her eyes and looked up at him. "Your exes are really nice. They barely even talked about you." She leaned farther into him and felt like she might die from happiness when he put his arm around her. "We should hang out next weekend too."

"I'll be at football camp next weekend."

"Oh." She frowned. "When do you leave?"

Kai looked down at her. "Monday."

"Monday." That was only two days away! "How long does camp last?"

"Two weeks." He bit his lip. "I forgot you don't go to Cedar and wouldn't already know that. I'm sorry, I should have told you before now."

He was going to be gone for *two weeks*?

It dawned on her that summer was coming to an end, and

soon she and Kai would go back to their separate lives. Him at Cedar High and her at St. Catherine's. No more shifts at Sailor Joe's. No more car rides.

"That's terrible news," she finally said.

"I know." Kai's voice was soft. He leaned down and placed his chin on her head.

She turned her body toward his and breathed him in. "If I knew you were going to miss the end of summer, I would have hung out with you tonight instead of spending so much time with your exes."

Kai laughed. "I guess you'll just have to make it up to me once I get back from camp."

"I guess I will." Zyla looked up at him and smiled. He really did make her feel so comfortable. So much so, she yawned.

"You ready to go?" Kai asked.

She shook her head. She didn't want to go home yet. She closed her eyes and leaned against him again. She wanted to stay here with him because he'd be gone for two weeks.

"You're falling asleep," Kai said, and she could tell from the tone of his voice that he was smirking. "Come on, I'll get everybody together."

Soon, Zyla found herself in the passenger seat of Kai's Jeep. Alanna, Jamal, and Darius were in the back. She glanced at Kai as he typed an address into his phone's GPS, and she finally let her eyes close, smiling.

———

Kai gently shook Zyla awake. She lived closest to him, so it only made sense to drop her off last. It's not like he wanted any privacy with her or anything.

My guy, you can't date. She doesn't want to date. You really need to give it up.

Zyla sat up and looked around, confused. Then she blinked at him and smiled. "Thanks for getting me home safely."

"You're welcome." Kai cleared his throat. He wanted to say something profound. Something that would make her think about him while he was away at football camp.

He was being mad extra. It was only two weeks. She couldn't forget about him that quickly.

That was the logical way to look at this, but he sat there racking his mind for the right thing to say anyway.

Then Zyla suddenly leaned forward and hugged him tightly. He tried to hold on to the moment for as long as he could. To remember how soft her skin felt, the smell of her hair. But it ended too quickly as she pulled away.

"See you in two weeks, Kai Johnson," she said, opening the door and getting out.

"See you in two weeks, Zyla Matthews."

He thought about that hug the whole way home.

After Alanna Thomas and her friends hear the news of Zyla and Kai's alleged fight with the Hopkins Prep boys and their subsequent disappearance, they stand by the waterslide, now holding their own flip-flops and towels and tote bags. Jamal is no longer here to do so for them. As the rest of the group discusses Zyla and Kai in loud, intrigued voices, Alanna watches Jamal's retreating form. She wonders where he's going. Probably to look for Kai. Jamal is very loyal in that way.

I'm sorry, he simply said before leaving. What does Jamal have to be sorry for? Truly, Alanna knows that she is the one who should be sorry. She didn't make any time for Jamal today, not in the way she promised. After stringing him along for a year, she sort of expected that he'd always be there. Ready to do whatever she asked.

"Do y'all think Brandon is lying with that story?" Ashley West asks. "Kai and Zyla fighting and then running off like that? It sounds too wild."

"I don't know," Whitney Brown says. "Remember how they got into that fight with that customer or whatever at the amusement park last summer?"

"I wouldn't be surprised if Kai saw her talking to a Hopkins Prep boy and got jealous," Deja Foster adds. "Wasn't he ready to fight Raheem at Brandon's beach party when he asked if Zyla was single? And remember their argument at Will's house? So much drama."

"What I want to know is why any of this is happening if they're broken up," Whit says.

"But is that even true?" Ashley asks. "You remember how they spent months telling everybody they were just friends. Even when they were posting on Instagram and in each other's face at Brandon's party. Then, boom. Next thing you know, they're together."

"It *was* weird that they kept lying about that," Deja says. "It was so obvious they were more than friends."

Whit nudges Alanna. "What do you think happened?"

"Well," Alanna says, trying to establish a diplomatic tone. "I don't think they got into some big brawl with Hopkins Prep. At least I hope they didn't."

Alanna has rooted for Zyla and Kai ever since she rode with them to Brandon's house in Wildwood last summer and saw the way they kept sneaking glances at each other for the duration of the drive. In Alanna's opinion, Zyla was exactly what Kai needed. Alanna isn't a big fan of Camille and was relieved when her and Kai's relationship finally ended. Then came Zyla. Sweet and funny. New. Alanna was so disappointed when they broke up.

Suddenly, the slight drizzle turns into a steady rain. The girls squeal, throwing their towels over the heads and running for shelter. Soon, they each receive an alert that the students must return to the lodge immediately to escape the storm.

"Well, there goes our trip," Whit mumbles.

"Don't worry. I'll think of something else for us to do before graduation," Alanna says. It is her job, after all, as student council president, to lift the morale of her classmates.

She forces a smile as they run quickly through the rain back to the lodge, but she is thinking of Jamal and how she mishandled their relationship, or lack thereof. She isn't sad, necessarily, because while she liked Jamal and enjoyed his company, she didn't have very deep feelings for him. She should have just told him the truth.

They finally reach the lobby and rush through the doors, huddling inside with everyone else. Zyla and Kai are the topic of everyone's whispered conversations.

It makes Alanna think about something she told Zyla last summer when she noticed Kai staring at her from across the backyard at Brandon's.

You gotta learn to play it cool.

You see, playing it cool is a motto Alanna has lived by. Play hard to get. Let them know you have options. It worked with Jamal for a while, but that's clearly over now.

Is playing hard to get what Zyla was doing the whole time? In the beginning, when she kept insisting that she and Kai were just friends, even though her feelings for Kai were written all over her face? And today, by flirting with some random kid from Hopkins Prep, was she trying to teach Kai a lesson? To show him that there were more boys in the world?

Alanna wonders if maybe Zyla took her advice to heart after all.

Chapter Thirteen

Another Saturday, another walk for Zyla with Bartholomew, the prima donna.

"Will you please just pee already?" Zyla begged.

Bartholomew sat on the sidewalk and sniffed his butt. He looked up at Zyla with contempt. *No, I'm not ready yet, human.*

"Ugh." They were only two houses away from Aunt Ida's, and Bartholomew was already having a hissy fit. Who knew how long she'd be stuck out here with him this morning.

She wiped the sweat off her forehead. It was September, but Mother Nature thought it was August, apparently. School started in two days, and Zyla cringed thinking about how hot she'd be wearing her St. Catherine's uniform in this weather.

It was wild that summer was basically over. She'd finished out her last few shifts at Sailor Joe's sitting alone at the Balloon Darts booth. She'd had more time to work on her portfolio in peace. But she'd missed Kai and their everyday routine. How when they weren't talking, she sketched while he read. Or once they got too bored, they'd roam around the park.

She hadn't seen him since Brandon's party. He returned

from football camp a couple days ago, but he'd been busy with his aunt and uncle and getting ready for school. They texted a lot. Like while he was at camp, he'd sent her pictures of the football field and his cleats, and an image of Jamal snoring, openmouthed in their shared room. She'd sent him pictures of the empty park at dusk, and some of the new designs she was working on. He'd particularly enjoyed a picture she sent of Bartholomew glaring at her by his food bowl.

The pictures they exchanged made her feel his absence less. But the simple truth was that she missed him. Even more, she couldn't stop wondering when she might see him again. God, this crush was taking too long to go away. These feelings were starting to scare her.

What if they didn't leave? What would she do then?

Regardless of her fears, she found herself contemplating how thirsty she'd look if she casually walked Bartholomew by Kai's house, when a black Mercedes pulled up alongside her. The driver rolled down the window, and a Black girl with long, straight extensions lifted her designer sunglasses and smiled, her mouth full of braces.

"Hi, I'm here to pick up my best friend," she said.

"BEATRICE." Zyla ran over and pulled the car door open. "I thought you wouldn't be back until tomorrow!"

Beatrice Moreau jumped out of her seat and wrapped her arms around Zyla like she wanted to squeeze the life out of her. "I came home early! I wanted to surprise you!"

"Oh my God!"

"I know! Surprise!"

They jumped up and down, clutching each other. Bartholomew took offense to the disturbance of peace and ran over to bark at them.

"Oh, shut up, will you?" Zyla said, scooping him up into her arms. To Beatrice, she said, "I'm just gonna change and pack a bag. It'll take two seconds."

They ran to her house, and as Zyla burst inside, she called out, "Beatrice is back!"

Beatrice added, "And she comes bearing gifts."

Zyla deposited Bartholomew on the floor, and he ran over to resume his place at Aunt Ida's feet. Aunt Ida reclined in her La-Z-Boy and frowned at Beatrice.

"You stay out of trouble over there in that foreign country, girl?" she asked.

"Yes, Ms. Ida." Beatrice smiled sweetly and walked toward Aunt Ida, digging in her Marc Jacobs purse. She pulled out packets of tea. "French tea from the market near my dad's house. Just for you."

Aunt Ida continued to frown but leaned forward and inspected the tea. "Put it in the kitchen for me, will you?" That was basically her way of saying thank you.

Beatrice then followed Zyla into the kitchen, where Jade was busy working in her math book. Jade turned her head as they got closer, and her eyes lit up at the sight of Beatrice.

"Beatrice! You're back!" Jade ran over to Beatrice and gave her a fierce hug.

"And I have a treat for you, miss." Beatrice handed Jade a small box filled with macarons of different colors and flavors. "Don't share them with anyone."

Jade held the box to her chest and grinned. "Thank you so much!"

On their way to Zyla's room, they paused at her mom's doorway. Zyla's mom was lying on her bed with her eyes closed, having just freshly applied a face mask.

"Mom, Beatrice is here," Zyla said. They'd since gotten over their argument about Keith and Philly, but her mom was in a mood today because Keith was on another "work trip" and wasn't returning any of her calls.

Zyla's mom sat up in bed and smiled at Beatrice. "If it isn't my favorite Parisian beauty queen. Welcome home, Miss Beatrice."

"Hi, Ms. Leanne." Beatrice sauntered into the room and handed Zyla's mom a small bag of cosmetics. "These are from my dad's girlfriend. She's a makeup artist and swears by this stuff."

Zyla's mom looked like she might cry. "You're a godsend."

Beatrice shrugged and smiled. "Yeah, I know."

"I'm staying the night at Beatrice's," Zyla said. "I'll be back tomorrow."

Zyla's mom lay back down again and waved her hand. "All right. Have fun, girls."

Zyla quickly threw a bag together, and then she and Beatrice ran back outside to her car.

Beatrice lived in Hamilton Heights, which was one of the wealthier neighborhoods in their county. Her house could only be described as a mansion. Zyla never failed to feel astounded whenever she visited.

Beatrice's mom owned a home goods line, and her furniture and household items were sold in stores throughout the country, so the inside of Beatrice's house was immaculate, of course. Zyla sometimes liked to pretend she was walking through a fancy IKEA.

Zyla hadn't been to Beatrice's dad's chateau in Paris, but apparently it was even bigger than Beatrice's Hamilton Heights house. Her dad owned a string of popular restaurants that were frequented by France's biggest celebrities. Beatrice's parents met when her mom studied abroad in Paris during college. They fell in love, and Beatrice's dad moved to the United States to marry her mom. They got divorced before Beatrice's first birthday, which meant she'd spent every summer of her life in France with her dad. She was bilingual and cool and cultured. All the things Zyla aspired to be.

Beatrice's housekeeper, a petite white woman named Helene, smiled at them on their way upstairs and told them to call down if they needed anything.

Beatrice's room was head-to-toe millennial pink with accents of white and light gray. She had a walk-in closet and her own bathroom. Whenever Zyla came over, which was often, she felt like she was entering another world.

Beatrice's life inspired Zyla. When Zyla became a famous

designer, living life on her own, she'd work really hard to have a nice big house just like this one, and while she might have to travel a lot to make custom outfits for important people, that big house would be her home base. No moving from place to place every year. That's why she was putting everything she had into her portfolio. She needed to make her dreams a reality.

She and Beatrice ran and landed in a heap on her plush queen-sized bed.

"Tell me everything," Zyla said, as if they hadn't talked every day this summer. "Don't leave out a single detail."

"Okay, let's see. I ate way too much and went shopping too much, which reminds me . . ." Beatrice climbed off her bed and ran over to her closet. She emerged holding a huge tote bag that spilled over with fabric. "I got all of this for you, my dear."

"Beatrice!" Zyla sorted through the bag of fabric. Silk, satin, cotton, velvet, chiffon. "Oh, my Godddd."

"Only the best for my bestie."

Zyla looked up at Beatrice, so happy, she thought she might cry. "I really, really missed you."

"I missed you more."

Then they hugged for the ten thousandth time that morning.

Zyla had started her freshman year at St. Catherine's in October, which meant she'd missed orientation and the first days when everyone got to know each other. When she walked into the cafeteria during lunchtime, she stood with her tray in her hands and surveyed the room. She was used to being the new kid. Used to being ignored. Used to finding small, unoccu-

170

pied spaces to squeeze into, both literally and figuratively. But on her first day at St. Catherine's, as she stood there trying to decide where to sit, the decision was made for her.

"Hey, you're new, right?" A Black girl with dark brown skin and long hair appeared at Zyla's side. She had braces, but she didn't look awkward. If anything, the braces added an extra layer of coolness. Zyla could tell this girl had money from her crisp white polo, blue blazer, and the dainty gold cross she wore around her neck. It seemed like the majority of the girls at St. Catherine's were rich. But only a handful of them were Black.

"Yeah," Zyla answered. "Today's my first day."

"Come sit with me," the girl said. "I'm Beatrice, by the way."

"Okay. I'm Zyla."

And they'd been inseparable ever since. Sometimes friendships were simple that way.

"Oh, and I have more news," Beatrice said now. She held up her hand, and on Beatrice's ring finger, Zyla noticed a silver ring with small diamonds encrusted around the band. "Look at this."

Zyla gaped at Beatrice's hand. "Oh my God. Is that what I think it is?"

"Hugo *finally* gave me a promise ring." Beatrice beamed. "I don't think I've ever been more in love with him, Zy."

"I'm so happy for you," Zyla said, smiling at her lovestruck best friend. And Zyla meant it. She *was* happy for Beatrice. She and Hugo, her Parisian boyfriend, had been dating since Beatrice was fourteen and Hugo was sixteen. Their relationship was an interesting one, though. During the summers when Beatrice was in France, she and Hugo were exclusive. But during the school year, all bets were off, and they could hook up with whoever they wanted to. If Zyla was being honest, Beatrice was a bit of a player. But she didn't put anyone above Hugo. She loved him something fierce.

"But tell me what *you've* done," Beatrice said, getting up and walking over to her vanity mirror. She began running a brush through her hair. "Any interesting amusement park stories? I mean, other than the ones you've already told me about Kai Johnson, of course." She glanced over her shoulder and flashed a sly smile. "How is he, by the way? Still strictly in the friend zone?"

"Yes," Zyla said, giving Beatrice a pointed look. "I've already talked to you about this."

Beatrice grinned. "I know, I know. There is no way you'd break your no-dating rule for the football star who drove you to and from work every day like a dedicated chauffer. The same boy who *bought* you a *piece of fabric* simply to protect your hair in the rain. You couldn't possibly fathom changing your mind for the reformed player who you once thought was conceited and walked around the amusement park like he owned it, even though you've since come to learn that he is nice and surprisingly sweet. I think those are the descriptions you used, right?"

"Oh, shut up." Zyla threw a pillow at Beatrice, and she dodged out of the way, laughing. Zyla rolled her eyes. "I regret telling you that."

Beatrice continued to laugh and plopped back on the bed beside Zyla. "No, you don't. You love telling me your deepest, most personal thoughts. That's why we're best friends."

Zyla winced a little at that. Because she purposely hadn't revealed the confusing feelings of her crush on Kai. She didn't want to dissect it, and she knew Beatrice would.

"Anyway, if you and Kai did start hooking up, I'd fully expect hell to freeze over," Beatrice said. "You've made it this far without breaking your rule. Why stop now?"

Zyla was struggling to come up with a response when Beatrice's phone vibrated on the bed. There was a text from someone named Xiomara.

"Who's Xiomara?" Zyla asked.

Beatrice's eyes quickly scanned the message, and she grinned at whatever Xiomara said. "A new girl I added to the rotation. She wants to meet up to tonight, but I'm telling her no, obviously. Wanna go to the mall? I need new cardigans for school."

Zyla hopped up and held out a hand to help Beatrice stand. "I thought you'd never ask."

They ended up at Nordstrom, Beatrice's favorite department store. Zyla much preferred shopping at thrift stores and consignment shops, but she did take this opportunity to buy some colorful hair bows from H&M on their way to Nordstrom.

She sat outside of the dressing room as Beatrice tried on clothes. She was in the middle of scrolling through pieces she'd photographed for her portfolio when her phone vibrated with a text from her dad.

Zy Zy, been trying to get ahold of you. How you been? Call me back.

She winced at the nickname he'd given her when she was a toddler and stared at his message. Her dad was currently living in Denver with his most recent fiancée, Jackie or Justine. It definitely started with a J. And he'd most likely already cheated on her by now. If Zyla called him, she'd have to sit on the phone and suffer through awkward conversation as he asked her questions that parents who were regularly involved in their children's lives would already know the answers to. She'd rather call him when she was with Jade. That way Jade would be the focus of his attention and Zyla wouldn't have to say much.

Her thumbs hovered over her keyboard as she wondered how to respond.

"Zyla? I thought that was you."

Zyla looked up and blinked. Standing in front of her was Camille Vaughn.

"Oh," Zyla mumbled, surprised. "Hi."

"Hey." Camille smiled and sat down right beside Zyla, gracefully flipping her hair over her shoulder. She placed a huge Forever 21 bag in her lap and sloshed an iced coffee around in her hand. "Back-to-school shopping?"

Zyla nodded.

"Same. I'm here with my older sister, but she's being a huge bitch, so I ditched her in the shoe section. I don't have time to deal with other people's attitudes. Know what I mean?"

"Um, sure," Zyla said. Camille had literally never spoken to her before, and now she was talking to her with such familiarity, like they were old friends. Like she hadn't spent the month of August giving her the stink eye.

Camille took a long slurp of her iced coffee. This close, Zyla could see her perfect cat-eye eyeliner and the shimmery blush on her cheeks. "You here by yourself?"

"No. My best friend is trying on clothes." Zyla nodded her head at the dressing room and tried not to stare at Camille suspiciously. Nordstrom was a huge store. She could have easily found somewhere else to sit. Why was she here?

"Oh, okay. Nice," Camille said. Then she smiled, flashing her straight, white teeth. "So, Zyla, there's something that's been weighing on my mind since summer, and I debated saying anything to you, because I felt like maybe it wasn't my place because you and I don't know each other very well. But what are the odds that I'd see you today, you know? It's almost as if it happened for a reason. So, woman to woman, I feel like I just need to finally come out and say it."

"Okay." Zyla's palms were beginning to sweat. Her mouth suddenly felt dry.

"You should really be careful with Kai," Camille said gravely. She glanced around and lowered her voice. "I know he seems really charming and sweet, and it's easy to fall for him. But it's an act. In reality, Kai is a liar and a player. And as his most recent ex, I feel as though it's my responsibility to warn you about him so that you don't end up like me, feeling tricked and betrayed."

Zyla quickly shook her head. "Oh, no. It's not like that."

"I know, I know," Camille said, smiling at Zyla with sympathy. "You probably can't believe that he's pretending to be different than how he really is. Trust me, when he finally showed his true colors, I couldn't believe it either. But I'm just trying to spare you the time and heartbreak, girl. Leave him alone before you get in too deep."

Silently, Zyla stared at Camille's pretty, heart-shaped face. She didn't believe that Kai was a player or a liar. He'd been nothing but honest with her since the beginning. And of the exes that she'd met, Camille was the only one who had bad things to say. Zyla saw right through her.

However, there *was* some truth to Camille's words. Kai was sweet and charming and easy to fall for. It was why she was having the hardest time shaking her crush, and it was beginning to freak her out.

"Camille, thank you for looking out for me," she said, "but Kai and I are just friends. You don't have to worry about him playing me."

Camille practically snorted. She raised an eyebrow and flatly said, "Just friends, huh?"

"Yes. Thank you, though."

Camille stared at Zyla and narrowed her eyes. Then she smiled, slowly and slyly like a tiger who isn't very hungry at the moment but who might eat you later. "Right. Well, just think about what I said, okay?"

"Of course," Zyla said.

Beatrice came out of the dressing room, holding her clothes. She paused, looking back and forth between Zyla and Camille. Her gaze settled on Camille's sly smile, and there must have been something about it that she didn't like, because she uttered a very cool "Hello."

"Hi," Camille chirped back. Then, without ceremony, she stood. "See you around, Zyla," she said. Then she turned and sauntered off in her graceful, confident way, her bright yellow Forever 21 bag bumping against her hip.

"Um, okay. Who was that?" Beatrice asked. "I don't even know her, and I already don't like her."

"*That* was Camille Vaughn."

Beatrice's eyes widened. "Kai's ex? The stink-eye girl?" Zyla nodded and Beatrice rolled her eyes. "Gross. What did she say to you?"

"Uh." Zyla was still trying to process their conversation. "She basically warned me away from Kai."

"Oh, of course she would," Beatrice said, gathering her clothes. They walked toward the register.

"She made it seem as though she was doing me a favor," Zyla continued. "Saving me from future heartbreak or something."

Beatrice rolled her eyes. "Yeah, sure. She probably just wants him to herself, and now you're in her way."

"I'm not, though. He's not allowed to date."

"And if he *could*, who do you think he'd be after?"

Too quickly, Zyla said, "Not me."

Beatrice laughed. "Okay. Well, you know him better than I do."

As the cashier rang Beatrice up, Zyla pulled out her phone and opened her text thread with Kai. She wanted to tell him about the run-in she'd had with Camille. She almost began to type out their conversation word for word, but what would Kai even have to say about it? Knowing the bad things Camille said would only upset him, and he didn't need to deal with that while he was trying to focus on starting his senior year and football. She didn't even know why she wanted to tell him. Did she want him to confirm that what she'd told Camille was right? That she'd had no reason to warn Zyla away from him when they were only friends?

Kai, who was only her friend. Kai, who she missed.

So instead, she typed: I miss you.

Her fingers hovered over the Send button. Should she say that? She told Beatrice that she missed her when they were apart. But in a way, Zyla knew this was different. Kai could easily think her intentions were romantic, which they weren't . . . And anyway, how many girls had ever told Kai Johnson that they missed him? Did she want to be added to that list? Maybe he read the words "I miss you" so often, they didn't even affect him anymore.

But something told her that wouldn't be true. At least not in her case.

Before she could talk herself out of it, she hit Send and held her breath as "Delivered" appeared under her message. Well, there was no going back now. She felt like she might barf. She shouldn't have said that. What had she been thinking?!

Not even a minute passed before her phone vibrated in her hand. Heart in her throat, she read Kai's response.

I miss you too.

Giddy and lightheaded, she wondered if it was possible for your entire body to smile. And she wondered if everyone felt this happy when their "friend" said they missed them back.

"Why are you smiling like that?" Beatrice asked. "Who are you texting with?"

"Um, nobody. Just Kai."

Beatrice tilted her head, looking intrigued. "I want to meet your new friend Kai."

Zyla stilled. She hadn't imagined that her friendship with Kai and her friendship with Beatrice would collide at some point.

"I'll see if he wants to hang out soon," Zyla said.

"Cool."

Beatrice's opinion of Kai was largely based on things she'd heard about him through St. Catherine's grapevine. But once she met Kai, she'd see how different he was. At least that was what Zyla hoped.

And, of course, the one point she kept trying to ignore was that this gave her a reason to see him again.

Chapter Fourteen

I miss you.

Almost a week had gone by, and Kai read Zyla's text over and over every day. Each time, the sensation he felt in his chest was stronger than a runner's high. He felt weightless, like the world was a wonderful and easy place.

It was a nice alternative to his reality, which wasn't exactly easy. During the school year his schedule was intense. He constantly found himself rushing from one place to another. He was student council vice president, and twice a week before classes started, he had morning meetings. Then he gave the morning announcements with Alanna every day. Then he had classes, and once a week during lunch, he had honor society meetings. Then in the fall after school, he had football practice, which is where he was rushing to now. On top of that, sometimes on weekends when he didn't have a game, he volunteered with Cedar High's Habitat for Humanity group. These activities would look great on his Morehouse application. Plus, Aunt Brenda and Uncle Steve liked that he was so involved. He didn't have time to get in trouble when he was this busy.

Yet his packed schedule didn't keep him from thinking

about Zyla and how much he missed seeing her every day. He'd hoped she felt the same way, but he hadn't dared to ask because doing so would only scare her off. Turned out she did miss him too. He couldn't wipe the smile from his face even if he tried.

He stepped into the locker room, and a sneaker went soaring over his head. He ducked absentmindedly, and the sneaker hit its intended target: Frank Guerra's back. Frank cursed and launched his practice jersey across the room at Rich Wallis, and it hit Rich right in the face.

Everyone in the locker room burst into laughter, and the Let's Throw Whatever We Can Find at Each Other fight continued. Kai made his way to the back of the locker room, where his usual crew was waiting: Jamal, Brandon, Chris, and Will. They'd each been on the starting lineup since sophomore year. Kai was the wide receiver; Brandon, the quarterback; Jamal, the running back; and Chris and Will were both safeties.

Jamal was in the middle of throwing a pair balled-up socks across the room, dodging out of the way just as someone tossed a T-shirt at his head. The team usually had this kind of energy at the beginning of the school year. Their first game was next week, and they'd gone undefeated through their scrimmage season. Basically, it was mayhem. Not that Kai noticed.

As team captain, he should probably say something so that everyone would chill out before the coaches got here, but now that he had a moment to himself, he sat down in front of his locker and scrolled through his text thread with Zyla. She'd started her senior year at St. Catherine's a couple days ago, so they hadn't really talked much. But today she'd texted, **My best friend Beatrice wants to meet you**. Kai had stared at his phone, surprised. If she wanted to introduce him to her best friend, didn't that mean something? Maybe she was coming around to liking him too. Or was he putting too much into that, seeing what he wanted to see?

It didn't matter, though. Even if she liked him back, he couldn't date her. He'd agreed to his aunt and uncle's rule.

He found himself scrolling back to when she'd said **I miss you**. After he responded **I miss you too**, she'd sent back a smiley-face emoji. It was officially the dopest emoji in emoji history.

"What in the world is going on in here?" Coach Jeffries suddenly appeared in the locker room, angry and red faced.

It was dead quiet. Everyone stared at Coach Jeffries. The team was wide-eyed and clearly guilty.

"We'll start practice with sprint drills, since you clearly need discipline," Coach Jeffries said, walking to his office, followed by Assistant Coach George.

"Damn," Jamal hissed beside Kai. "More sprints. My legs are gonna fall off."

Kai looked at Jamal and sucked his teeth. "Man, you're probably the one who started throwing stuff in the first place."

"Okay, and?" Jamal shrugged. "That doesn't mean I wanna do extra work."

Kai laughed and shook his head. He needed to hurry up and change into his practice clothes.

"Hezekiah," Coach Jeffries called, "come here for a minute, please."

Jamal, Brandon, Will, and Chris went "oooh," as if Kai were in trouble. Kai waved them off but secretly he wondered if he had done something wrong. He squared his shoulders and walked across the locker room.

"Close the door," Coach Jeffries said once Kai reached his office. "Take a seat."

Kai sat down and glanced between Coach Jeffries and Coach George. Jeffries was white with a mop of graying hair and a thick mustache. He'd been the head coach at Cedar High since the early 2000s, and he taught PE and driver's ed. Jeffries was cool, and so was Coach George, a tall, heavyset Black guy who taught special education classes. They both eyed Kai, and he waited to learn why he'd been called over.

"Why aren't you dressed for practice yet?" Coach Jeffries asked.

"I was running late from a Habitat for Humanity meeting," Kai said. Technically, it wasn't a lie.

Coach Jeffries stared at him and then leaned back. Kai assumed he'd given an acceptable excuse.

"The first game of the season is upon us," Coach Jeffries said. "How do you think the team is looking?"

"Good," Kai said, earnest. "Especially the offensive line."

Coach Jeffries nodded. "And your speed is up too. You've kept up with your running this summer?"

"Yes, sir."

"During practice today, we want you to lead some of the others in their workouts," Coach George said. "Particularly the underclassmen."

"Okay. I can do that."

Then they just stared at him. Kai realized he was being assessed. Awkwardly, he cleared his throat.

"Hezekiah, we think very highly of you," Coach Jeffries said. "You know that, don't you?"

"Yes, sir." They'd made him captain this year, so Kai figured that much was obvious.

"A captain leads," Coach Jeffries said, "and I trust you will lead your team well this year. So when I walk into the locker room and see chaos happening, I don't want to find you somewhere in the corner, texting on your phone. I want you to get your team in order. Understood?"

"Yes, sir." Kai tried not to wince.

"And we're going to do everything we can to make sure your GPA stays at a 3.8 or higher," Coach George said. "If you need a tutor or anything this year, you let us know."

Kai nodded. He probably wouldn't need a tutor. In fact, *he* tutored *other* students in between basketball season and spring track. But there was always room for him to improve.

Coach Jeffries leaned forward and smiled. "We know Morehouse is the goal, and we're going to do everything we can to get you there. Whether it's an academic or athletic scholarship. Maybe both. Either way, Hezekiah, we just want you to know that we're invested in your future."

Coach George nodded solemnly in agreement.

"Okay." Kai took a deep breath, feeling slightly overwhelmed. "Thank you, sir."

Sometimes, Kai thought about his eight-, nine-, and ten-year-old selves who had lashed out at authority for the smallest things and was deemed overall as a troublemaker, and he wondered what his younger selves would think to see him now. A football team captain and honor student with a future his teachers and coaches were invested in. Honestly, it was kinda trippy how he'd managed to turn his whole life around. No one was more surprised about this than him.

Without Aunt Brenda and Uncle Steve and therapy, who knew where he'd be right now. One thing he did know was that he'd probably be playing football. Some of his earliest memories were of sitting on the couch beside his dad as he cheered on the Philadelphia Eagles during NFL season, and Morehouse or Penn State if it was college ball. When Kai was a toddler with chubby little legs, his dad would take him in the backyard and they'd throw a football around. Kai loved to run for the ball, and he was fast. That's when his dad realized he'd make a good wide receiver.

Whenever Kai played football, he thought about his dad. Sometimes he wondered if that strong connection was what made him such a good player.

"Now, keep the team in line. All right?" Coach Jeffries said. "Get your head out of the clouds and focus on the field. And those books."

"Yes, sir," Kai said, standing.

He made his way back to his locker, berating himself the entire way.

You knew better than to just sit there while the team goofed off. You're a leader. You have to lead.

He opened his locker and retrieved his clothes. Jamal, Brandon, Will, and Chris stared at him, waiting for an explanation. But Kai was trying to process the conversation himself. Coach Jeffries and Coach George basically said the same thing as Aunt Brenda and Uncle Steve: Focus on school and sports. Ignore other distractions.

He hadn't stopped the team's silly game because he was too busy reading his texts with Zyla. Did that mean she was a distraction? He didn't want to think so, but he wondered if that was the case. He itched to text her now and see what she was doing, even though he'd just talked to her a couple hours ago. He was low-key obsessed.

"Come on, bro," Jamal said, nudging him. "What did Coach Jeffries say?"

"Y'all gotta chill on playing around," Kai said diplomatically. "And we need to help the freshmen more during practice." He narrowed his eyes at Will specifically. "No hazing."

"What?" Will held his hands up. "Did I say anything about hazing?"

"You didn't have to," Kai said. "Look, y'all, we're seniors this year. We have to set an example. Do we want to be remembered as the ones who goofed off or the ones who created a winning legacy with a perfect season?"

"Okay, we hear you." Jamal clapped Kai on his shoulder. "No more stupid shit. I swear. We won't let you down, Barack."

Kai snorted and they all laughed. They got dressed, and soon they were running out onto the football field. Kai was determined to practice what he preached and to not let down those who believed in him. He was going to try really, really hard to focus.

During practice, his attention was on the field one hundred percent, but afterward, as they trudged back to the locker room, he felt an emptiness in his chest. The idea that Zyla might be a distraction bothered him. Spending less time with her made him feel lonely. He'd felt that ache since the last time he saw her at Brandon's beach house.

There could be no harm in hanging out every once in a while, could there? Plus, she'd asked him to meet her best friend. What, was he supposed to say no? That was rude. As his friend, she deserved more than that.

Then he got an idea. At his locker, he grabbed his phone and typed a quick text to Zyla.

Want to meet up at the fall festival this weekend?

Every September, the town of Cedar held a fall festival at Sailor Joe's, and Kai and Jamal always went together. Wait, this was perfect. He and Jamal could hang out with Zyla and Beatrice, and Jamal would definitely take the edge off things because he was funny and easy to talk to. It could be like a group outing. That way Kai wouldn't have to feel pressure for Beatrice to like him. Or like he was asking Zyla out on a date.

Immediately, Zyla texted back, **Yes.**

The empty feeling in his chest evaporated right away.

The rumors surrounding Zyla and Kai's disappearance have not yet reached Beatrice, who is completely over Senior Day. Her hair got wet in the rain, and now she's stuck in the lodge with a bunch of other kids from Cedar High and Hopkins Prep. She could go find her friends from St. Catherine's, but she doesn't really feel like doing so. The teachers keep mentioning movie night and how students can play games in the lounge if they would like, but that sounds worse than staring out at the rain, which is what Beatrice is doing now in the half-empty food hall. Her papa would say that she is moping. And that moping is unladylike.

But she isn't moping. She's just . . . confused.

You see, she knows Zyla is mad at her about what happened earlier today, and that's why Beatrice is here in the food hall, staring out at the rain, wearing her bathing suit and cutoffs instead of getting a hot shower in her and Zyla's shared room. She wants to give Zyla her space.

Truth be told, Beatrice isn't even sure what happened earlier. About an hour ago, she and Zyla had been standing by the wave pool, talking to some boys from Hopkins Prep. There was Seth Peterson, whom she'd recently added to her rotation, and his two friends, Mike and David. Seth was freakishly tall and talked too much, but he took Beatrice to fancy restaurants, so she was keeping him around for the time being. They were in the middle of listening to Seth drone on and on about baseball season or something, and Beatrice was tuning him out when she stepped away to use the bathroom. When she returned, Kai was there, Mike had a bloody nose, and Zyla was crying. Kai was standing in front of Zyla, apologizing repeatedly as she continued to cry, and Beatrice ran over and told Kai to go away. He'd already caused enough trouble for Zyla. Why couldn't he just leave her alone? Kai looked at Beatrice a little wildly, then he turned and left. Zyla went to go after him, and when Beatrice tried to stop her, Zyla said, "Beatrice, just don't get involved!" And then she ran off too.

It made absolutely no sense.

Beatrice thought that Zyla hated Kai. They broke up back in March because Zyla caught him cheating on her at that St. Patrick's Day party. As far as Beatrice knows, they haven't spoken to each other since. She'd assumed Zyla basically erased Kai from her memory based on the way she acted.

But then again, what does Beatrice know, really? It's possible there have been signs all along and she just ignored them. Like with Hugo. They'd been dating for exactly four years, two months, and eleven days when he called her out of the blue and said he'd met someone else. Beatrice didn't see it coming at all. They'd had an open relationship, yes, but the deal was that at the end of the day, she and Hugo put each other first.

He broke up with her in March. It's May now, and every time she thinks about him, she feels a twist in her gut.

"I need to talk to you."

Beatrice turns, and somehow, her day gets even worse.

It's Jamal Smith, Kai's best friend, aka the most annoying person on planet earth.

"Ugh," she says in response.

Beatrice can't stand Jamal. He is arrogant, his jokes aren't funny, and he calls her "your highness." They were forced to hang out back when Zyla and Kai dated. It was torture.

"Ugh yourself." Jamal moves into her line of sight and blocks her view of the rain. "Look, the last thing I want to do is talk to you. But I'm looking for Kai and someone told me you were one of the last people to see him."

"That's not true," Beatrice says, pushing Jamal aside so she can continue to stare at the rain. "I have no idea where he is."

Jamal resumes his place in front of her. "Well, somebody told me that Kai got into a fight with three Hopkins Prep boys because Zyla kissed one of them and you were there and saw the whole thing."

Beatrice snorts. Another thing her papa would say is unladylike. "Zyla did not kiss one of those boys, and Kai didn't fight three of them at once! How ridiculous. Even more ridiculous that you'd believe such a story." She rolls her eyes.

"Then tell me what really happened," Jamal huffs.

"Kai only fought with one boy, and I'm not even sure it was a full-on fight." She sighs and shakes her head. "I don't know what caused it because I was in the bathroom. But Kai ran off and Zyla went after him, and I have no idea why because she hates him."

"No, it's the other way around. Kai hates Zyla."

"*No.* Kai literally begged her to take him back after she broke up with him. He's obsessed with her."

Jamal frowns so hard, Beatrice almost laughs. "No. After they broke up, Kai left her alone, and she's mad he didn't try to change her mind."

"That is such a lie!" Beatrice throws her arms up. "You don't know anything!"

"It's the truth! And I know everything about everything!"

The few other students in the food hall are watching their shouting match. Finally, some entertainment after being forced indoors.

"Just go away, okay, Jamal?" she hisses, noticing that they're being observed. "I don't know where Kai is. If he has any sense, he'll be in your room, avoiding trouble for breaking someone's nose."

Jamal scoffs. "Why are you so extra, your highness? I'm sure he didn't break that kid's nose."

"What did I tell you about calling me that?"

Jamal grins. "Sorry. Old habits die hard. I thought you liked the nickname."

All of Beatrice's frustrations suddenly come to a head. Being dumped by Hugo. Her weird, confusing fight with Zyla. Literally having any interaction with Jamal.

"Jamal, you'd better beat it or I'll—"

But Beatrice doesn't get to finish her sentence. Because she and Jamal are soon surrounded by a small cluster of teachers, who say they need to speak with them concerning Zyla and Kai immediately.

After they are pulled into an office, Beatrice and Jamal are informed that Zyla and Kai have run away.

"What the fuck?" Jamal says, and he is swiftly reprimanded for his language.

"No way," Beatrice says, stunned. Zyla and Kai would never do something so reckless. The teachers are clearly taking this overboard. But she can agree that Zyla and Kai *are* MIA.

Beatrice and Jamal turn to each other, and it dawns on Beatrice that there is obviously something both she and Jamal have failed to understand about their respective best friends: They haven't been entirely truthful lately. Were there any signs that would indicate so before today?

Beatrice thinks hard and is taken back to the night of the fall festival when she met Kai (and unfortunately Jamal). When Zyla and Kai had hugged, they'd looked at each other as if they shared some kind of secret. It was the first time Beatrice felt as though Zyla had kept something from her. Because there she was, clearly infatuated with Kai, when she'd insisted to Beatrice all summer that Kai was only her friend.

Maybe Zyla and Kai disappearing shouldn't surprise her so much. In the end, isn't a relationship just a matter of choices? Beatrice was willing to choose Hugo again and again, despite their open relationship. But that had been the wrong choice. By choosing Kai, Zyla is making the wrong choice. Especially given everything that Kai put her through. It's not worth it.

If Beatrice knows one thing it's that heartbreak is for suckers. Look at what it's done to her. And God, look at what it's done to Zyla.

Chapter Fifteen

"Damn, that's Zyla's friend?" Jamal asked.

Kai turned. Zyla and her best friend, Beatrice, were walking toward them. Kai smiled, and his stomach started doing weird flips. This was the first time he was seeing Zyla since the end of summer. He and Jamal were standing by the food court, and he'd been searching the crowd for her for the last ten minutes, and now she was here.

"She looks *good*," Jamal continued. "What's her name?"

"What? Who?" Kai could barely focus. His palms were sweating. Why the hell was he so nervous?

"Zyla's friend, bro. What's her name?"

"Oh." They were getting closer. Zyla was wearing a sleeveless white button-up and jeans with rips in the knees. Her hair was parted down the middle and pulled back in a curly ponytail just like on the first day they met. She smiled at Kai and waved. "Beatrice. Her friend's name is Beatrice."

"Beatrice," Jamal repeated, smiling. "Okay, cool."

Kai looked at Jamal, and something clicked. "Bro, I wasn't trying to play matchmaker when I invited you to chill with us tonight."

Jamal nodded, staring at Beatrice as they approached. "Right, right. You know I'm stuck on Alanna even though she dissed me for her friends tonight."

Kai didn't hear a thing Jamal said. Because Zyla was a few feet away, and he walked to meet her.

"Kai!" she said and jumped to give him a hug.

He was momentarily shocked at her excitement, to feel her arms wrap around him.

"Hey," he said, closing his eyes and hugging her back. She smelled like shampoo and maybe body spray or whatever. It felt so right to hold her this way, close to his chest. Like she belonged there.

Oh shit. He was in trouble for sure.

———

Zyla leaned her head against Kai's chest. She could hear the sound of his heartbeat. The skin on his neck was soft and smooth. She relished the feel of his arms around her waist. They could stand here like this for the rest of the night and she wouldn't care.

But that couldn't be.

Someone cleared their throat. Zyla turned, and Beatrice was watching them, raising her eyebrow. She grinned at Zyla, and Zyla knew that from Beatrice's perspective, it very much seemed like she and Kai were indeed hooking up after all.

And Jamal was watching them too, looking equally amused.

Zyla bit her lip and slowly slid away from Kai, regretting it when he retracted his arms.

"Um, hi," she said to him.

He smiled. "Hi."

She couldn't handle that beautiful smile right now. "This is my best friend, Beatrice," she said, beckoning Beatrice closer. "Beatrice, this is Kai and Jamal."

Beatrice quickly ran her eyes over Kai, similar to how she assessed her car for scratches every day. "I've heard a lot about you," she said, smirking.

Kai's gaze darted to Zyla. "All good things, I hope."

"Of course." Beatrice glanced at Jamal. "I've heard nothing about you, though."

"Well, I can tell you everything there is to know," Jamal said, extending his arm for Beatrice to take. "Can I interest you in a game of shooting baskets?"

Beatrice looked down at Jamal's extended arm and laughed. Zyla wasn't surprised when Beatrice slid her purse up onto her shoulder and looped her arm through Jamal's. He was being added to her rotation at this very moment and didn't even know it.

"You're funny," Beatrice said. "I'm not big into basketball, but I'll watch you play."

Arm in arm, Beatrice and Jamal began to stroll to the Games section, and Zyla and Kai fell into step behind them.

At the same time that Zyla said, "So, how's football?" Kai asked, "So, how's your portfolio coming along?"

They both stopped talking and laughed.

"You first," Kai said.

"I was just asking about football."

"Oh, it's fine. We should have a good season."

"Nice." She didn't know what else she was supposed to say to that. What did she know about football? "Are you a quarterback?"

"No, I'm a wide receiver."

Zyla's eyes popped. What the heck was a wide receiver?

"I make the touchdowns," Kai explained as if he could read her mind.

"Oh." She laughed. "Right. I knew that."

Kai smiled, seeing right through her lie. "You should come to our first game next week."

She'd gone to a couple Hopkins Prep games with Beatrice over the last few years, and she usually didn't pay attention to the games themselves. Instead, she sat there and wondered what her own line of football jerseys would look like.

Regardless, she said, "Yeah, okay."

"Cool." He was smiling. It caught the attention of her esophagus butterflies.

They stood aside and watched as Jamal played shooting baskets. Beatrice cheered him on, and her Cartier bracelets jangled loudly every time she clapped her hands.

"You have any exciting end-of-summer stories for me?" Kai asked, leaning closer to Zyla.

Zyla once again considered telling him about her conversation with Camille. Before, she hadn't wanted Camille's comments to upset Kai. But now, she wondered what Kai would think about Camille assuming he and Zyla were a couple. Would he think it was funny? Or maybe he'd think the idea was absurd. He'd asked Zyla out on the first day they'd met, so he had been interested in her at one point. But what if he strictly looked at her as a friend now?

Wait, what did that matter? She and Kai *were* friends! These esophagus butterflies were screwing with her mind!

"Everything was cool," she said calmly. "Boring. The usual."

Kai looked like he was about to say something else, but he paused when Beatrice suddenly appeared at Zyla's side.

"I think I like this Jamal kid," she whispered in Zyla's ear. "He's hilarious."

That was fine and dandy, but Zyla wanted to make sure that Beatrice liked Kai.

"What about Kai?" Zyla whispered back, knowing full well that Kai was trying his hardest not to eavesdrop.

Beatrice shrugged and whispered, "He's fine, I guess. You're just friends, aren't you?"

Zyla nodded. But why did she feel like she was lying?

"Bro, I think I'm into Beatrice," Jamal said.

Kai had walked away from Zyla and Beatrice to give them space. They were whispering about something. Not him, he hoped. Or maybe, if they *were* talking about him, he hoped it was because Zyla liked him and Beatrice knew.

Wait, nah. He didn't want that. He couldn't date. Even if Zyla did like him, nothing could come of it.

"Did you hear what I said?" Jamal asked, nudging Kai.

"Yeah, Beatrice seems cool," Kai answered. "And bougie, but not in a bad way. What about Alanna, though?"

"Eh, I don't know. She doesn't wanna make it official." Jamal shrugged. "And there's just something about Beatrice. I can't explain it, but I gotta see this through."

Beatrice returned to Jamal's side, her mini conference with Zyla apparently over.

"Would you like to ride the Ferris wheel?" she asked Jamal.

From the way Jamal's eyes lit up, you would have thought she'd asked if he'd like to win a million dollars.

"Absolutely."

They looped arms and strolled in the direction of the Ferris wheel.

Zyla laughed as she and Kai once again followed behind.

"Is Beatrice the friend that you said would eat Jamal alive?" Kai asked.

"Yes." She nodded, smirking. "Maybe I was wrong?"

Apparently, she spoke too soon.

"Can you move your big bag to your other arm?" Jamal asked Beatrice. "It keeps hitting my side."

Beatrice suddenly stopped, and Kai held his arm out to keep Zyla from crashing into Beatrice's back.

"My big bag?" Beatrice repeated. "I didn't realize the size of my bag was a problem."

"I mean, I don't know why you felt you had to bring it to an amusement park," Jamal said. "But I'm only asking for you to move it to your other arm so that we can continue to walk together."

Beatrice narrowed her eyes. "I'm just trying to figure out why you felt it was necessary to comment on the size of my bag. All you had to say was, 'Can you move your bag to your other arm?' Like, why did you have to mention that it's big?"

Jamal looked confused, then he crossed his arms and grinned.

Shit.

Kai knew that look. Jamal was fixing to argue.

Kai stepped forward, attempting to defuse the situation. "Y'all, we're about to get on the Ferris wheel. Beatrice, you can put your bag in your lap, and it won't matter."

"Nah," Jamal said. "Her bag is big as hell, and it's annoying me. Did you just want everyone to know you can afford Michael Kors?"

"It's *Coach*, thank you very much," Beatrice snapped.

Zyla put her hand on Beatrice's shoulder. "Okay, I think—"

"Oh, well, excuse me, your highness," Jamal said, interrupting Zyla. "Please move your *Coach* bag out of my way."

"You won't have to worry about my bag hitting you anymore, because this," Beatrice said, pointing between the two of them, "is over."

"Over?" Jamal laughed. "It barely even started!"

"Good! Because I wouldn't want to start anything with you!"

"Good!"

"Ugh!" Beatrice spun and looked at Zyla. "I have to walk away now or I'm gonna murder him."

"Beatrice, wait," Zyla said, beginning to follow her. But Beatrice said, "No, you stay. I'll find you later. Your night doesn't have to be ruined too."

"I didn't ruin your night," Jamal called after her. "You ruined your own night!"

"Bro, are you serious?" Kai said, shaking his head. He and Zyla were finally reunited and this shit was blowing everything.

"What? She started it!" Jamal huffed like a little kid. "I'm over this. I'll hit you up later. Bye, Zyla."

Then he stormed off in the opposite direction of Beatrice.

Zyla and Kai stood there, stunned.

"What should we do now?" Zyla asked.

The answer seemed pretty simple to Kai. "Still want to ride the Ferris wheel?"

She smiled. "Yes."

Chapter Sixteen

The esophagus butterflies had formed a mutiny. It was the only explanation for why Zyla couldn't stamp them down as she and Kai stood in line to ride the Ferris wheel.

It was only the two of them now. No Beatrice or Jamal to act as buffers. It wasn't like she and Kai ever needed buffers before. Why did it feel different now?

"Oh hey, Bonnie and Clyde." Miranda Pérez, who was working the Ferris wheel, gave them a sly smile. Antonio rehired some employees for the fall festival. It was the last night the park would be open until next spring.

"Summer is over," Zyla said, frowning. "Enough with the nickname."

"What's up, Miranda." Kai calmly ushered Zyla forward until they were seated in their two-person pod. He smiled at Zyla. "I don't know why you let them get to you."

"It's just annoying," she said. But now that he was sitting beside her, smiling, she didn't feel annoyed at all.

Miranda quickly checked that everyone was buckled in, and then Zyla and Kai were lurching higher into the air. They paused once they reached the top so that more people could board, and Zyla could see the whole park from this angle. With the lights and smiling faces below them, the park didn't look so run-down. She realized she missed this place. She missed seeing Kai every day too. Terribly.

She turned to him, and he was already looking at her. Studying her, really. The esophagus butterflies were practically flapping out of her ears.

She liked him.

That was the plain truth that she'd been trying to avoid. But she couldn't escape it anymore. The knowledge of it gripped the hem of her shirt and wouldn't let her run any farther.

She felt her face get hot. Kai blinked at her and took a deep breath. Could he tell what she was thinking? Were her feelings that obvious?

"Zyla," he said softly. And then he paused. Her heart pounded desperately as she waited for him to keep talking. Instead, he moved closer to her, and his expression suddenly grew very serious.

He lifted his hand and pushed a few stray curls behind her ear, and then he cupped her cheek. He leaned closer and she stared at his brown eyes and full lips. He was going to kiss her. She *wanted* him to kiss her. God, she wanted it so badly.

But then if he kissed her, what would happen next? She'd probably become obsessed with him, like how her mom became obsessed with each of her partners. And then Kai would have power over her. He'd be able to break her heart so easily, and she'd be left devastated. Wasn't that inevitable? She'd seen it happen so many times.

She wanted Kai to kiss her. But she was so very afraid of him and her feelings that she couldn't contain.

Kai closed his eyes, and his mouth was less than an inch from hers when she turned away at the last minute.

"Oh," he said, quickly leaning back. His eyes widened. "Shit, Zyla. I'm sorry."

"No, it's okay. I'm sorry. Um. Yeah." She laughed nervously, anxiously. Miserably. "Sorry."

"No, seriously, Zyla," Kai said. He looked just as anxious as she felt. "I shouldn't have done that. I misread the whole thing."

You didn't misread anything. I'm just a coward!

They sat in excruciatingly awkward silence until their pod reached the ground again. They unbuckled their seat belts and Zyla stood up immediately.

"I . . . I have to go find Beatrice."

She could barely think straight. Kai stared at her, looking pained.

"Right, okay," he said, raking a hand over his head.

What are you doing? Don't walk away from him!

She felt like she might throw up as she turned away, trying her hardest not to break into a run.

———

What the fuck. What the fuck. What the fuck.

Kai had ruined everything. *Everything.*

How had it even happened? They were on the Ferris wheel, and they were smiling at each other, and then Zyla turned away to look down at the park, and Kai felt this overwhelming sensation in his chest as he watched her. There was no one like her in the world. And despite the fact that he wasn't supposed to date, and he didn't want to disappoint Aunt Brenda and Uncle Steve, and he was supposed to focus on himself and football and getting into Morehouse, and he didn't even have time to be someone's boyfriend with his busy schedule, and she was planning to study abroad in *Paris*, he didn't care. All he wanted to do right now was focus on Zyla.

He liked her, and he was tired of trying to fight it. But what would that mean for their friendship? What if she didn't feel the same way? Toward the end of summer, at times he'd felt like she might have liked him too, or that she at least found him attractive, because every now and then he'd catch her staring.

Then up there on the Ferris wheel, she'd looked at him and he could tell that she did feel the same as him. He'd felt so happy, like the luckiest dude in the universe. Because Zyla Matthews liked him back. He'd been so encouraged by this assumption that he'd tried to kiss her.

Damn idiot.

How could he have misread the situation so badly?

He was the one who'd had fifty thousand freaking girlfriends. He knew what it was really like when a girl was interested. Dr. Rueben would say Kai was *projecting* that Zyla had feelings for him.

He needed to apologize to her again, needed to save their friendship. He hoped he hadn't fucked things up so badly that she wouldn't even want to be friends. Because that would really break his heart.

Taking a deep breath, he pushed through the crowd and tried to catch up to Zyla. She was walking so quickly, her arms clenched at her sides. Fuck. He'd made her so uncomfortable, she had to walk around this way?

"Zyla," he said, catching his breath once he reached her.

He came around to stand in front of her. She froze and stared at him, eyes wide.

He was supposed to apologize again, to beg her not to end their friendship because he'd fucked it up. He wanted to be her friend, and he hoped she still wanted to be friends too.

But as he stared down at her upturned face, he couldn't bring himself to say those words. Because he'd be lying.

"Zyla." He took a step forward. They weren't touching. Not yet. But she was very close, and he felt her everywhere, surrounding and overwhelming him. "I like you more than I've ever liked anyone in my life. I'm sorry that I tried to kiss you, but I'm not sorry for the way that I feel. The truth is that I don't want to just be friends. I like you too much for that, and I don't want to pretend otherwise anymore. If you feel the same way at all, even a little bit, please just tell me. Because I really want you to be my girl."

Zyla stared at Kai. She couldn't speak. He liked her more than he'd ever liked *anyone*? More than Whit and Ashley and Deja? Even Camille?

He liked her, and he wanted her to be his girlfriend.

"But your aunt and uncle said you can't date," she said, holding her hand over her heart as if she could slow it down.

People continued to swarm around them, laughing and running from Games to Rides and back again. But it was like they were the only two people in the entire park.

Kai shook his head, not breaking eye contact with her. "I don't care about that. They'll understand. I care about *you*."

Zyla absorbed his words. Suddenly, everything became very simple. She felt the tension leave her body.

Distantly, she knew there were many reasons she should tell Kai no. But as she stared into his eyes, she no longer felt the weight of those reasons. She liked him too much.

"Yes," she said.

Kai's eyes widened. "Yes, what?"

"I like you," she said. "And I will be your girl."

Kai let out a deep breath like he'd just finished a marathon. And then he was pulling her close and covering her mouth with his.

Kai's lips were warm and soft, and Zyla would have thought she was floating if Kai hadn't been holding her so tightly, reminding her that gravity kept them on the ground.

Kai would have to tell his aunt and uncle that he'd broken their rule. That would cause trouble.

Aunt Ida would be so disappointed in her. That would cause more trouble.

Her mom would probably be thrilled, and that would cause a different kind of trouble.

But Zyla couldn't care less right now.

Because she was kissing a boy for the first time, and he *liked* her. And she liked him.

She hoped they'd be able to stay this happy forever.

Part Two:
Girl Loves Boy

NOW: May, Senior Day Trip, 5:57 p.m.

Before Leanne, Zyla's mother, is alerted to her daughter's disappearance, her focus is completely on Denise Claremont, a new prospective partner. They are on a date at Il Forno, the fanciest Italian restaurant in town. There was once a time when Leanne kept track of the amount of dates she went on per year. She even kept a separate list of how many first dates led to second and third dates. But then there came a point when the lists got too long, and she was still single. It became too disappointing.

However, her date tonight seems slightly promising. Denise Claremont is the director of the Cedar Planetarium. You see, it was Denise's idea to bring Leanne to Il Forno, and that already puts her leagues ahead of Leanne's previous dates this year. Leanne doesn't consider herself to be high maintenance in the slightest. She simply wants her partner to have basic manners. Like opening the door for her and pulling out her chair before she sits down. Denise had already done both of those things without having to be prompted. She is a great conversationalist and has asked Leanne questions instead of talking about herself the whole night.

The way Leanne met Denise was a little weird. It wasn't at a bar or on a dating app. She and Denise met after Zyla and Kai got in trouble for deciding to be little criminals on Valentine's Day. Leanne doesn't understand why they did something so stupid.

The morning after Valentine's Day, Leanne went to see Denise, and she'd been so stressed and confused that her darling, bright daughter had somehow turned into a delinquent, she burst into tears as she begged Denise not to press charges for Zyla and Kai's actions. Denise had kindly comforted her and promised that she hadn't planned to do anything of the sort. Weeks later when Leanne ran into Denise in the supermarket, Leanne felt very embarrassed. But Denise had been so gracious, only asking if Zyla was okay and if she was doing well in school. They stood in the parking lot chatting, and then they went and got coffee, and now here they are on a romantic date at Il Forno.

Leanne should be delighted that her love life might be looking up. But she can't feel as happy as she'd like to.

Zyla has been withdrawn ever since that trouble on Valentine's Day. Even more withdrawn than usual. Leanne and Zyla don't have the easiest relationship. She knows that Zyla is disappointed in her and her choices when it comes to her love life. Sometimes Leanne watches television shows like *Gilmore Girls* and *The Parkers*, shows with great mom-and-daughter relationships, and she wishes she and Zyla could have that. She wishes that Zyla didn't look at her like she was waiting for her to be better someday. Like the current version of Leanne wasn't the mom she deserved.

Maybe it would be different if things had worked out with Zyla and Jade's dad, Terrance. Leanne had met him when she was a senior at St. Catherine's. She'd gone to a basketball game at Cedar High and fallen in love as soon as she saw him run out onto the court. He was tall and lean and more handsome than anyone she'd ever seen. Boldly, she'd waited outside of the boys' locker room and introduced herself to Terrance after the game. Then they were together, then she became pregnant, and then after graduation, she moved with him to Florida. It happened so quickly. One minute she was young, carefree, and in love. The next, she had a baby and a cheating husband.

She'd stayed with Terrance because she'd loved him. Despite his constant infidelity. Despite the fact that Aunt Ida called her almost every week and encouraged her to come back to New Jersey with Zyla. Leanne wanted her relationship with Terrance to work. Their vows were sacred, and she took them seriously. But even another baby six years later couldn't change him.

She doesn't know if things will work out with Denise past this first date, but she is being naively hopeful that they will. She wonders if her terrible love life has affected Zyla. For the longest time, she assumed Zyla wasn't interested in dating at all, but suddenly Kai came along and changed everything.

Leanne likes Kai. She thinks he's much sweeter than some of the other boys who are Zyla's age. But she doesn't want him getting Zyla into trouble, not when Zyla has such big plans for her future, like studying fashion all over the world. It's a good thing that they broke up.

But Leanne hates that Zyla is so heartbroken. She looked so off this morning as she got ready for her senior trip. If Leanne could spare Zyla from anything in this world, it would be heartbreak. In Leanne's opinion, it is truly one of the worst things a person can experience.

Young love is stressful. Old love is stressful too. Leanne wonders if love can ever be easy.

"Sorry I took a while. There was a long line." Denise sits down across from Leanne and smiles, returning from the bathroom. Leanne's stomach flips.

"Oh, it's okay," Leanne says.

"So, what were we talking about before I left?"

"I don't remember," Leanne says. But suddenly she gets the urge to ask Denise her thoughts on love. Would that be too forward? She doesn't want to scare Denise away. But now she's thinking about her daughter, and she could use some perspective at the moment. "What do you think—"

She abruptly stops when her phone vibrates loudly in her bag.

"I'm so sorry," she says, reaching for her phone. "It might be my aunt or one of my daughters."

Denise waves her hand. "Please, go ahead."

But it's a number that Leanne doesn't recognize.

She figures it might be Terrance. He used to call her from random numbers every now and then, depending on wherever his new girlfriend or wife lived. But ever since he moved back to New Jersey, he often asks Leanne if she wants to hang out, like they are best friends instead of exes and coparents. If it's Terrance, he can wait.

Leanne lets the call go to voicemail. Whoever it was leaves a message and calls back just as Leanne begins to put her phone away.

"Maybe you should answer," Denise says, very serious.

Leanne sighs. If it is Terrance, she's going to be quite annoyed that her ex-husband is ruining her date.

"Hello?" she answers.

"Hi, Ms. Matthews? This is Sister Joellen from St. Catherine's."

Oh no. Leanne's stomach drops.

"Ms. Matthews, are you there?"

"Yes," Leanne says. "I'm here. Is everything okay?"

"Well, no, it isn't. Zyla disappeared earlier this evening with another student. We have reason to believe that they've run away together."

"Run away?" Leanne practically shrieks. Denise's eyes widen, and she immediately waves over the server to get their check. "Are you sure?"

"Yes, ma'am. We have the park rangers here now, and we've spoken to some of Zyla's classmates."

Leanne is gathering her things at the speed of light, not even bothering to take her food to go. She stands up and rushes to the door, Denise following close behind.

"Who was the other student?" she asks, running to Denise's car, even though she already knows the answer to this question.

"His name is Hezekiah Johnson," Sister Joellen says. "He

attends Cedar Regional High School. We're told that he is Zyla's ex-boyfriend."

"I'll be there as soon as possible," Leanne says on the verge of frantic tears, fumbling to open Denise's passenger-side door.

She hangs up and calls her daughter. It goes straight to voice-mail. She begins to text Zyla angrily. **How dare you run away? What do you think you're doing? Are you out of your mind?!**

She erases the message and sends another text instead. **Zy, please just let me know that you're safe.**

The message fails to deliver.

"It's going to be okay," Denise tries to assure her.

Leanne nods, but she can't believe this is true. She thinks of the stupid things she's done for love. If she had set a better example, could this have been avoided? Never in a million years did she think that her daughter would *run away* with the boy she loved.

Chapter Seventeen

Zyla didn't know the first thing about being someone's girl-friend. But here she was, trying her best.

She sat beside Beatrice on the crowded Cedar High bleachers. It was the football team's home game against Yardley High. Cedar was up by nine points in the second quarter.

Zyla watched as the quarterback, Brandon, launched the ball through the air. On the other end of the field, Kai, number twenty-eight, ran to catch it. Zyla sucked in a breath. *You've got this. You've got this.* Kai caught the ball and took off running, dipping, dodging, and spinning to evade being tackled. And then he ran into the end zone, scoring a touchdown. The bleachers erupted into cheers.

Zyla jumped up and shouted at the top of her lungs, her long box braids hanging down her back. Watching Kai score gave her the most exhilarating rush. She was so proud of him, although she had nothing to do with how good he was at sports. And she loved when he did his little victory dance, like right now. He shimmied his shoulders and moved his feet, and his teammates ran over and joined him.

Months ago, if you would have told her that she'd be at a football game, cheering her head off because her boyfriend scored a touchdown, she would have laughed in your face. Especially if you'd have said that the boyfriend in question was Kai Johnson.

But she and Kai had officially been dating for five weeks and two days. He picked her up for school in the morning sometimes when he didn't have meetings, and he called her every night after football practice. One of her favorite things to do was go to the movies with him and sit way in the back so that they could make out in the dark without anyone seeing. The only thing she didn't like was that they were both so busy. Kai had his extracurriculars, and Zyla was now working part time managing the front desk at the salon where her mom worked. And every spare minute she had, she worked on her portfolio. It was hard sometimes when the only thing she wanted to do was see him and there was no space in their schedules. But the moments that they were together, she felt like she was the star of her very own romantic comedy. Zyla, of all people. She'd gone and broken her no-dating rule, but she didn't regret doing so, because Kai already knew why she'd had the rule in the first place, and he was taking things slow, which she appreciated. Life could be really trippy sometimes.

Apparently, Beatrice felt the same way, because as Zyla sat back down, Beatrice grinned at her.

"What?" Zyla said, looking at her reflection in Beatrice's cat-eye sunglasses.

"Nothing." Beatrice shook her head innocently. "I'm just happy to see you having fun."

"Are *you* having fun?"

"Sure." Beatrice shrugged. "Nothing like watching America's favorite pastime."

"That's baseball. And why are you wearing your sunglasses at a night game? Can you even see anything?"

"Not really. But I cheer when everyone else does," she said. "And I'm wearing the shades because I'm tired of being watched."

"Oh," Zyla said. She glanced over her shoulder. Whenever she and Beatrice came to Kai's games, Cedar High girls watched them like hawks. It's exactly what they were doing now.

A group of them currently sat in the upper right corner of the bleachers. Zyla didn't know who they were. Alanna usually sat down in the front and wore bright yellow and blue, showing her school spirit. Whit was on the dance team, and she hadn't seen Ash or Deja at a game yet. The girls staring at Zyla now were strangers. But *they* clearly knew who *she* was.

Zyla turned back around and sighed. This was the cross she had to bear as Kai Johnson's girlfriend. She'd be lying if she said it didn't make her feel a little uncomfortable. Even at St. Catherine's, classmates whom she'd never spoken to had suddenly taken an interest in her. And they wanted to know what it was like to date Kai. At least once a week, they tried to gather around her during lunch and toss out questions like she was at a press conference. Beatrice practically had to beat them away with a stick. Or in her case, a Fendi bag.

"Just ignore them," Zyla finally said to Beatrice.

Beatrice pushed her long hair over her shoulder and scoffed. "Oh, trust me. That's what the sunglasses are for."

The halftime buzzer rang, and the teams jogged off the field. Zyla looked for Kai's number-twenty-eight jersey and followed him with her eyes until they disappeared inside the school, heading for the locker room.

Then the dance team ran onto the field. They performed a routine to a Megan Thee Stallion song. Both Whit and Darius looked great out there. But Camille stood right in the center of the squad, and Zyla couldn't focus on Whit or Darius without glancing at Camille too.

She hadn't ended up telling Kai about her weird conversation with Camille. Camille probably thought Zyla was a huge liar now. But at the time, she *had* been telling the truth. On the day she spoke to Camille, she and Kai were just friends.

She wondered how Camille and Kai acted around each other in school. Kai had said that in the beginning of their relationship, he liked Camille more than any of his exes. Was it weird to see someone you used to like in the hallways every day?

Sometimes if Zyla wasn't careful, she caught herself thinking about Kai and his exes. How had he acted when he dated them? Was he kind and polite and charming like he was with Zyla? How many times had he taken a girl to the movies and then to dinner? How many times had he driven around with a girl riding shotgun as she held his hand? How many times had he sat outside of a girl's house, kissing her until she felt like her lips might fall off, telling her, *I really don't wanna leave yet*?

It was a dangerous train of thought, so whenever Zyla caught herself going down that path, she pivoted and focused on how much she adored Kai, how he seemed to adore her just the same. And she thought about the words he said to her at the fall festival. *I like you more than I've ever liked anyone in my life.*

He wouldn't have told her that if he didn't mean it. She'd convinced herself that Camille was wrong. Kai wasn't a liar.

Zyla snapped back to reality when Beatrice nudged her. She dug in her bag and produced a Kind bar.

"Want half?" she asked. "I don't feel like going to get a gross hot dog, but I'm hungry."

Zyla laughed and hugged her best friend, who couldn't be less interested in their current activity. "Yes, I'd like half. You're the best for coming with me tonight. You know that, right?"

"Mm-hmm," Beatrice said, smiling. "I'm always the best, even when I'm not doing things that make other people happy."

After the game, Zyla and Beatrice waited outside of the school for Kai and Jamal.

When the team emerged and Zyla spotted Kai, her stomach fluttered. He just played a whole game and scored three touchdowns, helping Cedar High win. All that work, but he didn't even look sweaty or gross or winded. When he caught sight of Zyla, he grinned and made a beeline for her.

"Hey," he said, approaching. He wrapped her in a tight hug and pulled back to steal a quick kiss.

"Hi. Good game." She was a little breathless. She felt that way whenever Kai kissed her. She wondered if she'd ever get over the excitement.

"Hey, Beatrice," he said, nodding at her best friend. "Thanks for coming."

Beatrice smiled and waved her hand. "Oh, I wouldn't miss it for the world."

Kai laughed at her sarcasm, and Beatrice laughed too. But she stopped when Jamal showed up.

"Your highness," Jamal said, "You decided to grace us with your presence tonight. I'm *honored*."

Beatrice glared at him. "I hate you."

Jamal smiled. "Aww, how sweet."

"Guys, please," Zyla said, wishing their bickering would stop. Whenever they got together they had to pick at each other. Last weekend they'd argued on the entire train ride to Philly because they couldn't decide on whether the train went over the Benjamin Franklin or Walt Whitman bridge. Neither of them thought to use the internet to find out the real answer. It was ridiculous. Zyla wondered if they secretly enjoyed arguing so much.

"What? I'm innocent," Jamal said, holding his hands up. Beatrice scoffed. "*Anyway*, Brandon is having people over. Are we going or what?"

Kai looked down at Zyla. "You wanna go?"

"I have to be up extra early for work." Zyla bit her lip. "My mom's boss wants me to help count product inventory. But you should go."

"Nah, that's okay. I'll drive you home." He squeezed her hand.

Zyla perked up at the idea of having some alone time with Kai, but she'd come here with her best friend. Chicks before . . . well, you know the saying.

Zyla turned to Beatrice. "What are you going to do?"

"Well, I don't want to go home yet." Beatrice frowned and looked at Jamal. "I guess I'll go with him."

Jamal grinned and bowed deeply. "After you, your highness."

"Ugh." Beatrice rolled her eyes and walked toward the parking lot. Jamal hurried to catch up with her. Over her shoulder she called, "Zy, if I end up in jail tonight it's because he drove me to commit murder."

"I'd die a happy man if I were killed by you," Jamal said, dodging away just as Beatrice moved to swat at him.

"What are we going to do with them?" Zyla asked, turning to Kai.

"I don't know." He was staring at her in that intent way he did sometimes. Like he couldn't believe she was here with him, that she'd said yes to being his girlfriend.

No one had ever made her feel so special. Beatrice had informed Zyla that she and Kai were in a honeymoon phase, but Zyla didn't agree with that. She and Kai were just *happy*.

He drove her home, and they made out in his car for twenty minutes or twenty years. She lost track of time during these sessions. Kai had, like, the best lips in the universe. She couldn't believe she'd gone years without kissing anyone. No, not just anyone. Kai, specifically. Was she a good kisser? Did Kai think she was a good kisser? How did her kissing skills compare to that of his exes?

Stop that. Seriously!

Kai looped one of her curls around his fingers and smiled at her. God, he had such a perfect face.

"Can you make yourself free a couple Sundays from now?" he asked.

"Sure. Why?"

"My aunt and uncle want you to come over for dinner." He was looking at the strands of her hair curled around his finger, but his eyes shot to hers when she sucked in a breath.

"Oh," she said. *Yikes.* Apparently, his aunt and uncle hadn't been mad, exactly, when she and Kai started dating. But they had been disappointed that Kai broke his promise before summer even ended. She was afraid to meet them, and yet she wanted so badly for them to like her. To prove that she was worth Kai breaking his promise. "Um, okay. Yes."

"You don't have to be nervous," Kai said, searching her face. "They'll love you."

"I hope so."

"Trust me," he said. Then he pulled her close and kissed her again. "You should go before your aunt comes out here and yells at me again."

A week ago, she and Kai were sitting in his car when Aunt Ida let Bartholomew outside and caught Kai kissing Zyla's neck. She'd been furious, of course.

Zyla laughed. "She only did that *one* time."

"Once is definitely enough for me. She's scary as hell."

She leaned over and kissed him before she opened the passenger door. "Text me before you fall asleep?"

He nodded. "I'll do better than that. I'll call you."

"Okay, bye." She got out and shut the door.

Kai rolled down the window so that he could see her. "Okay, bye."

She grinned at him. "Okay, bye."

He started the engine. "Okay, bye."

They could stand there doing this forever.

"Okay, bye for real this time," she said, backing away, smiling huge.

Kai smiled at her too. He waited until she'd let herself inside before he beeped his horn and drove away.

She leaned against the door and sighed wistfully. Starring in your own romantic comedy was thrilling.

"Out late again, I see," Aunt Ida said from her La-Z-Boy. She raised an eyebrow at Zyla.

"It's only a little after nine," Zyla said, taking off her shoes and heading for the stairs.

"How was the game?" her mom asked, walking out of the kitchen. She had a dreamy-eyed look on her face. "Games used to be so exciting in high school! I remember going to your dad's games. They were so much fun."

Speaking of her dad, Zyla needed to call him back. The problem was she rarely felt like talking to him, especially now when she was so preoccupied with Kai and senior year. But if she didn't call him back soon, he'd say something to her mom, and then her mom would give her a long talk about how her dad tried his best and she needed to make space for him in her life.

"The game was cool," Zyla said. "Kai's team won."

"Fabulous. Tell Kai I said congratulations. And bring him over for dinner one night, will you?"

"Sure," Zyla said, wincing at the thought of subjecting Kai to sitting through an entire meal while her mom asked him a million questions and Aunt Ida glared at him with suspicion.

She retreated to the sanctuary that was her room. She spent about an hour making notes on her portfolio, and then she wrapped up her braids and got in bed, climbing under the covers.

Her phone buzzed, and Kai's name flashed across her screen.

"Hi, Kai Johnson," she said.

"Hi, Zyla Matthews," he said. "Did you miss me?"

She laughed. "Maybe."

"You don't have to play it cool with me. I know you've been staring at the phone, waiting for me to call." She could tell from the sound of his voice that he was grinning.

They talked about nothing and anything until she dozed off, clasping her phone to her ear, secretly wondering what his aunt and uncle would think of her when they eventually met.

Chapter Eighteen

"You seem in high spirits today," Dr. Rueben said to Kai as he bounded into his office.

Kai smiled and shrugged, sitting down. "I don't know. I guess."

He was downplaying it. Lately, he felt like he was walking on a cloud. Or, what were the words to that cheesy song they played on commercials sometimes? Walking on sunshine or whatever? Yeah, that's how he felt.

Dr. Rueben nodded. He crossed his leg over his knee, and Kai saw a flash of bright orange pumpkin-print socks. Halloween was next week, and he and Zyla were going to Chris's costume party together. They hadn't decided on a costume yet. Kai was leaving it up to Zyla. She wanted to make the costumes or thrift them. He'd been hesitant because he knew she was busy working on her portfolio, but she said it was fine.

"Things are going pretty good with Zyla," Kai said.

"Ah." Dr. Rueben nodded again. "It's been almost a month and a half, yes?"

"Yeah."

When Kai had first told Dr. Rueben he'd had a new girlfriend, he'd expected Dr. Rueben to sift through his mental folder of Kai's history and point out that Kai had promised his aunt and uncle that he wouldn't date until graduation. But Dr. Rueben only nodded and said, "As people, we're allowed to change our minds."

It was true. And even several weeks later, Kai kind of couldn't believe that Zyla was his girlfriend. Sometimes he thought back to the fall festival at Sailor Joe's when she'd said, *I like you. And I will be your girl.* At first, he'd thought he'd misheard her. Because there was no way he was finally getting what he wanted so badly. But she had said those words, and then he'd kissed her, and now he got to keep kissing her. And chilling with her and calling her and seeing her whenever they had time. "I feel really lucky."

Dr. Rueben smiled and tilted his head. "Lucky. Why did you use that word?"

Kai paused, not expecting that this would lead to a "deeper meaning" conversation. "I guess I said lucky because Zyla didn't want to date anyone at all. That was her rule or whatever, but she broke it because she liked me. And she didn't break it for anyone else before. So I feel special. Because I was worthy enough for her to change her mind. And *she* was special enough for me to break the promise I made Aunt Brenda and Uncle Steve. I guess we both made compromises."

"That's understandable," Dr. Rueben said. "We all want to feel special, particularly with those we care about."

"Yeah," Kai said. Then he bit his lip and looked down at his Nike PG 4s. "But I think I also feel a little bit of pressure. I'm her first boyfriend, so I want to make sure I'm doing everything right. That she doesn't feel like she made the wrong choice by dating me."

Dr. Rueben placed his chin in the palm of his hand. "It's impossible to do *everything* right, wouldn't you say? You could be setting yourself up for failure from the beginning if getting everything right is your overall goal."

"I know," Kai said. But he didn't *like* making mistakes. He wanted to do everything right for Zyla.

"You're frowning," Dr. Rueben said. "Tell me what you're thinking right now."

Kai began bouncing his knee, but he stopped as soon as Dr. Rueben noticed. He took a deep breath and tried to sort through his thoughts. "I guess my goal is to do everything right because if there are no mistakes or mess-ups, not only will Zyla not regret dating me, but I won't give her a reason to dump me."

"Ah." Dr. Rueben leaned back. "What kind of mistakes and mess-ups do you mean here?"

"I don't know. If we go out to a party and she doesn't have a good time. Or if I accidentally say something to piss off her aunt, which I wouldn't do. It's just an example."

"You've been together for a month and a half," Dr. Rueben said. "Has Zyla ever given you a reason to believe that she'd break up with you over any of those things?"

Kai thought about his girlfriend, who so far in their relationship had been sweet and understanding.

"No." Kai sighed. "I'm projecting."

Dr. Rueben smiled and nodded. "What if we reframe the idea of doing everything right? What if instead of focusing on doing everything right, you focus on trying your best? How does that sound?"

"That sounds good," Kai said because he felt like this was what he should say. In reality, he didn't like the idea of not getting everything right.

"It gives you a little more freedom, wouldn't you say? Trying to do everything right, or to achieve absolute perfection, can be very limiting in some cases."

Kai let Dr. Rueben's words sink in, mulled them over. He wasn't sure how he felt about them, but he nodded.

Dr. Rueben was quiet for a few minutes. He glanced at his clock. "Before our session ends, I do want to ask you about school. Would you say that you're making progress on your ability to focus in class?"

"Um, I'm trying," Kai said.

Somewhere in between his many duties, he had to eat and sleep and run and find as much time as he could to spend with Zyla. Which is why he'd taken to texting her during sixth-period study hall. He should have been doing homework during this period because he was always exhausted when he got home after football practice. But he missed Zyla constantly, and he wanted to talk to her. It was really ass that they went to different schools.

Last week, his study hall teacher, Mr. Cartwright, caught Kai texting and kindly asked him to put his phone away. High

School Kai wasn't known for getting into trouble, so he was let off easy. But as soon as Mr. Cartwright went back to grading papers, Kai pulled his phone out again. He and Zyla were sending pictures of their shoes back and forth. It sounded stupid, but it was a funny thing they did to let each other know where they physically were in the world. So Kai snapped another picture, and Mr. Cartwright caught Kai with his phone again. This time, Mr. Cartwright threatened to take Kai's phone away, so Kai slipped his phone in his pocket and bounced his knees, staring at the clock, waiting for study hall to end.

As soon as the ball rang, he grabbed his books and sprang out into the hallway. He rushed to seventh-period AP History, and as soon as he sat down, he pulled out his phone and snapped another picture for Zyla. Unfortunately, Mrs. Deaver had a very strict no-phones policy, and she snatched Kai's phone right out of his hand and put it in "phone jail," aka the small wicker basket on her desk.

Kai was embarrassed to get in trouble, and he was disappointed in himself, to be honest. Mostly, though, he was annoyed that she'd taken his phone, because it was really the only time he'd have to talk to Zyla until later that night. He barely paid attention to whatever Mrs. Deaver was saying at the front of the classroom. They were discussing the Space Race between America and the Soviet Union in the late fifties. History curriculum in most American high schools was taught through a white lens. Kai's dad, and later Aunt Brenda and Uncle Steve, made sure that Kai learned the history of his people. The history that schools didn't teach. Like how Katherine Johnson, a Black woman and extraordinary mathematician, calculated trajectories that were critical to the success of NASA's Friendship 7 mission. Yet, in Kai's textbook, there were only photographs of white men at NASA's headquarters during this time. Most people didn't learn about Katherine, or the many other Black women at NASA, until the movie *Hidden Figures*.

The erasure of Black history in the American high school curriculum bothered Kai, but he always tried his best not to be disrespectful to Mrs. Deaver. However, she'd taken his phone, so he wasn't in the mood to listen to her. He stared out the window and bounced his knees, trying his best to be patient and wait for class to end.

Then Mrs. Deaver called on Kai and asked his thoughts on a point she'd made. A point that Kai hadn't even heard. Usually, Mrs. Deaver could count on Kai to answer discussion questions when the rest of the class didn't want to participate. But that day, he just wanted his phone back and he didn't feel like doing Mrs. Deaver any favors.

He shrugged. "I don't know."

The whole class went quiet. Kai always had an answer.

"Well, let's think about it this way," Mrs. Deaver said. "Do you think astronauts would be seen as American heroes if the American public wasn't able to have easy access to them through the television?"

Kai turned to look out the window again. "I don't know."

He was being childish, he knew. He imagined what Aunt Brenda and Uncle Steve would think if they saw him behaving this way. He sighed and decided he'd give an actual answer, but then Mrs. Deaver was already calling on someone else.

After class, when Mrs. Deaver returned Kai's phone to him, she said that his behavior took her by surprise, and she expected him to come back ready to focus the next day. And because Kai was honest to a fault in therapy, he'd told Dr. Rueben the whole thing.

"There were no incidents this week," he said to Dr. Rueben now.

Instead of texting Zyla during study hall, he texted her during lunch. It meant he missed out on ninety percent of whatever Jamal and the crew were saying, but they mostly talked shit anyway, so it was fine.

"I'm glad to hear that," Dr. Rueben said. "Let's keep up this good progress."

"Okay," Kai said. "I will."

After their session ended and Kai was halfway home, he realized he forgot to tell Dr. Rueben that Zyla was having dinner at his house next Sunday.

Zyla had been nervous about it, and Kai told her everything would be fine. But honestly, he was nervous too.

Kai hadn't wanted to spring Aunt Brenda and Uncle Steve on Zyla as soon as they'd started dating. It could scare her off. But a month and a half into their relationship felt like enough time. At least he hoped that was the case. His aunt and uncle wanted to meet her. He felt shitty for breaking his promise to them, and even shittier because of their response. Uncle Steve had been disappointed, remarking that the school year had barely even started before Kai found a new girlfriend. He'd asked Kai if he'd even tried to keep his promise, to which Kai swore that he had. He'd tried so hard to resist his feelings for Zyla. Aunt Brenda had been a bit more understanding. She only asked that he prioritize school.

He needed them to like Zyla, to know that he didn't go back on his word for just anyone. That what he'd done had been worth it.

He wished he didn't have to prove his reasoning for being with Zyla to anyone, though. Sometimes, he imagined the two of them alone on an island in the middle of the ocean. Away from school and jobs and parents and guardians and expectations. Just the two of them, sitting in the sun, holding hands.

He pulled into his driveway, and his phone buzzed in his pocket. Zyla sent him a picture of Bartholomew snoozing in one of her fabric bags. **My model is taking a break.**

Kai smiled and texted back, **Camera ready even when he's sleeping.**

He'd told Zyla the truth at the fall festival. He liked her more than he'd ever liked anyone. That was just the truth of it.

He prayed Aunt Brenda and Uncle Steve would like her too.

Chapter Nineteen

In Zyla's opinion, the costumes she'd planned for herself and Kai were absolutely brilliant. Halloween was her favorite holiday, particularly because she loved creating costumes, whether she hand sewed them herself or carefully thrifted the pieces and put them together. She didn't shop at the Spirit of Halloween or Party City. Where was the fun in that? When Kai said he wanted to take her to Chris's Halloween party, she jumped at the chance to find a couple's costume. It meant she'd lost a few nights to work on her portfolio, and the stress of it lingered in the back of her mind, but once Halloween was over, she'd focus her attention on her portfolio one hundred percent. Did she ever expect that she'd put herself in charge of something like creating a couple's costume for herself and a boyfriend? No. Not a chance. But life was strange and full of surprises, apparently.

Zyla had been stumped for a little bit on a costume idea. Should they dress up as a famous couple? Or maybe a couple from a movie? Then the idea came to her: They should poke fun at that annoying nickname they'd earned over the summer and go as Bonnie and Clyde. That way, they could reclaim the narrative or whatever. In pictures, the real Clyde wore a shabby suit and Bonnie wore dresses and long skirts. Zyla didn't really like that idea. Bonnie and Clyde were gangsters, weren't they? She could play that up. She spent an entire Saturday in Philly with Beatrice, scouring thrift stores until she found two pinstripe suits and wide-brimmed fedoras. When Kai tried on his suit, it fit him pretty perfectly, which shouldn't have surprised Zyla because everything looked perfect on him. Her suit was slightly baggy, but that was okay. It only added to her gangster appeal.

Now, on Halloween night, she and Beatrice sat in her living room and waited for Kai to pick them up for Chris's party. Zyla couldn't wait to debut their costumes.

"How's my lipstick look?" Beatrice asked, pursing her lips, which were painted a deep matte red. She was dressed as a devil in a red catsuit and pointy devil ears. Her pitchfork lay at her feet.

"You look like you rule over minions in the underworld," Zyla said.

Beatrice smiled in a way that could only be described as devilish. "Perfect."

Zyla's phone vibrated with a text from Kai saying that he just pulled up. She called upstairs to Aunt Ida and her mom to let them know she was leaving, and she and Beatrice hurried outside, eager to start their night.

Jamal got out of the passenger seat for Zyla, and when Zyla saw him, she burst out laughing. Jamal was dressed like a devil too. He wore black and a long red cape. His pointy ears looked just like Beatrice's. When he saw Beatrice, he glared and pointed his pitchfork at her.

"You gotta be kidding me," he said.

Beatrice held up her pitchfork too, like they were about to have a duel. "You're a poor man's devil. I'm the real deal."

Jamal smirked. "Of course I'm the poor one in this scenario."

Beatrice huffed, ready to argue, but Zyla quickly put an end to it. "Both of your costumes are great!" She ushered Beatrice into the back seat and hopped up front with Kai. Kai smiled, looking her up and down. "What's up, Bonnie?"

"Nothing," Zyla said, grinning. "What's up, Clyde?"

"You two are so sweet, I have a toothache," Beatrice said, and Jamal laughed. She turned to him and narrowed her eyes. "I didn't say you could laugh at my joke."

Kai turned up the radio to drown out the sound of their bickering.

Chris's house was packed, which Zyla expected. Anytime she went to a Cedar High party with Kai, she wondered if the whole school had been invited. Not to mention, moving through the party with Kai made her feel as though she was walking with Barack Obama. Everybody and their mom wanted to talk to him. She'd gotten a lot better at remembering names, though. That's what happened when you dated someone for two months.

Two months. She'd been dating someone for that long. Not just someone. Kai. She couldn't believe it sometimes, honestly.

Beatrice dipped off to find Xiomara, the girl she was currently hooking up with, and Jamal disappeared almost as soon as they walked inside. With his fingers woven through hers, Kai led Zyla into the kitchen and got her a beer. He drank a Coke, since he was driving. Zyla noticed that even when he wasn't driving, he didn't really drink that much at parties.

"Let me guess who you are," Brandon said, strolling over to them, wearing a banana suit. "You're bank robbers."

Kai smirked. "Technically, that's right."

"We're Bonnie and Clyde," Zyla said.

Brandon snapped his fingers. "Oh shit! I get it. Wowww. Nice." He turned around and spoke to the others in the kitchen. "Ay, y'all, look, Kai and Zyla are Bonnie and Clyde. Get it?"

Some people looked at them and laughed, but others just ignored Brandon, who was well on his way to being wasted. That didn't stop him from trying to have a full-blown conversation with Kai, though. Zyla tuned them out as they talked about football or something, and she scanned the people standing in kitchen and those lingering in the hallway. Halloween costumes said something about a person. From what they chose to be to the amount of effort they put into it. She spotted Darius, Whit, and Alanna standing at the entrance to the living room. Darius was dressed as Rihanna, circa her *Loud* phase, with red hair, a colorful bustier, and denim shorts. Whit and Alanna were Thing 1 and Thing 2. Cute.

She spotted lots of people dressed as Where's Waldo. That was a pretty easy costume. What she mostly noticed, though, was that the girls' outfits tended to be tighter and showed skin. There was nothing wrong with that. Even last year, Zyla had dressed up as Chuckie, the possessed serial-killer doll, and she'd worn really short overall shorts and a striped red crop top. She looked at the girls around her dressed as sexy bees and butterflies, and even sexy nuns (the sisters at St. Catherine's would have a heart attack), and she looked at her own baggy suit and wondered if maybe she'd gone the wrong route this year.

She hadn't questioned her sense of style before. Not even when she was teased in middle school for her thrift-store shopping. She loved the way she dressed. Her fashion sense was the one thing she could count on when so much else in her life was so up in the air. But right now, she couldn't shake the feeling that maybe her costume just looked stupid.

She looked down at her wide pants and bit her lip. Insecurity wasn't something she usually struggled with. But when it came to being Kai Johnson's girlfriend, she had to admit that sometimes she felt a little inadequate. Kai didn't make her feel that way, of course. It was other people. From the way they looked at her, at the two of them together, she could tell that she wasn't necessarily the type of girl they expected Kai to date. It was how the Cedar High girls looked at her whenever she came to Kai's games. It was even the way that Camille had looked at her during their awkward conversation in Nordstrom. Kai's exes—or at least the ones Zyla had met—were beautiful and unique. Zyla thought she was unique and beautiful in her own way, but she also knew that people might describe her as quirky or offbeat or whatever stupid things people said about girls who wore weird glasses and spent most of their time with their head down in a sketchbook.

She was Kai's tenth girlfriend. *Tenth*. Meanwhile, she'd never dated anyone. It was so tricky to navigate.

"Hey, you okay?" Kai whispered in her ear.

She shrugged him off, irritated at her own thoughts. Kai jerked away and blinked at her.

"Sorry," she said quickly. "Yeah, I'm fine."

He stared at her. Quietly, he said, "You sure? You look upset."

She nodded and forced a smile. Kai smiled back, a little hesitantly. Zyla gave him a once-over. Of course he looked gorgeous in his suit, while she looked like a frumpy 1920s wannabe. Ugh.

"Do you want another beer?" Kai asked.

"No."

"You wanna play flip cup?"

Zyla glanced at people gathered around the kitchen table. She wouldn't put her stupid costume on display, not while standing next to immaculate Kai for everyone to see.

"No," she said.

Kai's eyebrows drew together. He was confused. She was being confusing, she knew. But she couldn't kick her sour mood.

And then her mood got worse when Camille Vaughn sauntered into the kitchen, in a witch costume. Witches were a basic go-to for Halloween, but Camille looked great. She'd stuffed her hair inside of her tall, pointy witch hat, and she wore a black leather bodice, black tutu, and black fishnets with high-heeled boots. Great, just great. Of course Camille looked amazing. And Kai looked amazing. And Zyla looked like she'd robbed a thrift store with her eyes closed.

One of the boys playing flip cup whistled, and Camille rolled her eyes. She paused when she noticed Zyla and Kai by the kitchen sink, but she only smiled tightly and grabbed a beer before disappearing back into the hallway. Zyla thought of how Camille walked away after their conversation in Nordstrom, sporting the same smug, tight smile. Beatrice had assumed that Camille had wanted Kai back and Zyla was in her way. Was that true now?

Zyla looked at Kai to see his reaction to Camille's presence, but he was only staring down at her, frowning.

"Are you sure you're okay?" he asked. "Do you wanna leave or do something else?"

"I'm fine, Kai," she snapped. "Please stop asking."

Kai winced like he'd been slapped. Zyla immediately regretted her tone. He didn't deserve to be snapped at. She should apologize.

"Well, damn, okay," Kai said, shrugging, annoyed. "Say no more." He turned away and started talking to Brandon again.

Never mind. She wouldn't apologize if that's how he was going to be.

You know what she'd do? Go find Beatrice.

She walked away without a word, ignoring the sinking feeling in her stomach. She and Kai never fought. What was happening? But it was too late. Their first fight had already started, and she was too proud to say sorry now.

Zyla found Beatrice in the basement, standing by the dryer, but she wasn't with Xiomara. She was with Jamal.

"My costume is better than yours. Just admit it!" Beatrice was shouting.

Jamal cackled like a true devil. "It isn't! It's just spandex! You don't even have a cape!"

God. The last thing Zyla wanted to do was stand by while the two of them argued for the millionth time. Instead, she went upstairs and found her way onto the back porch. It was chilly, but there were people outside smoking and talking. Zyla spotted Whit and Alanna sitting side by side on deck chairs. She waved at them, and Alanna beckoned her over.

"Wow, girl, love your costume," Whit said, scooting over to make room for Zyla in her chair. "Gangster. Very classic."

Zyla plopped down and let out a deep breath. She didn't even feel like explaining that she wasn't just any old gangster. She was Bonnie, and Kai was Clyde.

And they were in a fight.

"Thanks," Zyla mumbled. She tried to lose herself in Alanna and Whit's conversation, but she couldn't keep up. She kept thinking about how she should just swallow her pride and apologize to Kai. She needed to go find him.

But she took too much time mulling this over, because before long, Kai came to find her.

"It's almost curfew," he said, not really looking at Zyla. He nodded at Alanna and Whit. Both girls glanced back and forth between Zyla and Kai and quickly fell quiet, obviously picking up on their tense vibes.

Zyla stood. "Where are Beatrice and Jamal?"

"Jamal's getting a ride home with Brandon. Beatrice said she wanted to stay with Xiomara."

"Oh." So it would just be the two of them on the ride home. "Okay."

Kai walked with stiff shoulders as she followed him to his car. His face looked so different when he wasn't smiling, less alive. She hated that she'd caused him to look that way. He didn't say anything for the few first minutes of the drive. Then when they reached a stoplight, he turned to her.

"Zyla, what is going on?" Kai asked. He was confused as fuck. "We're in a fight, and I really don't get why."

At his next session, he'd have to ask Dr. Rueben what happened when trying your best wasn't good enough, especially when you had no idea what you'd done wrong. Kai had "tried his best" to make sure that Zyla was having the perfect night, and he didn't understand what he could have done differently to make it so that she wasn't upset.

The night had started off fine. Their costumes were fire. Zyla seemed proud that she'd picked them out, and Kai was happy that she was happy. He didn't give a fuck about costumes, honestly. Last year, he wore a black T-shirt and jeans to Chris's party. On his T-shirt, he wore a name tag he'd found that said "Dave." When people asked Kai who he was supposed to be, he pointed at the name tag and said, "I'm Dave, obviously." *That's* how much he cared about Halloween. But Zyla loved it, so he would love it for her too.

And he loved bringing her to parties with him. He didn't look at her as a trophy wife or anything, but he loved that she walked around holding his hand. That people would look at her and know she'd chosen Kai.

They'd posted up by the kitchen sink, per usual, and before he could really even start talking to her, Brandon came over, already buzzed. He'd derailed Kai with a conversation about agility drills, of all things, and by the time Kai returned his attention to Zyla, she was pissed about *something*. Was it because of Brandon? He didn't think so. She was pretty used to Brandon at this point. But when Kai tried to talk to her, she gave him one-word answers, and her posture was weird, like she was closing herself off to him. For what? What had he done? Then she'd gone and snapped at him, just for asking if she was okay. His temper flared up quick and hot before he could stop it. "Say no more" rolled off his tongue, and he turned his back on her. He knew it was the wrong thing to do even as he was doing it. They should be able to talk about whatever was bothering her. They hadn't had communication problems before. But when he turned to face her, she was already walking away.

He was tempted to chase after her. But then he'd risk looking like a fool in front of everyone. He tried to let it go, to focus on whatever Brandon was talking about. He tried to play flip cup with Chris, just opting not to drink. He wondered where the hell Jamal was. And all the while, his heart was in his stomach. Why had he thought that he and Zyla were immune to arguments? He hadn't even seen this one coming, and that was what scared him, even though he knew that abandonment could happen without warning. One minute, everything was fine, and the next, the rug was pulled out from under you.

Zyla sat beside him in the passenger seat, biting her lip. He waited for her to answer his question. His mouth was dry, and his tongue felt heavy. What was she going to say?

"Our costumes are stupid," she blurted. Then she shook her head. "No, *my* costume is stupid. You look fine."

What?

Kai stared at her, baffled. The driver in the car behind them honked their horn, and Kai realized the light had turned green. He put his foot on the gas and switched into the slow lane.

"You're mad at me because you think I look better in my costume?" he asked.

"No, no." She shook her head again, quicker this time. "We were at the party, and I was thinking about how stupid my costume looked in comparison to everyone else. And how people were probably looking at you and wondering what you were doing with me. And then I was thinking about your exes, and how no one probably ever asked that question when you'd dated the other girls. And then I thought about how you have so many exes, and I'm your tenth girlfriend. All of this is new to me, but you've done it before. Those thoughts bothered me. They *always* bother me, and I was trying to sort through them, but you wouldn't stop asking what was wrong, and then I snapped at you, and I shouldn't have done that."

Her words came out in one big whoosh, and when she finished speaking, she had to stop and catch her breath.

Kai tried to sort through everything she'd said. He didn't even know where to begin.

"I don't think the costumes are stupid," he said. "And I doubt anyone looks at me and wonders what I'm doing with you, if anything it's the other way around." Then he paused. "You haven't said anything to me about my exes before. I didn't even know you cared."

Wasn't she the one who'd gone and become friends with at least half of his exes at the same party? In fact, tonight, he'd found her talking with Whitney Brown after she'd ditched him in the kitchen.

Zyla shrugged, staring down at her hands. "I just think about it sometimes."

"I've had girlfriends before you, but what's happening between us is new to me." He'd told her that he'd never liked anyone as much as he'd liked her. He still felt that way. Did she think he'd been lying? Did she think he was a liar in general? His heartbeat sped up. Involuntarily, he began drumming his fingers against the steering wheel, and he forced himself to stop. "I don't care about my exes, and you shouldn't either. I'm with you now, and that's what matters."

Zyla was staring down at her hands, quiet. He turned onto her street and slowed to a crawl as he pulled up in front of her house. He hoped her aunt Ida had already fallen asleep in her chair. The last thing he needed was for her to flash the porch lights while he and Zyla were in the middle of possibly the worst conversation they'd ever had.

He cut the engine. Zyla wouldn't look at him. She was still biting her lip, frowning. What was she thinking? What was she struggling to say?

Then it hit him. She was having second thoughts. She was probably thinking of how to tell him it was over. She'd leave him behind.

He felt himself deflate just like those stupid balloons at their Sailor Joe's booth. He couldn't let it end this way, not this quickly. He'd change her mind, show her that they'd get through this, whatever *this* was.

"We don't need to break up," he said, hating the desperation in his voice. "Just talk to me. What do you want me to do? How can I make it better?"

Zyla's eyes widened. Her mouth fell open. "Break up? Kai, I don't want to break up with you. Why are you saying this?"

Huh? He froze. "Because . . . you were talking about my exes, and you didn't like that I had so many."

"That doesn't mean I want to break up with you. No, oh my God." She sprang out of her seat and threw her arms around him, squeezing him close. "I don't want to break up. I was just being stupid. You're right. You and I are together now, and that's what matters."

Shocked, Kai wrapped his arms around her too.

"I want to stay together," Zyla whispered. He felt her breath on his neck. He pulled away so that he could see her face. Her eyes were wide. She looked scared, knowing that she'd scared him. "I'm sorry for the way I acted earlier tonight."

"It's okay." He kissed her. She wanted to stay together. She wasn't dumping him out of nowhere. "Please know I don't care what anyone else thinks when they see us. I only care about you."

"I *do* know that." She kissed him back harder. "I'm sorry. I don't know what I was thinking."

They were frantic, reaching for each other, kissing, hugging. Kai felt overwhelmed by the quick turn of the conversation. She wasn't mad at him. They weren't breaking up. They were okay.

Aunt Ida flashed the porch lights.

"Damn," Kai whispered.

"I can stay out a few minutes longer," Zyla said.

"I don't want you to get in trouble." He held her hands and looked into her eyes. "Can we make a promise to talk through our problems? If you're upset, just tell me. Don't walk away. And I'll do the same."

She nodded. Her cheeks were flushed. "Yes, I promise."

The porch lights flashed again. Kai quickly grabbed her face and kissed her. Zyla kissed him back for as long as she could. Then she was rushing away into her house. She texted him once she was inside. **Call me when you get home?**

He sighed, relieved. **I will.**

They'd survived their first fight. If they were lucky—and Kai hoped they were—this fight would be their first and last.

248

Chapter Twenty

Zyla was so nervous, her palms had basically turned into tiny swimming pools.

"How do I look?" she asked, staring at her reflection in the mirror.

Jade was lying on her bed, her chin propped up in her hands. "I think you look beautiful."

Zyla turned around and smiled at her sister, letting out a deep breath. "Thanks."

She was wearing a navy-blue short-sleeve baby doll dress with a white Peter Pan collar. Her hair was slicked back in a low bun and she'd borrowed a pair of Aunt Ida's pearl earrings. On her feet she wore a pair of vintage brown leather Mary Janes that she'd thrifted last fall.

Tonight, she was having dinner at Kai's house. Her nerves could energize a small planet.

This was her first dinner with her first boyfriend's family. She had no idea what to expect. She wished there was a handbook or something that told her the correct protocol for this kind of thing. It was another reminder of her inexperience. But maybe her inexperience didn't matter in this situation. After she and Kai had their first fight, their connection had been shaken, but it came back stronger. Here was proof: Kai hadn't brought a girlfriend over for dinner before. It didn't matter if she was his tenth girlfriend or hundredth. This was new for him as well. At least that was comforting.

"Wow, Zy, you look gorgeous, babe." Zyla's mom leaned in her doorway and smiled. She walked over and smoothed down the stray curls around Zyla's bun.

Zyla looked at her mom's reflection in the mirror. Her hair was wrapped in a scarf. She was planning to cook Sunday dinner, at Aunt Ida's behest. Keith was officially old news. She was supposed to go out on a date tonight, but they'd canceled last minute.

"Thanks, Mom."

"Oh, stop pinching your face like that," her mom said, squeezing her shoulders. "Just relax. I was nervous when I met your dad's parents for the first time too."

"Really?" Zyla asked. "Why?"

Her mom's smile turned sly. "You've met your grandparents. You know how prickly they are. They thought I'd distract Terrance from his dreams of going to the NBA." She sighed and laughed. "I guess they were right at the end of the day. I wound up pregnant, and we moved to Florida so that he could work with his uncle at the marina. Your grandparents *loved* that."

Zyla frowned. "Mom, why would you think that story would make me feel any less nervous?"

"Well, last time I checked, you don't have plans to get pregnant and move to Florida." Her mom paused and narrowed her eyes. "Right?"

Zyla groaned, not even bothering to answer that question.

Her mom turned around and looked at Jade, shrugging. "What did I say?"

Jade laughed, and Zyla went to grab her phone. Kai would be there in two minutes, and he was rarely late. She did one more mirror check and took a deep breath. Then the doorbell rang.

"That would be Kai," her mom said.

Jade hopped up and ran downstairs. She'd become Kai's number-two fan in this household over the last couple months. Zyla, of course, was number one.

"It'll be fine," Zyla's mom said, kissing her on the forehead.

Zyla followed her mom downstairs, where Kai was waiting in the living room on the couch beside Jade, who was excitedly telling him about the things she'd done so far today. Bartholomew sat on the rug in front of him, passive-aggressively growling, and Aunt Ida was narrowing her eyes at him from across the room in her La-Z-Boy. So much chaos, and Kai took it in stride.

He stood up when Zyla and her mom walked into the room. He was wearing an olive-green button-up and black jeans.

"Hey," he said, smiling at Zyla, warm and handsome. He hugged her politely, taking care not to squeeze her too closely because her family was watching. But her heartbeat sped up regardless. He pulled away and then politely hugged her mom. "Hi, Ms. Matthews. It's nice to see you."

"Nice to see you too, Kai. Please tell your aunt and uncle I said thank you for inviting Zyla into your home."

Kai nodded. "Sure, of course."

"And tell them we're unhappy with the way the two of you sit outside in that car of yours every night," Aunt Ida grumbled.

"Aunt Ida!" Zyla hissed, mortified.

"Auntie, cut it out." Zyla's mom laughed and shook her head. "She's in a mood today, Kai. Just ignore her."

Kai made a face. It was clear that Aunt Ida was in a mood *every day*, but he quickly covered it up and said, "I'll have Zyla back before curfew."

They said their goodbyes, and as they walked to his car, Kai pulled her in for a quick kiss. Zyla had seen him yesterday afternoon after his game, but she'd missed him like crazy.

"Ready?" he asked.

No. I'm terrified that your aunt and uncle won't like me.

But there was no more time to be terrified.

Sink, *then* swim.

"Yep," she said. "I'm ready."

———

Kai had been thinking hard about Dr. Rueben's advice to shoot for his best as opposed to striving to get everything right, but there was a lot riding on tonight's dinner. He hadn't brought a girl to meet Aunt Brenda and Uncle Steve in such a formal way. He was sweating bullets under his button-up. He wanted Aunt Brenda and Uncle Steve to like Zyla so badly. He wanted Zyla to like them in return. He wanted his aunt and uncle to realize they didn't have a reason to be disappointed in him.

As they walked up to his front door, he squeezed Zyla's hand. She smiled at him. She looked so pretty tonight. He kissed her one more time before he opened the door. The hallway smelled like Aunt Brenda's cooking: baked chicken, collard greens, and yams.

Aunt Brenda and Uncle Steve both emerged from the kitchen. Kai wondered how they appeared to Zyla, with their matching burgundy sweaters. They looked like they'd walked right out of a catalog.

"Zyla, this is my aunt Brenda and my uncle Steve," Kai said.

"Zyla," Aunt Brenda said, smiling and holding out her hand for a shake. "It's so nice to finally meet you. Welcome."

"Thank you so much for having me," Zyla said. "You have such a lovely home."

Kai tried not to smile at that. This wasn't the first time Zyla had been inside his house, of course. A few weekday evenings when Aunt Brenda had her night class and Uncle Steve stayed late at work, Zyla had come over so they could do homework together . . . and make out on the living room couch.

Aunt Brenda beamed at Zyla's good manners. "Thank you, sweetheart."

"It's nice to finally put a face to a name," Uncle Steve said. "I hope you like chicken."

Zyla nodded. Her eyes were slightly wider than usual, which let Kai know that she was nervous. "I love chicken."

They sat around the table, Zyla and Kai on one side, Aunt

Brenda and Uncle Steve across from them. They held hands as Uncle Steve blessed the food, and then began to eat. Kai was shoving food in his mouth because that's what he was supposed to be doing right now, but he could barely register what he was eating. He was too nervous, watching everyone's faces to gauge what they were thinking. Zyla was quiet as she ate. They caught eyes for a quick second, and she smiled and looked away.

"So, Zyla, Kai tells us you live in the neighborhood?" Uncle Steve said.

Zyla nodded. "Yep, a few blocks away. Kai runs by my house a lot."

"Oh?" Uncle Steve glanced at Kai and raised an eyebrow. Kai could see him calculating each of Kai's late-night runs, possibly assuming that he stopped at Zyla's house every time. Which wasn't true. At least it hadn't been since school started.

"During the summer, yeah," Kai said quickly. "Not so much now because we're both busy with school."

Aka they were focusing and not distracting each other.

Uncle Steve kept his eyes on Kai, nodding. Thankfully, Aunt Brenda jumped in before Uncle Steve could ask a follow-up question.

"Zyla, I taught at St. Catherine's years ago before I got my master's," Aunt Brenda said. "Is Sister Joellen still there?"

"Yes, she teaches senior English," Zyla said, smiling. "She's my favorite teacher."

Aunt Brenda nodded knowingly. "The students loved her back then too."

"St. Catherine's is a fine institution," Uncle Steve said to Zyla. "They have one of the highest graduation rates in the county. Have you thought about which colleges you're going to apply to yet?"

Ah, Uncle Steve with the serious questions already. Kai tried not to suck his teeth. Wait, this could be good, though. Zyla's answer would impress them.

"Um, yes, I have," Zyla said. "I want to study fashion design. I'm applying to some programs in the US, like FIT, Parsons, and FIDM. But I'm really hoping to go to Parsons Paris or the London College of Fashion."

"Fashion design!" Aunt Brenda clapped her hands together, delighted. "Oh, Kai did tell me that you made your own clothes. Did you make that dress you're wearing now?"

Zyla shook her head. "I thrifted this one. But I could make something similar if I wanted to."

"That is so impressive. I admire people who can be so creative. Kai's mom used to sew her own dresses sometimes. She even made a few of Kai's onesies."

"Really?" Zyla turned to look at Kai. "I didn't know that."

Kai shrugged, glancing at Aunt Brenda. "I mean, she mended my clothes when I ripped holes in them and stuff."

Zyla was staring at him. He didn't talk about his parents that much, and she didn't push him to do so, but he could tell she was hanging on to his every word right now.

"Zyla, I'd love to see your work sometime," Aunt Brenda said. "I'm sure your pieces are as beautiful as Kai says."

"Of course, whenever you want to see them, I'd be glad to show you." Zyla bit her lip, and she and Kai shared a quick glance. She grinned at him and he grinned too, leaning back in his chair.

What had he been so nervous about? Of course this night was going to be perfect, or "the best" it could be. Why had he ever assumed differently?

"So, London and Paris," Uncle Steve said. "That's pretty far."

"I know," Zyla said, turning to look at him. "I think it's kind of exciting to go to college in another country."

"I studied abroad in Rome one semester," Aunt Brenda said. "Some of my best memories happened in that city."

Uncle Steve nodded at Kai. "Kai will be at Morehouse next fall, God willing. That'll be a big time difference. At least six hours. What's your plan for keeping in touch?"

Kai froze. Their plan? When they first got together, they'd both known each other's goals for the future and how far apart they'd be, but they didn't focus on it because they'd been too caught up in the now. He'd been so happy that she was finally his girlfriend, he didn't think about what they'd do *after* graduation.

He and Zyla exchanged another glance. She blinked at him, clearly as dumbfounded as he was. He could be in Georgia next year and she could be in Europe. It *was* far, just like Uncle Steve said. He couldn't imagine having that distance between them.

Their sweet bubble had been plucked by their argument, and now it was being pricked.

Kai didn't know what to say, and apparently, neither did Zyla. They both sat there until the silence between them started to get awkward.

"Who wants ice cream?" Aunt Brenda asked, standing up. Kai noticed that she shot a quick, reproving look at Uncle Steve. Uncle Steve shook his head, confused. He had no idea what he'd just done. Because now Kai couldn't get that question out of his head. What *would* he and Zyla do next year?

No, no. He could worry about that later. Fixating in the middle of dinner wasn't gonna help anything.

Over dessert, Zyla talked about her family, and Kai willed himself to focus and listen. And later as Aunt Brenda gave Zyla the heartiest hug goodbye and Uncle Steve seemed genuinely happy to have met her, Kai tried to focus on those positive things too. In their eyes, the dinner had been a success.

He and Zyla were quiet as he drove her home. Was she thinking about how far apart they'd be next year too? Kai glanced at her, and she was staring out of the window with a pinched expression. Fuck.

He pulled up in front of her house and cut the engine. He took a deep breath, thinking of what to say, how to smooth over whatever weirdness they were experiencing.

"There are different kinds of ways that we can keep in touch," she suddenly said, turning to him. "FaceTime and Google Chat and Zoom, and whatever new app they'll have by next year."

"Yeah," he said, nodding, desperately grasping onto her words. "And we can find specific times to talk. Like when it's

257

eleven a.m. in Europe and five p.m. here. When you think about it, Paris isn't *that* far. It's not like Australia or something."

"Exactly! And we can write letters too." She smiled at him, bashful. "You'd write me a letter if I wrote you one, wouldn't you?"

"Of course." He was so overwhelmed with relief. They were on the same page. "We'll be okay no matter where we are."

"Exactly," she repeated, nodding.

She scooted forward and kissed him. They stayed like that for a while until Aunt Ida flashed the porch lights.

"Gotta go," Zyla said, slipping away.

Reluctantly, Kai unlocked the doors and watched her hurry up her driveway. She turned around and waved at him before she walked inside.

They *would* be okay, no matter what.

Kai had to believe that.

NOW: May, Senior Day Trip, 5:58 p.m.

Before news of Kai's disappearance reaches his aunt Brenda, she is at home cleaning her office, as she's wont to do on Friday evenings. It is how she unwinds after a long work week filled with grading papers and lecturing students on the works of James Baldwin and Maya Angelou and Toni Morrison. Lauryn Hill's "The Sweetest Thing" plays softly from Aunt Brenda's mini speaker as she roams the room, wiping away dust and organizing her papers.

She pauses when she picks up a framed photograph of her fraternal twin sister, Barbara, holding Kai when he was an infant. Brenda and Barbara were as close as any two sisters could be. Brenda's face was more oval shaped while Barbara's was round, and Barbara was at least two inches taller, but they barely noticed those differences. Brenda used to feel as though she and Barbara shared the same skin. They knew everything about each other, inside and out. When Barbara decided she wanted to go to Spelman for college, Brenda decided that's where she wanted to go too. And when Barbara started dating Tim, Brenda soon met his best friend, Steve. After college when Steve got a job in Philadelphia, Brenda gave up her life in Atlanta to be with him. Tim and Barbara shortly followed behind and bought a house in New Jersey. The couples were married within months of each other.

Brenda and Barbara tried to get pregnant at the same time so that their kids could grow up together. Barbara got pregnant with Kai quickly, but Brenda struggled to conceive. She and Steve had been disappointed but ultimately came to accept this, and sweet baby Kai made everything so special. Brenda loved watching him grow up, and she loved her role as the cool aunt, taking him to bookstores and libraries whenever she could. She longed for a child of her own, but she had Kai, and that was enough.

Then Barbara and Tim died, and by tragic fate, Kai was Brenda's permanently.

Those first few years were hard. Kai was so angry, understandably so, and Brenda had no idea what to do because she was struggling with her own grief. She'd lost her sister, her other half. Yet somehow, they managed to work through it. Brenda knows she can't replace Barbara, and she doesn't want to. She just hopes she's done a good job raising Kai.

Kai is special. Every parent or guardian probably thinks that about their child. But in Kai's case, Brenda knows this is true. Kai is kind and compassionate and intelligent. Sometimes he feels things so strongly, and she wishes he would spare himself of that. Lately, since his breakup with his ex-girlfriend, Zyla, he's been in a deep funk, distant. He doesn't like to talk to her and Steve. She isn't sure if he talks to anyone other than Dr. Rueben. He goes to school, goes to track practice, runs late at night, and sleeps.

Brenda surmises he's acting this way because he misses Zyla. Brenda had met Kai's other girlfriends briefly at sports games and other school events, but Zyla was the first girlfriend who came over for dinner. Brenda could tell by the way Kai and Zyla looked at each other that their feelings ran deep. And she saw the fear in their eyes when Steve brought up how far apart they'd be once they went off to college. That was the saddest thing. They'd found one another, but their timing was completely off.

Zyla is a sweet girl, and Brenda can understand why Kai liked her so much, but she can't in good conscience support a relationship between the two of them, not after the trouble they got into on Valentine's Day. It's probably for the best that they broke up. Brenda just wishes it didn't make Kai so sad.

You see, Brenda knows love is important to have a successful life. She knew that when she left her job in Atlanta to be with Steve in Philly. But she made that decision when she was an adult. It was sad that Kai and Zyla found each other and this bond so young because it meant their relationship would be so much harder to maintain.

Earlier this morning before Kai left for his trip, Brenda passed by his room on her way downstairs, and what she saw gave her pause. Kai was lying on his bed with a bright smile on his face. She was surprised to find him this way after his days of moodiness. He looked, in one word, elated. Or in other words, relaxed, bright-eyed, hopeful. Yes, that was it. Absolutely filled with hope. Originally, Brenda thought this was because Kai was excited to get away on an overnight trip with his friends. And then, naturally, as a guardian to a seventeen-year-old boy, Brenda grabbed Steve and they sat down to give Kai a lecture on safe sex. Kai sat up and stared at the two of them, raising an eyebrow. He looked bemused, but he listened patiently, nodding his head, that hopeful smile on his face. Then he thanked them for the talk, grabbed his duffel bag, and left. She hopes he's having fun today. After what he's been through, he surely deserves it.

She places the framed photograph of her sister back on her desk and sits in her chair to take a quick break. She closes her eyes and leans back, letting out a deep sigh, wondering what Steve is doing downstairs. Probably working. He often brings work home from the office. He says that if he has to work late, at least he'll do it at home where Brenda and Kai are close by.

Her cell phone vibrates on her desk, and a number she doesn't recognize pops up on the screen. She reaches to answer it immediately, remembering the Thai takeout she ordered not too long ago.

"I'll get my husband to come to the door in two seconds," Brenda says when she answers.

"Mrs. Washington, this is Mrs. Deaver from Cedar High."

Brenda gets a chill as she hears the serious tone of Mrs. Deaver's voice.

"Is everything okay?" she asks. "Is Kai okay?"

"We're not sure. We think he may have run away from the resort. The last—"

"*Run away?*" Brenda stands and fists her thick curls. "What do you mean he ran away?"

"The other students tell us that he got into an argument with some boys from another school, and he was last seen getting onto the ski lift with a student named Zyla Matthews."

"Are you out there looking for them?!" Brenda is shrieking now.

"Yes, Mrs. Washington, the park troopers are searching for them now. But the ski lift operator also noted that they were carrying backpacks and weren't dressed in bathing suits like the other students. He said they were acting very suspicious. His account is the only one we have to go on. We're so sorry that this happened on our watch."

Brenda is shoving on her loafers, trying to piece together the information she is receiving. And she suddenly thinks back to that day over twenty years ago when Steve called her from his hotel room in Philadelphia. "I got the job," he said. "Will you come be with me?" Without a second thought, Brenda threw a bag together and hopped on a bus in the middle of the night. Because she simply knew. Because she was a hopeless romantic who was willing to do anything, even run away in the middle of the night, to be with the one she loved, because the thought of being apart was too painful to bear. A hopeless romantic, just like Kai.

That elated smile on his face this morning now makes so much sense. Maybe and he and Zyla had been planning to run away together all along.

"We're coming now," Brenda says. "Please keep me updated on *everything*."

Ms. Deaver promises that she will and apologizes once again.

Brenda rushes out of her office and into the hallway, searching for her husband. "Steve, grab your car keys!"

Chapter Twenty-One

The overwhelming gloom always surprised Kai, although it shouldn't have. It was something about the air. The crisp smell of fall, the chillier gusts of wind. The lawn decorations and radio stations that played Christmas music too early. Thanksgiving would be here in a couple weeks. A time for family and togetherness. Yet Kai felt very alone.

It was during this time of year that his parents died nine years ago. Dr. Rueben often told Kai that it was okay to be sad, to grieve. During the month of November, Kai tried to allow himself to lean into this, to accept that sometimes he was a sad person who was grieving the loss of his parents. Eventually this feeling of sadness would ease and no longer feel so heavy. But for some reason, this November, Kai felt like the gloom was a cloak he couldn't shrug off. He couldn't understand why, and he thought really hard about it too. Then he realized it was because this was his last November being home with Aunt Brenda and Uncle Steve. Next year, if everything went to plan, he'd be at Morehouse, and when he'd start to feel sad, thinking about his parents, he wouldn't be able to sit with Aunt Brenda to be near her comforting presence. He wouldn't be able to go in the backyard and toss a football around with Uncle Steve. And, shit, he'd no longer have easy access to Dr. Rueben. Zyla might be in Europe. Kai would be alone. *All alone.* He'd been thinking about this the day before and had a panic attack while sitting in his backyard. He was still reeling from it.

"Kai, hello? Are you listening? I asked what your thoughts are on the homecoming budget."

Kai blinked. He'd been staring into space. For how long? He had no idea. Camille was currently waving her hand in his face, trying to get his attention. He looked around at the other student council members, who were waiting on his opinion regarding . . . what was it? The homecoming dance?

"Um, it's fine," he said.

"Is it?" Alanna asked from the other end of the table. "Because Camille wants to spend over a thousand dollars on a DJ, and just last week you said we needed to be better at conserving our cash."

Kai blinked again. Had he said that? It was hard to think through the fog. He was the vice president. He needed to get it together. "Oh, yeah. Right. Um, a thousand dollars for music? I don't know, Camille."

Camille looked at Kai and raised an eyebrow. He expected her to fight him on this. She was the student council treasurer, and how they spent money was technically her decision unless otherwise vetoed by himself or Alanna. At the beginning of the school year it seemed Camille picked fights with Kai simply to get under his skin, but lately she'd cooled down. They'd been almost civil, which was a relief. He hoped she didn't revert to her old ways today. He didn't think he could handle it.

"Okay, whatever," she said. "I'll find a cheaper DJ."

Kai sighed, relieved. The rest of the meeting went by in a blur. He'd have to check in with Adam, who served as secretary, to get the meeting minutes.

The first-period bell rang, and his fellow council members sprang up to dash into the hallway. Kai stood slowly. He felt sluggish. Sleepy. He needed a nap.

"Are you okay?" Camille asked. She was eyeing him with something that could have possibly been concern. "You look, I don't know, off or whatever."

"I'm just tired," Kai said, gathering his books.

He and Camille walked side by side to the door. Kai wondered what people might think if they spotted the two of them together. Then he realized he felt too blah to care.

"You should go to the nurse's office and lie down," Camille said. "That's what I do when I'm tired. She doesn't ask questions."

"Huh." Kai thought about how strained he'd feel trying to pay attention in first-period calculus. Maybe he'd go to the nurse for a bit, just for the beginning of class. "Okay."

Nurse Iverson didn't ask any questions, just like Camille said. Kai told her he had a headache and needed to lie down. Because he was seventeen, she'd need to contact his aunt or uncle if he wanted ibuprofen, but he could rest on a cot until he felt better. One of the four cots was occupied by a freshman with a bloody nose, but the other three cots were empty. Kai chose the cot closest to the wall and rolled over onto his side. He pulled out his phone and saw he had a text from Zyla. He managed to smile for the first time today.

Catholic school chic. She sent a picture of the weird loafers she wore with her school uniform.

Nice, Kai responded. He sent her a picture of his classic black Vans.

Her reply was immediate. **Where are you? Why are you lying down?**

Nurse's office.

Are you okay? What happened??

Kai's thumbs hovered over his keyboard. He wanted to tell Zyla how he was feeling. But he didn't want her to feel bad for him. He hated pity more than anything, and he didn't want it from Zyla of all people.

After they'd decided they were going to stay together no matter where they went to college, their connection got stronger once again. Sometimes when they kissed, they'd pause and just stare into each other's eyes, and it might sound corny or like some cheesy shit you saw in a movie, but when Kai looked at Zyla, he saw his present and future. When they held hands, their connection just vibed. It was difficult to describe. In a way, she was becoming an extension of him, and he wanted to think that she felt the same. A few weeks ago, they'd been watching television in his living room and she randomly turned to him and said, "Kai Johnson, you are my favorite person." It was the best thing anyone had ever said to him in his whole life. He adored her. He adored them. And he wouldn't mess it up with his sad shit.

Everything's cool. I just have a headache, he texted.

Oh no 😞 that sucks. feel better.

It bothered him that he wasn't being truthful. But his funk would pass soon, so there was really no need to bring it up. Or maybe he should? He took too long deciding. His phone vibrated with another text from Zyla.

Okay, about to take my English exam. I'll text you after.

Good luck <3

Thank u <3333

He stared at those four hearts for a while. The lightness in his chest lifted the cloak of gloom for a good ten minutes. But inevitably, it returned. Kai lay on his back and stared at the ceiling. He imagined himself doing this alone in his freshman dorm room at Morehouse. Did they decorate freshman dorms for the holidays? His mom had loved the holidays. She went above and beyond with her decorations every year. Their Christmas tree was decked with ornaments, and she had a thousand miniature Black Santas that she'd put throughout the house. On Thanksgiving she hung a cardboard cutout of a turkey on their front door, and her favorite dish to make was stuffing. To this day, Kai hadn't tasted anything better. He thought of his dad mumbling "I'm up, I'm up" when Kai would barge into their room on Christmas morning. He was an only child. He got hella toys every year. And then he thought of how the air smelled that day all those years ago when his coach called him off the field and his aunt Brenda was waiting for him, crying.

He squeezed his eyes closed. *It's okay to feel sad. It's okay to feel sad.*

The bell rang for second period. Kai's eyes popped open. Shit. He'd fallen asleep. He hadn't meant to stay in the nurse's office for the whole period! Now he'd have work to make up. He was an honor student, not someone who skipped class.

He checked his phone, and there was another text from Zyla, sent eight minutes ago.

I think I aced the test, idk. I guess we'll see. How are you feeling?

Kai felt drained. He couldn't even text her back. Zyla, his favorite person to talk to. He slid his phone into his pocket and rolled onto his side again. He hated that he couldn't get himself together, that he knew he wouldn't go to second period either.

He felt someone shake him awake. It was Nurse Iverson. She was frowning at him. She took his temperature. He didn't have a fever. She told him it was lunchtime. He'd slept right through second, third, and fourth period. Did he want to go home?

Kai had been having his stress dream again. The one where he ran through an empty house, knowing he'd been left behind.

The school day was only halfway through, and he had football practice later. He was captain, he had to be there. But he just couldn't do it.

"Yeah," he said, "I'd like to leave."

After a call to Aunt Brenda, Kai drove home. The house

was empty. He trudged upstairs and got right into bed. Aunt Brenda called to check in on him. He assured her that he was fine. He stared at the ceiling and tried not to let his gaze drift to the photograph of his parents on his dresser. The one of them when they were young, wearing their Spelman and Morehouse sweatshirts. Smiling, happy. With no idea what would eventually happen to them. To Kai.

He closed his eyes and rolled over.

A few hours later, Uncle Steve got home first. He usually did. When he found Kai lying on his bed, gazing at the ceiling, he paused in the doorway.

"You okay? Brenda told me you left school early because you had a headache."

"I don't have a headache. I just feel . . ." He trailed off and shrugged.

Uncle Steve came and sat down on the edge of Kai's bed. "I know this time of year is hard. We miss them too. Do you want to talk about it?"

"No." Even if Kai had wanted to talk, he didn't have the energy. "But thanks."

Uncle Steve sat quietly and watched Kai. Finally, he stood up. "I'm right down the hall if you change your mind."

Kai nodded and waited for his uncle to leave before he closed his eyes again. An hour or so later, he dragged himself out of bed to eat dinner because he'd missed lunch and was hungry, and more importantly, he didn't want Aunt Brenda and Uncle Steve to become more concerned. Throughout the meal, they didn't force him to talk, but as he tried to follow their conversation about one of Aunt Brenda's students, his inner battery drained.

At one point, he felt Aunt Brenda looking at him. When he glanced up, she asked how he was feeling and if he wanted to call Dr. Rueben. Kai shook his head. He just wanted to get back in bed. She said maybe he should speak with Dr. Rueben if he was feeling this way tomorrow. Kai nodded and agreed, if only to make her happy. He hoped he'd feel better tomorrow and that the call wouldn't be necessary.

He showered, which did offer some improvement, and got back in bed. He checked his phone. One missed text from Jamal.

Bro where were you today?? If the plan was to skip practice you shoulda let me know bc I woulda been right there with you. You good?

Kai would have laughed if he had the energy. He responded that he'd gone home early, that he'd felt off today. Jamal quickly texted back to say he was always there if Kai wanted to talk, and Kai thanked him.

And there were two missed calls from Zyla. Shit. He hadn't texted her back earlier. It was unlike him. He didn't want her to think something was wrong. In the past, around this time, when he told a girlfriend he was fine even though he acted otherwise, they believed him. He knew that wouldn't be the case with Zyla. She was much more perceptive.

She answered on the first ring when he called her back.

"Hey, I was worried about you," she said.

The sound of her voice washed over Kai. It was a salve. "Sorry, I've just been sleeping."

"Do you have a headache? Are you okay?"

"Yeah, yeah." He attempted to brighten his voice. He didn't know if it worked.

"You don't sound okay."

Guess not.

"It's cool," he said. "I'm cool. Tell me about your day."

She was quiet on the other end, and Kai prayed that she wouldn't push him on this. Finally, she said, "Well, Beatrice got us in trouble with Sister Michaela during morning mass because she accidentally started playing Saweetie's new song on her phone's speaker."

The deep hole in Kai's chest began to fill as he listened to Zyla. It didn't fill entirely, that wouldn't be possible. But she was pouring into him, and he accepted it gratefully.

He didn't know how much time had passed once Zyla finished talking, but he'd listened to the tale of her day with as much attention as he could muster. And he felt a little bit lighter, maybe light enough that he'd fall asleep without cycling through the memories of the worst day of his life, which had been a day in the middle of fall not unlike this one.

"Are you sure you're okay, Kai?" Zyla asked softly. "Do you want me to come over? I can walk there and sit with you on the porch."

"No, it's okay. You should be working on your portfolio." If

273

she saw him, she'd know right away that he was *not* okay. Then what would she think? And she really *should* be working on her portfolio. She would be sending out early-decision applications next month.

"I have time for that. I really don't mind."

"I'm good," he said. "I'll feel better after I get some sleep."

She paused. Then, "Okay. Text me when you wake up?"

"I will."

He wished Zyla good night and hung up, scolding himself for his inability to stay on the phone. He turned off his room light and got back into bed.

He hoped he'd be back to his old self by tomorrow.

Chapter Twenty-Two

Zyla's favorite moment of the day was when she woke up and saw a good-morning text from Kai. Even though St. Catherine's school day started before Cedar High's, Kai was usually awake before Zyla because he had club meetings or something else. He was constantly busy with one thing or another, and his attention was often being pulled in different directions. The fact that he woke up thinking of Zyla, and made sure to let her know, was the sweetest thing.

He was growing on her, or *through* her, like a vine, wrapping around her, hugging her closely. They had been together for almost three months. Sometimes she marveled that this boy, who had become her favorite person, had only lived a ten-minute walk away for the past three years. Why had it taken so long for them to connect? In only a few months' time, they'd both be going off in different directions, and that scared her. She tried to put on a brave face for Kai so that he wouldn't think she was freaking out. She learned her lesson after their first big fight. He assured her that she didn't need to feel insecure about their relationship, so whenever she had insecure thoughts, she tried her best to push them aside. She needed to get out of her own way.

Kai, and her intense feelings for him, sort of snuck up on her. She hadn't thought she'd be in this position. Sheesh, she never thought she'd even have a boyfriend. But she was beginning to understand the love songs and romance novels and romantic dramas, and if she kept this up, she might even begin to understand her mom and how she often lost herself in relationships. Zyla didn't want to lose herself, but she couldn't deny that when you cared about someone this intensely, they stayed at the forefront of your mind. And that scared her too.

So when Zyla woke up the next morning and didn't see a good-morning text from Kai, her stomach twisted. He'd sounded so off the night before. He'd claimed to have a headache, and because Aunt Ida got bad migraines, Zyla knew headaches could be brutal. But Kai didn't just sound like someone who was exhausted from battling a headache. He sounded *sad*. Zyla could tell the difference. Kai was a glass-half-full kind of person, and she appreciated that, since she could be so cynical. Something was wrong, but she didn't want to push him, because he clearly didn't want to talk about it. But shouldn't she try a little harder? She was his girlfriend, after all. Wasn't that her job? She was constantly learning things on the fly.

She decided to text him first. **Good morning <3 how are you feeling?**

She got out of bed and showered. She woke Jade and then woke her mom, who was notorious for oversleeping. She got dressed in her school uniform—a white button-up and navy-blue skirt—and took Bartholomew out for a walk around the block. She came back just as Beatrice was pulling up in front of her house. She ran inside, grabbed her backpack, and shouted goodbye to her family. In the time that passed, Kai hadn't responded to her text.

"I think something's wrong with Kai," she said to Beatrice.

"What do you mean?" Beatrice pushed her sunglasses up on top of her head and checked her rearview mirror as she backed out of Zyla's driveway. "Is he sick?"

"I don't know." Zyla stared at her message. Kai didn't have his read receipts on, so she didn't know if he'd seen her text. "Maybe he's sleeping."

"Could be," Beatrice said.

They sat through morning mass, and Zyla was very conscious to keep her phone out of sight, because the sisters eyed the students like hawks. But her phone buzzed in her cardigan pocket.

"Cover me," she whispered to Beatrice. Quickly, Beatrice leaned forward and placed her elbow on the pew in front of them so that Sister Michaela wouldn't see Zyla texting.

Hey, sorry for the late reply. I stayed home today. Still not feeling great.

Earlier this year, Kai had gone to school even though he figured he might have had bronchitis, because he didn't want to miss some honor society event that wasn't even mandatory. Zyla had been right to think that something was wrong.

She responded, **Is the headache bad?**

Nah, not a headache. I'm just feeling blah. Idk.

Zyla stared at her phone, trying to think of how to respond. He felt blah? What did that mean? Then, as if he could read her mind, which he probably could do by now, he sent a follow-up text.

Don't worry.

Don't worry? Fat chance she wouldn't do that. Telling her not to worry only made her worry more.

Do you need anything? I can come by after school.

She had to work after school, but she'd squeeze in time to see him first. She watched the text bubbles pop up as he began to reply, and then they disappeared. She stared at her phone, anxiously waiting for his response that didn't come.

Had she pushed him too hard by asking if he wanted to talk? Had that been the right thing to do?

She worried for the rest of mass and throughout the morning. Instead of going to the cafeteria during lunch, she went to the bathroom, closed herself in a stall, and googled "what to do when someone says they're feeling blah." All the hits pointed to depression.

Was Kai depressed? Was that what this meant? She looked at the symptoms: fatigue, insomnia, or sleeping too much. Even headaches were a symptom, but now she wasn't sure if he'd ever had a headache. She wondered if he'd only said that so she wouldn't be concerned. But *why* was he feeling this way? Had something happened that he didn't want to tell her about?

She googled "what to say to someone when they're

depressed." Some of the suggestions: *I'm here for you. Take as long as you need. Everything is going to be okay.*

She reopened their text thread and typed out, I'm here if you want to talk. Anything you need, I've got you.

And it was true. She did have his back, and she would have it through anything. She tried not to feel afraid for him. He had a therapist. She didn't pry too much into the nature of their relationship, but she knew that Kai had been seeing his therapist since he was a kid and he liked him. He had access to professional help, and that was a good thing. She should probably give him space.

Her worry didn't abate by the time the school day ended, and Kai hadn't responded to her. She just wanted to know that he was okay. She paced outside of St. Catherine's as she waited for Beatrice. What could she do? Was there someone she could ask for more information? She didn't have his aunt's and uncle's numbers. Who else could she talk to in Kai's circle?

Jamal sounded like he was running when he answered the phone. "What's up, Matthews?"

"Hey, are you busy?"

"A little. Running late to practice. What's up?"

Zyla took a deep breath. "Um, have you talked to Kai today? I know he wasn't in school. He seems kind of off, and . . . I don't know, I guess I'm concerned."

Jamal's heavy breathing slowed down. It sounded like he'd stopped running. "Ah, yeah. He gets that way this time of year. Because of his parents."

"What do you mean?"

"They died in November, a few weeks before Thanksgiving. The holidays are kind of hard for him."

Zyla could have smacked herself in the forehead then. She *knew* Kai's parents had died in November, and here she was absolutely clueless about Kai's behavior. She was a terrible girlfriend.

"I usually check in with him and let him know I'm here to talk if he needs it," Jamal continued. "He usually comes around in a few days."

"Okay," Zyla said weakly.

"He's probably talking to his therapist right now," Jamal said. "Don't stress, Matthews. He'll be good."

"Okay," Zyla repeated.

Then Jamal hung up because he had to get to practice.

Jamal knew things about Kai that Zyla would probably never know. That was the nature of friendships versus romantic relationships. But she couldn't take Jamal's advice not to stress.

Beatrice dropped her off at the hair salon, and Zyla sat behind the front desk, so preoccupied with Kai that she accidentally hung up on two clients when she'd meant to put them on hold. When one client threw a fit because Zyla accidentally overcharged her credit card, the salon owner, Ms. Patricia, came to the front desk and gave Zyla a look.

"Everything okay today, Miss Zyla?" she asked.

Zyla nodded profusely. "Yes, sorry. I'm just, um, thinking about school and stuff."

"Okay, well, I need you to focus on that phone a little better for the next two hours. All right?"

"Yes, ma'am."

As Ms. Patricia walked off toward the back room, Zyla caught eyes with her mom, whose station was across the salon. She tilted her head and raised an eyebrow. Ms. Patricia had hired Zyla as a favor to her mom to help with college expenses. It didn't look good for either of them that Zyla was screwing up her basic front desk duties.

She needed this job. But she also needed to see that Kai was okay. She stood and went to her mom's station.

"Mom, I don't feel good," she said.

"What's wrong?" Her mom paused in the middle of curling her client's hair and set down the curling iron. She reached out to touch Zyla's forehead, and Zyla backed away.

"My stomach hurts." She wrapped her arms around her midriff for emphasis. "I think I need to go home. Can you tell Ms. Patricia I had to leave early?"

Zyla's mom squinted, suspicious. "Why don't you run over to Walgreens and get some ginger ale? That should do the trick."

"I don't think it will help. I think I need to lie down."

Her mom opened her mouth, then glanced down at her client, who was staring at both of them, all in their business. Finally, she asked, "How will you get home?"

"I'll take the bus."

"All right," she said evenly. She picked up the curling iron again. "I'll call you in a little to see how you're doing."

From her tone, Zyla knew her mom didn't believe her. But she would have to deal with that later. She caught the bus to their neighborhood, and as she walked toward Kai's house, she told herself she was just going to make sure he was okay. He didn't have to talk to her if he didn't want to. She only wanted to get a glimpse of him, and then she'd go home.

Ms. Brenda answered the door when Zyla rang the bell. She looked surprised to see her.

"Oh, Zyla. Hi, sweetheart." She glanced behind her. "Let me see how Kai is feeling . . ."

But then Kai appeared at his aunt's side, pulling the door wider. Zyla was seized with nerves. There were bags under his eyes, and his shoulders sagged. But when he looked at her, he smiled a little. It was more like a small smirk, just a quirk in the corner of his mouth. But for the first time today, Zyla felt a bit of hope.

"Hey," he said.

"Hey," she said.

Kai wasn't surprised to see Zyla at his door, given the way he'd ghosted her all day. She'd probably been worried sick, and he felt shitty for it. But he didn't want to freak her out any further, so he just didn't respond to any of her messages or calls, which he now realized was the opposite of making the situation better.

An hour ago, Jamal texted, **Zy just called me asking about you. Maybe talk to her?** And Kai had been gearing up to call her back. He was just trying to figure out what to say, and then the doorbell rang and he heard Zyla's voice.

Now, she stared at him, wide-eyed, biting her lip. It was how she looked when she was scared or nervous. Maybe both. *Shit*. He'd done that.

"I just wanted to see that you were okay," she said. "I can go home now."

"No, wait." He reached out and gently grabbed her arm, stilling her. He opened the door wider. "I want you to stay. Come in."

She followed him into the living room, and Aunt Brenda quickly gathered her papers and went upstairs, giving them privacy. This morning, once she realized Kai didn't wake up feeling much better, she chose to stay home and teach her classes virtually. She was the one who suggested an emergency session with Dr. Rueben. Kai spoke with him about an hour ago, and he felt less heavy now, but he wasn't at a hundred percent.

Once he and Zyla were alone, he sat down on the couch and she sat beside him. He took a deep breath. What could he say?

"I'm sorry I went MIA on you."

"You don't have to apologize." Zyla looked down at her hands, which were clasped together in her lap. When she returned her gaze to his face, her eyes were watering. "I should have known you were feeling upset about your parents. I'm so sorry. I hope you know that you can always talk to me about how you're feeling, but I understand if you don't want to."

"I know that," Kai said.

They fell quiet. After a few moments, Zyla scooted closer and reached out her hand, weaving her fingers through Kai's. They continued to sit in silence. He realized Zyla was giving him the space to talk if he wanted to, or not. He'd never shared this vulnerable side of himself with a girlfriend before. The thought of doing so scared him. But she was here and ready to listen. He could try to meet her halfway.

"My parents died out of nowhere," he said. "I learned at a young age that the people you care about can leave at any time, whether by choice or some other reason. This time of year is hard for me, but it's been rough these past few days, and it's because next year and every year after that, I'm going to be far away from the people I care about."

Zyla gripped his hand tighter and continued to listen quietly. He could tell she was trying to hold back from speaking, that she wanted him to keep talking.

"Every time one of my relationships doesn't work out, I feel left behind, just like when my parents died," he admitted. "It's not that bad, of course. Nowhere near. But I hate that feeling." He looked down at their hands and rubbed his thumb over her knuckles. "Sometimes I worry about what would happen if we broke up. You're so smart and independent and you don't need anything from me, which is a good thing, and I admire you so much, but then I feel insecure because if for some reason we ended things, you could leave me and be perfectly fine, but I would feel really fucking gutted."

"What? Kai, no." Zyla threw her arms around him. "We're not going to break up. We have no reason to."

She was holding him so tightly, he couldn't easily pull away to look at her face. But she was sniffling and the skin on his neck was growing damp, so he knew she was crying.

"I'm not going anywhere, I promise," she said fiercely. She sat back and firmly placed both of her hands on his shoulders. "It doesn't matter if I'm in New York or Paris or freaking Antarctica. I'm in this with you."

Hearing her say this was a huge relief. The entire weight didn't lift from his chest, but she'd eased a large piece of it.

"Okay?" she said.

He nodded. "Okay."

She reached for both of his hands this time and grasped them in her own. It grounded him.

"I'm in this with you too," he said.

She leaned forward and kissed him softly. "Okay."

He didn't know how long they sat facing each other and holding hands. But it helped. That's what he knew.

He walked her home some time later, and her hand didn't leave his. When they reached her front porch, he kissed her once, twice.

"Thank you for coming over," he said.

"You don't have to thank me, Kai. I'll always be here for you. But please promise me that if you're feeling down like that again, you'll let me know. If you need space, that's okay. All I'm asking is that you don't leave me in the dark."

"I promise," he said. "No more headache lies."

"Thank you."

She kissed him again and rocked back onto her heels. She seemed reluctant to leave him.

"I'll be okay," he said. "I'll call you when I get home."

She nodded and walked inside, waving before she closed the door behind her.

She'd seen the side of him that he hadn't wanted to show anyone, and she hadn't shied away. If anything, she'd held on to him tighter.

He was so damn grateful.

Once he got home, he called her like he said he would.

Chapter Twenty-Three

Was there a more quintessential high school experience than going to a homecoming dance? Zyla didn't think so.

"Zy, you are gonna be the baddest girl at this dance," Beatrice said. She was lying across Zyla's bed, smiling. "You won. Everybody else can go home."

Zyla stared at herself in the mirror. Tonight, she was Kai's date to Cedar High's homecoming. It was going to be her first school dance ever. She'd almost made it her entire K–12 career without going to a dance. Was that sad? Maybe to some people. Zyla didn't care that much. But her boyfriend was a big man on campus, and going to school dances came with the gig.

"She won? What's that mean?" Zyla's mom asked, sitting at the foot of Zyla's bed. "Zy, can you win homecoming queen at a school you don't go to?"

Zyla and Beatrice both laughed. "No, Mom," Zyla said. "It's a saying."

Beatrice elaborated, "Basically, Zy is going to look better than everyone else, so they might as well not bother showing up."

"Ah." Zyla's mom nodded. "Well, Zy, you do look absolutely beautiful, babe."

"Thanks, Mom."

Zyla and her mom were being exceedingly polite to each other lately. After she left work early to see Kai a couple weeks ago, she and her mom got into a big argument. Her mom thought she was being irresponsible for choosing a boyfriend over her job. Zyla tried to explain that wasn't exactly the case. It's not like she ditched work so that she and Kai could go to the movies. But she wanted to respect Kai's privacy, so she hadn't told her mom the truth about why she'd gone to see him. After their argument, they'd given each other the silent treatment for days until it bothered Jade so much, she burst into tears during dinner a few nights ago. So now they were choosing to be polite, but her mom's comment about ignoring her responsibilities nagged at Zyla. She glanced at the discarded fabric draped over her mannequin, pieces for her portfolio that she hadn't created because she'd spent almost the entirety of Thanksgiving and Black Friday perfecting her homecoming dress, which was a deep emerald green made of silk. The thin straps were braided, and the bodice was low cut. A slit went up her left leg. It was a simple style, yet regal and modern. She was going to include it in her portfolio even if it didn't end up going with her theme. She had to justify all of the time she'd spent on it somehow, if only to prove that her mom wasn't right. Her relationship wasn't causing her to be irresponsible.

Beatrice stood up and surveyed her handiwork on Zyla's hair and makeup. She'd helped Zyla take out her box braids, slicked her hair back, and added a jumbo braid that went down her back. Zyla wore a nude matte lipstick and layered it with her shimmery lip gloss. She found a pair of gold platform heels at Genie's that matched perfectly with her thick gold hoops.

Beatrice was right. She did look good. She couldn't wait for Kai to see her.

"Babe, your dad's FaceTiming me," Zyla's mom said, holding up her phone. "He wants to see you dressed up. I told him you were going to your first dance tonight."

"*Mom,*" Zyla groaned. "Why?"

"Because he is your father, and he has resorted to contacting me for updates on your life since you barely answer any of his calls."

Zyla sighed. It wasn't that she was purposely avoiding her dad. It's just she'd been really busy with school and hanging out with Beatrice, and then of course she was spending so much time with Kai.

Actually, that was a lie. She *was* avoiding her dad. Recently, she realized she was old enough to know she didn't need to have her dad in her life, so she didn't see the point in trying to foster a relationship with him. But if she told her mom the truth, it would only upset her.

Zyla glanced at Beatrice, and Beatrice shrugged. Beatrice often went through phases when she didn't feel like talking to her own dad. Her face said, *Girl, do whatever you want*. Then Zyla looked at her mom, who was patiently waiting for her daughter to open up a space in her life for her dad.

"Okay, fine." Zyla took the phone from her mom and swiped

to answer. Her dad's face appeared on the screen. Her dad had dark brown skin and a low-cut afro. He was handsome, which was something he often used to his benefit.

"Zy Zy, baby, you look so beautiful!" he said, grinning, showing off the small gap between his two front teeth. The same gap that she had.

"Thanks, Dad."

"Let me see your dress," he said. Zyla flipped the camera so that he could see the entire look in her full-body mirror. "Wow, Zy Zy. You really outdid yourself this time. Damn gorgeous! Now who's this knucklehead that's taking you to the dance?"

"Dad. I'm going with Kai. I told you about him already, remember? He's my boyfriend."

"Right, right. Your mom says he's nice. But I'll decide if he's good enough for my baby girl once I meet him."

Zyla tried not to roll her eyes. She hadn't seen her dad in over a year. He was living in Denver and chances were very slim that he'd make his way to New Jersey to meet Kai.

The doorbell rang downstairs, and Zyla was quite literally saved by the bell. She heard Jade open the door and greet Kai.

"Dad, I have to go. Kai's here." She handed the phone back to her mom and rushed out of her room.

Beatrice followed behind and yanked Zyla's arm. "Girl, what are you doing?" she said. "You have to make an entrance. Go down the stairs slowly like those girls in the movies. Let Kai get the full effect."

"Oh, right. Okay."

Beatrice touched up Zyla's hair and then walked downstairs. Zyla tried to shake off her nerves as she heard Beatrice talking to Kai. She pulled her shoulders back and held her chin high. Slowly, like Beatrice said, she began walking down the stairs.

Kai stood in the hallway. He wore a black tux and a vest and bow tie that matched her emerald-green dress. She should have been used to Kai's beauty by now. But sometimes, it still surprised her. Like right now. She sucked in a breath at the sight of him, even though she was the one who was supposed to be making an entrance.

Kai turned and looked up at her. His mouth fell open, almost comically. Beatrice and Jade both giggled. He blinked at Zyla, trailing her with his eyes as she descended the steps. Then she was standing right in front of him.

"Hi, Kai Johnson," she said.

He smiled wide, showing his teeth. "Wow, Zyla. You look amazing. I mean . . . wow. You look beautiful."

"Thank you," she said, feeling giddy at his praise. "You look beautiful too."

His smile softened, and he stared at her. This was the first time they'd seen each other in over a week. There were midterms and then Thanksgiving and then Kai had been busy with basketball tryouts. She'd missed him. She stepped closer to give him a kiss.

"Aht, aht. None of that in my house," Aunt Ida said, wagging her finger. Zyla hadn't even noticed that Aunt Ida had emerged from the living room. "Now, you have her back here at a decent time, young man."

"Yes, ma'am," Kai said. He looked at Zyla. "Ready?"

Zyla nodded but paused when her mom came rushing down the steps.

"Wait! You can't leave without taking pictures!" she shouted.

They obediently posed for Zyla's mom, and Beatrice crouched down, taking pictures too. When her mom was finally satisfied, they were able to leave. Jamal and Alanna were waiting in the back seat of Kai's Jeep. Jamal rolled down the window when he spotted Beatrice walking to her car.

"What's the problem, your highness?" he called. "Too good to come to Cedar High's homecoming?"

Beatrice narrowed her eyes, most likely ready to fling back an insult. But she paused when she spotted Alanna beside Jamal. She frowned, then quickly covered it up. "Have fun, Zy. Kai, I'm trusting you to show her a good time."

Kai opened Zyla's door for her and smiled down into her face. "I will," he said.

Kai was a really good dancer. Zyla added this new knowledge to the list of things she loved about him, along with his sense of humor, his face, his kissing skills, and his patient and kind personality, among other things.

The DJ was lit, and the gymnasium made for a great makeshift dance floor. Somehow, they'd hooked up a disco ball to the ceiling. "EARFQUAKE" by Tyler, the Creator, played through the speakers. Kai had ditched his blazer and Zyla was barefoot. They danced together, sweaty and exhilarated.

Kai smoothly shimmied his shoulders toward her and moved his hips. She was glad to see him so carefree and happy after the rough couple weeks he'd had at the beginning of November. He'd gradually been opening up to her more about his parents. He told her his favorite memories about them. He was more honest with her when he was feeling sad. Zyla realized that Kai was a precious person, and he'd chosen to give her his heart. She'd have to guard it with everything she had.

The song changed, and they went back to their table to get water. Alanna and Whit were talking and laughing. Jamal sat beside them with his chin propped in his hand, looking bored. The most animated Zyla ever saw Jamal was when he was arguing with Beatrice. She'd bet Jamal would be having a good time if Beatrice were here. It kind of sucked that they disliked each other so much. In another universe they might make a good couple.

"Are you having fun?" Kai asked, leaning closer to her.

She smiled and nodded. "Are you?"

"Of course. I'm with you, ain't I?"

The esophagus butterflies swarmed, happily flapping their wings. Kai threw his arm around Zyla and kissed her forehead. She leaned into him and then had the weird sensation that she was being watched. She turned her head and spotted Camille a few tables over with Darius and another boy she didn't recognize. She figured he must have been Camille's date, because he wore a gold tie to match her halter-top gown. She wore long, dangly earrings, and her curly hair fell loosely around her shoulders. She was frowning at Zyla and Kai, but she quickly looked away once she and Zyla caught eyes.

Zyla compared herself to Camille, and any of Kai's exes, less than she used to. Because she was the one who was with Kai now, and that was what mattered. But she didn't like that Camille had been watching them.

"I'll be right back," she said to Kai, nodding her head toward the bathroom.

He squeezed her hand. "Okay."

After taking a minute to cool off and check her makeup in the bathroom mirror, Zyla walked out in the hallway and bumped right into Camille.

"Oh," she said, stumbling backward. "Sorry."

"It's no problem." Camille said. Her eyes quickly swept Zyla from head to toe. "You look pretty."

"Thanks," Zyla said. "So do you."

Camille shrugged. "Yeah, I look good in gold. My sister wanted me to wear this ridiculous silver dress, which was hideous, but that's because she's a hater."

"Oh." What the heck was she supposed to say to that? She began to sidestep Camille.

"Have you met my boyfriend, Rob?" Camille asked, pointing over her shoulder to the boy at her table with the matching gold tie. "He's cute, right?"

It felt like a trick question. Either way, Zyla was smarter than that. "You guys look nice together."

"Thanks." Camille smiled, slightly tigerlike. "It's funny, because I always thought I'd go to senior-year homecoming with Kai and we'd be crowned king and queen. I guess you never know how things will turn out."

Zyla paused and leveled her eyes at Camille. "I guess not, seeing as though I'm here with Kai, and we've been together for months."

"Of course," Camille said quickly. "Kai and I are just fellow classmates now. I see him every day on student council. Sometimes I feel like I see him too much." She laughed, but Zyla knew it was fake, that Camille was really trying to get under her skin. She wasn't going to put up with any of her games, not today.

"Have a good night, Camille," she said.

Camille blinked, slightly taken aback by Zyla's curtness. But Zyla didn't care. She walked off, her sights set on Kai, who was standing by their table talking with Jamal. Her annoyance at her conversation with Camille eased away once she was next to him again.

"You okay?" he asked, hugging her to his side.

She nodded, absorbing his warmth. "I'm okay."

The DJ stopped the music, and one of Kai's teachers took the mic and announced that it was time to crown the homecoming king and queen. Right, that was a thing that happened at homecoming dances. There were voting cards on a table at the door when they first walked into the gym. Alanna and Jamal had both cast their votes, but Kai had walked right by the table, so Zyla had too. Now, everyone stood and gathered on the dance floor. Jamal and Kai's other friends crowded around him.

"You ready to be king?" Jamal asked, clapping Kai on the shoulder.

Kai smirked and shrugged him off. "You know I don't care about that."

Oh, right. Duh. Kai was probably going to win homecoming king. But then who would be homecoming queen?

Anyone but Camille.

Zyla hated that this was her first thought. It didn't matter who was crowned queen. *She* was Kai's girlfriend at the end of the day.

His teacher Mrs. Deaver walked to the center of the dance floor. She held a crown for the king and a tiara for the queen. She urged the students to quiet down, and a hush fell over the crowd.

"This year's homecoming king is . . . Kai Johnson!"

Everyone cheered, and Zyla cheered too. She's been expecting as much, but to see Kai crowned homecoming king was pretty exciting. His friends were jumping up and down, shaking his shoulders.

"That's my boy!" Jamal said, grinning and pointing.

Kai smiled bashfully and squeezed Zyla's hand before making his way to Mrs. Deaver. The crowd cheered as Mrs. Deaver placed the crown on Kai's head. Kai thanked her and smirked at his classmates. He looked a little embarrassed to have so much attention on him, but Zyla was probably the only one who could tell.

Mrs. Deaver quieted the crowd again, and Zyla tried not to feel anxious knowing the homecoming queen would be announced next.

"And this year's homecoming queen is . . . Alanna Thomas!"

"Yasssss," Whit cheered, ushering Alanna forward. And Zyla clapped too, because Alanna was the nicest person she'd ever met and if anyone should be crowned a queen, it was Alanna, for sure.

And Zyla felt relieved that Alanna was queen and not Camille. She wondered if that made her evil. If her inner insecurity dragon had been ready to rear its ugly head.

The DJ cued up "At My Worst" by Pink Sweat$ and Kehlani, and Mrs. Deaver left the dance floor so that Kai and Alanna could slow dance together. Kai and Alanna laughed as Kai placed his hands on her waist and Alanna hooked her arms around his neck. They smiled at each other politely and swayed side to side.

Zyla felt herself moving farther away to the outskirts of the crowd. Her stomach was doing something strange, watching Kai dance with Alanna.

He was homecoming king! It was perfectly normal for him to be dancing with Alanna, the homecoming queen. So why did Zyla feel so irrational? Alanna and Kai were friends. Zyla knew that. She'd spent enough time around both of them to know they'd never been into each other that way. Plus, Alanna was kind of dating Jamal. These were facts. So then why did Zyla feel weird watching them dance together? To see him share this moment with someone else. Maybe she felt off-kilter from her stupid conversation with Camille.

Stop it, it's fine. Don't be stupid. It's just a dance. It doesn't mean anything. You couldn't be queen! You don't go to Cedar High! God, why is this song so long?

She shook off her annoyingly intrusive thoughts.

When the second verse started, Kai dropped his hands from Alanna's waist, mumbled something to her, took a step back, and bowed. Alanna smiled at him. Confused whispers spread through the crowd. What were they doing?

Smoothly, Jamal materialized in the center of the dance floor. He stepped toward Alanna and held out his hand, which she accepted. She grinned as he pulled her into his arms and resumed the dance.

Zyla was lost. Was this normal? Did stuff like this usually happen at homecoming dances?

She watched as Kai turned in a circle, scanning the crowd. And then she realized he was looking for *her*. He spotted her in the back, and her breath hitched as he approached her. The crowd split for him like the Red Sea.

He was grinning from ear to ear when he reached her. She felt everyone staring at them, but he didn't seem to care at all.

"What are you doing?" Zyla whispered breathlessly. "You can't just stop your dance. You're homecoming king."

Kai continued to smile. "This homecoming king would like to dance with his girl." He gently took Zyla's hand, brought it to his lips, and kissed her knuckles. "Will you dance with me?"

She stared into his brown eyes, absolutely shocked. "Yes," she whispered.

The esophagus butterflies were throwing a rave as she let Kai lead her out to the dance floor. He pulled her against his chest, and they swayed in time to the music. She looped her arms around his neck.

He leaned down to kiss her, and when their lips met, Zyla had the terrifying realization that she was falling head-over-heels in love with Kai Johnson, and there wasn't a thing she could do about it.

Before Ida discovers that her grandniece Zyla has gone missing, she is sleeping soundly in her beloved La-Z-Boy. She is dreaming of her late husband, Herald, as she often does, fifteen years after his death. It is the same dream every time. She is yelling at Herald, distraught and angry. *Where were you? Who is she? Why do you lie to me?* And Herald stands in front of her, palms upturned, then palms together in prayer, asking for forgiveness. Even in her dreams, Ida knows she will forgive him.

Ida is not like her niece, Leanne. She has been in love once and only once. She was sixteen when she met Herald in the church's youth group. He was tall and slim, with a rich baritone. He loved the Lord, and Ida loved watching him express that love through song. Every Sunday, she sat in the pews, eyes locked on Herald in the middle of the choir. She'd naively pray for Herald to love her the way that she loved him. It took a while, two years, actually, until God heard her prayers. On her eighteenth birthday, Herald came to the party her mother threw in the church's backyard. After her years of pining, Herald finally paid Ida some attention. Soon, she was his girlfriend. A year later, when they graduated high school, Herald proposed. Ida thanked God. Could she be any more blessed in this life?

Herald's love for the Lord did not translate to keeping to the commandment thou shalt not commit adultery. During their marriage, he became a professional groveler, an eloquent apologist. So often he broke their vows that Ida's intuition flared up in the middle of the most mundane tasks, like cooking dinner or gardening. She'd be knee-deep in soil, and she'd get a tingling sensation. *Herald is out messing around.* Her intuition didn't let her down. Except when it failed to warn her that marrying someone so charming and handsome could lead to no good.

She is still dreaming. Herald is on his knees, reaching for her, begging. Then his face changes. He is no longer Herald. He is Kai. And Ida has become a spectator in her own dream, now watching as Zyla looks down at her ex-boyfriend. Zyla frowns, indecisive. *Leave him alone,* Ida shouts. *Don't forgive him.* But Zyla can't hear her.

When Ida wakes, her throat feels strained from yelling. She is disoriented to find herself in her La-Z-Boy, to discover that she isn't a twenty-year-old housewife but a seventy-three-year-old matriarch. She and Herald didn't have kids of their own. Maybe she was barren, maybe he was sterile. After a while she didn't care to learn the real reason, because she didn't want his children. He'd only lie to them too. Leanne is Herald's niece. Her mother died when she was young from a disease misdiagnosed by a doctor who, like many, did not listen to the pleas of a Black woman about her health, so Ida became Leanne's mother. She gave Leanne the "men are good for nothing" speech many times during her teenage years. Not that it mattered. Leanne met Terrance, and Ida's advice subsequently went out the window.

At least Zyla listens. Except in Ida's dream just now. You see, Ida knows that dreams have meanings, symbolism to our real lives. Ida had been suspicious of Kai in the beginning, as she would have been of anyone interested in her grandniece. She remembered when she first met him last summer. He'd stood in the living room, handsome, charming, charismatic. He called her "ma'am" and didn't break Zyla's curfew. Not once did she hear a negative sentiment come out of his mouth. He was so unlike Terrance, who was arrogant and had to be prompted to shake Herald's hand the first time Leanne brought him home. Ida could tell that Terrance was more in love with the idea of Leanne than Leanne herself. But that didn't seem to be the case with Kai.

He was attentive to Zyla in a way that Herald hadn't been with Ida, nor Terrance with Leanne. And she saw the clear love in his eyes when he came to pick Zyla up for that school dance back in November. She didn't let on, but Kai had started to grow on her too. She wondered if maybe he wasn't a wolf in sheep's clothing after all. Then he went and broke Zyla's heart.

"Auntie!"

Ida jumps in her chair as Leanne blows into the house, shrieking. Of course, Bartholomew starts barking, causing absolute chaos.

"What's the matter, child?" Ida asks, softly bopping Bartholomew on the head to quiet him. "I can't hear you when you're yelling like this."

Leanne kicks off her heels at the front door and slides on her sneakers. She is crying, which concerns Ida, but Leanne is prone to cry at anything, so Ida will need more information before she becomes alarmed.

"Zyla and Kai ran away while on that school trip and nobody can find them and Zyla isn't answering her phone! I have to go up to the resort now. Terrance is gonna ride up with me. Where's Jade? Please keep an eye on her."

Ida grips the arms of her chair and struggles to stand. Her arthritis has been acting up today because of the rain, but to hell with that.

"I'm coming with you," she says. "Jade! Get down here and put your shoes on!"

"Auntie, no," Leanne says. "You don't—"

Ida holds up her hand. "I'm coming with you and that's that."

Bemused, Jade comes downstairs and puts on her sneakers, asking questions as she follows Leanne and Ida outside to Leanne's car. Leanne informs Jade that her big sister is in big trouble, that she's done something dangerous and silly while on her trip and they are going to get her.

Terrance, newly single and newly local, pulls up in seconds. He rushes to Leanne's car with his lanky limbs and holds Leanne as she frantically tells him what's happened.

"I knew it," Terrance says. "I knew they'd get into some kind of trouble again."

On the drive, Ida sits in the back seat with Jade, rubbing her wrists, which have become irritated. Now her dream makes sense. A wolf is a wolf is a wolf. They show their true colors eventually. Kai is a wolf, just like Terrance. Just like Herald.

As Leanne speeds down the highway, Ida wonders if maybe the women in her family are simply cursed to fall in love with the wrong people.

Chapter Twenty-Four

Zyla had no idea what to get Kai for Christmas, and it was only a week away. Somehow, time was moving so quickly, when last summer it seemed to move in slow motion. Before, Zyla would have welcomed the quicker pace because it would put her one step closer to graduation, but now she wished everything would slow down for her and Kai to have more time together.

She and Jade were at the mall, which was overcrowded with last-minute shoppers. Jade was simple. She went to Claire's and bought everyone a pair of earrings with the money she'd saved up doing Saturday chores. Now, Zyla and Jade sat in the food court, eating pizza. Zyla smiled at her little sister as she let gooey cheese slide down her chin.

"You're making a mess, you know," Zyla said.

Jade grinned and shrugged. "Is Kai going to meet us?"

Zyla laughed. Jade was a little infatuated with Kai. "No, he can't, because if he did, he'd see what I was getting him for Christmas."

"Oh, right," Jade said, nodding. "Do you know what you're gonna get?"

"No," Zyla sighed. "I have no idea."

When she'd asked what Kai wanted, he'd said, "You." And he'd been dead serious. It was sweet, of course, but unhelpful. Now, Christmas was right around the corner, and she was stuck on a gift. Growing up, she'd mostly received necessities for Christmas. Socks and underwear. Maybe a doll or two if she was lucky. She and Beatrice usually went to the diner on Christmas Eve and splurged on desserts, and that was their gift to each other. She made items of clothing for her mom, Jade, and Aunt Ida every year. Simple things like scarves and a matching hat-and-mitten set. She thought about making something for Kai, because when she gave it to him, she could say in a cheesy way, "Merry Christmas. This was stitched with love."

Love. She was pretty sure she loved Kai.

It was freaking scary to think about. She'd promised herself that she'd never fall in love with anyone. But Kai had made it too easy. She should have seen it coming on the first day they'd met, when he'd easily wrapped her in his charismatic web.

If she admitted to Kai that she loved him, that meant he had the power to hurt her, to break her heart. She liked to think he wouldn't do either of those things, that he cared about her too much. But then again, wasn't it better to be prepared for that possibility so that it didn't hit her out of nowhere? She didn't want to give that power to anyone. Yet every time she saw Kai, she became overwhelmed with the desire to blurt out her feelings and to hear him say he loved her too. And she was trying not to be anxious over the fact that he was stopping by on Christmas day to spend some time with her and her family.

She hoped Aunt Ida could keep the stink-eyeing to a minimum in the name of Jesus's birthday. She also hoped that her mom wouldn't be moping over another partner who'd failed to show up on one of the most important holidays of the year.

She'd been so caught up lately in Kai, she'd almost missed Parsons Paris's early-decision deadline a few weeks ago. She'd mixed up the dates in her head, and on the day it was due—December 1—she got a reminder alert on her phone while she and Kai were at the movies. They'd had to leave in the middle of the film, and Zyla pulled an all-nighter to finish her portfolio. She couldn't understand how she'd confused the dates even when she'd correctly noted them in her phone. It was so unlike her.

In the end, the focus of her portfolio was how Black women were original trendsetters, and that high fashion often stole from Black culture for their own profit. She had her mom, Beatrice, and Jade model her outfits for her photographs. She'd sent in her application with minutes to spare. Just to be safe, she'd stayed awake to submit her applications for FIT in New York, FIDM in LA, and the London College of Fashion, which weren't due until December 15.

She didn't think that her and Kai's relationship was a distraction. Just her feelings for him. And maybe Kai felt the same way, because last week, the night before he took the SATs, he'd stayed too late at Zyla's, sitting with her in his car. He hadn't wanted to leave, even when Zyla mentioned he had to get up early. He insisted he'd be fine, and then the next morning, he woke up late and they almost didn't let him take the test. Luckily one of his coaches stepped in to help. His aunt and uncle had not been happy about it. Zyla had felt crappy, of course. It was partially her fault because he'd been out with her.

Afterward, she'd made sure Kai knew his college application dates too, and she was more conscious of how late they stayed up talking. They weren't distracting each other. They were helpful, supportive.

Her phone buzzed in her pocket then, breaking her train of thought. She pulled it out and sighed once she saw who was calling. Her dad. It was too close to Christmas. She couldn't ignore him. She handed the phone to Jade.

"Here," she said. "It's Daddy."

Jade eagerly took the phone and answered. Jade and their dad had a good relationship. She didn't have any memories of their mom crying every night over their dad coming home late. Zyla didn't want to ruin the bond they shared. She made sure not to bad-mouth him to Jade. She saved that for her inner dialogue.

"Really, Daddy?" Jade suddenly said. Her eyes popped open in delight.

Zyla immediately became skeptical. She looked at Jade and raised an eyebrow, prompting her to share.

"Daddy is coming to stay with us for Christmas! He's on his way to the airport now!"

"What?"

"He and Janine called off the wedding," Jade continued. "So he's staying with us. He already talked to Mommy. Here, he wants to talk to you." She held out the phone, and Zyla furiously shook her head.

Her dad did this whenever he was newly single around the holidays. He was alone, so he'd suddenly decide to show up and spend Easter/Thanksgiving/Christmas with his "girls." He hadn't done so for most of Zyla's high school years, and she thought maybe he'd outgrown that phase, but she was wrong, clearly.

It wasn't even her dad's presence that annoyed her, although that was part of the problem too. She *hated* the effect he had on her mom. It was almost as if her mom hadn't gotten over him. Whenever he came around, she was at his beck and call, and she acted giddy and starry-eyed. It drove Zyla nuts. She couldn't imagine being so devoted to someone who'd cheated on her. Plus, Aunt Ida and her dad argued whenever they were in each other's presence. Sometimes Aunt Ida picked fights with him just because. And now this was going to happen over Christmas, when Kai was supposed to be there too.

This was going to be *terrible*.

"Tell him I'll call him back," she said to Jade.

"Zy said she'll call you back. Mm-hmm. Yeah. Okay. Bye, Daddy. See you soon."

Jade was on cloud nine, cheesing as she handed Zyla her phone. Who could blame her? She was spending Christmas with her dad for the first time in years. Zyla sat on her hands and tried not to show Jade how angry she was.

Her dad was going to ruin everything.

Chapter Twenty-Five

The ice skating rink at the waterfront in Philly was packed the day before Christmas Eve. Kai, Jamal, and the rest of their crew had made a tradition out of going on the twenty-third. This year, Zyla and Beatrice joined them.

"Yo, who's that clown Beatrice is talking to?" Jamal asked as he and Kai waited in line for hot chocolate.

Kai glanced over his shoulder, searching for Beatrice. She wasn't hard to find. She was wearing a silver bubble coat and huge white earmuffs. She stood by the edge of the rink, talking to a white boy Kai recognized from Hopkins Prep's spring track team. According to Zyla, this was the new dude Beatrice had been chilling with lately.

"I think his name is Travis," Kai said.

Jamal huffed. "I guess she likes 'em rich."

"What do you care?" Kai asked, grinning. "You're here with Alanna."

"Never said I cared."

Kai laughed as they moved up in line. He glanced back at the skating rink and spotted Zyla holding on to both Brandon and

Whit, struggling to stay upright on her skates, while Alanna followed closely behind to catch Zyla in case she fell. Brandon said something that made Zyla laugh, and Kai was relieved to see her smile. She'd been stressed since her dad came to visit a few days ago. Apparently, he planned to stay until New Year's Day.

Kai hadn't met her father. He could only go on information he'd received secondhand. He knew that her dad was unfaithful to each of his wives/fiancées/girlfriends. He knew that Zyla didn't feel as though her dad made a real effort to be in her or Jade's life. He knew that Zyla wasn't a big fan. But soon, Kai would get to form his own opinion about her dad because he was going to spend a few hours with Zyla and her family on Christmas Day. Regardless of whether or not Zyla liked her dad, Kai needed to make a good impression.

He'd spent a long time thinking about Zyla's gift, and he finally found a pair of fancy new shears for her to use whenever she made clothes. She could take them with her to college next year, and every time she sat down to make a new piece, she'd pick up her shears and think of him. It was perfect.

Christmas was a hard holiday for Kai without his parents, and while he loved spending it with his aunt Brenda and uncle Steve, there was a shadow hanging over the day. Maybe that would be different this year, since he'd be able to spend some of it with Zyla.

He and Jamal returned to the group and passed around

the hot chocolates. Everyone huddled outside of the rink in a circle, and Zyla stood close to Kai and sipped her drink. She'd been quiet most of the day. It kind of sucked that her mood was ruined because of her dad.

Kai leaned down and whispered, "You okay?"

Zyla looked up and nodded. "You okay?"

"I'm okay."

They held hands and went out onto the ice. Zyla wobbled and squealed as Kai smoothly led her around the rink.

"Are you good at everything athletic?" she asked.

Kai snorted. "I don't know. I haven't tried everything yet. Never played lacrosse or golf."

"Mm-hmm," she said, eyeing him.

He was happy to see her sarcastic nature briefly resurface.

Later, on the car ride home, she was quiet again. He wished he could make her stress go away. The radio station was playing an oldies Christmas song by the Temptations, and when Kai pulled up in front of Zyla's house, he waited for the song to end before he spoke.

"So," he said, "what time should I come over on Christmas?"

Zyla bit her lip. She was silent for a long time. Then, "You don't have to come over anymore."

Kai blinked. "Wait, what? Why not?"

"I know you probably want to spend the day with your aunt and uncle, and they probably want you home most of the day. So it's okay. You don't need to come by."

Kai felt like he'd been punched in the gut. Zyla stared straight ahead and wouldn't look at him. He leaned forward, trying to catch her line of sight.

"Did I do something to piss you off?" he asked, racking his brain for any possible reason that she might not want him to come over.

"No! No. It's not like that." She finally turned to face him, shaking her head. She looked a little desperate. "You've done nothing wrong."

"Then why are you telling me not to come over on Christmas? I was looking forward to spending the day with you . . ." He trailed off, knowing he sounded pathetic. But he was hurt. And confused. He wanted answers. "Are you embarrassed of me or something?"

"No!" This time she shouted even louder. "Kai, you could never embarrass me. You are perfect. You're the only perfect thing in my life."

She was tearing up, and now Kai was really fucking confused. And touched, because she'd called him perfect, and that made him feel good. But she was crying, and none of this made sense.

"Zyla." He gently took her hands in his. She didn't resist him. She looked down at their intertwined fingers and bit her lip again. "Hey, look at me." She glanced up, eyes glistening with tears. Quietly, he said, "Tell me what's wrong."

She sucked in a deep breath and let it go. "My dad being here for Christmas throws everything out of whack, even more so than usual. Maybe if I had a normal dad and a normal family,

313

I would bring you around all the time. I'd present you to them like a trophy—well, not a trophy because you're not just this, like, brainless thing to be paraded around, but I'm just really proud of you as a person and I'm glad to be your girlfriend and I wouldn't hide you from anyone. But if you're around my whole family, maybe you won't want to be with me anymore because maybe you'll see that I'm kind of out of whack just like them."

She was talking at the speed of light, not even pausing to wipe the tears running down her face.

Kai didn't let go of her hands as he sorted through her words, turning them over in his mind.

"Please say something." Zyla sniffled, staring at him.

Kai didn't know what to say. And yet . . . he knew exactly what to say. It was startlingly clear to him then. He felt kind of stupid for not realizing it sooner.

He leaned forward, held Zyla's face in his hands, and kissed her.

"I love you," he said.

Zyla froze. Her mouth fell open, but she was speechless. She blinked over and over.

"I love you," Kai repeated. "I don't care about what your family is like or if you're kinda like them. I just love you. So it doesn't matter."

He felt the truth of his words as he said them. He loved Zyla. This was a fact. Like how the sky was blue and water was wet. Kai loved Zyla.

She started to cry harder.

Oh shit. Okay, maybe admitting his love wasn't the right move. Shit. Shit. Shit.

"Um, hey. No, don't cry." He tried to think of how to back-track. But saying *I love you* wasn't something he could take back, and he didn't want to.

Zyla shook her head and waved him off. She wiped her eyes and cleared her throat.

"I love you too," she said.

Then she kissed him, hard. They kept kissing even when Aunt Ida flashed the porch light twice and then opened the front door and shouted, "Zyla Leanne, get in this house now, girl!"

"I love you," she repeated, scrambling out of the car.

"I love you too," he called back, not caring if her aunt Ida heard him.

He felt like a shaken-up bottle of soda as he drove away, ready to burst at any moment.

Zyla loved him!

Zyla *loved* him.

He wanted to climb a mountain and shout it to the world. He wanted to make a gushy-ass post for Instagram and let his followers know. This was the best day of his life, no lie.

He carried that joy with him until he saw Zyla on Christmas day. And he held on to his joy as Zyla's dad grilled him during Christmas dinner and when Aunt Ida remembered to stop scrutinizing Zyla's dad in order to scrutinize Kai, per usual. His joy grew as he watched Zyla gleefully unwrap his gift and then kiss him right in front of her entire family. And when she gave him a hand-knit maroon-and-white sweater, Morehouse's colors, Kai legit almost cried a little bit.

It was the best Christmas he'd had in a really, really long time. Because he loved Zyla and she loved him back.

Chapter Twenty-Six

Zyla sat in front of her mirror, flat twisting her hair. Kai would be here in half an hour to take her to Beatrice's New Year's Eve party. The esophagus butterflies happily swarmed and spread through Zyla's limbs. She was going to see Kai soon. Kai, who loved her. She and Kai loved *each other*. She felt brand new. To know that she was a girl who was loved by her mother and sister and aunt and best friend, and now by Kai.

Don't be fooled. It scared her something serious. She thought of her mom and wondered how many times she'd exchanged those words with someone, and how often those words weren't true or didn't matter in the end. And she wondered how many times her dad had thrown those words around, knowing he didn't mean them. But Kai was different. She knew he would protect the pieces of herself that she'd given to him. The same way she'd protect what he gave to her.

"Knock, knock."

Zyla glanced up. Her dad leaned against the doorframe. "Partying tonight?" he asked. Her dad was long and lean. He looked young for his age, not like someone who had a seventeen-year-old daughter. Maybe it was because he had a youthful smile. It used to be one of Zyla's favorite things about him.

Zyla nodded and kept doing her hair. She didn't really feel like talking to her dad. She was grateful that she'd be spending the night at Beatrice's and that she'd get a break from the drama. Just as she'd suspected, her dad's presence in their household was causing fissures everywhere. Aunt Ida didn't have a kind word for him. Her parents were acting like a weird quasi couple, going on dates to the movies and the mall, and Jade thought they might get back together, which was terrible because they wouldn't, and Jade would only end up disappointed. And Zyla wasn't sure where her dad slept every night. He was supposed to sleep downstairs on the basement couch. But the other night, when she woke at 3:00 a.m. to use the bathroom, she heard her parents in her mom's room, whispering to each other. What did they have to whisper about at 3:00 a.m.? Zyla didn't want to know. It didn't matter anyway. In a few days, her dad would be gone, and they wouldn't hear from him for weeks.

Maybe that was what bothered Zyla the most about him being there. Soon, he'd just leave. Why did his presence in her life have to be so temporary? She wished they could be a real family, that her parents could have a marriage like Kai's aunt Brenda and uncle Steve.

"Who you going out with?" he asked, walking over to sit down on her bed.

Zyla smoothed down her baby hairs and glanced at his reflection in her mirror. "Kai."

"You're pretty serious about this boy, huh."

It wasn't a question.

Zyla adjusted the collar of her oversized silver button-up and finally turned around to face him.

"Why?" she asked.

Her dad chuckled and shook his head. "No need for the attitude, Zy Zy. I just want you to be careful is all."

Be careful? What right did *he* have to tell her to be careful?

How could he just stroll into her room and sit down on her bed and start giving advice when she didn't even ask for it? When she didn't ask him to be here, period? What did he think this was? Her blood boiled. She spoke before she thought better of it.

"I don't need to be careful with Kai. He's not like you."

"Like me?" Her dad laughed and tilted his head. "What's that mean?"

"You know what it means."

"I really don't," he said calmly. "You care to explain?"

This was the tone he used with her mom whenever they had disagreements. If he was calm, it was easier for him to gaslight others.

"I don't want to argue with you," Zyla said.

"We're not arguing. We're just having a conversation."

"Dad." She just wanted him to get out of her room. "I'm trying to do my hair."

"So you're too busy to talk to your dad, who you hardly see?"

Zyla narrowed her eyes. "Yeah, well, whose fault is that?"

Her dad sighed and leaned forward, placing his hands on his knees. "Just be careful with that boy, like I said."

"Like *I* said, I don't need to be careful. Kai isn't a liar or a cheater."

"Oh, okay. So that's what you meant." He looked at her closely. "And let me guess, you think the two of you are in love."

"We *are*."

"And how do you know he loves you? Because he told you so?"

She hated the way he was trying to water down her and Kai's relationship. When they'd said I love you, it had been beautiful. The words grew more beautiful every time Kai said them. And now her dad was trying to make it seem so basic.

"I just know, okay?" Zyla snapped.

Her dad held up his hands in surrender. "Listen, don't get riled up, baby girl. I'm just saying, I was a seventeen-year-old boy once too. I know how it is. He's probably a lot more like me than you think. Is it too much for me to ask you to be careful? I'm your pop, ain't I?"

Zyla sat there seething. She was so angry, she couldn't even speak.

Then Jade appeared in Zyla's doorway. Their mom stood behind her. She took one look at Zyla's face and frowned.

"Everything okay in here?" she asked.

Zyla turned back toward the mirror, saying nothing.

"Everything's cool," her dad said. "We cool, right, Zy Zy?"

Zyla mumbled, "Mm-hmm." Because she wanted to keep

whatever peace currently existed between her parents. And she didn't want Jade to see any of them arguing.

"Daddy, the movie's starting," Jade said, grabbing their dad's hand and leading him out of the room. He glanced back at Zyla and gave her a look. One that said, *Remember what I told you.*

Zyla couldn't wait to get the heck out of the house.

Her mom walked closer and surveyed Zyla's hair. "Looks good, babe." She paused. "You sure you're okay? Did he say something to upset you?"

"It's fine, Mom," Zyla said with as much calm as she could muster. She gathered her phone and overnight bag. She'd rather sit outside on the porch and wait for Kai than linger any longer under the same roof as her dad.

As Zyla moved toward the door, her mom hugged her. "Have fun tonight, okay? Be safe."

Zyla closed her eyes and let her mom hold her. Even when her mom made her angry, Zyla knew that she would be there at the end of the day. Zyla didn't know if she'd ever be able to say the same for her dad.

"Thanks, Mom. I'll see you tomorrow."

As she waited outside for Kai, her dad's words ran on a loop through her mind.

He's probably a lot more like me than you think. Just be careful.

It wasn't true. It couldn't be. Her dad only met Kai once. He didn't even know him. Who was he to form such an opinion? This was exactly why she couldn't wait to go away to college. It was highly unlikely that her dad would randomly

321

show up at her dorm room in New York or Europe.

Kai pulled up in front of her house at 9:00 p.m. on the dot. As soon as she opened the passenger door and was settled inside, Kai kissed her and said, "I love you." All the anger seeped out of her body.

Her dad didn't know anything. Least of all anything about Kai.

———

Kai could legit get lost in Beatrice's house. That's how big it was. He stood in the kitchen with Zyla, Beatrice, and what felt like fifty other people. Beatrice's party was well under way, and she was tripping because apparently she'd invited one too many special guests.

"How could I have done this, Zy?" Beatrice asked, running a hand through her bone-straight hair. "I invited Xiomara, Travis, *and* Shana, and I somehow forgot that I invited all three of them?"

Zyla bit her lip and rubbed Beatrice's arm in an attempt to calm her. "I'm not gonna lie, this is kinda bad."

"Zy! You're supposed to say something to make me feel better." Beatrice poured a shot, took it, and winced. She looked at Kai. "What should I do?"

Kai shrugged. "I don't know. Who do you like best? Chill with them tonight."

"I like them each the same," Beatrice groaned. Then she raised an eyebrow. "Where's Jamal tonight? Too cool to come to my party?"

"He had a family thing," Kai said, confused at her question.

Beatrice couldn't stand Jamal. Why would she want him here?

"Whatever," she said. Then the doorbell rang. "I'll be back." And she was gone, shoving her way through the kitchen and into the hallway.

"What's the deal with Beatrice and her boyfriend again?" Kai asked.

"They're in an open relationship," Zyla said. "It seems to work for them."

That was interesting. Kai respected that love looked different for everyone. But he didn't think that open relationships were for him. He was so overwhelmed with his feelings for Zyla. He couldn't imagine being able to pay attention to anyone else.

Zyla looped her arm around his waist and leaned against him.

"You okay?" he asked.

She nodded. "I'm okay. You okay?"

"I'm okay."

Then she stood on her tiptoes and kissed him. Tonight, she was heavy on the PDA. Not that Kai minded. While kissing her, he could easily forget that they were in the middle of a New Year's Eve party, surrounded by a crowd of people.

That was kind of how it felt to be in love with Zyla in general. He had tunnel vision. She was the only thing he could see or think about. The way he felt about Zyla didn't compare to anything or anyone.

This must have been how his parents felt about each other. Now Kai could finally experience it too.

A group of St. Catherine's girls crowded into the kitchen and huddled around the island close to Zyla and Kai.

"It's so loud in here," Zyla said. "Want to go somewhere quieter?"

"Quieter?" Oh shit. That was what people said to each other when they wanted to dip from the party and . . . do things together . . . right?

Shut up. Get your mind out of the gutter.

"Yeah," Zyla said.

"We could go to my house," he heard himself suggest. "I can bring you back here after midnight. My aunt and uncle aren't home."

Great. Yeah, go ahead and tell her nobody's home so she'll just think you want to get in her pants.

"I mean, only if you want to leave," Kai quickly added.

To his surprise, Zyla grabbed his hand. "Yeah," she said. "Let's go."

———

Zyla hadn't been in Kai's room before. He had a poster of LeBron James taped to his wall, right next to his bed. His sneakers were lined up in perfect rows at the foot of his closet, which she appreciated. His room was organized and clean, which wasn't a surprise. It was the put-together room of a good student. It smelled like the cinnamon-spice cologne he often wore.

His bed was neatly made with a maroon comforter, pillow, and sheet set. Kai kicked off his sneakers and sat at the edge of his bed, watching Zyla. He looked slightly nervous. Now that she thought about it, she was nervous too. She was here in Kai's bedroom. What would happen next? Was he thinking about sex? Because suddenly that was what she was thinking about. Kai had done some things with his exes before, but he hadn't gone all the way. Zyla was *for sure* a virgin. Kai was the only person she'd even kissed.

She tried to keep her cool and walked over to Kai's dresser. She picked up a photograph of his parents. He looked a lot like his mom, with his wide brown eyes and full lips. He had his dad's deep-brown complexion and strong jawline. They must have been in college when the photo was taken, because they were young and wearing Spelman and Morehouse sweatshirts. They looked so content, joyful. Looking at them, she suddenly understood what Kai hoped to capture at Morehouse. A bit of their essence.

"They were beautiful," she said.

"Thank you." Kai was watching her, a soft smile on his face.

She placed the picture back down, glancing once again at his dad's Morehouse sweatshirt. Suddenly, she felt herself become anxious. "What do you think it will be like for us next year? You know, with you in Atlanta and me in Paris . . . hopefully."

"It'll be good," Kai said easily. "We'll figure out the time zone thing and talk when we can. I'll be busy with football and you'll be busy with fashion and exploring Europe and that cool stuff, but we won't feel bad about it because we'll both be doing what we love and we'll see each other on breaks."

Zyla felt her anxiety disappear, hearing Kai's vision for their future. It was simple, attainable. What they had could continue to be successful. She felt herself smile.

"Okay," she said. "Sounds like a plan."

Kai scooted backward on his bed until he was leaning against the wall. "Sit down with me?"

She sat close to him. Their arms were touching, and she felt the warmth of his sweatshirt sleeve. It was *so* quiet.

"Where are you aunt and uncle?" she asked.

"My uncle's coworker had a party."

"Oh, okay."

Kai turned toward her and smiled. Her stomach flipped. Four months together and being this close up to his face was a sight to behold.

"Want to listen to some music?" he asked.

She nodded, and he pulled out his phone and began playing a 6lack song. He put his arm around her and she rested her head against his chest, listening to the constant rhythm of his heartbeat. She intertwined her fingers through his, and he drew circles in her palm with his thumb.

"It's almost midnight," he said quietly.

They stared at his phone. When the clock hit 12:00, Zyla turned to Kai.

"Happy New Year," she said.

"Happy New Year." With his index finger, he tilted her chin up. He kissed her softly at first. Then the kiss deepened. He pulled her closer, and she interlocked her fingers behind his neck, leaving no space between them. His hand trailed down her side and onto her thigh. She felt him finger the hem of her long shirtdress. Almost like a question. In answer, she moved her thigh higher, and he put his hand under her shirt, skimming her stomach and stopping over her bra.

This wasn't new. Kai had put his hand up her shirt many times when they kissed in his car. But that was sitting in his car, not lying on his bed.

She didn't want him to stop, though.

He began kissing her neck, feather light, and then with his tongue. He reached for the buttons on her shirt.

"Is this okay?" he asked.

She nodded and watched as he unfastened the buttons one by one. Then he slipped off his sweatshirt and his ribbed tank underneath, leaving his torso bare. Nervous and giddy, she fumbled with the hook of her bra and slowly slid it off. Kai stared at her in quiet wonder, and her heart beat fast in anticipation. He came closer and kissed her again. His hand slowly crept down her stomach to her waist. He looked up at her with hazy eyes.

"Is this okay?" he repeated.

Zyla nodded again. "Yes."

Then she felt his hand in a place that was new. And he was kissing her breast, which was also new.

They melded into each other, entwined together. Kai shifted until he was completely on top of her, and she wrapped her arms around his back. Then she realized she might not be ready for what came next.

"Wait," she said, reaching up and gently placing her hand on Kai's chest.

Kai stopped immediately and moved off her, propping himself up on his elbow. *Shit shit shit.*

"Shit," he said. "I'm sorry. Are you okay?"

"I'm fine," Zyla said breathlessly. "I'm just not ready for . . . everything else."

"Of course. I'm sorry." Kai dragged his hand over his face. He'd pushed her and completely ruined the moment. "I'm really sorry, Zy."

"It's okay. I'm okay." She sat up and looked at him. "I want to, you know, do it. Just not today. But in the future."

"Okay, yeah. Sure, sure. Me too."

Kai had to remember that Zyla was more inexperienced that him. Not that he knew much more than she did, to be honest.

"You sure you're okay?" he asked.

"I'm okay. I promise." She kissed him on the cheek. "I love you."

He sighed in relief. "I love you too."

Quietly, they put their shirts back on. It wasn't awkward between them. That was probably a testament to how much they vibed with each other.

Kai was about to suggest that they watch a movie when he heard his aunt and uncle pull into the driveway.

"Oh, fuck." He jumped up and ran to the window. Sure enough, his aunt and uncle were home early from their party. What the hell would they say if they saw Zyla here at this hour? "Fuck, um, okay. My aunt and uncle are home."

"What?" Zyla scrambled to put on her Docs. "Oh my God. What should we do?"

"It's cool," Kai said calmly, although he didn't feel calm at all. "We'll just have to sneak out."

"Oh my God," Zyla hissed.

They rushed downstairs and slipped out of the back door just as his aunt and uncle stepped into the hallway. They crept around to the front yard and climbed into Kai's car. When he started the engine, he hoped his aunt and uncle wouldn't wonder why his car mysteriously disappeared. Maybe he'd just tell them he'd decided to go back to the party, and that way he wouldn't have to lie.

He and Zyla held hands as he drove her back to Beatrice's house. The party was winding down when he pulled up. Beatrice stood at her front door, waving to her leaving guests. When she spotted Zyla and Kai, she grinned in a way that said she knew exactly what he and Zyla were just doing at his house.

"I'll call you before I go to sleep," Zyla said. She kissed him goodbye.

He placed his hands on either side of her face and held her lips against his for a second longer. Then he let her go. "Okay. I love you."

"I love you too."

He drove away, thinking that next time—and he really hoped there would be a next time—he and Zyla would have to be more careful.

NOW: May, Senior Day Trip, 6:14pm

Kai's ex-girlfriend, Camille Vaughn, is not yet aware of Kai and Zyla's disappearance. At the moment, Camille is wrapped up in a towel, about to take a shower in her room at the Roaring Rapids lodge. She desperately wants to wash the chlorine smell from her hair and skin. She wonders whose great idea it was to force three high schools together and take the students to a second-rate resort in the Poconos. Why couldn't they have gone to Disney World like other high schools? On student council, she'd pushed Alanna to ask for Disney World, but Alanna had argued that Roaring Rapids was tradition, and the rest of council agreed with her. Camille lost that battle to Alanna the same way she lost the homecoming queen title. It is just one of the many things Camille expected to have senior year that didn't come to fruition. Unwarranted, an image of Kai slow dancing with Zyla at homecoming flashes in her mind. That was supposed to be *her*. She pushes that image away, deep, deep down into the recesses of her memory. She made a decision to move on after what happened on St. Patrick's Day. She just wishes her brain would get with the program.

As soon as she steps into the bathroom, her best friend, Tyesha, bursts into their room, out of breath.

"Oh my God, guess what happened?" Tyesha yells.

Camille rolls her eyes because Tyesha can be dramatic sometimes. "What?"

"Kai got jumped by some boys from Hopkins Prep over Zyla, and he and Zyla ran away together and now everybody is looking for them!"

"Excuse me?" Camille blinks, staring at Tyesha. "Are you serious?"

"Yes!" Tyesha flops down onto her bed. *"Everyone* is talking about it."

Camille narrows her eyes, skeptical. You see, she doesn't know if she can believe this news since it is coming from Tyesha.

Last summer, Tyesha was the same person who told Camille that Kai had been flirting with another girl at Sailor Joe's while she and Kai were still dating. Camille felt embarrassed. How dare Kai flirt with someone else while she was his girlfriend, and while she was working at the same park? At the time, she and Kai were going through a bit of a rough patch, but she expected his fidelity.

When she confronted him at the Tilt-A-Whirl that day, Kai truly seemed to have no idea what she was talking about. He claimed he didn't flirt with anyone else. Camille realized he was telling the truth, and then she questioned the validity of Tyesha's story. But she'd walked across the park to call Kai out. She was already causing a scene, and she was going to finish it. She didn't expect that little kid to get sick on the ride or for that camp counselor to get involved and yell at Kai, and she definitely didn't expect Kai to snap on both of them. Despite her telling Kai "Good luck not getting fired," she didn't really want him to lose his job. In fact, later that day, she went to talk to Antonio and admitted that she took some part in the whole situation. She'd antagonized Kai, and she pleaded with Antonio not to fire him.

Then Antonio told her that Kai had been moved to the Games section. Knowing that Kai hadn't been fired relieved Camille.

You see, Camille has a different opinion about love. To her, love is not easy and unconditional. On the contrary, love is full of conditions. Love is having a screaming match with your partner and ignoring them for days, and then choosing forgiveness for the sake of keeping the peace. Love can be expressed through expensive gifts that say I'm sorry. This is what her parents do when they fight, which is often. Love is when someone takes you to the mall to shop for school clothes or a homecoming dress and offers unwanted opinions on your appearance. This is what her older sister, Priscilla, does when she feels bad for calling Camille an annoying spoiled brat who lives in her shadow. Love is putting up with people even though they're mean to you. Love is not letting your partner see you at your most vulnerable because you can't show weakness or assume their unconditional support.

So last summer, when Camille gave Kai a hard time for the simplest things, she didn't think much of it. That, to her, was normal. And the day when Kai saw her crying after yet another fight with Priscilla, and he wrapped Camille in his arms, Camille knew she'd made a mistake. Kai would see this weakness and think she was a leech for comfort, or even worse, someone who literally couldn't stand on her own two feet with the way she fell into him. The next day she said they needed a break, that Kai didn't pay her enough attention. It was a lie, of course. Kai paid her plenty attention. She just needed an excuse, a reason to give herself a few days to regrow her tough exterior.

Following the scene at the Tilt-A-Whirl, Camille fully expected that after a week or so, it would blow over and she and Kai would be boyfriend and girlfriend again. She'd seen her parents have much worse fights. After all, she and Kai were a power couple. People looked at them and knew they belonged together.

But afterward, Kai completely ignored her. And then to make matters worse, he started hanging out with Zyla Matthews. They spent weeks telling everyone they were only friends, but Camille knew that wasn't true. She'd dated Kai. She knew how he looked at someone when he was infatuated.

She tried to warn Zyla away from Kai, telling her about his past player ways, hoping that Zyla would back off and Camille could finally have him for herself. But Zyla had been innocent and sweet, claiming that she and Kai really were just friends. It was such a joke. And it drove her nuts that Kai was choosing to be with someone else over her.

Something to know about Camille is that she is driven by

competition. In addition to being student council treasurer, she is the debate team captain and cocaptain of Cedar High's competitive dance team, and she fully intends to be a criminal defense lawyer one day, spending her life arguing with others and consistently proving her point. So . . . when she decided that she was going to get Kai back, it wasn't so much that she wanted *him*, exactly. It was that she'd lost him to another girl, and that was something she couldn't accept. She thought that Zyla and Kai's relationship would fizzle out after a couple months. They were too different; it wouldn't last. So she gave it some time. But when she realized their bond was only getting stronger—like that stunt they pulled dancing together after Kai was crowned homecoming king—she realized she needed to put a real plan in motion to break them up.

She is not proud of the things she did in order to achieve this goal. She doesn't like looking at those ugly parts of herself, but she has a feeling that she will have to face them soon.

She sends a quick text to Darius. **Did Kai and Zyla really run away?**

Darius responds immediately. **Idk. That's what the teachers are saying. Why aren't you in the lounge? Everyone else is here.**

"Okay, let's go," Camille says to Tyesha.

She bites her lip as she gets dressed. She is struggling with an emotion that she can't name. They reach the lounge and it's filled with students from the three high schools, and everyone seems to be talking about Zyla and Kai. She and Tyesha spot

Darius right away, and he fills them in on the recent developments. People have different theories and stories about what has or hasn't happened. Some say Kai started the fight because Zyla's new boyfriend is some kid from Hopkins Prep. Others say that Zyla started arguing with a Hopkins Prep boy and Kai jumped in and threw a punch. And then there's the story Tyesha heard about Kai getting jumped. No one can agree on the specific details. But the students at least can agree that the idea of Zyla and Kai running away seems farfetched, and the teachers are grasping at straws. Zyla and Kai are probably just being their normal drama-causing selves, secretly hiding out somewhere in the park. Drama seems to follow them wherever they go. From the fight they got into with a customer at Sailor Joe's to the time they did or didn't get caught breaking and entering on Valentine's Day (no one really knows what happened with that incident, except for Zyla and Kai, of course), and a couple months ago when they got into an argument at Will's St. Patrick's Day party and broke his mom's fancy china. They didn't earn the nickname Bonnie and Clyde for no reason. They'd even dressed up like them on Halloween.

The unnameable emotion continues to brew in Camille's gut as people chatter around her. It's starting to make her nauseous. Then a hush falls over the room when Jamal Smith and Zyla's friend Beatrice arrive. Jamal has his arm around Beatrice, and he's whispering in her ear. It almost looks like he's comforting her, most likely because she's upset that her friend is missing. When Beatrice notices that everyone is watching them, she shrugs away from Jamal and glares around the room, as if she dares anyone to question her about Zyla.

Then Beatrice's eyes land on Camille, and she scowls so deeply, Camille can feel Beatrice's hate manifesting like a physical being. Camille is used to being hated for one reason or another, so she isn't deterred as she makes a beeline for Jamal. When he spots her, his eyes widen. He looks around like he's planning to escape. Camille is definitely the last person he wants to speak with, but he doesn't move quickly enough.

"Is Kai okay?" Camille asks him.

Darius is right beside her. "Yeah, what's going on?"

"I don't know," Jamal says. "We don't know where they are. The teachers don't know either."

"Has anyone talked to his aunt and uncle?" Camille asks.

Jamal nods. "They're on their way here now."

"That's good," Camille says. She feels more nauseous now. Kai's aunt and uncle are probably worried sick.

"Why do you care?" Beatrice suddenly snaps. She looks Camille up and down with a fiery gaze. "Kai doesn't want you, okay? What will it take for you to get that through your head? You need to leave him and Zyla alone."

"She's not wrong," Darius says, folding his arms and looking pointedly at Camille.

Darius is supposed to be Camille's best friend. He took her side when she and Kai broke up, but after what she did on Valentine's Day *and* St. Patrick's Day, he hasn't been too hot on her. She can't even blame him.

Usually, if someone spoke to Camille the way Beatrice just did, it would be on and popping. But she simply stares at Beatrice, because Beatrice is right, and she deserves Beatrice's anger. Camille realizes now that she didn't stand a chance at getting Kai back. Kai was never going to choose her. He loves Zyla so much that he ran off with her in the middle of a monsoon-like storm. Maybe love *is* unconditional. For some people.

Guilt. That is the nausea-inducing emotion she was unable to name. She feels so, so guilty for the way she tried to weasel herself between Zyla and Kai.

If they ever come back, she'll apologize for her terrible actions.

Maybe.

Chapter Twenty-Seven

Technically, St. Catherine's students were only supposed to eat lunch in the cafeteria. But Zyla and Beatrice didn't pay much attention to technicalities, which is why they were currently sitting in Beatrice's car eating the turkey-and-Swiss-cheese sandwiches Helene packed for them that morning.

Beatrice smiled widely as she texted with Hugo. She was flying to Paris next month to attend the opening of her dad's newest restaurant, and she'd be seeing Hugo for the first time this year.

Zyla grinned, watching as Beatrice cheesed and snapped a selfie for Hugo.

"Hey, is it cool if I stay over again tonight?" Zyla asked.

Beatrice glanced up from her phone. "Duh. You should move in until graduation. My mom won't care."

"*My* mom would." Zyla sighed.

She'd been spending a lot more time at Beatrice's lately. Being at her own home was weird. After New Year's, her dad didn't go back to Denver. Well, he did go to Denver to move his things out of Janine's apartment. Then he came back to Cedar, because he'd made the decision to stay in New Jersey so that he could be closer to Zyla and Jade. He was sleeping in Aunt Ida's basement, which Aunt Ida hated, but he'd already found a full-time job delivering parts for AutoZone. Soon, he'd have enough saved to get his own apartment nearby.

Her parents weren't back together or anything. In fact, her mom was pretty adamant about keeping their relationship strictly to coparenting, which had surprised Zyla. It could be because her mom was currently dating a woman named Cheryl who she'd met at the bank while standing in line for the ATM on New Year's Day. But either way, her parents' relationship wasn't romantic.

Her dad was present for every dinner unless he was working a night shift, and he sat at the kitchen table with Jade while she did her homework, and he gave Zyla and Jade lunch money, and he even washed Aunt Ida's car and fixed her La-Z-Boy when it stopped reclining. He was doing the things that Zyla had always wished for. But she couldn't fully enjoy him being there for two reasons. One, she was worried this was temporary. He might meet someone new, and then, poof, he'd be gone. And two, she was pissed at him for the things he'd said about Kai.

Awkwardness lingered between Zyla and her dad now. She didn't like that he felt as though Kai was someone she needed to be careful around. Especially not now when for the past month or so she and Kai had been getting closer and closer to having sex.

And they'd finally planned to do it on Valentine's Day, only a few days away. She hadn't imagined that she'd care about a person enough to even consider having sex with them. The fact that she was finally at this point was exciting, but it also made her super nervous.

Beatrice finished her sandwich and balled up the aluminum-foil wrapping. "Do I have anything in my teeth?"

Zyla examined Beatrice's braces. "No, you're good."

Beatrice blew a kiss in thanks and turned up the radio. But not too loud, because they didn't want to get caught in the parking lot during school hours.

"Hey," Zyla said, then paused. "Um. Question."

Beatrice raised an eyebrow. "I'm listening."

"When you lost your virginity, it hurt, right?"

"I mean, yeah. It was more uncomfortable than painful, though. I think it's different for everyone . . ." Beatrice squinted. "Are y'all finally gonna do the do?"

Zyla nodded. "Yeah. On Valentine's Day. Kai has something special planned. It's a surprise."

"Ha!" Beatrice held a hand over her heart. "How romantic. When I lost my virginity to Hugo, we took a train to the beach and got a hotel room with this huge bed. He put rose petals everywhere. I mean, the way I'm telling it to you, it might sound basic, but it wasn't."

"How can losing your virginity in a French beach town sound basic to anyone?"

Beatrice smirked. "I guess you're right."

"Do you, um, have any advice for me?" Zyla asked.

She wasn't, like, completely ignorant when it came to sex. She knew which parts went where, and years ago, her mom sat her down for a very informative and surprisingly frank sex talk. But Zyla wanted to get the real scoop from her best friend, who also happened to be the most experienced person she knew.

"Well, use protection, of course," Beatrice said. "Make sure to tell him what you like and don't like. It should be enjoyable for both partners . . . or for however many partners are involved depending on the situation. You don't have to do anything you don't feel comfortable doing. Um, what else, what else. Oh, make sure you pee afterward. That way you won't get a UTI."

Zyla nodded, mentally taking notes. "Right, okay."

Beatrice turned, fully facing Zyla. "I have to say, I didn't see this coming."

"See what?"

Beatrice shrugged. "You and Kai. The two of you falling in love. You were so against relationships and anything remotely romantic. Now look."

"I know," Zyla said. "I don't think I would have changed my mind for anyone else."

"I'm happy that you're happy, Zy." Beatrice sighed and smiled at her friend. "And I'm happy that you're staying over tonight. Just move in, like I said."

Zyla laughed. "Yeah, maybe."

Distantly, they heard the bell ring, signaling the end of lunch. They hustled back toward the building, slipping through the side door by the locker room that none of the sisters bothered to pay attention to.

As Zyla hurried up the steps to sixth-period marine biology, her phone buzzed in the pocket of her cardigan. It was a text from Kai accompanied by a picture of his new white Reebok Classics.

Hey <3

Zyla smiled and paused on the stairs as she quickly took a picture of her clunky yet very cool loafers.

Hey <3

Kai grinned at his incoming text from Zyla. Only she could wear low-key ugly shoes and make them look dope.

He felt someone nudge him and glanced to his left at Alanna.

"Pay attention," she whispered, smirking. "This meeting is *very* important."

Kai held back a snort. They were in the middle of a student council meeting, which Camille had called at the last minute before lunch. Apparently, she wanted the okay to purchase roses to hand out to the student body on Valentine's Day, as opposed to carnations, which she claimed were "cheap and tacky."

Kai didn't care one way or another. Zyla didn't go to Cedar High, so he didn't have to worry about buying her a carnation or rose. Well, he was planning to buy her a bouquet of roses because that was classic Romance 101, but he had something big planned for Valentine's Day. Bigger than flowers. He couldn't wait.

Lately, he'd been feeling weightless, like nothing could hold him down. He and Zyla were good. Better than good. He was anxious that they were finally gonna have sex, but only because he wanted everything to go perfectly—or he wanted to try his best to make the experience good for Zyla. There could be no mistakes, he'd make sure of that.

And in addition to how well their relationship was going, senior year had been pretty smooth sailing. Except, of course, for that time he almost missed the SATs in December, and the one time he was late to basketball practice because he was up on the phone talking to Zyla until the early morning hours. She had been stressed about her dad, and she'd kept apologizing the whole time for talking to Kai about it, attempting to hang up so he could sleep, but he refused to leave her hanging. The next morning was the first and only time he'd been late to practice the entire season, but it was for an important reason. Plus, the big things had been accomplished. Kai finished his Morehouse application and applied to some safety schools like Rutgers and Rowan University, but he made sure to apply to more selective schools like UPenn, and Villanova too. The varsity basketball team was having an okay season. Jamal and the rest of the crew were doing well and ready to graduate. For the most part, shit was sweet.

"Everyone who votes on roses over carnations, raise your hand," Alanna said, bringing Kai back to reality.

Kai looked around at the other members of student council. Camille had her hand raised, and so did Adam, the secretary. Alanna's hand wasn't raised, and Vivian, the parliamentarian, didn't raise her hand either. Camille narrowed her eyes, and Alanna shrugged.

"We don't need roses, Camille," she said. "Sorry. That money can go to better causes. Like our fundraiser for those who can't afford suits and dresses for prom."

Camille took a deep breath, and Kai knew this was what she did when she was trying not to roll her eyes. Suddenly, Camille looked at him. "Kai, you're the deciding vote," she said.

Ah, shit. He didn't want to be put in the middle of this. He glanced at Alanna, who quirked an eyebrow. Alanna most likely thought Kai was going to side with her, being that he and Camille weren't on the best terms, and Camille had tried to ruin his reputation over the summer. And Alanna did have a point. It would be better to help those in need for prom as opposed to buying roses that would die in a few days.

But then again . . . Camille had once told Kai that people liked to receive beautiful things because it made them happy. When they were dating, he'd taken that very literally and went and bought her a charm bracelet like a sucker, but she'd loved it. Maybe she was applying this philosophy to the roses. Roses were more beautiful than carnations . . . Maybe Camille was just trying to make the student body happier on Valentine's Day. That wasn't so bad, right? And Kai had felt differently about Camille since that day in November when he had felt like shit and she had asked if he was okay and suggested he go to the nurse. She probably didn't realize that she'd been doing him a favor, but he could do her a favor in return.

"Uh, the roses are cool, I guess," he finally said, raising his hand.

Alanna blinked. Across the table, Camille smiled wide and triumphant, almost slyly. Kai kinda wondered if he'd made the right choice.

"O-kay, then," Alanna said. "You'll get your roses, Camille. Meeting dismissed."

As Alanna stood, she gave Kai a pointed look.

"What?" he whispered, shrugging. "They're just flowers."

Alanna sighed and gathered her books. "It's never 'just' anything with Camille."

Great. Now Alanna was disappointed in him, and that was annoying because he valued Alanna's opinion. He started to follow after her, ready to enact damage control, but when he stepped into the hallway, he felt someone tug on his shirtsleeve.

"Hey," Camille said, "thanks for voting on the roses."

"Oh . . . sure," Kai said, startled. "No problem."

Adam and Vivian skirted around them, heading toward the cafeteria. Kai itched to get there too. He needed to talk to Alanna, and he was hungry as hell.

"I'm guessing you're going to get a rose for Zyla," Camille said. "That's why you voted yes."

"Nah, I've got something else planned. I mean, yeah, I'm gonna get her roses. But not from the school . . ." He trailed off.

Talking to Camille about Zyla was weird. Camille *was* his ex-girlfriend. Other than their brief conversation in November, they hadn't talked since last summer.

Kai took this opportunity to look at Camille, *really* look at her. She was definitely one of the prettiest and smartest girls in school. He could recognize that he found her attractive, but otherwise, he felt . . . nothing. Wild. It was funny how once you met the right person, you realized why your other relationships didn't work.

"What are your plans?" Camille asked him now.

"Plans for what?"

She raised an eyebrow. "Valentine's Day?"

"Oh, nothing too crazy. Just gonna hang out."

That wasn't exactly true. Kai had something dope planned, but he hadn't told anyone other than Jamal, who'd called him Loverboy and said that the plan was over the top but typical for Kai.

"Rob wants to go Il Forno," Camille said. She smirked and snorted a little. "I guess he's kinda basic, but it's whatever."

Rob Cruz was Camille's new boyfriend. He ran indoor track, and sometimes Kai saw him in the weight room when their practices overlapped. From what Kai could tell, or from the PDA displays in the hallway, Camille and Rob seemed happy.

"I don't think it's basic," Kai said. "Il Forno has good food."

Camille laughed. "I know. We went before, remember?"

Kai nodded, glad that the moment didn't feel awkward. "I remember. You ate a bunch of those garlic knots before they brought out your pasta and you lost your appetite, so you had to sit there and watch me eat my steak."

"Oh my God, my stomach hurt so bad! I couldn't even think about garlic knots for days."

Now Kai was laughing too. "Days? More like weeks. You wouldn't let me take you back there again."

"Well, I guess we'll see if I've gotten over my garlic knots fear in a few days, huh."

"I guess so." Kai nodded in the direction of the cafeteria. "I'm heading to the caf, if you want to walk there."

Camille blinked at first. Then, "Yeah, sure."

They were quiet as they made their way down the hallway. "So you're telling me that you don't have anything extravagant planned for Zyla?" Camille asked. "I don't believe that. On our first date, you gave me a corsage."

Kai winced. "I definitely did the most."

"Oh, for sure. But I appreciated it."

Camille grinned at him. It still wasn't awkward. Was it possible that he and Camille could be friends one day?

"Actually, I'm taking Zyla to the planetarium," Kai said. "Remember Phil Watkins, who graduated a couple years ago? He's a security guard there, and he's gonna let us in after hours. I slid him some money."

"Wow." Camille slowed her walk. "What are you going to do once you're inside?"

Kai's plan was personal, just between him and Zyla. So to Camille he only gave one small detail. "We're gonna have dinner."

Camille nodded. "Ah, there's the romantic Kai that I know."

Kai shrugged and smiled. "Yeah, I guess."

They reached the cafeteria doors and turned to each other.

"Hey, listen, I'm glad we're cool now," Kai said.

"Me too." Camille smirked in a way that Kai had once found mad seductive, but now it was just a normal smirk. "See you around."

She sauntered away and glanced back at him once before joining her friends at their lunch table and sitting down next to Darius. Darius caught eyes with Kai and mouthed, *What just happened?* Kai simply shook his head and walked toward his table at the back of the cafeteria with Jamal and the rest of the crew. He didn't have anything to tell Darius because nothing happened. He and Camille had a conversation, and they were cool now.

Kai could finally say that he was on good terms with each of his exes. Perfect.

Chapter Twenty-Eight

On Valentine's Day evening, Zyla sat in the living room with her mom, Aunt Ida, and Jade, wondering if it was obvious to her family that tonight was the night she was going to lose her virginity. She was wearing a simple black turtleneck sweater dress and tights with her white Docs, and underneath, she wore a brand-new bra-and-panty set that Beatrice helped her pick out at the mall. Her armpits were drenched in sweat, and her palms were clammy. She'd need to reapply some deodorant before Kai picked her up, for sure.

Her mom and Jade sat on the living room floor, sharing a bag of Valentine's chocolates that Jade received from her classmates. Zyla's mom turned to her and held a handful of Hershey's Kisses in her palm. "Want some, Zy?"

Zyla shook her head. She was too nervous to speak. She had an irrational fear that as soon as she opened her mouth, her mom would know right away that she was keeping a secret.

For a brief second, she thought about how her mom got pregnant at her age. What if that happened to Zyla? No, no. She and Kai would be careful. They'd use protection.

"You okay?" Zyla's mom asked, tilting her head. "You're being so quiet today."

Both Jade and Aunt Ida turned to look at Zyla then. Oh no. Too much attention.

Zyla cleared her throat. "I'm fine. Just tired."

Luckily, before her mom could dig any deeper, the front door swung open and her dad stepped inside, carrying four huge teddy bears.

"Happy Valentine's Day," he sang, smiling.

Jade hopped up and ran over, wrapping her arms around their dad and the bears. "Thanks, Daddy!"

Zyla's mom stood and smirked. "And who are those for?"

"My girls, of course," he said. "Got one for Aunt Ida too."

"Don't want it," Aunt Ida grunted, eyes on the television.

Zyla stayed put on the couch, conflicted. On one hand, she was glad to see Jade so happy, glad that her father was the cause of Jade's happiness. And she could tell that her mom was pleased as well. Like Jade, Zyla wanted to run up to her dad and thank him for the bear. But she couldn't trust his presence. She didn't want to get too attached.

"This one's for you," her dad said. He walked over and placed the bear in Zyla's lap. It was light brown and soft. Easily half Zyla's size.

"Thank you." She leaned back and stared at the bear. She ran a hand over its fluffy belly.

Her dad sat down beside her. "You like it?"

Zyla nodded and bit her lip. She felt emotional suddenly,

like she might cry. For what? It was just a silly bear.

"I do like it." She held on to the bear's paws and avoided looking at her dad. She had a feeling that her mom was watching her too, watching how this conversation unfolded.

Her dad smoothed his hands over his jeans. The silence between them was turning awkward. "So what's Kai got planned for you tonight?"

Zyla's cheeks got hot. She hugged the bear and hoped it wasn't obvious that she was trying to hide her face. "I don't know. Dinner? It's a surprise."

"Oh, that's sweet!" her mom said, propping her teddy bear on her hip like it was a baby. "I hope he takes you somewhere nice."

"Me too," her dad said. He smiled, and it seemed genuine.

Lately, it seemed as though he was trying to make peace since the conversation he and Zyla had on New Year's Eve. When Kai came over, her dad made an effort to sit and talk to him about sports and whatnot. And there were no more warnings that Zyla should be careful.

"I don't see why you and Kai can't have dinner here with us," Aunt Ida chimed in. "That way we could keep an eye on you. I don't like this *surprise* business."

"Oh, Auntie, stop it," Zyla's mom said.

Zyla and her dad exchanged a look and laughed. Wow, exchanging looks? That was new.

The doorbell rang, and Zyla's heart sprang up to her throat. Kai was here, and she hadn't reapplied deodorant!

"Can someone get that?!" she said, dashing upstairs.

She glanced at her reflection for a final once-over. The next time she looked at her herself in this mirror, she'd no longer be a virgin.

Nervously, she made her way down the steps. Kai stood in the hallway, holding a bouquet of pink roses. Jade had one rose and she held it to her nose. Zyla's parents were both standing in the hallway, chatting with Kai, and it was weird for Zyla to see them as a united front, welcoming her boyfriend into the house.

"Hey," she said to Kai, unable to keep from smiling.

"Hey." He handed her the roses. "Happy Valentine's Day."

She took the bouquet and wanted to jump on him. But her parents were watching. So instead, she said, "Thank you. These are beautiful."

Her mom swooped in and said she'd put the roses in some water.

"Have fun tonight," her dad said. He pointed between them. "But not too much fun."

"Bye," Zyla said, grabbing Kai's hand.

Once they were in his car, they kissed for real. Then Kai held up one of his ties.

"What's that for?" she asked.

"Okay, so I have to blindfold you for the surprise," he said. "That way you won't know where we're going."

Zyla smirked. "Should I be nervous?"

"Nervous to have the best night of your life? Yes."

She giggled as he covered her eyes with the tie. On the drive over, she kept trying to guess where they were going, but Kai wouldn't budge. Finally, Kai turned into a parking lot and cut the engine.

"Can I take this off now?" she asked.

"Nope, not yet."

Kai opened her car door and led her to . . . wherever he was leading her to. Then they stopped.

"Thanks for doing this," Kai said to someone. "I owe you one."

"It's all good," a guy with a deep voice replied.

Kai ushered Zyla into a building. Or at least, she figured it was a building, because a heavy door closed behind them and it was cold inside. And quiet. They were alone, as far as she could tell. They walked and walked until she heard Kai open another door. The anticipation was killing her. Where the heck were they?

Then they stopped. She felt Kai reach around and untie her blindfold. He was smiling.

She blinked, letting her eyes adjust to the dark room. They were in a theater.

"Look up," Kai said.

And Zyla froze at what she saw. The entire galaxy was displayed across the ceiling.

She turned in a circle, staring up at the moon, planets, and stars. It was huge, like she was really in space. "Kai," she whispered. "How are we at the planetarium right now?"

"Don't worry about the details."

She returned her gaze to his face. That's when she noticed the blankets and pillows set up on the floor behind him. He bought takeout from Ishkabibble's, the first restaurant they ever ate at together.

She was going to float right on up to the ceiling with the stars.

"Oh my God," she said, stepping closer to Kai. "This is perfect. *You* are perfect."

You are perfect. It was practically music to Kai's ears.

He'd thought really hard about the perfect place to take Zyla on Valentine's Day, especially given what they planned to do. Being with Zyla made him feel infinite, as big as the galaxy. He wanted to lie beside her underneath the stars. But it was February in New Jersey, and it was way too cold to spend the night outside. Then he realized the planetarium offered a good alternative.

He was determined to make it the best night of their lives.

Once they sat down on the blanket, Kai was too nervous to eat, even though he'd driven to Philly to get food from Ishkabibble's. Zyla nibbled at her cheesesteak and glanced up at him every now and then. What was with this nervous energy between them? Maybe it was the whole sex thing that was throwing them off.

"Wanna listen to some music?" he asked. Zyla nodded, and he put on an R&B playlist. He tried to make it seem casual as he scrolled on his phone, but the truth was that he'd specially curated this playlist for tonight.

"I love this song," Zyla said, humming along to Khalid's voice. Suddenly, her eyes widened. "Wait, I didn't give you your gift!"

"You didn't have to get me anything," Kai said, surprised.

Zyla waved him off and dug around in her bag. She produced something small, wrapped in red crinkly paper. She bit her lip as she handed the gift to Kai. Slowly, he removed the paper and was left with a football-shaped enamel pin in his open palm.

"I saw it at Genie's," she said. "You'd asked about my pins before. I thought you might want one of your own. I know it's silly."

"Nah, nah. It's not silly." Kai pinned it on his shirt right away. "When I get home, I'm going to pin it on the sweater you made."

"I'm glad you like it."

"Thank you," he said softly.

She nodded. Kai moved closer and gently placed his hand over hers. Her skin was warm. They stared at each other, and then Kai ducked his head and kissed her. The kiss began soft and hesitant but quickly turned intense, their hands moving everywhere. All their nervous energy finally found an outlet.

Then their clothes were gone, and they lay side by side.

"Are you sure you want to do this?" Kai whispered. His heart hammered away in his chest. He watched her pulse throb quickly at the hollow of her throat.

"Yes, I'm sure," Zyla said. "Are you?"

Kai nodded. He put on a condom and reached for her. She was in his arms, and they moved together.

Afterward, Zyla curled up beside him, and Kai whispered I love you, and she whispered that she loved him too. Whether or not the sky above them was real didn't matter. In that moment, Kai was in the center of the universe with the girl he loved. He finally knew the feeling of all-encompassing happiness. Or even better, perfection.

Then the alarm sounded.

Chapter Twenty-Nine

When the lights cut on, Kai's first instinct was to cover Zyla. He wrapped his arms around her, and she grabbed on to him with a frantic look in her eyes. A look that said, *Oh shit*.

"Fuck, fuck, fuck," Kai hissed. He tried to stay calm as he shoved Zyla's sweater dress into her hands and scrambled to put on his own clothes. If they didn't get out of here soon, they'd be caught. But what the hell was he supposed to do with this food and shit?!

They both stood, and Kai scooped everything into the blanket. He grabbed Zyla's hand, ready to run, and the theater doors opened. A short Black woman stood beside a tall, burly security guard. A security guard who wasn't Kai's friend, Phil Watkins, who'd let them inside.

"Hands up where I can see them," the security guard shouted.

Kai immediately dropped the blanket and held up his hands. Zyla quickly did the same. She sucked in a breath, and Kai wanted to reverse everything about this night. Even finally having sex, because he never wanted to see Zyla look this afraid ever again.

Shit, shit, shit.

The woman and security guard approached them. When they got closer, Kai realized the woman was Denise Claremont, the director of the planetarium, who just so happened to be Uncle Steve and Aunt Brenda's friend. Phil had promised that Ms. Claremont wouldn't find out about tonight. Great, this was going so fucking great!

"Hezekiah Johnson, is that you?" Ms. Claremont asked, coming closer.

"Yes, it's me," Kai said. He took a shaky breath. "We weren't doing anything bad, just having dinner, I swear."

"Dinner?" Ms. Claremont stood only a few feet away now. She looked at the blanket, which was covered in spilled food. Then she looked at Kai and Zyla. "It's okay, I know him," she said to the security guard, and he nodded.

"You can put your hands down," she said to Kai and Zyla, and they obeyed. "I got a random call that someone thought suspicious activity was happening at the planetarium. I thought I'd come here and investigate myself before risking getting the cops involved. And you're here having dinner? What on earth made you think sneaking in here for that was a good idea?"

"I don't know," Kai said. Beside him, Zyla stared wide-eyed at the security guard. Kai wished he could hug her and tell her it would be okay, but he knew that wouldn't be the truth. "It was really, really stupid."

Ms. Claremont shook her head. "I didn't expect something like this from you, Hezekiah," she said. "You know I'm going to have to tell your aunt and uncle."

Fuuuuuck.

This felt a thousand times worse than almost getting fired last summer.

Kai and Zyla were dead silent as they left the dome theater, followed closely behind by Ms. Claremont and the security guard. Once they were inside Kai's car, Zyla held her hands to her face.

"Kai," she said quietly, "this is so, so bad."

"I know. I'm so sorry." He felt like he might throw up. "I didn't mean for any of this to happen."

"Who would call the director? Was it your friend who let us inside?"

Kai shook his head. "I have no idea."

Ms. Claremont flashed her lights, reminding Kai that he was going to be followed in order to make sure that he and Zyla both went home. And so that she could tell Uncle Steve and Aunt Brenda about what Kai had done.

Kai started the car and tightly gripped the steering wheel as he drove out of the parking lot.

It was over. He'd told his aunt and uncle that he wouldn't get distracted by his relationship with Zyla. He'd tried to prove that he and Zyla were good for each other. And he'd come so far without getting into any real trouble in years. Now he was being escorted home by the director of the planetarium and her security guard. There'd be no coming back from this.

What if they grounded him until graduation? What if this was the last time he'd see Zyla in who knows how long?

He gripped the steering wheel tighter and fought the urge to bounce his knee as he drove.

No, don't spiral right now. Hold it together while Zyla is right here.

"Hey," he said, suddenly turning to her when they reached a stoplight. He glanced at his rearview mirror and saw Ms. Claremont's car behind them. "I don't know what's gonna happen, but I want you to know—"

"No, don't do that," Zyla said, squeezing his hand. "We're going to be fine. *We're* going to be fine."

She spoke with such conviction, but who was she trying to convince? Herself or Kai?

Kai had hoped Zyla could easily slip inside once he dropped her off. They didn't both need to get in a shit ton of trouble. But he realized that wouldn't be the case as he pulled in front of her house with Ms. Claremont on his heels and Zyla's dad sat in Aunt Ida's rocking chair on the front porch, smoking a cigarette. Her dad stood, eyeing their cars. He peered at Zyla and began walking down the porch steps.

"Oh no," Zyla whispered.

She looked at Kai, and her anxious expression finally matched his own.

He felt like he was gonna puke.

She kissed him hard and desperate. "I love you," she said, and then she was gone, darting out of the car to meet her dad halfway on the front lawn.

Kai wanted to go with her and explain to her dad what

happened, but he froze when Ms. Claremont got out of her car and motioned for Kai to stay put. Kai watched miserably as Ms. Claremont spoke to Zyla's dad, who listened intently to whatever Ms. Claremont said. Then he turned to Kai and glared.

Fuuuuuck.

Ms. Claremont walked back to her car and signaled for Kai to get a move on. Zyla locked eyes with Kai as her dad ushered her inside. Kai touched the football pin on his jacket and hoped she knew what he was trying to say. He was sorry. He loved her. There were a few instances in the past when he felt as though she could read his mind. He hoped that was the case now.

When he pulled into his driveway, he sent a prayer up to his parents. He willed his mom's words to come to him. *It's gonna be all right, Hezekiah, baby.* But they brought no comfort.

Ms. Claremont followed Kai to the door. Aunt Brenda and Uncle Steve were both sitting at the kitchen table when Kai and Ms. Claremont walked inside. Uncle Steve stood up so fast, he almost knocked over his plate.

"Denise, what are you doing here?" he asked, looking from Kai to Ms. Claremont. "What's happened?"

Kai kept his eyes on the floor as Ms. Claremont explained how Zyla and Kai broke into the planetarium. That wasn't even the truth, though. They didn't break in. It was more accurate to say that they *snuck* inside. "Breaking in" made him think of smashing windows and busting doors open with crowbars. They weren't criminals, damn.

Aunt Brenda's feet suddenly appeared in Kai's line of sight.

He looked up, and she was frowning at him in a way that said she wasn't just sad; she was disappointed too. Kai sighed. This shit was his fault. Why was the floor taking so long to swallow him whole?

Uncle Steve thanked his friend Ms. Claremont for letting Kai off the hook, for not getting the cops involved. And he promised, on Kai's behalf, that something like this wouldn't happen again.

Once Ms. Claremont left, Kai didn't wait for Uncle Steve to dig into him.

"We didn't break in," he quickly said. "I planned a dinner for Valentine's Day. I didn't think we'd get caught. It was stupid. I'm so sorry."

"You're damn right it was stupid," Uncle Steve said. "Kai, what the hell possessed you to do something like this? You know what, don't answer that. Because I know the answer. You were too busy worrying about that girl to think straight."

Kai winced, but he was smart enough not to interrupt and say "that girl" had a name.

"Now do you see why we told you not to date and focus on school?" Uncle Steve continued. "You almost missed the SATs, and you've been late to basketball practice. Now this! Imagine if the director of the planetarium wasn't Denise Claremont but someone who would have called the cops instead. Imagine what could have happened to both of you!"

"I know. I'm sorry." Kai closed his eyes, thinking of how

terrified Zyla looked when they were caught, and how terrified he'd felt. He sucked in a breath and tried not to cry, because that wouldn't make the situation any better.

Uncle Steve shook his head. "I don't even know what else to say to you, Hezekiah. You're grounded, though. I hope you know that."

Kai nodded.

Softly, Aunt Brenda, said, "Kai, why don't you go up to your room. We'll finish talking about this tomorrow."

"Okay," Kai said. "I'm sorry."

He turned to walk upstairs, and then the doorbell rang.

Zyla's parents couldn't agree on a freaking thing when she was growing up, but now, suddenly, they both seemed to think it was a great idea to confront Kai and his aunt and uncle to get the story of tonight's events straight. And now they stood at Kai's door, waiting for someone to answer.

"I warned her about that boy. I did, didn't I?" her dad said to her mom.

"Dad, stop it!" Zyla shouted, furious, yet feeling guilty that any of this had to happen in the first place.

Zyla's mom shook her head and stepped in between them. "Cool it, Terrance, okay? Let's see what Kai has to say."

The planetarium director, who apparently knew Kai and his family, told Zyla's dad that she and Kai had broken into the planetarium, which was a freaking lie. Well, wait, maybe *technically* that was true. But it wasn't like they'd stolen anything! They just wanted to have sex for the first time under some fake stars!

When Kai's uncle Steve opened the door, Zyla wished she could disappear. But her mom grabbed her arm and pulled her inside of the hallway. Kai's aunt and uncle stared at Zyla and her parents. And Kai stood at the foot of the steps, his gaze locked on Zyla. His eyes were red. Had he been crying? She wanted to run to him.

"I'm so sorry to barge in on you like this," Zyla's mom said. "But I think we need to talk about what happened tonight."

Kai's uncle Steve nodded and crossed his arms over his chest. "You're right, we do."

"Ms. Claremont told us they were caught eating inside," her mom said, "but we want to get the whole story from Zyla and Kai together."

Zyla glanced at Kai, who'd come closer to their circle. He stood beside his aunt Brenda, looked at Zyla, and tightly shook his head. She knew what he meant. They wouldn't admit the real reason they were at the planetarium. Their parents couldn't know the whole story. It sounded so stupid now that they'd been there to have sex, but Zyla knew that Kai's intentions had been pure when he planned this night for them. What they'd done was nobody's business but their own.

"It was just dinner," Kai said.

Zyla nodded. "That's all."

The adults stood around quietly, watching Zyla and Kai,

waiting for them to share more. The heavy silence bordered on awkward.

"I think we can agree that these two could do with some time apart," Zyla's dad suddenly said.

"What?" Zyla said.

"What?" Kai said.

They locked eyes again. What the heck was happening?

"I agree," Kai's uncle Steve said. "I feared this relationship would distract Kai, and that's clearly what's happened here."

"Distract Kai?" Zyla's mom said, incredulous. "Do you know that Zyla has skipped work to see your nephew? That she almost missed her college application deadline because of him?"

Kai's aunt and uncle turned to Kai, wide-eyed, and Kai cringed.

"Mom," Zyla cried. "Stop!"

"I told *Zyla* to be careful around *Kai,"* her dad said. "And *clearly* I was right, because tonight was his idea."

Uncle Steve blinked. "His idea? I'm sure Zyla influenced him in some way."

"Now, hold up, why does that have to be the case?" Zyla's mom asked.

"I think everyone needs to calm down," Kai's aunt Brenda said, attempting to referee.

"Come on, Zy. I think it's time for us to leave, and you're not coming back here either." Her dad steered her toward the door, but Zyla twisted, trying to look at Kai.

Kai stepped forward toward her, but his uncle Steve stopped him. Zyla's parents pulled her outside, furious.

"Can't stand uppity Black folks like that," her dad was saying. "Just assuming Zy convinced their nephew to do some shady shit because we don't have degrees or walk around wearing button-ups like they do?"

"Terrance, not now," Zyla's mom said, holding Zyla's hand. "You okay, babe?"

"No, Mom, I'm not okay!" Zyla felt like she was losing her mind. "None of you know what you're talking about! Kai and I don't need time apart!"

Zyla wanted to shove her parents and Kai's aunt and uncle into oblivion. They said they wanted for Zyla and Kai to tell them what really happened, but they didn't listen to them at all!

Frantically, she glanced back up at Kai's house, and he was watching her from his window. He placed his hand against the windowpane, and Zyla waved desperately, hoping it could convey what she felt but couldn't say. She loved him. She was sorry.

Her mom basically dragged her into the back seat, and the whole time Zyla complained about how this was so ridiculous. Once she was away from them at college, she wouldn't have to deal with this craziness!

As they drove off, her phone vibrated with a text from Beatrice.

Zy . . . is this you and Kai??

Zyla gasped at the screenshot Beatrice sent. Somehow, somebody snapped a picture of her and Kai being escorted out of the planetarium by the security guard. It was being shared all over social media with captions like, "Look at Bonnie and Clyde out here committing crime."

"Oh my God," Zyla moaned.

She sent the picture to Kai. **Did you see this?**

Within seconds, Kai responded, **I'm grounded and they're taking my phone. I love you.**

She texted, **I love you too.** But the message wouldn't deliver.

This was supposed to have been the best night of her life. And now it was the worst.

Chapter Thirty

You'd have thought people didn't have other shit to talk about.

Kai closed his locker and focused on spinning the lock as two girls walked by him, whispering and giggling. He glanced over his shoulder and caught them staring before scurrying off down the hallway.

Everyone was so concerned with trying to find out what had happened with him and Zyla at the planetarium on Valentine's Day almost a week and a half ago.

He took a deep breath and walked to the cafeteria. He avoided making eye contact with his classmates, but he felt them watching. The Cedar High rumor mill was even worse than the one at Sailor Joe's. People were saying the nuttiest shit. Like that he and Zyla had planned to rob the planetarium, or that they'd been about to throw a secret Valentine's Day party but got caught before anyone could arrive. The stupidest rumor he'd heard was that they'd both been kicked out of their houses and had been sleeping at the planetarium at night for weeks. Why did people care so much?

It didn't matter. Kai wasn't going to tell anyone the truth. It was nobody's damn business. It was between him and Zyla.

The only people who knew what happened that night were Beatrice and Jamal. And Dr. Rueben, sort of. For the first time in years, Kai didn't tell Dr. Rueben the full truth about why he'd gotten in trouble, just that they'd been caught having dinner. This weighed on Kai, but he didn't need Dr. Rueben to point out that Kai's plan to sneak into the planetarium had been stupid. Kai already knew that well enough by now.

Kai walked straight to the lunch line as soon as he entered the caf. It was for the sake of normalcy. In reality, he didn't have the slightest appetite. And why would he? His aunt and uncle low-key thought he was a delinquent. And between being grounded without his phone, unable to talk to Zyla, and basically bombing his Morehouse virtual interview the previous week, Kai didn't know which was worse.

He felt like a stretched rubber band, ready to snap at any moment. He struggled to ground himself.

It's lunchtime, and I'm standing in line to buy food. After this, there are only three more periods left in the day. Even though it's been a week and a fucking half, people will stop talking about Zyla and me soon.

He clenched and unclenched his fist and focused on his breathing. He spoke calmly to the lunch ladies when he paid for his chicken parm sandwich, and as he walked to his lunch table, he kept his gaze forward.

The usual crew was there waiting for him. Jamal and Brandon were deep in conversation about last night's game between the Sixers and the Clippers. Across the table, Will was busy trying to eat lunch and skim through his copy of *Things Fall Apart* for an English test, and Chris was leaning over to the table beside theirs flirting with some girl who did color guard.

As soon as Kai sat down, Jamal slid over his phone.

"Thanks," Kai said quietly. Jamal had been letting Kai use his phone during lunch now that he didn't have access to his own.

Kai quickly texted Zyla.

Hey, it's Kai.

Her reply came within seconds. Hey. I miss you so much.

Kai's stomach clenched. I miss you too. This shit sucks.

I know. I can't believe they're being so ridiculous.

Zyla's parents and Aunt Brenda and Uncle Steve had assumed that Zyla and Kai were broken up now, simply because they'd said that Zyla and Kai could do with some time apart. Sneaking into the planetarium had been stupid, but it didn't mean he and Zyla needed to break up. What kind of twisted logic was that? He and Zyla didn't bother telling them that they were still together. Let them think whatever they wanted. After a few weeks, they'd cool off, and he and Zyla wouldn't have to pretend they were broken up anymore. For now, he had to do his best to get back in his aunt and uncle's good graces.

A burst of laughter sounded from the table beside them. Kai glanced up and noticed that the color-guard girls were looking at him and chuckling. Chris was laughing with them. *Chris.* One of his friends. That was what really set Kai off.

"What the hell is so funny?" he asked.

Everyone froze. Over the past week and half, Kai hadn't

said a word in response to the rumors and whispers.

"Nothing, bro," Chris said, leaning away from the other table. The color-guard girls turned away and busied themselves with eating their lunch.

"Nah, nah," Kai said. "I wanna laugh too."

"Kai," Jamal warned quietly, "let it go."

Kai shrugged Jamal off. "Chris, what's the joke?" He leaned forward and shouted to the color-guard girls, "Come on, y'all. What's the joke?"

Distantly, Kai realized that the cafeteria suddenly grew quiet. Everyone's attention was focused on his lunch table. He didn't give a shit.

Chris glanced around at the other boys hesitantly before he answered. "It was stupid. Earlier today I heard someone say that you and Zyla really were like Bonnie and Clyde because y'all were careless enough to let yourselves get caught."

"Ha," Kai said, bouncing his knees under the table. "That *is* funny. So funny."

He forced a hollow laugh. Chris grinned, looking relieved, and he laughed too. That's when Kai snapped and lunged across the table.

"Whoa, whoa, whoa!" Jamal shouted, pulling Kai back just as he swung at Chris, grazing his nose.

Will and Brandon both shot to their feet to intervene, and the cafeteria broke into pandemonium.

"What the fuck, bro?" Chris said, stumbling back. He readied his fists, squaring up.

"What's up, then?" Kai shouted, trying to push Jamal away. "You wanna fight, let's fight since you think shit's so funny!"

But the teachers showed up before Kai could beat Chris's ass like he wanted to. The next thing Kai knew, he was being escorted to the vice principal's office and then straight to in-school suspension, where he'd have to spend the remainder of the day.

He had no one to blame but himself. He'd let his temper get the best of him. But seeing Chris, one of his closest friends, feeding into those stupid rumors really fucked with him. Now that he'd gotten in trouble *again*, his aunt and uncle had even more reason to be pissed at him. He was doing *such* a great job at proving how responsible and focused he was.

There were only a handful of students spread out in the in-school suspension classroom. Kai didn't look at anyone as he made a beeline for the back of the room. It was the first time in his entire high school career that he'd been suspended in any form. But in-school suspension had been no stranger to him in middle school. The principal used to joke that Kai had a reserved desk back then.

Kai flopped into his seat and stared out the window. He'd been in the middle of texting with Zyla before his stupid almost-fight with Chris. He'd meant to confirm their plans for tonight and now he'd just have to hope that she remembered.

He didn't know how long he'd been staring out the window before he heard someone hiss his name. He looked over and blinked in surprise at Darius, who sat a few desks away. He'd been so focused on finding a seat in the back of the room, he hadn't even noticed that Darius was there too.

Darius glanced at the aide, who'd fallen asleep at the front of the classroom, and he quietly made his way to the desk beside Kai.

"What'd you do to get in here?" he whispered.

Kai shook his head. He had no energy to explain. "Something stupid. You?"

"During third period I said to Ms. Gregory, and I quote, 'Lady, I'm not gonna read another chapter of racist-ass *Huck Finn*. Fuck that.' Been here ever since."

Kai smirked. "Good for you."

Suddenly, Darius leaned closer and lowered his voice. "Look, I know since you and Cami broke up, you and I haven't talked much, because Cami's my girl, and I felt like I had to choose between y'all."

Kai narrowed his eyes. Why was Darius randomly bringing this up?

"But you and I have been cool since diaper days," Darius continued. "So I feel like I owe it to you to tell you the truth, even if Cami gets mad at me."

"Huh?" Kai said, confused. "What are you talking about?"

Darius glanced around like they were being watched. "Camille is the one who tipped the planetarium director off about you and Zyla on Valentine's Day. She got her personal number somehow. You know her mom's on Cedar's Arts and Sciences board."

"What?"

Kai shouted so loudly, he woke the teacher's aide.

"Hey, what's going on back there?" he called. "Darius, move back to your seat."

Darius took his sweet time returning to his desk, and Kai stared at him in shock. *Camille* had called Ms. Claremont on him and Zyla. But how would she even know—oh, shit. Kai had told Camille he was taking Zyla to the planetarium after it closed on Valentine's Day. He'd thought they'd finally squashed their beef, and here Camille had been playing him the whole time. How could he have been so stupid?

Kai squeezed his eyes closed and counted down from ten. He wanted to flip over his desk. He wanted to find Camille and give her a piece of his fucking mind. But he'd already caused enough trouble for himself today.

He took a deep breath, then another. "Did Camille take the picture too?" he whispered to Darius.

Darius shook his head, looking apologetic. "I don't know who took the picture, but it wasn't Camille. The planetarium is in the middle of town, Kai. Anybody could have seen y'all."

The aide shushed Kai and Darius and threatened to send them to the principal's office if they didn't stop talking.

Kai made himself stare out the window. He bounced his knees, revving up to take off. He felt sick to his stomach. Fucking Camille. But she was the least of his worries.

Zyla was gonna kill him when she found out the truth.

As suspected, Aunt Brenda and Uncle Steve were pissed about the in-school suspension. Kai stared down at the table as Uncle Steve lectured him, warning Kai that if he didn't get it together soon, he could kiss his bright future goodbye. Once Uncle Steve finished speaking, Kai asked if he could be excused, but Aunt Brenda made him finish his dinner, being that he'd barely had a chance to eat his lunch. Kai knew he should be grateful that Aunt Brenda was paying such close attention to his welfare, but he really just wanted to be left alone.

He ran the dishwasher after he forced himself to eat at least half his plate of pork chops and macaroni and cheese, and as he turned to go upstairs, Aunt Brenda gently tugged at his shirt-sleeve, stopping him.

"You want to check your email?" she asked.

Right. Kai's decision letter from Morehouse was due to arrive any day now.

"Okay," he said.

He followed Aunt Brenda into her office and sat down at her desk chair. Robotically, he opened his email account, and what do you know? There was an email from Morehouse. Kai opened the email and peered at the screen.

Dear Hezekiah,

It is our pleasure to inform you that . . .

Kai read the rest of the email in a daze. He'd been accepted to Morehouse. His dad's alma mater. He'd achieved one of his biggest goals. So why wasn't he hype as hell right now?

"Oh my God, you got in!" Aunt Brenda said, leaning over Kai's shoulder. "Steve get up here!"

Uncle Steve jogged upstairs and ran into the room, looking concerned, but his face lit up in pure joy when Aunt Brenda shared the news. All of his disappointment for Kai forgotten, Uncle Steve pulled Kai out of his seat and wrapped him in a warm, tight hug.

"I'm so proud of you," he said. "Your dad would be proud too."

Kai sniffled and closed his eyes. After the trouble he'd gotten into recently, he was so happy to hear his uncle say these words. Despite everything, he was able to make him proud at least in this way. "Thanks, Uncle Steve."

They celebrated by going for ice cream, which was kind of pointless because Kai didn't have an appetite, but he was glad to see his aunt and uncle so happy.

The Morehouse letter had come right on time. Because it meant Aunt Brenda and Uncle Steve were sleeping contently and soundly when Kai snuck out of the back door after midnight to meet up with Zyla.

Chapter Thirty-One

Relief washed over Zyla when she spotted Kai waiting for her on the old swing set at the park in between their houses. Funny they hadn't thought to come here before when they'd actually been allowed to see each other.

"Hey." Kai stood and met her halfway.

She broke into a run, knowing how dramatic she looked, and wrapped her arms around him. He smelled the same, like his cinnamon cologne. He looked the same, but tired. Not that much time had passed since she'd last seen him on Valentine's Day, but she'd felt as though it had been years.

"Hey," she said, pressing her face into his coat. Kai held her close and rested his chin on top of her head. She closed her eyes as they swayed a little. She tried to imagine that they were dancing together like at homecoming, when everything was easy and simple.

Eventually Kai pulled away and led her over to the swings. They held hands once they sat down. Zyla could see her breath clouding in front of her every time she exhaled. It was cold, but she didn't care. She'd have met Kai tonight even if there was a snowstorm.

"I'm sorry, Zyla," Kai said. "This is my fault."

"No, it's not," Zyla said fiercely. "It's *their* fault. Yeah, we got in trouble, but that doesn't mean we need to break up! It's so absurd. I'm not talking to my parents."

Zyla had been giving both her mom and dad the silent treatment in the days since, especially her dad. How dare he think he could tell her not to see Kai anymore, as if she had any real reason to listen to him? The only upside was that her parents hadn't grounded her, which meant she was able to text Kai whenever he borrowed Jamal's phone during school or after basketball practice. Aunt Ida was the only one who seemed to think that Zyla should be punished, but Zyla's mom had brushed off Aunt Ida's suggestion, most likely remembering the times Aunt Ida grounded her for silly things when she was Zyla's age.

Zyla's mom said Zyla would thank her in the future. That she didn't want Zyla making the same mistakes she'd made in high school with boys.

None of them knew what they were talking about. Zyla wouldn't talk to them until they came to their senses. How were her parents or Aunt Ida pretending to know anything about love?

"My aunt and uncle are still mad," Kai said. He bit his lip and glanced away. "I got in-school suspension today, so it's not like that helped."

"*What?* Why?"

"Um . . . I almost got into a fight with Chris."

"Chris?" Zyla shook her head, confused. "What happened?"

"He made some joke about us being like Bonnie and Clyde. Usual stupid shit."

"I can't believe people won't let this go," Zyla said, frustrated. Her classmates at St. Catherine's were treating her like some sort of celebrity because, of course, rich Catholic-school girls thought getting in that kind of trouble was *so cool*. "It's annoying."

Kai kicked his sneaker into the dirt and nodded. "Really fucking annoying."

"My mom apologized to the planetarium director. She says we're lucky she didn't decide to press charges." Zyla sighed and zipped her coat up higher. "I just wish we knew who called the director that night. Maybe someone drove by and saw us?"

Kai looked down at his feet and shifted in his swing seat. He was fidgety suddenly.

"Are you cold?" Zyla asked. Meeting up at midnight in February definitely wasn't ideal.

"Nah," Kai said quietly. He took a deep breath and finally looked at her. "I know who called Ms. Claremont."

Zyla froze. "Who?" she asked even though, somehow, she knew she wasn't going to like his answer either way.

"It was Camille," he said.

A fire lit up inside of Zyla. Her insecurity dragon knew it was finally time to shine.

"What?" Zyla's voice echoed off the trees. "How did Camille even know?"

Kai winced. "I told her. It was stupid, I know that. Trust me.

379

But I thought she and I were becoming cool, and she asked what we had planned for Valentine's Day, so I mentioned the planetarium."

Zyla couldn't believe what she was hearing. How could he ever think that Camille would want to be "cool" with him? Why would he even entertain the possibility? Her insecurity dragon was ready to burn down the entire park and then find Camille's house next.

"Does she know that we had *sex* too?" Zyla asked.

"No! Of course not. I wouldn't tell her that. Come on, Zyla. What the fuck?"

"Well, you said you told her your plans!"

Zyla suddenly pushed to her feet, and Kai quickly followed suit.

"I'm sorry," he said. "I'm really fucking sorry, Zyla."

She stared at Kai and knew he meant what he said. He looked torn up about it, and she hated to see him so stressed and upset. Yet she couldn't wrap her mind around his thought process.

"Camille is manipulative, Kai," she said. "Why is that so obvious to everyone in the entire world except for you?"

"It is obvious to me! Don't you think I'm pissed that she tricked me?" Kai dragged his hands over his head. "I'm sorry. I'm so fucking sorry, and I don't know what else to say. I won't speak to Camille ever again for the rest of my life."

Zyla sat back down and huffed out a deep breath. It was the first time she and Kai had seen each other in over a week, and here they were arguing about Camille freaking Vaughn. If Zyla let this come in between them, Camille would win. Because that's clearly what she wanted so badly. She wanted them to fight and break up so that she could have Kai back.

Well, Camille could kick rocks. Zyla was in love with Kai, and she wasn't giving him up.

She took another deep breath. "Okay," she said softly.

Kai peered down at her, searching her face. "You're not mad anymore?"

"I'm mad. Just not at you. I'll get over it."

"Okay." Kai watched her warily for a second, then sat down beside her. They twisted in their swings until they faced each other, bumping knees.

"I got into Morehouse," he said.

The Camille drama was quickly forgotten—for the moment.

"Kai, that's amazing!" Zyla threw her arms around his neck. "Congratulations!"

"Thanks." Kai leaned into her hug and rested his head on her shoulder. "I'm kind of surprised, to be honest. I thought I fucked up in my interview."

"Of course you were going to get in."

Zyla had been sure that Kai would kill his alumni interview, but when his interview took place last week, she hadn't been able to talk to him. So she sent him good vibes via good thoughts. And out of curiosity, she'd looked on Morehouse's website. She'd heard of Morehouse before, of course. It was one of the most popular HBCUs in the country. And of course she'd also heard of Spelman, the girls' college right across the street from Morehouse. Somehow, she'd then found herself browsing Spelman's website, and as she scrolled through photo after photo, she soon realized that apparently every girl who attended Spelman was beautiful, smart, and accomplished. And these were the girls that Kai would be around on a daily basis. In Georgia. While she was in Paris, if she was lucky.

In the week since Zyla lost her virginity to Kai, she'd been thinking a lot about how Kai was her first everything. First kiss. First boyfriend. First time . . . She'd officially given away all the pieces. She didn't regret having sex with Kai, not at all. She thought he would safely secure the pieces of herself that she'd given to him. But then again . . . how could he do that while he was in Georgia and she was in Paris (maybe)? Would he get bored with not seeing her? Would the time zone difference make him lose interest? She'd been struggling with these feelings for days, and it sucked because she couldn't even talk to Kai since her parents and his aunt and uncle were being so ridiculous. She'd felt slightly lost without Kai, and she'd come to rely on his presence without even realizing it. That alarmed her. Her mom's relationships tended to go south once the partner in question started to become a permanent fixture.

But she and Kai weren't like her mom and her partners. They loved each other. They would be *fine*. This would be easier once they were past the planetarium drama.

Zyla wondered how many times she'd need to repeat that in order to feel like it was true.

"When will you hear back from your schools?" Kai asked, pulling back to look at her.

"Over the next few weeks. I'm hoping to hear back from Parsons Paris first."

Kai paused. "If you get into the programs in New York or LA, do you think you'd consider going?"

"If I don't get into Parsons Paris, yeah."

"But if you get into Parsons, that's where you're going for sure?"

Zyla nodded. Kai fell quiet and looked away.

"What?" she asked. His body language was making her anxious.

"Nothing," he said. "It's just that Paris is so far. I know we talked about it before, but . . . I don't know." He shook his head. "Forget it. The distance doesn't matter."

Zyla stared at him. Apparently, she wasn't the only one who'd been thinking about the distance. They were both possibly going to their dream schools, and it should be something to celebrate. But why didn't that feel worth celebrating?

"You're right," she said, grasping his hand. "It doesn't matter."

His hands were cold. He wasn't wearing any gloves.

"We should probably go back soon," Zyla said reluctantly.

"I know." Kai leaned forward and kissed her. Zyla realized it was the first time that they'd kissed the whole night. His lips were cold but soft.

They held hands as they left the park, and Kai walked her home. They stood in front of her house, staring at each other.

Zyla prayed Aunt Ida or her dad wouldn't suddenly come to the front door and catch them. She wanted to milk these last few minutes with Kai for as long as she could.

"I love you," Kai said. He kissed her, placing his cold palms on either side of her face.

"I love you too." She held her hands over his on her cheeks and kept them there for a few seconds. She didn't want him to leave. But it was almost 1:00 a.m., and they both had school in the morning.

Kai promised to text her on Jamal's phone tomorrow, and he waited for her to sneak back inside before he turned to walk home.

Zyla stood in the hallway for a long time, thinking about Kai and their future. She wished everything could go back to normal and that they didn't have to sneak around.

She wished they were as carefree as they'd been over the summer.

Chapter Thirty-Two

Two things happened at the beginning of March. Zyla got into Parsons Paris, and Hugo dumped Beatrice.

"I can't believe this," Beatrice said, sobbing. She lay across Zyla's bed with her head in Zyla's lap. Zyla held a box of tissues at the ready. "He said he loved me. We were supposed to get married! And then he goes and falls in love with *someone else*? How could he do this to me?"

"He's an idiot," Zyla said, smoothing a hand over Beatrice's hair. After years of comforting her mother post-breakup, Zyla knew the right things to say. "You're better off without him. You know that, right?"

"Of course I know that." Beatrice sniffled. "But it still hurts."

According to Beatrice, when she'd gone to Paris last week for the opening of her dad's newest restaurant, Hugo was being distant. She thought he was stressed about university exams, but it turned out he'd met another girl in one of his classes. They'd started seeing each other casually, in the same way that Beatrice often dated other people, but soon Hugo realized things weren't casual with this girl. He loved her even more than Beatrice. He waited to break the news until Beatrice was back home in New Jersey.

"He didn't tell me in person because he didn't want to hear what I'd have to say," Beatrice moaned. "He wanted to have the chance to hang up on me, which is exactly what he did!"

Zyla hugged her friend hard. "I'm so sorry. You deserve so much better than this."

Beatrice nodded and sighed through her tears. "You were right this whole time. Love *is* stupid."

Zyla didn't want to point out that her opinion had changed on the subject. Now definitely wasn't the time.

"Hey, girls." Zyla looked up and her mom was standing in her doorway, holding a bowl of popcorn. "Just made this fresh. Want some?"

Zyla started to say no, but Beatrice jerked upright and said, "Yes, please."

Zyla's mom walked over and joined them on the bed. "What's wrong, Miss Beatrice?"

Beatrice began telling her breakup story, and Zyla's phone vibrated on her pillow. It was a text from Kai. Last week his aunt and uncle finally lifted his punishment and returned his phone.

You coming to Will's party tonight?

Zyla glanced at her mom, who was fully preoccupied listening to Beatrice. Since Zyla's acceptance into Parsons Paris, everyone in her household was so proud, they seemed to have forgotten the drama that transpired on Valentine's Day. Granted, they thought Zyla and Kai were broken up. Zyla

386

hadn't thought of how to tell them the truth yet, and Kai hadn't said anything to his aunt and uncle either. They were walking on eggshells, sneaking around to meet at the park every few days. It was becoming stressful. Zyla feared they wouldn't ever find the right time to tell everyone the truth.

Idk, she responded. **Beatrice is upset about Hugo. I'm probably gonna stay with her tonight.**

Not even a minute passed before Kai called her. She stared at her phone as it vibrated in her palm. She couldn't talk to Kai while her mom was sitting right here, and if she got up and left the room, it might make her mom suspicious.

She let the call go to voicemail and willed her mom to leave so that she could call Kai back, but now her mom was hugging Beatrice and letting Beatrice cry on her shoulder. Zyla sighed. She wanted her mom to leave, but Beatrice badly needed the comfort. When Kai called again, Zyla excused herself and hoped her mom was too wrapped up in Beatrice to pay her any mind. She went into the bathroom and turned on the faucet so that no one would be able to overhear her.

"Hey," she answered. "Sorry I didn't pick up before. My mom's in my room talking to Beatrice."

"Are you coming?" Kai asked. His background was loud.

"I don't know, Kai. It depends what Beatrice wants to do. I doubt she feels like partying tonight."

"I didn't ask about Beatrice," he said. "I asked if *you're* coming."

Zyla blinked, taken aback at Kai's tone. "I can't just leave Beatrice alone after she's been dumped. She needs me."

"Okay, but I need you too."

The sneaking around was already weighing heavy enough on them both. But the weight increased once Zyla got her acceptance letter to Parsons Paris. She'd been rejected by the London School of Fashion and FIT, but she did get into FIDM in LA. Parsons Paris was her ultimate dream, but she was starting to wonder if maybe FIDM might be more ideal. At least then she'd be in the same country as Kai. There was already so much stacked against them. The knowledge that they'd officially be apart next year was too much to handle. Maybe moving to Los Angeles for school would be easier. She hadn't shared these thoughts with Kai or her family yet. She wanted to wait until she was absolutely sure.

"I'm sorry, Kai," Zyla said, feeling miserable. And slightly annoyed that he was making her choose between him and Beatrice, which was unfair. "It's just a stupid party."

"Just a stupid party?" Kai repeated, his voicing turning icy. "Who cares about the party? We barely see each other. That's why I want you to come out. But you know what? Forget it. Stay home. I'll see you whenever."

"Kai, wait—"

But he'd already hung up. Zyla pulled her phone away from her ear and stared at it in shock. Kai hadn't hung up on her before. He'd hadn't ever been so short with her. She felt crappy, because it was her fault, and Kai was right. They hardly saw each other, and Will's party would be the perfect opportunity for them to hang out without worrying about getting caught by her parents or his aunt and uncle. But what was she supposed to do? Beatrice was in a crisis, and she didn't want to leave her or force her to go out.

I'm sorry, please don't be mad at me, she texted Kai.

She watched his response bubbles pop up and then disappear.

Ughhh. First their argument over Camille calling Ms. Claremont, and now this. She hated that they were arguing, and that it might become consistent. It reminded her too much of when her parents had been married.

She stepped into the hallway and bumped right into her mom.

"She's pretty upset," her mom said, meaning Beatrice. "It sucks to see her that way, huh?"

Zyla nodded. She was still kind of giving her mom the silent treatment. Her mom's response to this was to keep talking anyway.

She suddenly hugged Zyla. "I'm gonna miss you once you're at college."

"You'll be okay," Zyla said, trying to squirm away.

"I know I'll be okay. I'll just miss you." She kissed Zyla on the forehead and continued down the hall into her room. It was a Saturday night, and her mom didn't have a date, which was unusual.

Her mom and dad were continuing to coparent only, nothing more. Tonight, her dad was across town moving things into his new apartment. Having both of her parents around would finally be the new normal, and months from now she'd be away in Paris or LA. Ironic.

When Zyla returned to her room, Beatrice was applying makeup in Zyla's mirror.

"I don't want to sit around crying anymore," Beatrice declared.

"Okay," Zyla said, coming to stand behind Beatrice. She looked at her best friend's red-eyed reflection in the mirror. "What do you want to do? Order food? Watch a movie?"

"No, no. None of that." Beatrice brushed her long extensions over her shoulder and turned around to face Zyla. "I want to forget about Hugo and this whole shitty thing. I want to *go out*."

———

Kai stood alone in Will's backyard and stuffed his hands in his pants pockets. He didn't care that it was chilly as hell, and that he'd forgotten his coat inside, only wearing the Morehouse sweater Zyla had knitted him for Christmas. He didn't care that Will's St. Patrick's Day party was usually the best party of the year and his friends were inside having fun without him. He found that he didn't care about a lot of things lately.

What he cared about was Zyla. And the fact that they barely got to see each other anymore, and soon they would *never* see each other, and that clearly didn't bother her as much as it bothered him.

He'd been an asshole to hang up on her earlier, but how could she say this was just a stupid party, when the party was obviously not even the point? He wanted her to come and see *him*. Fuck the party.

Maybe he was tripping, but he could feel her pulling away

already. She wasn't even in Paris yet, and he was already being dissed. After she'd promised that she was in this with him. Before, he'd had such a clear plan for how they could work things out next year. He'd tried so hard to get everything right—or as best as he could, if you wanted to rephrase that to please Dr. Rueben—and it didn't fucking matter. And on top of that, Aunt Brenda and Uncle Steve might not approve of their relationship again. Everything was messed up now, and he had no idea how to fix it.

He held his face in his hands and massaged his temples. He was getting a headache agonizing over this shit. After a while, he checked the time on his phone. He'd been standing alone out here for a good twenty minutes.

"Kai?"

He spun around and came face to face with Camille.

"I don't have shit to say to you," he said, turning away.

"I know you hate me," she said. "You have every right to."

She walked around until she was standing right in front of Kai. She wore a red peacoat and a matching red knit hat. Kai's blood boiled looking at her.

"Camille, I'm serious. I don't want to talk to you. Leave me alone."

Camille bit her lip and cringed. "I just want to say I'm sorry for getting you and Zyla into trouble. It was so stupid to call Ms. Claremont on you, and it was terrible and shitty of me."

Kai shook his head. Camille was too confusing to be real. "Why, Camille? Why did you do it? Do you get some weird thrill out of ruining my life? What the fuck is the issue? Please tell me, because I don't get it."

"I like you, okay?!" she suddenly shouted. "And I was jealous. I've been jealous for months. I even broke up with Rob because of it. I thought we'd get back together last summer, and we didn't because you got with Zyla. You moved on so easily!"

Kai was silent as he stared at Camille. Finally, he said, "The reason that you and I didn't get back together isn't because I started going out with Zyla. We didn't get back together because I realized I couldn't be with someone who would try to get me *fired from my job*. Or who treated me like shit throughout our whole relationship. We weren't meant to be, Camille."

"I know," she said quietly, looking down. "That much is clear now."

Kai sighed. He was so tired all of a sudden. Honestly, he'd been tired since Valentine's Day. When would this drama in his life end? He just wanted to be happy.

"I'm so sorry," Camille said, tearing up. "I don't want to have beef with you or Zyla anymore. Can you please forgive me?"

Seeing Camille cry shook him up. It was just like that time he'd seen her crying after the fight she had with her sister last year before they broke up. Camille made *other people* cry. Seeing her be so vulnerable threw him.

Then he started to feel sorry for her as she stood there sobbing. Damn. She must feel bad if she was acting this way. He didn't want to be an asshole and just stare at her. He patted her shoulder.

"I forgive you, okay?" he mumbled. "Just . . . stop crying."

"Thank you." Camille sniffled and wrapped her arms around Kai, surprising him. "I promise I won't get in between you and Zyla again."

Kai held his arms at his sides, unsure if he should hug her back. The truth was that he wanted to believe Camille wasn't a completely terrible person. Because then what did that say about him? He was the one who'd dated her.

Camille is manipulative. Why is that so obvious to everyone in the entire world except for you?

Maybe Zyla had been wrong about Camille. Zyla's track record wasn't great. She'd been wrong about a lot of things. Love. Whether or not the two of them would ever get together. And she'd been wrong about being in this with him. Because where was she tonight? Nowhere to be found.

Kai gave Camille a friendly pat on the back. "It's cool. We're cool."

Camille leaned away, then stood on tiptoe and kissed Kai on the cheek. She lingered there for a second, and slowly, almost imperceptibly, she moved her mouth closer to his. Oblivious, Kai took too long to realize what she was doing. He didn't catch on until Camille's lips brushed against his.

By the time he pushed her away, it was too late.

Jamal was the first person Zyla saw when she stepped inside of Will's house. He was sitting on the steps wearing a bright green T-shirt. He leaped up at the sight of her and Beatrice.

"Matthews! I thought you weren't gonna make it," he said, grinning.

"I'm here after all." Zyla glanced past him. "Where's Kai?"

"Out back, I think." He turned to Beatrice and bowed. "Your highness, you've decided to grace us with your presence once again. May I provide you with a beverage from the kitchen?"

Zyla tensed, waiting for Beatrice to wail on Jamal for the "your highness" nickname, especially since she was in such a bad mood. To Zyla's surprise, Beatrice only frowned and rolled her eyes.

"Ugh," she said. "A wine cooler will do."

Jamal was quick to escort Beatrice to the kitchen. Zyla was relieved that Beatrice was momentarily occupied so that she could go and find Kai.

Will's house was packed with people dressed in green. Jamal said that Kai was out back, so Zyla maneuvered her way to the back door. She spotted Alanna sitting with Whit and Ash over in the corner of the living room. Alanna waved excitedly, but Zyla smiled and kept going. She'd say hi to Alanna after she talked to Kai. She needed to apologize for saying it was just a party. And she'd have to explain to him that she couldn't abandon Beatrice. She wasn't the kind of girl who ditched her friends for a boyfriend. But still, she didn't have to get so snippy with him on the phone. They'd already been through so much together. Surely they'd be able to get over this too.

She opened the back door, and the porch light wasn't on, so it was hard to see if anyone was outside at all. Then she spotted two people standing in the center of the yard. There was a girl who wore a bright red jacket and a matching hat pulled low on her forehead. And the other person was tall, with their back to Zyla. It looked like they were kissing. Yikes. She definitely didn't want to crash anyone's moment.

Zyla backed away, then froze. Because she realized the tall person was a boy. And she recognized the colors of the maroon-and-white sweater he wore. She'd knitted that pattern herself.

Time slowed as Zyla walked down the porch steps toward the couple. They weren't faceless anymore. The girl was Camille Vaughn. And the boy was . . . no. *No.* She didn't want to believe what she was seeing. It wasn't true. It *couldn't* be true.

"Kai?" she whispered.

Kai pushed Camille away and whipped around to face Zyla. He froze, eyes wide.

"Zyla," he said, coming toward her. "It's not what it looks like."

Zyla stared at him, shocked into silence. She looked at Camille, who had the sense to back far, far away from them.

Kai was coming toward her, reaching for her. His mouth was moving, but Zyla couldn't understand a thing he said. She barely heard him at all. A loud static took over her brain, but Aunt Ida's speech, the one Zyla knew by heart, cut through.

Men are good for nothing, and they'll run you into the ground ... Steer clear of men like that. You hear?

Zyla evaded Kai's arms and walked back toward the house. She wanted to run, but she wouldn't embarrass herself any further. She'd already done enough of that. She'd been an *absolute idiot* not to listen to Aunt Ida. She'd been an *idiot* not to listen to her dad, who'd told her to be careful around Kai. And she'd been an *idiot* not to listen to herself. She'd known better than to delude herself into falling in love. She was a huge freaking idiot!

"Zyla, please," Kai begged, grabbing onto her arm. "I didn't kiss her, I swear! She kissed me!"

Zyla shook him off. She knew what she'd seen. Kai had been *hugging* and *kissing* Camille. *Camille,* of all freaking people! How? How did she continue to worm her way between the two of them?

Suddenly, the answer was crystal clear.

"You like her, don't you?" Zyla said. "You've probably liked her this whole time and were *playing* me. Get off me! Don't ever touch me again!"

"What?!" Kai jerked away. "Are you fucking kidding me? I don't like her. I *love* you! Zyla, stop, let me explain!"

Zyla forced her way back into Will's house, bumping into the people who were standing by the back door. She didn't care. She needed to get the heck out of here right now. Where was Beatrice? The static in her brain was getting louder. She couldn't focus. She felt like she might puke at any second. Kai had been kissing Camille. *Her* Kai. The one she'd lost her virginity to. She was such an idiot!

Kai pulled on her coat sleeve, and she stumbled back into his arms.

"Zyla, please, listen to me for one second," he said, a desperate edge to his voice.

Zyla struggled to get away from him. "You were cheating on me!"

"No, I wasn't!"

The entire party was staring at them now. They were a spectacle.

Kai let go of Zyla, and she turned to face him.

"I can't believe you would do this to me," she said. When the heck had she started to cry? Her cheeks were covered in tears. "I can't *believe* you."

"I didn't do anything! You won't even let me explain!" Kai gripped either side of his head, like he was literally trying to keep from losing his mind.

"I don't care what you have to say! I know what I saw!"

Zyla turned, blindly searching for the quickest way out the front door. In her stumbling haste, she knocked into the living room china cabinet, and a handful of small dishes went crashing to the floor. Suddenly, the music cut off and Will came running into the living room.

"What the hell happened?" he asked, his pale cheeks turning red.

"I'm so sorry," Zyla said. Could this night get any worse? "I'll pay you back for them, I promise."

Will ignored her and opened the china cabinet, crouching down to look at the broken plates. He glanced behind him at Zyla and Kai and at the partygoers-turned-spectators.

"Everybody out!" he shouted. "Party's over!"

Everyone around Zyla groaned. "Thanks, Bonnie and Clyde," someone yelled. A few others echoed the line, but Zyla didn't care. She'd pay Will back for the dishes, and she wouldn't come near any of these Cedar High people ever again.

Especially not Kai, who followed her outside to the front yard. Zyla turned in a circle, trying to remember where Beatrice had parked her car. She had to get away *now*. Now, now, now.

"Zyla, please, I love you, just listen to me," Kai said. *"Please."*

He was crying too, which surprised her. But it was an act. She knew what she'd seen, and she couldn't get rid of that image of Kai's arms wrapped around Camille, their lips pressed together.

Zyla squeezed her eyes closed and covered her face with her hands. "This is over, Kai. Please leave me alone."

"What? No, Zyla, don't do this."

She felt Kai stand in front of her. Before he could say anything, Beatrice came to her rescue.

"Zy! Come on!" she called, storming toward them. She pushed herself in front of Kai and grabbed Zyla's hand, leading her away.

"Zyla, wait," Kai begged, but Beatrice held up her hand, stopping him.

"You're such a fuckboy, Kai," she hissed.

Kai froze, his mouth fell open. *"What?"*

"You heard me," Beatrice said. "Fuck. Boy."

Kai didn't try to stop Beatrice and Zyla as they hurried to her car.

"I'm so stupid," Zyla cried as Beatrice pulled off. How did she get here? Crying in the passenger seat over love gone wrong like her mom. Someone she'd promised herself she'd never be like.

"You are not stupid," Beatrice said fiercely, gripping Zyla's hand. "He is stupid. And you are better off without him."

What Beatrice said was true. But the truth really freaking hurt.

Now Zyla finally knew how her mom had felt throughout the years, but unlike her mom, she wouldn't go through this again and again. She'd learn her lesson. Because this pain was deep, and she wouldn't wish it on anyone.

Not even Kai, the boy she loved. And now hated.

———

Kai stood in Will's front yard, reeling. Beatrice called him a fuckboy. A fuckboy. He'd been called a lot of things in his life, but not that. Is that what Zyla thought of him now?

He'd made a mistake. But not even, really! Camille had kissed *him*. If he was at fault for anything, it was believing that Camille hadn't been manipulating him.

He'd pushed Camille away as soon as he realized what was happening. Zyla just showed up at the wrong time. And he didn't love Camille. How could Zyla say some bullshit like that?

He had to fix this. He *had* to. He wiped away the wetness on his cheeks. When had he started to pace? He looked up, and his classmates were staring at him as he walked back and forth across the front lawn.

"Bro," Jamal said, jogging over, handing Kai his coat. "What the hell happened?"

"I need to go to Zyla's house," Kai said, patting his pockets for his keys.

"I'm coming with you," Jamal said. "Just in case."

Just in case what? Kai didn't have time to ask.

He had to make things right with Zyla.

When he pulled up to her house, Jamal stayed in the car. Kai stood on the sidewalk in front of Zyla's window, just like he'd done months ago back in July. He called her name, but she wouldn't come to the window. Then he FaceTimed her, and she didn't answer. He contemplated going up and ringing her doorbell, her parents and Aunt Ida be damned, but then Zyla opened the door and came outside.

She rushed toward him, and he felt such relief, he didn't notice the blank look on her face. Except her eyes. They were hard and furious.

"Kai," she said quietly, stonily. "I don't want to see you anymore. Don't come back here."

Then she left, just as quickly as she'd come.

Kai stared in silence as she slammed her front door.

It was over. It was really fucking over.

He felt hollow as he somehow made his way back to his car. He climbed into the driver's seat and fumbled with his keys.

Eventually he gave up and dropped his forehead against the steering wheel.

"Fuck," he mumbled. *"Fuck."*

"You're good, bro," Jamal said quietly. "You're better off without her."

Kai barely heard a word his best friend said. But he managed to start his car and drive off.

I don't want to see you anymore. Don't come back here.

The gloom descended over him before he even got home.

Chapter Thirty-Three

Zyla sat on her bedroom floor surrounded by a sea of fabric. She'd promised Jade that she'd make her a custom vest for her mathletes competition, but Zyla hadn't been able to work on it in almost two weeks. Every time she pulled out her material and sat at her sewing machine or opened her sketchbook, her mind went blank. She didn't know where to start.

Maybe that was the worst thing about the breakup. It sapped her creativity.

She lay down on her side, resting her head on a pile of acid-wash denim. *You're going to be in Paris soon. You'll be out of here. Away from everyone and on your own like you've wanted.* Months ago, those words brought her comfort, but now it only made her sadder. She couldn't believe she'd considered choosing LA over Paris because of Kai. How stupid. She closed her eyes and let the rain cloud of sorrow hover above her. She pulled her hoodie over her head and cried into her fabric.

This was so exhausting. How did people do this? How did her mom constantly battle this feeling of heartbreak?

She needed a nap, the comfort of her sheets and pillows. Eventually, she got up and crawled into bed, because that's when she did her best thinking about Kai. About how much she hated him. Or rather, how much she wished she could hate him. About how stupid she felt for letting him trick her into falling in love.

She replayed the scene of him kissing Camille over and over in her mind, because she was conducting an analysis. She wished she had shot-by-shot stills. For example, here was where Camille leaned in. Here was where Kai inched forward to meet her. Here was the *exact* moment where their lips met. She figured once she'd finally thought this through enough times, she'd be one step closer to getting over him.

The worst thing about Kai breaking her heart was that she missed him. Missing him was worse than wishing she could hate him. The feeling of being without him permeated her. In her most desperate moments, she'd turn to her window and look outside, willing him to appear beneath the streetlight. Because she missed him so much, and if he apologized to her, she'd forgive him.

But in the moments when she regained some semblance of strength, she imagined living a life like her mother had when her parents were married. Or like Aunt Ida with her husband. She imagined being skeptical of Kai every day moving forward, not being able to trust him. Watching over her shoulder for Camille Vaughn, or a new girl, because there would always be a new girl. She wouldn't do that to herself.

Plus, Kai had stopped trying to contact her. At first, he called and texted multiple times a day, begging Zyla to talk to him, but she didn't respond. Eventually, he must have taken the hint, because by the end of the first week, the calls and texts stopped. She wondered if he'd already gotten back together with Camille. If so, she hoped they were miserable.

She snuggled against her tearstained pillow, ready for another nap. Then someone opened her bedroom door. And she heard the sound of Beatrice's distraught groan.

"Okay, so this is what we're not gonna do," Beatrice said, walking closer.

Zyla sighed and pulled the covers over her head. She heard the sound of Beatrice kicking off her shoes. Then she felt a dip in her bed under Beatrice's weight. Beatrice crawled up to Zyla and lay beside her. Zyla relaxed, inhaling the citrusy smell of Beatrice's perfume.

"Zyla, my dear sister-friend," she said, "it's been two weeks. You must rejoin the population."

"I don't want to."

"I know you don't," Beatrice said, sympathetic. "But you have to try. Otherwise, you'll sit here like this forever."

Zyla turned her face into her pillow. "Not forever. Just a little longer."

"No, come on. Get dressed. It's Saturday. Let's go to the mall."

Beatrice hopped up and pulled the covers away. Zyla almost hissed like a vampire exposed to sunlight. She just wanted to lie here and be sad, but here was Beatrice, forcing her to go outside and be a functioning human being.

What a terribly good friend.

Beatrice waited patiently while Zyla showered. And she didn't say anything when Zyla dragged her feet and poked through the clothes in her closet. Then Zyla went to grab a pair of sweatpants, and Beatrice practically shrieked.

"Sweatpants? *You?* Absolutely. Not. Absolutely not!" Beatrice hip checked Zyla out of the way. Zyla shrugged, uninterested in arguing. She sat on her bed and watched as Beatrice looked through her clothes, mumbling that Zyla was a *fashion major* and she'd better not forget it. She picked out a cream turtleneck and black boot-cut jeans. "Put this on."

Zyla groaned. "Okay, fine."

The mall was busy because it was a Saturday in suburbia. Zyla followed Beatrice from store to store, hoping and praying she didn't run into Kai. Or anyone from Cedar High for that matter. No doubt they were still talking about her and Kai's big *public* breakup. How embarrassing. Even some girls at St. Catherine's had heard about it. The only person that Zyla wouldn't mind running into was Alanna, who'd texted Zyla the day after and asked if she was okay.

As Zyla followed Beatrice out of a sunglasses shop to the food court, Beatrice chatted about whether or not she needed a new bag specifically for spring, and Zyla watched her best friend with intense scrutiny. Beatrice had been with Hugo for *four* years. He'd been the love of her life, and when they'd broken up, it had been such a huge blow.

Yet here Beatrice was, determined to survive, putting one

foot in front of the other, intent on buying a purse simply because the seasons were changing. Zyla envied her best friend and her ability to adapt. Because Zyla felt like a zombie. Not even one of the zombies that ran fast and dodged bullets. She was the type of zombie that moved in slow motion, dragging one broken leg, their jaw detached and hanging open. She wasn't even the kind of zombie that wanted to eat your brains. She had no energy. No will. God, when was this going to end?

At the food court, she and Beatrice shared a huge order of chicken tenders and cheese fries. Midway through the meal, Beatrice reached out and squeezed Zyla's hand.

"Zy, you'll get over him," she said. At this point, Kai was no longer mentioned by name. "I promise."

Zyla sighed, hoping Beatrice was right. "Are you over Hugo?"

"No," Beatrice said softly. "But he's proved that he was unworthy of me, so I'm not going to waste any more time wishing we were together."

"You're so strong. I wish I were more like you."

"You *are* strong," Beatrice said. "Don't ever let anyone tell you different."

Zyla started tearing up. "I legit don't know what I'd do without you."

"I don't know what I'd do without you either. But get it together, girl. Don't cry on our cheese fries."

Zyla snorted and Beatrice laughed.

Who needed romantic love when you had friendship?

Later, after dinner, Zyla washed dishes at the kitchen sink. Behind her, Aunt Ida chewed sunflower seeds while Bartholomew sat obediently at her feet. Her dad and Jade were in the living room watching television. Zyla's mom stood beside her, drying dishes with a rag.

"I noticed you've been spending a lot of time in your room lately," her mom said. "Even more so than usual."

Zyla shrugged and continued to focus on scrubbing the lasagna pan.

"And you seem sadder, babe. Want to talk about it?"

"No," Zyla said.

"Is it Kai?"

Zyla froze and glanced at her mom. Her mom stared back.

"I know the way things ended between the two of you on Valentine's Day was messy," her mom said. "I'm sure you miss him."

Zyla bit her lip. She'd cried enough already today. She wanted to tell her mom the truth. She and Kai hadn't broken up on Valentine's Day like they thought. They'd broken up two weeks ago because he'd cheated on her with his ex.

"I do miss him," she heard herself say.

Her mom nodded. "Well, maybe he can come by for a visit one day soon. We might have overreacted about the planetarium situation. I'll talk to your dad about it."

Zyla shook her head and turned away. "We're not getting back together."

"You never know. You might be able to work it out."

Zyla held back a sob. "There's more to the story. I don't want to talk about it, but it isn't something we can work out."

Zyla's mom was quiet for a few minutes, watching her. Then she rubbed Zyla's back in soft, slow circles.

"I just don't want to feel sad anymore," Zyla whispered, leaning into her mom.

"You gotta take it day by day, babe," her mom said. "It'll get easier."

Take it day by day. It became a mantra that Zyla lived by. Some days were easier than others. She'd be in class and go an entire period without thinking of Kai. And then there was a day when she accidentally stumbled across Brandon's Instagram account and saw Kai tagged in a picture taken after a track meet. He was standing beside Brandon, smiling. Like he was perfectly fine. Zyla had sat in the bathroom stall and cried for half the period.

But gradually, it got easier, like her mom said. She stopped feeling like a zombie. She started sketching. She finished Jade's vest. She ate dinner with her family and paid attention to what they were saying. She laughed with Beatrice, and they stayed up watching movies on Friday nights. She went to work at the salon and didn't mix up any appointments or overcharge customers. She finished her paperwork for Parsons Paris, applied for loans to cover the rest of her tuition, and created mood boards for how she wanted to decorate her dorm room.

She still thought about Kai. She thought about how it had

felt to hold his hand and the sound of his voice, muffled and deep, as they'd talked on the phone at night. She thought of his handsome face, and how lucky she'd felt to call him hers. But thoughts of him stung less and less every time.

She realized she was pretty close to normal when she came home from school one day and found Bartholomew snoring on her bed.

"Get down and get out of my room," she ordered.

Bartholomew picked up his little head and glared at her before rolling over, showing her his back. She laughed so hard then that she had to bend over to catch her breath.

I'm happy, she thought. *Wow.*

And then on an absolutely ordinary Tuesday morning in April, while she and Beatrice pretended to pay attention in morning mass, Zyla's phone vibrated in her pocket. She pulled it out and saw a message from a number she'd deleted but knew by heart. The text was three simple words.

I miss you.

Chapter Thirty-Four

Track practice. Kai's favorite time of day. The only part of the day that didn't monumentally suck.

Today the sprinters were practicing handoffs for relay races. Kai was the anchor on the four-by-four team. He stood on the track, bouncing from foot to foot, watching as Jamal ran one hundred meters and handed the baton to Devon Smith, and Devon passed it to Brandon. As Brandon got closer, Kai started to run, holding his arm behind him. He felt Brandon slap the baton into his palm, and Kai took off. The baton slipped through his fingers, and their coach blew his whistle.

"You're supposed to pass me the baton, not throw it, B, damn," Kai snapped.

Brandon held up his hands, backing away. "Bro, *you* dropped it. How am I supposed to fix what you're doing wrong?"

"I've been running track since I was damn near in diapers. You think I don't know how to grab a baton?"

"Okay, okay, that's enough," Coach Peters said, coming to stand in between Kai and Brandon. "We're gonna run it again. *Both* of you pay attention to what you're doing. We can't mess up in our meet against Hopkins Prep next week."

Brandon mumbled something about how it wasn't his fault and walked back to his place at the three-hundred-meter mark. Kai sighed and looked across the field at Jamal, who was slightly shaking his head.

Kai knew damn well it was his fault that he'd dropped that baton. Didn't have shit to do with Brandon. Everyone else knew it too. He'd been doing the most since he and Zyla broke up. Two weeks ago. Two weeks of being cranky, irritable, and mad. Just really damn mad.

Jamal started them off, and this time when Brandon passed the baton, Kai held on to it and kept going. Once he was in motion, his mind blessedly went blank. He didn't think about a thing but putting one foot in front of the other. Make it to the finish line. Breathe in and out. Pump your arms.

When he went soaring over the finish line, Coach Peters called their overall time, which had been better than yesterday, and he ended practice early. The rest of the boys cheered. Kai, however, was sad. Practice was over early, so what the hell was he supposed to do now? Go home and stare at the ceiling and think about how much he missed Zyla? How she'd dumped him over a stupid-ass misunderstanding? How he'd utterly failed at their relationship? How he felt lonely and empty?

He wanted to keep running. Because running was pushing. He'd been trying his best to push through everything that happened with Zyla the same way he pushed himself to beat yesterday's time.

In the locker room, everybody was hype as hell about

practice being over. It was a Friday night, and they began planning an impromptu party at Brandon's. Kai stayed out of the conversation as he took off his cleats. He closed his locker and shouldered his duffel bag.

"Yo, you coming out with us?" Jamal asked.

"Nah, I think I'm gonna chill at home tonight."

Jamal eyed him. He lowered his voice so that the rest of the boys wouldn't overhear. "Look, I know what you're going through is ass. But you gotta try to get over her and get out of your room. It's senior year. We graduate in three months. You don't wanna look back on this time and regret missing out on everything." He paused. "You wanna talk about it?"

"No," Kai mumbled, looking down. "I'll try to come out next weekend, though. Okay?"

Jamal nodded and smiled sadly. "Cool. Hit me up if you change your mind about tonight."

"I will," Kai said, knowing he wouldn't.

He went home and camped out in the living room, flicking through channels. He couldn't settle on anything to watch. Nothing interested him. Everything was boring. Not that he could tell, really. He was having a hard time focusing lately. He'd be in class, staring pointedly at his teacher in the front of the room, and it was like they were speaking another language. He couldn't focus, so he spent more time at the nurse's office. Skipping class this way should have bothered him, but . . . it didn't. Because weirdly, he focused better in the nurse's office. He'd lie back on a cot and count the water stains in the ceiling.

He'd mentally catalog the items he'd need to take with him to Morehouse. He played a guessing game about why other students were visiting the nurse. A girl who walked in with her head held back? Nosebleed. A boy hobbling in wearing a T-shirt and mesh shorts? Twisted his ankle in PE. Kai got pretty good at that game.

Kai told Nurse Iverson that he got intense headaches due to senior-year stress. Whether she believed him or not, she didn't say. He was quiet and offered up his cot when a student came in that needed it.

He was grateful that Nurse Iverson didn't kick him out. Because the time he spent in her office was time spent not thinking about Zyla. About how much she probably hated him.

His other favorite game to play was Pretend Camille Vaughn Doesn't Fucking Exist. During student council meetings he didn't even look at her. Everyone at school either thought Kai did cheat on Zyla with Camille or that Camille had tried to break them up. Alanna fell into the latter group, which is why she sat beside Kai during every student council meeting and fielded each of Camille's questions. To Camille's credit, she didn't try to talk to Kai either.

Sometimes Kai replayed the events from that night and wondered how he could have handled the situation better. Obviously, he could have ignored Camille when she'd apologized. He shouldn't have let her hug him. He shouldn't have been so damn nice.

He would be mean to Camille a million times over if it meant he'd no longer have the memory of Zyla staring him dead in the face and saying she never wanted to see him again.

"Are you going to choose a channel?" Aunt Brenda asked.

Kai jumped. When the hell had Aunt Brenda even sat down? "Um, here, you pick." He passed the remote.

Aunt Brenda landed on the Lifetime channel. A movie was playing about a wedding planner who had become obsessed with a groom and kidnapped the bride. The plot was so ridiculous, it actually held Kai's attention. During a commercial break, Aunt Brenda turned to him and he immediately tensed.

"How's everything going?" she asked.

It was a simple question, yet Kai fumbled for an answer. He didn't want her to think anything was wrong. He forced himself to smile and felt the action stretch the skin around his mouth.

"Good," he said.

"Yeah?" She paused, staring at him. Assessing him. "Things don't seem good, honey. Are you okay?"

"Yes." He sat up straighter. Would a person who wasn't doing well have good posture? "I got an A-minus on my calculus test today."

"I'm glad to hear that. You're such a good student. But you can be a good student and also be unhappy."

Kai gave her a sidelong glance. "I'm fine, Aunt Brenda. I really am."

"I know that things haven't been easy since you and Zyla broke up on Valentine's Day, but—"

Kai suddenly shot to his feet. "I, uh, think I'm gonna go for a run."

Aunt Brenda blinked. "Didn't you just leave track practice?"

"Yeah, but we have an important meet next week," Kai said, already leaving the living room. "Gotta stay in shape."

"Okay . . ."

He was out the door before she could say anything else.

He had a new running route. One that didn't go by Zyla's house. Or the park where they used to meet. He ran around Cedar, past the school, by Jamal's house, over to the other end of town, where Brandon and Chris lived. He ran by the movie theater and saw some of his classmates enjoying a Friday night like normal people.

He hated running without music. He'd been in such a hurry to leave, he'd left without his phone and headphones. Now, he was stuck with his thoughts. He ran and ran and ran until the balls of his feet started to get sore. He didn't stop then. And he didn't stop when his breathing turned jagged. Finally, his right leg cramped up so bad, he fell down on the sidewalk.

"Fuck," he hissed, holding his leg, waiting for the spasm to end. This shit *hurt*.

Everything hurt.

Out of nowhere, he started crying. He'd fucked everything up. He'd lost his aunt and uncle's trust. He missed Zyla something wild, but she wanted nothing to do with him. How did *this* not work out? He loved her so much, too much. More than he'd ever loved anyone. Wasn't that the only thing that mattered? He thought his love for her should be able to fix this, but it couldn't, and he had no idea what to do. He'd never been this heartbroken in his life. Would he ever be able to move on? It felt impossible.

He held his leg to his body and rocked back and forth. He wished his life were different. He wished his parents were alive, that he could talk to them about this. But they'd left him behind, and now Zyla had left him too.

How long had he been sitting on the sidewalk, crying and holding his cramped leg? He had no idea. Eventually, a nice old lady pulled over and lowered her window and asked if he was okay.

"Yes," Kai said, wiping his eyes. He stood, putting his weight on his good leg. "I'm just on my way home."

The old woman smiled at him. "Chin up, young man. You've got so much life left to live!" Then she waved and pulled away.

Kai blinked and stared at her old Cadillac. Was that a message from the divine? Maybe; maybe not. He decided to see it that way regardless.

He had a lot of life to live, even in the wake of heartbreak.

He kept trying to focus in class and continued to show up to track practice. As the weeks went by, his teachers stopped speaking gibberish, and he spent less time in Nurse Iverson's office. New drama became the topic of the rumor mill, and he and Zyla were forgotten. He continued to ignore Camille. He tried to participate in real conversations with his aunt and uncle, to continue making them think that he was fine, just fine. Hoping that he'd regain their trust.

He tried not to stalk Zyla's Instagram page, which was public because she posted pictures of her sketches and clothes. He tried not to stare at the Morehouse sweater and think it was low-key cursed because he'd been wearing it on the day that everything went to shit. And, most importantly, he stayed in therapy.

"I went four periods straight without thinking about Zyla today," he told Dr. Rueben.

Dr. Rueben nodded and adjusted his thermostat. April was turning out to be a warm month.

"That's progress," Dr. Rueben said.

Kai slid down in his chair. "Yeah . . . I miss her, though. I wish I could talk to her."

"Is there something you specifically want to say?"

Kai stared at the floor and thought for a while. Without Zyla, he felt incomplete, like a shell of a person. But he couldn't admit that, not even to Dr. Rueben.

"I would say that I didn't cheat on her, and that I was sorry I put myself in a position where she thought I did," he said. "That we broke up for a stupid reason, and I love her." He sighed. "Mostly, I would say that I'm sorry. I've been thinking about texting her, but I don't know. It's not like she responded to any of my other texts. She doesn't want to talk to me."

"Okay," Dr. Rueben said. "There's nothing wrong with apologizing to someone when you feel as though you're in the wrong. But say you send Zyla this message and she doesn't respond. What then?"

"I guess . . . I guess I would feel okay knowing that I'd told her how I felt? And that she knew the truth? Even if she doesn't speak to me again, I want her to know that I would never have disrespected her that way."

"There's nothing wrong with trying to clear the air so that both of you can move forward. It's possible that Zyla is hurt, and apologizing to her might be helpful to both of you. But if you apologize and she doesn't respond, you should be respectful of her choice."

"Yeah," Kai said, nodding. "Yeah, you're right."

He took Dr. Rueben's words as a green light. Dr. Rueben thought it was a good idea for him to text Zyla, so he would. *Finally*, some hope.

All night, he thought about what he'd say to her, how he'd say it. The next morning, while grabbing books from his locker, he pulled out his phone and started to compose the text before he could talk himself out of it. He drafted it over and over, and finally the bell rang. He'd be late to homeroom if he spent any more time in the hallway. Finally, he texted what was in his heart. I miss you.

It wasn't the apology he'd talked about with Dr. Rueben, but hopefully it was a conversation starter.

Hours later, when track practice started and Zyla hadn't responded, Kai knew he'd gone the wrong route. He wanted to slap himself in the forehead. He should have just said he was sorry! Why did he have to get soft and say he missed her? That was probably the last thing she wanted to hear. He could follow up with an *I'm sorry* text, but he didn't want to blow up her phone. She most likely didn't want to receive one text from him, let alone two.

He agonized over it as he stretched, did drills, and ran lap after lap.

After practice, he was so drained, mentally and physically, he felt like he could fall asleep right there on the locker room bench. He opened his locker and was shocked to see he had a missed alert on his phone. His text finally had a response.

Hi.

He spent a long time staring at that one word. It was simple, but it was enough.

Then he thought about how he might see her on Senior Day.

Reggie, the ski lift worker, has never seen so many people gathered in his boss's office. And there for sure has never been so much *yelling*.

"Where is my daughter? How have you not found her yet?" Leanne, Zyla's mom, shouts at Reggie's boss and the teachers. "This is ridiculous!"

"It's been almost two hours," Brenda, Kai's aunt says. Her voice is quieter, but she's just as angry.

Reggie's boss looks like he might have a heart attack. "The park rangers and police are in the mountains looking for your children as we speak. We are *so* sorry. Something like this has *never* happened at Roaring Rapids."

"This is that boy's fault," Aunt Ida says. "Zyla wouldn't have done something like this on her own. Just like how that mess on Valentine's Day was his little surprise."

"How dare you blame Kai for this?" Kai's uncle Steve says, aghast. "Kai has goals! He wouldn't simply throw them away! He stopped dating Zyla months ago and has hardly been in trouble since. This is her doing."

"My baby girl doesn't have shit to do with this," Terrance,

Zyla's dad, says. For once, he and Aunt Ida have something to agree on.

"Please, stop with the arguing," Brenda begs, glancing at Zyla's younger sister, Jade, who is standing quietly and obediently behind Terrance and Leanne. "We need to focus on the children." She looks at Reggie. "Tell us again what you remember from when they got on the ski lift."

Every angry and exasperated face turns to Reggie. He gulps. How did he get into this? He is supposed to be having a makeup dinner with Nicole right now. Then he remembers exactly how he became so deeply involved. He is the one who originally said the students ran away. He was trying to save his own neck, and look what he's done. Then again, the students haven't come back yet. Even if they didn't run away, something fishy has happened.

"I . . . um. Their behavior was kind of shifty, like they were being sneaky," Reggie says. "They said they were going to walk down the trail instead of taking the ski lift back, and nobody ever does that. And they had bags and stuff, so I kind of put two and two together . . ."

One of the teachers, Mrs. Deaver, speaks up. "The students told us that Kai got into a bit of a scuffle with a student from Hopkins Prep, and that's the last any of them saw him or Zyla."

"The students," Leanne repeats. "Where's Beatrice? That's Zyla's best friend. Have you talked to her?"

"And what about Jamal?" Brenda adds. "What did he say?"

Beatrice and Jamal didn't expect to be pulled back into the Roaring Rapids main office to retell their version of events, but here they are.

"One of my boys told me that Kai got into a fight with a Hopkins Prep kid because he saw Zyla kissing one of them and he got mad," Jamal says.

"And that is *untrue*," Beatrice says, angrily rolling her eyes. "Zyla wouldn't have kissed any of the boys we were talking to. What I know is that when I returned from the bathroom, Kai was there and one of the boys had a bloody nose. Then Kai ran off and Zyla went after him."

"And I tried calling Kai," Jamal says. "But his phone must be off."

"Zyla isn't answering either," Beatrice adds. "They probably lost service."

Zyla and Kai's families look disappointed that Beatrice and Jamal don't have more information to offer.

Beatrice internally begins to freak out. She doesn't think Zyla and Kai have run away, but *where are they*? She can't believe this situation has become so nuts. She thinks back to her interactions with Zyla since she and Kai broke up. Is there anything that she's missed? A clue that would help them understand what's happening? Then she remembers.

"A couple weeks ago, I saw Kai's name pop up on Zyla's phone," she says. "It was really random. He'd texted her out of nowhere, and Zyla ignored it. I think it was the first time he'd bothered to get in touch her with after they broke up on St. Patty's Day."

"St. Patty's Day?" Leanne repeats, confused. She looks at Terrance, then at Steve and Brenda. "I thought they broke up on Valentine's Day?"

Beatrice bites her lip, realizing her mistake. You see, she forgot the adults didn't know Zyla and Kai had been sneaking around behind their backs.

"Um," Beatrice says. "Um . . . well—"

"No, you've got it wrong," Jamal suddenly says, frowning at Beatrice. "Zyla texted Kai a couple weeks ago, and *he* ignored *her* text. We already talked about this. Zyla is the one who wanted to get back together, not Kai."

Beatrice glares at him. It's quite unfortunate that he had to start with her. For the first time since the day they'd met, they'd gotten along a bit today. Almost as if they'd called a truce. No such luck.

"No, *Kai* wanted to get back together," she says.

"No, it was Zyla."

"It was Kai!"

Their bickering is cut short when one of the teachers escorts them out of the office and instructs them to go back to the lounge with the other students.

Beatrice turns in a huff and storms off down the hallway. Jamal runs to catch up with her. Kai and Zyla's disappearing act has shaken him. And it's also made him think a lot about what he'd do for the person he likes. *Really* likes. He realizes there is a reason that things haven't worked out with Alanna. As beautiful and sweet and smart as she is, she is not the right one for Jamal. He watches Beatrice walk away from him and decides he's tired of playing games.

"Beatrice, wait," he says, grabbing her hand.

She whirls to face him, ready to rant, but something in Jamal's expression gives her pause. She thinks about how he comforted her today. She didn't know there was a side to Jamal that wasn't annoying. However, she has to admit that even when they argue, she secretly enjoys it.

"What?" she says, though it lacks her usual heat.

"I'm sorry for the way I've been acting today," he says. "How I've always acted. I've just been salty. Really salty because I like you, and I've liked you since the day we met, and I have a shitty way of showing it, and I'm probably not good enough for you, but—"

He stops short when Beatrice suddenly kisses him. When she pulls away, he stares at her wide-eyed. The look on her face is just as surprised.

"I guess I like you too," she says.

Their sweet moment is interrupted when the office door swings open and Kai's aunt and uncle and Zyla's parents storm by them, carrying flashlights, followed by Reggie the ski lift worker and his boss. Zyla's mom tells Jade to stay behind with Beatrice.

"What's going on?' Beatrice asks, hugging Jade to her side.

"We're going up on that damn mountain to find my baby," Leanne says. She pauses to give both Jade and Beatrice a kiss on the forehead. "I'll be back soon, babe," she says to Jade. "Stay safe, Miss Beatrice."

With one hand, Beatrice reaches for Jade, and with the other, she reaches for Jamal. They watch the adults leave the building and head for the ski lift, where allegedly Zyla and Kai's disappearing act began.

Part Three:

A Boy and a Girl

Chapter Thirty-Five

To truly answer everyone's questions about Zyla and Kai's location, it would make the most sense for Zyla and Kai to tell it themselves. Let's begin with Kai . . .

The minute that Kai steps off the bus at Roaring Rapids, he has one thing on his mind, and one thing only. Today, after weeks and weeks, he is finally going to spend time with Zyla.

It took work for them to reach this point. Hella work. After he texted Zyla that he missed her, and she responded with hi, he apologized, like he talked about with Dr. Rueben. He told Zyla that he didn't cheat, and he was sorry that he ever put himself in a situation where she could think something like that. He explained how Camille tricked him and how he was silly enough to fall for it. He wouldn't make the same mistake again. He hoped Zyla believed him and that she'd forgive him. He was very deliberate not to mention anything about getting back together. He wouldn't force the issue. He loved her something wild. However, if anything, he hoped they could at least be friends.

Zyla took days to respond to his apology text. And Kai wondered if she'd deleted it and decided to move on. A week went by, and she finally texted back, **I want to believe you. I hope what you told me is the truth.**

It is, he quickly responded. **I swear.**

From there, their text exchanges were tentative. There were no paragraph-long messages or pictures of shoes, like before. Most of the time, Kai was the one who initiated conversations about simple things, like graduation or even the damn weather. He didn't care that he was the one who texted her first. He only cared that she texted him back each time. He kept thinking about how they'd see each other at Senior Day, but he didn't want to bring it up.

Turned out he didn't have to, because Zyla ended up texting him first for once (!) and asked if he planned on going to Senior Day. When he said yes, *she'd* said, **Ok. Maybe I'll say hi.**

Kai had sent back the smiley face emoji and left it at that because he didn't want to seem too eager, when in reality, he was hype as fuck.

Soon, Zyla started texting him first more often. And then came the day when she sent him a picture of the bright yellow Keds she was wearing. **Found these at Genie's.** And Kai knew. He just knew he had a chance to get her back. He took the risk and asked if she wanted to hang out on Senior Day, and he hoped to God he wasn't shooting himself in the foot. To his surprise, and absolute fucking delight, Zyla said yes.

So when Kai steps off the bus, he is excited to finally see Zyla. Today is about regaining her trust. He'll see where things go from there.

After he and Jamal leave their things in their room, Jamal begs off and runs after Alanna and her crew. Kai is relieved. He hasn't told Jamal that he and Zyla have been talking. He doesn't want to say anything to anyone until he knows for sure that he and Zyla will work it out. A couple weeks ago during lunch, Zyla texted him, and Jamal saw the message pop up on Kai's phone. When Jamal shot Kai a surprised look, Kai shrugged and made it seem like he didn't care, like he wasn't going to respond. He doesn't like keeping secrets from Jamal, but Jamal has been so worried about him after the breakup. Kai doesn't want him to worry any further.

Zyla said she wanted to spend the first couple hours of the day with Beatrice, and Kai was quick to tell her that was totally okay. He learned his lesson on St. Patrick's Day, when he stupidly tried to make her choose between him and Beatrice.

So, he walks around the park for a few hours alone. He gets on some waterslides. At one point, he runs into Brandon, Chris, and Will, and they get in the wave pool together, then grab food. After he eats, he goes back to the lodge and changes out of his swim trunks into denim shorts and a black T-shirt. Apparently it gets chilly at night in the mountains, so he grabs his jacket and stuffs it in his backpack, along with a bottle of water. Wait, two bottles, just in case Zyla gets thirsty too.

Then he waits in the lounge, where he and Zyla planned to meet at 2:30 p.m. Zyla texts and says she's with Beatrice and will be late. Kai tells her it's fine, because it is. He plays games on his phone, browses social media. He drinks his entire bottle of water. He dozes off and wakes up. He looks at his phone, and it's almost 4:00 p.m. He has two missed texts from Zyla.

Still with Beatrice.

I'll be there soon.

Both were sent more than twenty minutes ago.

Kai suddenly realizes that the chances of Zyla leaving Beatrice on Senior Day to hang out with him are very slim. He's not sure why he didn't realize this before. He feels stupid for placing so much hope in today.

Well, he's not gonna sit around feeling sorry for himself. He'd rather *walk* and feel sorry for himself.

He slowly makes his way back toward the water park. He should get some ice cream. That's what Aunt Brenda eats when she wants to feel better. He turns the corner with the food court in his sights, and that's when he sees her. Zyla. But she's not with Beatrice. She's with three Hopkins Prep boys, and one is up in her face, smiling and laughing like a hyena.

Beatrice is legit nowhere to be found. It's just Zyla and these randoms. What's going on? Has she been lying to him all day?

Before he even knows what he's doing, Kai is walking toward them. Zyla spots him and her eyes widen.

"Hey," he says once he reaches her, completely ignoring the Hopkins Prep boys. "Zyla, can I talk to you for a second, please?"

"Um." Zyla's eyes dart past his shoulder.

Why the hell does she look so nervous? All he did was ask if they could talk.

"I think it's kind of obvious she doesn't want to talk to you," the hyena Hopkins Prep boy says.

Kai stares at the boy and his sunburnt cheeks and forehead. Then he looks at the other two Hopkins Prep boys who are grilling him. "Yeah, I wasn't talking to you." He turns back to Zyla. "Can we talk, please?"

Zyla moves toward Kai, and on instinct, he moves toward her as well. That's when hyena boy stiff-arms him.

"Hey!" Zyla says. "Don't push him! What's wrong with you?"

"He's bothering you!" hyena boy shouts. He shoves Kai away, and whatever self-control Kai had disappears. In one quick motion, he arches his fist and hits the hyena boy right in the nose.

Blood runs from the boy's nostrils immediately. "What the fuck, dude?" he shouts.

One of the other Hopkins Prep boys swings at Kai in retaliation, but Kai is quick to dodge him. A crowd is beginning to gather around them now. The other boy runs off, yelling that he's going to get park security, and Zyla bursts into tears.

And that's when Kai realizes he really, *really* fucked up.

"Zyla, I'm sorry. I'm so sorry." He reaches out to hug her but pulls back because he isn't even sure if she wants his hugs anymore.

"None of this was supposed to happen today," she says through tears. "It was supposed to be a *good* day."

Yeah, maybe a good day if he didn't come and ruin it. If he

hadn't let his anger get the best of him. When would he learn?

"Kai, what are you doing here?" Beatrice suddenly appears, pushing herself between him and Zyla. "Go away! Don't you get it? She doesn't want to talk to you!"

Zyla shakes her head wordlessly, wiping her eyes. Kai isn't sure if she's saying no to him or Beatrice's words. Either way, he figures Zyla is probably better off without him. That breaks his damn heart, but it's the truth.

"I'm sorry," he says to her one more time.

And then he runs away back toward the lodge, because he doesn't want to get caught by park security. They'll find him eventually, but he should give himself a few minutes to think about what he'll say. Better yet, forget about what he'll say to them. How will he possibly explain to Aunt Brenda and Uncle Steve that he punched someone and made their nose bleed? Regardless of how annoying that kid was, Kai feels shitty for hurting him. He deserves whatever trouble is about to come his way.

Then he hears Zyla call his name.

———

Zyla is almost out of breath, chasing after Kai. Why does he run so freaking fast? Thankfully, he stops when she calls him. He pauses and waits for her to catch up, watching her apprehensively.

"Why did you run away?" she asks, winded.

"I didn't want to get caught by park security."

"I would have vouched for you. Seth started it."

Kai snorts and shakes his head. "So his name's Seth?" He

starts to back away. "Zyla, listen, I don't want to ruin your day any further. I'll be okay, I—"

"Ruin my day?" she repeats, confused, stepping closer as he retreats. "What are you talking about?"

"Back there, you said today was supposed to be a good day, and then I came along and fucked it up."

"No, that's not what I meant."

"I thought you said you'd be with Beatrice," he suddenly says.

"I *was* with Beatrice," Zyla says, frustrated. He doesn't even know how overwhelming this day has been for her. For starters, she's been a nervous wreck at the idea that she and Kai were finally going to see each other. It's not like she could talk to Beatrice about it, because Beatrice has no idea that Zyla and Kai have reconnected. Now that she and Beatrice are both single for the first time during their entire friendship, Beatrice is determined for them to make the most of it, and Zyla doesn't have the heart to burst her bubble.

The whole single-best-friends summer is why she and Beatrice have spent most of the day with those Hopkins Prep boys. Zyla is supposed to be Beatrice's wing woman. Seth and Beatrice have kind of been hooking up for the past couple weeks, but today, whenever Beatrice would walk away, Seth would flirt with Zyla. He's a complete pig. That's exactly what was happening when Kai showed up. Kai was clearly upset that Zyla was an hour and a half late to meet him. It was incredibly rude. She'd been trying to get away. She'd even gone and changed out of her bathing suit into her normal clothes and stuffed her denim jacket into her mini backpack in case she got cold. Then when Beatrice asked why she changed, Zyla was afraid to tell her the truth, and she couldn't come up with a good enough excuse to leave. She doesn't want to tell Beatrice the truth about her and Kai until she knows for sure what's happening between them.

Not that it matters now. With the way Zyla ran after Kai, Beatrice has to know something is up. The way she told Beatrice not to get involved. She managed to leave right as park security was arriving. God. Too much drama.

"I'm sorry I made you cry," Kai says. "Everything is so messed up."

Zyla shakes her head. "You didn't make me cry. I was feeling overwhelmed. When I said I was supposed to have a good day, I meant because I was supposed to see you."

"Oh," Kai says, staring at her.

Wow. She's really missed looking at his face. Being in his presence. Does he feel the same? Should she care?

She believed Kai when he said that Camille kissed him and that he didn't kiss her back. But she doesn't like that it happened. She's here because she wanted to see him, despite everything.

"I wish we could go somewhere to talk in private," Kai says quietly. "Far away from everyone."

"Me too." Zyla looks around; they are halfway between the lodge and the water park. Soon, park security will come to get Kai, and possibly her too, to explain what happened only a few minutes ago. Where can they go to avoid everyone?

Zyla bites her lip and looks around, hoping an answer will come to her. Then she looks up and finds it.

"Let's go on the ski lift," she says. "We can ride it to the top of the mountain and walk down the trail."

That way they'll be completely alone, and no one can eavesdrop on their conversation while they're literally up in the air. And plus, park security and the teachers won't think to look for them on the ski lift.

"Okay," Kai says.

The boy working the ski lift looks like he's Zyla's age. If he weren't wearing a T-shirt that said Roaring Rapids, she would have assumed he went to Cedar High. He seems annoyed that she and Kai have requested to ride the ski lift so late in the day. He barely listens when Kai asks if it's okay for them to walk down the trail, and he rushes them onto the lift, busy texting on his phone.

As they rise higher and higher away from Roaring Rapids and everyone below, Zyla lets out a relieved breath. Then she feels a few raindrops hit her cheeks. She turns to look at Kai, and he is watching her. She simply stares back. Now that they are alone, she doesn't know what to say. The esophagus butterflies and the insecurity dragon are vying for her attention. She inhales his familiar cinnamon scent and glances at his pulse, beating quickly at the base of his throat. She wants to touch him there, to remind herself that he is flesh and bone and he once told her he loved her. She wants to hear him say it. But she also doesn't. She believes that Kai didn't cheat on her. The situation with Camille might not have been what she thought it was, but her heartbreak terrified her. She doesn't want to go through that again.

Yet she also loves him. She has no idea what to do.

"I miss you," Kai suddenly says. "So much. You have no idea."

Zyla's heartbeat speeds up. The esophagus butterflies are winning. They cheer in triumph.

"I do have an idea," she says. "I miss you too."

It is hard to tell who moves toward whom first, but then there is no space between them. Kai is cupping her cheek with his hand, and she places her hand on his shoulder. They kiss passionately, frantically, as they rise higher in the sky.

She missed Kai, and she missed *this*. The closeness.

Kai pulls away first and stares deep, deep into her eyes. She feels hypnotized.

"I want to get back together," he blurts.

Zyla's emotions come screeching to a halt.

"Back together?" She moves away, putting as much space between them as possible. His words have manifested her fear, a physical thing that sits in the middle of them. "Jesus, Kai. This is the first time we're seeing each other since we broke up."

"So what?" he says. "I love you. And if you love me, we should be together."

She shakes her head so quickly, it's a wonder she doesn't make herself dizzy. "We can't get back together right now."

"Why not, Zyla?" Kai rakes his hands over his head. "Why?"

"Because of what happened with Camille!"

"I thought you said you believed me?!"

"I do, but it still happened!"

Kai stares at her, wide-eyed, his nostrils moving as he breathes in and out. He puts his face in his hands for a second and then sits up.

"I don't know why I didn't realize it before," he mumbles.

"Realize what?" Zyla asks.

He looks at her. "You were just waiting for me to fuck up like your dad did with your mom so you could say that love was bullshit. What was it that you said to me last summer? That you don't want to end up like your parents, so you avoid dating altogether? You were projecting shit from their relationship onto us." He shakes his head. "We didn't have a chance."

Zyla literally gasps, she is so taken aback. "You have *no idea* what you're talking about. I never compared us to my parents, or you to my dad! You wanted everything about us to be perfect. You wanted a perfect love that would always be with you to fit your idea of the perfect relationship. It didn't matter if it was me or not. It could have been anyone who fit the role. You were living in la-la land, and when things stopped being perfect, you got caught up with Camille so easily and ruined everything we had."

"That's not true," Kai says fiercely. It's raining harder now, and he angrily wipes his face. "I didn't want us to be perfect, and it doesn't matter anyway. We couldn't be perfect because you'll be in *Paris* next year."

"That's right!" Zyla says, hopping off the lift as soon as their toes skim the ground.

The rain is coming down *hard*. She lifts her backpack over her head and walks toward the trail. How could she stupidly think today would be different, that they'd somehow work through their problems? She's so angry, she can't even remember how their conversation went left.

She is angry, but she is also so, so disappointed. Because this morning when she woke up, she'd been filled with hope. That maybe she and Kai would have a good day. That things wouldn't fall apart so quickly.

Kai is steaming as he watches Zyla storm away. How dare she say those things about him? That he wanted their relationship to be perfect? It's not even true! He only wanted them to be together and to be happy. Is that too much to ask? Apparently so.

He pulls his hoodie out of his bag and throws it on because this rain is doing the most. He takes a few quiet moments to breathe and cool off, and then gets concerned, because Zyla is out on the trail in the rain alone.

He calls her name, jogging to catch up with her, and at this point, he can barely see a few feet in front of him. His hoodie is soaked and sticking to his body. Zyla is shivering as she continues to walk, not looking at Kai, her yellow Keds completely covered in mud. Kai glances down at his J's and winces. They're ruined forever.

Thunder crackles overhead, followed by lightning, and this

shit is starting to get real scary. The rain is coming down in cold sheets, but they continue trying to find the trail, not speaking to each other.

Zyla abruptly stops. "We're lost," she shouts over the rain. She is drenched everywhere, including her glasses.

"If we keep walking downhill, we should find the resort," Kai shouts back.

"I can't see anything! Neither can you!"

"I can see perfectly fine!" But he can't see a damn thing. He's only saying that because he's mad and wants to disagree with her. He starts walking, only to slip and fall right on his butt.

Thunder crackles, louder this time. The wind slaps rain hard against his face. Zyla comes up behind him and holds out her hand.

"Are you okay?" she shouts.

Kai nods, but he's not okay. Neither of them are. How long have they been stuck up on this damn mountain? He has no idea. He accepts Zyla's hand, and they wobble, trying to right themselves.

Kai spots a fallen tree trunk, and they run to it, fighting the rain. The trunk is sheltered under the branches of another tree, so while they sit, they are being rained on, but it's nowhere near as bad as being out in the open.

Zyla wraps her arms around her torso. She looks so vulnerable and small, sitting there beside him. Kai's frustration seeps from his body. How did they get here? Literally. Figuratively.

They sit in silence for a long time, sheltering from the storm.

"I don't know why we can't seem to work it out," Zyla suddenly says, looking up at him with sad eyes.

"I don't know either," Kai says, feeling his heart beginning to break all over again. He loves Zyla so much. He'd thought that love was the simplest part of a relationship. Why did everything have to be so hard for them? "I wish things were different."

Zyla nods silently and shivers. She leans into Kai, and he wraps his arms around her. It is getting darker and the storm shows no signs up letting up, the wind blowing harder and faster. They'll have to wait it out before they can try to find the trail. Kai hopes there are no bears in these woods. He might be able to take on a Hopkins Prep kid, but not a grizzly.

He and Zyla huddle for warmth. Together, and not together. In love, and out of sync.

He doesn't know how much time passes as they sit and hold each other. Eventually, he sees flashlights and hears people shouting their names. He leans forward, peering through the rain. Wait a minute . . . is that Uncle Steve?

"Mom?" Zyla stands up and shields her face from the flashlights. Is she tripping? She swore she heard her mom call her name. But why would her mom be here?

"Zy, baby!" Her mom rushes toward her, breaking away from the crowd of people. Her dad, Aunt Ida, Kai's aunt and uncle, park rangers. *What the heck?*

Her mom squeezes her close, and soon her dad and Aunt Ida

are doing the same. Kai's aunt and uncle are hugging him too. The park rangers are radioing people to alert that Zyla and Kai have been found. *Found?* They weren't lost.

Their families are talking at the same time, rejoicing, then scolding. How dare they try to run away together, and in the middle of a storm? They gave everyone heart attacks!

"Run away?" Zyla says.

"Run away?" Kai says.

"We didn't run away!" Zyla says.

"We were just . . . talking," Kai finishes.

Whether or not they are believed doesn't matter. They are soon rushed into separate park ranger Jeeps.

Zyla looks over her shoulder, trying to catch Kai's eye. He climbs into the designated Jeep with his aunt and uncle, but he twists around and looks out the back window at Zyla. He lifts his hand and smiles sadly. Zyla lifts her hand too and holds it there until they pull off.

As they arrive back at the lodge, Zyla can't believe what she sees. Everyone: students, teachers, staff, standing at the windows, staring at them. She spots Beatrice and Jamal and Jade. Alanna and her crew, and Camille and Tyesha and Darius. Watching them like they're in a fish bowl.

Zyla wonders what the real Bonnie and Clyde would do right now. She almost wants to laugh when she realizes the answer. Surely they wouldn't let people pull them apart.

The real Bonnie and Clyde would have actually run away together.

Chapter Thirty-Six

When Zyla and her family got home, everyone was too tired and relieved that Zyla was safe to reprimand her. However, the next morning, the minute Zyla steps foot into the kitchen, her mom and Aunt Ida start in on her.

"Why would you and Kai ever try to run away like that?" her mom asks. Her thick auburn hair is pulled back in a high ponytail. It is a Saturday morning, and she is fresh faced, ready for a day of work at the salon. "Do you know what kind of stress you put us through?"

"And what have I told you about those boys?" Aunt Ida says, wagging her finger. "I thought *you'd* at least listen to me, Zyla."

Zyla looks at the women in her family, who have taught her so much, either from lectures or by example.

"I didn't run away," she says calmly. And then she explains yesterday's events. The argument between Kai and the Hopkins Prep boy, how they went on the ski lift for privacy and got stuck in the storm.

After she is done explaining, her mom is less rattled. Aunt Ida isn't quite satisfied.

"I told you about those boys," she repeats. Sighing, she leaves the kitchen and takes her usual spot in her La-Z-Boy.

At the same time, her dad walks through the front door and is obviously unaware that he's missed Zyla's first scolding, because he walks right up to her, shaking his head.

"Do you have any idea how afraid we were yesterday?" he asks, searching Zyla's face. "Do you?"

Zyla is momentarily stunned. She hasn't seen her dad afraid for her. Never in her entire life. Not even when she was a toddler and he taught her the sink-then-swim method by throwing her into a pool.

"Dad, I—" she starts, then falters.

"Dad, what?" he prompts, staring at her closely. He glances at her mom, who is standing by the sink, watching their exchange.

"I'm sorry," Zyla finally says. "I'm sorry that I scared you."

Her dad falls silent. Maybe he's surprised that for once, Zyla didn't argue with him.

"It's okay. I'm just glad you're safe."

And then, to Zyla's surprise, he hugs her. Tentatively, she hugs him back. They stay that way, embraced and unsure, until Jade walks into the kitchen and says, "I'm ready, Daddy."

Zyla pulls away and looks between her dad and sister. "Ready for what?"

"I promised Jade I'd take her to breakfast this morning." He pauses. "Do you want to come too?"

Normally, Zyla's answer would have a been a swift no. There

is a shift happening here. Her dad is extending an olive branch. Would it hurt so bad to try to accept it?

"I'll go," she says.

At the diner, her dad listens attentively to Jade's tales of middle school woes, and he knows the names of her teachers and friends. He knows that Jade likes scrambled eggs, not eggs over easy, and he reminds her that the bacon at the diner is pork, not turkey. He has already saved enough money to send her to another math camp this summer.

A tiny part of Zyla is jealous, watching her dad and sister interact. They have a bond that he and Zyla weren't able to have, because when Zyla was in middle school, she was too busy moving from city to city with her mom, and her dad was only present via the occasional phone call.

At least Jade has him now.

And Zyla has him too. Later than she wanted. He is here regardless, though, and he has stayed. Albeit months before she herself is leaving, but it is better than nothing.

When they order sundaes for dessert—something their mom wouldn't allow at breakfast—their dad gives Jade some coins to change the song on the jukebox. Jade excitedly darts from the table, and then it is Zyla and her dad, sitting across from each other. Silent. Wanting to connect, but not sure how.

"I've been meaning to apologize to you for a long time about what I said to you on New Year's Eve," her dad says.

Zyla stares at him, shocked. She assumed they both decided

to not bring up that conversation for the sake of peace.

"I shouldn't have told you to be careful around Kai," he continues. "Kai wasn't the issue. I was thinking about myself and how wild I was at seventeen when I got with your mom. I didn't want the two of you to end up like we did."

Zyla absorbs her dad's words, his apology. On the mountain, Kai accused her of projecting the terrible things about her parents' marriage onto their relationship. Her mother's unhappiness, and her continued unhappiness with her later partners. Her dad's dishonesty and infidelity. Had Kai been right?

Maybe. Maybe that's why Zyla got so upset when her dad told her to be careful around Kai, claiming that he and Kai might be more alike than she thought. And maybe that is why she kept comparing herself to his exes, wondering if Kai wanted to be somewhere else. Her dad was only voicing her own fears that she'd buried deep down. So deep that it later manifested itself as her insecurity dragon, finding fault with Kai when fault wasn't evident.

Wow.

"I'm so afraid to get it wrong," she says quietly. She looks up. "Love, I mean."

"Shit, me too. I got it wrong when it came to your mom. *Way* wrong."

"So you do love my mom? Or at least you did when you were together?"

Her dad leans forward and lowers his voice, like they are the only two people in the entire diner. "I love your mom more than anyone on this planet, except you and your sister, of course. You know what I mean."

Zyla shakes her head, desperately trying to understand. "Then why didn't you try to work things out with her?"

"Because I was young and stupid. I loved her, but I didn't love myself, if that makes any sense. I've looked for your mom in every woman I've dated since we split. That's no excuse for the way I've treated the other women I've been with, though. There's only one Leanne. But it's too late now. Your mom has smartened up. Friend zoned me, as she should. I don't deserve her, but I'm grateful to have her friendship."

"I used to wonder how different my life would have been if you'd stayed," Zyla says. "I don't know. I guess everything happens for a reason. Or maybe the two of you weren't meant to be together."

What about her and Kai, though? Are they meant to be together?

"Look, I'm not the philosophical type," her dad says. "I don't know about fate and who is meant for who. What I know is that people make mistakes. Sometimes you can come back from them, sometimes you can't. If I ever meet someone who I love as much as I love your mom, I'll try my best not to screw it up. Here is my real bit of advice to you: When you love someone, tell them. Treat them right while you have the chance. Don't be like me."

Zyla doesn't have a chance to respond before Jade returns, having finally picked "This Will Be (An Everlasting Love)," by Natalie Cole, on the jukebox.

"Good choice, baby," their dad says, and Jade beams.

In the car ride home, Zyla mulls over her dad's words. And not just his words, but the way he said them. The fact that the two of them sat down and talked about something real for the first time in . . . well, forever.

When they pull up outside, Jade gives their dad a goodbye kiss on the cheek and heads up the driveway. Zyla stalls in the passenger seat. Her dad is due to start his shift at work soon, but he doesn't rush her from his car.

"Dad," she says, turning to him. "I want you to know that I'm glad you're here, and I hope we can do this more often before I leave for college."

Her dad smiles. "Me too. I'd love that, Zy Zy."

As she gets out of the car, she doesn't even cringe at the nickname. "See you later, Dad."

Hours later, she finds her mom in the bedroom.

Her mom is sitting in front of her mirror, curling her long hair. Jill Scott is playing lowly from her phone's speakers. Zyla leans in the doorway, watching her mom. The woman who represents the epitome of beauty.

Her mom is not perfect. *Zyla* is not perfect. But even when they literally had nothing, they had each other.

"Hey, babe," her mom says, turning and catching sight of Zyla in the doorway. "What's up. Wanna talk?"

"Yeah," Zyla says, walking over and sitting pretzel style in the middle of her mom's bed. "Not if you're busy. Date tonight?"

"Yes, with Denise. I like her a lot. Feels different this time around." She turns off her curling iron and comes to sit beside Zyla. "I'm never too busy for you. I don't want you to ever feel that way."

"Okay," Zyla says. She pauses, wondering how to say what she wants to say. "I want to apologize to you."

Her mom blinks. "Apologize for what?"

"I think—well, wait. I *know* I've been really hard on you because I was so mad at how you'd let yourself get hurt in your relationships. I didn't understand you. But that's just it. I didn't understand love at all, or how it makes you feel and what it makes you do. So, I'm sorry."

"Okay," her mom says softly, smoothing a few thick curls away from Zyla's face.

"Watching you made me want to avoid love because I didn't want to end up heartbroken like you after your breakups," Zyla continues. "And I didn't want to end up with someone who would treat me poorly or lie like Dad. I was trying to keep myself safe. Then I met Kai, and he threatened that safety, and I let my fear of what he *could* do get in the way, and I think that kind of messed everything up between us."

Her mom is quiet for a long time, thinking.

"Well, babe, we can't let fear dictate our lives, especially when it comes to love," she says. "Not loving out of fear is the cowardly way to go. It's a brave thing to open your heart to someone, especially after you've been hurt before. You take that risk and extend your heart because you want to take that chance, and if it doesn't work out, you learn what you do and don't want in your next relationship. Love is a learning curve."

Zyla nods, listening, absorbing every word.

"You can't compare your relationship with Kai to the relationship I had with your dad or any of *my* relationships. They're just that. Mine. You have to focus on what your love with Kai *is*, not what you think it should be. A relationship is only between the people who are in it. At some point, you have to shut out the noise from everyone else. Does that make sense?"

"Yes," Zyla says quietly. "Love is important, and it makes our lives special, even sometimes when we have to go through heartbreak, it's worth it for the right person. I only wish I knew what to do about me and Kai. Everything felt so final when we were on the mountain, like our differences weren't something we could overcome."

They both have their problems. Zyla with her fears of love, and Kai with his need to strive for perfection. After everything they've been through, shouldn't that be something they can talk about and work out? If not, were the last eight months for nothing? It doesn't seem right that they found such a connection with each other, just to sever it.

Kai has repeatedly extended himself to Zyla. *He* asked her to be his girlfriend, and *he* said *I love you* first. He was the one who reached out and reconnected after they broke up. Maybe this time she has to be the one to extend herself.

"I want to make this right," she says. "But I don't know how."

Her mom sits quietly for a few seconds, which feels like hours to Zyla.

Finally, her mom says, "You love him, don't you?"

"Yes," Zyla says. "I do."

"Then you know his love language better than anyone. You'll think of something."

Kai's love language? Well . . . he is humble and smart. He can be over-the-top romantic, a little chauvinistic even, yet subtle at the same time. But above everything he wears his heart on his sleeve. Something a cynic like Zyla didn't initially understand but now appreciates. She wouldn't have fallen in love with him otherwise.

And just like that, the idea comes to her.

"Thank you," she says, throwing her arms around her mom. "I want you to know I think you're a good mom, and I'm really, really going to miss you once I go to Paris."

Her mom smiles, teary-eyed. "Thanks, babe. I'm going to miss you too."

Zyla kisses her mom on the cheek, wishing her well on her date and secretly hoping that Denise might be the one.

She rushes to her room and closes the door; she has a plan to execute.

Chapter Thirty-Seven

The morning after The Mountain, which is how Kai has taken to referring to the event, he receives the longest apology text in history from Camille Vaughn. He doesn't read the whole thing. He gets the gist of it: She caused hella drama and she's sorry. Really sorry, this time. Maybe he'll reply to her in a few days, maybe not. He has been thinking about Camille's role in his and Zyla's break up, and while Camille was the catalyst, for sure, there were deeper underlying issues that he and Zyla didn't address.

Funny to think that at this time last year, he, Camille, and Jamal had just finished up interviewing for summer jobs at Sailor Joe's. And apparently Zyla was there that day too and Kai didn't even notice her. How different would things be if he'd been standing in line behind Zyla and struck up a conversation, as opposed to Camille? He'd never know. No point in spending time on the shoulda-coulda-wouldas. It was time to face the music, aka Aunt Brenda and Uncle Steve.

Last night on the way home, they told Kai they'd have a *serious discussion* in the morning about yesterday's events. Kai is tired as hell, and he's nervous. Because how can he explain himself out of this one? They had the *park rangers* looking for them on that mountain. Big yikes.

Aunt Brenda and Uncle Steve are both in the kitchen. Aunt Brenda is sipping her coffee. Uncle Steve is standing by the sink, drinking his orange juice.

Kai clears his throat and sits down across from Aunt Brenda. "Good morning," he says.

"Good morning." She glances at Uncle Steve, who assumes his spot beside her.

"Hezekiah," Uncle Steve says. His voice is stern. "I need you to explain to me how you and Zyla got on that mountain and *why* you were up there."

Kai takes a deep breath and right away begins bouncing his knee. He is trying to think of a way to spin this, to tell the truth while also making things seem not so terrible, and—wait. Isn't this what Zyla accused him of yesterday? Always trying to make everything perfect. Not just letting things exist as they are?

To make himself perfect, unable to simply exist as he is.

He stares at his aunt and uncle, the people who he has desired to please and tried to be better for. No, better than better. Perfect. It is an unrealistic goal. If he doesn't stop this now, he never will. Perfection is not what he needs to achieve.

He takes another deep breath. "I did punch a kid from another school yesterday," he admits. "And Zyla and I did take the ski lift to have privacy from everyone, but not to run away." He then tells them the whole truth about him and Zyla planning to meet up, arguing on the ski lift, and getting stuck in the woods during the storm.

"Why didn't you tell us that you and Zyla were back together?" Aunt Brenda asks.

"We're not," Kai says, sighing. "I thought maybe we had a chance at getting back together yesterday . . . but that doesn't matter now. I didn't tell you that we were talking because I knew you wouldn't approve after what happened on Valentine's Day. And since Valentine's Day, it seems like I've messed up over and over, and I hate that because one of my worst fears is letting you down."

Uncle Steve starts to speak, but Aunt Brenda pats his shoulder, stopping him. It encourages Kai to keep talking.

"I've only ever wanted your approval, to make you proud," he continues. "It's why I work so hard to get good grades, and I did everything I could to get into Morehouse like my dad and Uncle Steve, and I sign up for sports year-round to keep me busy. It's like if I try my best to be perfect and keep you happy, then you won't leave me. I don't have my parents. You're all I have . . ."

He trails off, surprised at his own ramble. At the flood of sudden emotion. His throat feels tight. He takes a few deep breaths to steady himself.

Aunt Brenda reaches out and gently lays her hand over Kai's. Her eyes are red as she stares at him unflinchingly. "We don't want you to be perfect. We love you exactly as you are, and we are proud of you, no matter what. It doesn't matter how good your grades are or how many sports you play. And it has nothing to do with whether you got into Morehouse or community college."

"We love you like you're our son because you *are*," Uncle Steve says, voice heavy with emotion. "We won't replace your parents and we don't want to. But you are a son to us, Kai. And maybe this is something every parent says about their kids, but you're the best damn child there is. You don't have to do much to make us proud. We are proud of you for simply existing."

"Oh," Kai says, staring at them. "But . . . I acted out so much when I was younger, and I feel indebted to you for taking me in and everything."

"You were a kid who lost his mom and dad. We didn't hold your behavior against you," Aunt Brenda says. "We love you. You don't need to feel indebted to us."

"And we aren't going anywhere," Uncle Steve adds. "I feel terrible knowing this is how you've felt for so long."

Kai looks down at Aunt Brenda's hand, which is covering his own. He nods, accepting what they are telling him.

"I'm afraid to go away to college and be away from you two," he admits, "to be alone without you."

Aunt Brenda smiles softly. "You won't be alone. We'll be there regardless. Even if it means we have to take a road trip down to Georgia every month."

"And then you'll get sick of seeing us," Uncle Steve adds.

Kai laughs. The weight he's unknowingly been carrying for years begins to lift. It will probably take a while for it go away completely, if ever. But it's a start.

"I'm grateful for you guys," he says.

Aunt Brenda leans forward and kisses him on the forehead. "And we're grateful for you, Kai."

They sit in silence, smiling at each other. This blended family of three.

"So," Uncle Steve says. "You and Zyla. Are you two going to try to work it out or what?"

"I don't know," Kai says. With the way they left things, are they even able to make a comeback?

Uncle Steve laughs. "After sneaking around for weeks and then getting caught in a monsoon on a mountain, you might as well try."

Well . . . maybe Uncle Steve has a point.

"You'll figure it out, honey," Aunt Brenda says. "You will."

Kai nods, although he isn't sure Aunt Brenda is right.

Two days later, Kai is back in Dr. Rueben's office for his weekly appointment. As soon as he sits down, he begins discussing The Mountain, his conversation with his aunt Brenda and uncle Steve, and Zyla, period.

When he is done talking, his mouth feels dry. When his sessions start this way, he talks too fast to keep up with his own thoughts. He feels like a wrung-out washcloth, lighter after release, but disheveled.

"It sounds to me like you struggle with the idea of abandonment," Dr. Rueben says. A succinct response to Kai's ten-minute-long intro. "Your parents. Your aunt and uncle.

Even your past girlfriends, but most particularly Zyla. Even though you noticed that there were signs from the beginning that the two of you might not work well together, you put everything into it anyway. Then when she chose to end the relationship, you felt abandoned by her."

"Huh," Kai mumbles, thinking.

You wanted a perfect love that would always be with you to fit your idea of the perfect relationship.

Zyla's words. She was right about him. It was how he'd been with each of his girlfriends. Including Zyla. However, with Zyla, being together forever had felt tangible.

"I guess I've been looking for someone who would be with me always," he says.

Dr. Rueben nods, mulling this over. "The truth is, Kai, it's not possible to find someone to be with you forever," he says. "Your aunt and uncle love you. They will show up for you whenever they can. But one day they won't be here anymore, at least not physically. That's simply the way of things."

"Okay," Kai says, conceding. He takes a deep breath, because while that's true, it's a scary thought.

"It's natural to be skeptical of people when they say that they will stick by you, especially given the way your parents died so suddenly. But it's also okay to give those people the opportunity to show you that they mean what they say. Have your aunt and uncle ever shown that they would abandon you?"

"No," Kai says quietly.

Dr. Rueben nods. "Okay. What about Zyla?"

What about Zyla? Kai remembers how lonely he felt at Will's party when he called and texted, asking her to meet him. He was trying to make it work when it felt like everything was lost, and she wasn't meeting him halfway. But she did show up that night . . .

"I got so mad at her the night we broke up," he says. "Because she'd promised me we were in this together and that she wouldn't leave me, and I was upset that she didn't want to meet me at that party. I *did* feel abandoned. But she did show up. I was just too in my feelings to see the bigger picture." He pauses and stares down at his sneakers. "Our relationship wasn't as easy anymore. We'd gotten into so much trouble on Valentine's Day, and I was frustrated that we weren't living up to the idea of what I had in my head. I wasn't thinking about how regardless of the trouble we got into, we loved each other anyway. And she showed up in the middle of the night over and over to meet in the park."

"It's possible that both you and Zyla needed some space to get perspective," Dr. Rueben says. "Maybe the breakup wasn't a completely bad thing."

"Maybe," Kai says. "It made me feel empty, though. Incomplete."

"Incomplete," Dr. Rueben repeats, nodding. "Do you feel like you need Zyla in order to complete you?"

Kai sat quietly. The truth was he *had* felt that way. But after his talk this morning with Aunt Brenda and Uncle Steve, he was starting to get a better understanding of what unconditional love looked like. And maybe the best place for him to start was with himself.

"I don't think another person can really complete me," he says. "I have to focus on being whole on my own, without looking to somebody else. Next time, I should try not to get lost in my relationship or my idea of what I want the relationship to be. It might be better that way." He pauses. "I want to get back together with Zyla. I love her. After everything that's happened, I guess I just don't know how to move forward."

"Take your time to think it through. You aren't racing against the clock, even though it may feel that way."

"Yeah," Kai says, fidgeting in his chair.

Dr. Rueben smiles. "Remember, there is no 'perfect' way to be in a relationship. How about we focus on trying our best? Remember that?"

Ah, the same advice from months ago. This time around, Kai is really going to try putting it into practice.

"Thanks, Dr. Rueben," he says, per usual wondering where he'd be without therapy.

"Just trying my best," Dr. Rueben says, then points. "See what I did there?"

Kai doesn't know what surprises him more. That Dr. Rueben made a joke or that it was actually funny.

"Yeah," Kai says, chuckling. "Good one."

Later, he goes on a run. A light, steady jog. He's not trying to get a cramp or a charley horse.

And this time, he takes his usual route that goes by Zyla's house. He slows his pace as her house comes into view. The light is on in her bedroom. What is she doing right now? The urge to call her name is strong. Then he remembers what he said to Dr. Rueben. That he should try his best to be whole before he gets back together with her. He wants to give himself the time to be sure.

He picks up his pace, passing her house. His phone vibrates on his armband. He rarely ever stops to check texts when he runs, but this time he does. And it's from Zyla.

Sailor Joe's opening day at 7pm. Meet me where we started?

Chapter Thirty-Eight

If you would have told Zyla this morning that not only would she be standing in the middle of a run-down amusement park in the exact spot where she kissed Kai Johnson for the first time, where he asked her to be his girlfriend, but that in said spot she'd draw a heart around herself in red chalk, leaving enough space in the heart for Kai Johnson to come and meet her, well . . . she would have believed you. Because this has been her plan for days, and it's exactly what she's doing right now.

"Excuse me, sir, can you not step on my heart, please?" she says.

A short, disgruntled man who is trying to wrangle three young kids turns and looks at her. "Your what?" he says, scrunching up his face.

Zyla points down at her chalk-drawn heart. "You're messing it up," she says.

The man huffs and hurries his children along, muttering something under his breath about teenagers these days.

It is opening night at Sailor Joe's, and the park is packed. Maybe Zyla's plan is wild. Taking the leap to date Kai in the first place seemed wild at the time too. Yet it had been one of her best choices, and now she is standing here in the middle of this crowded park on opening night, because right here, about twenty feet away from the Ferris wheel, is the spot where she and Kai started.

Beside her, Beatrice laughs. "Girl, this idea is something."

"Remind me why we're standing here in the middle of the park instead of getting on rides on *opening night*," Jamal says.

Beatrice swats at him. "Zyla is making a grand gesture. Something you wouldn't know about even if it smacked you in the forehead."

"What you mean? I know everything about them," he scoffs. "I got you, didn't I?"

"No, *I* got *you*."

Jamal throws his arms around Beatrice and playfully kisses her cheek. She pushes him away, laughing, and they are so stinking cute. Zyla is happy for them, but their presence is increasing her stress. Because it's 6:57 p.m., and in three minutes, Kai may or may not show up. And if he doesn't come, she doesn't want Jamal and Beatrice here to witness her absolute embarrassment.

She tugs nervously at the hem on her long-sleeve T-shirt. It's not the ideal top for the beginning of June, but she needed a long-sleeve shirt in order to sew little red hearts onto her sleeves. Maybe that's way too cheesy and on the nose. Whatever, it's symbolic for her feelings. And anyway, it's too late to turn back now. She pats her back pocket for the sketch she drew for Kai. It's 6:58 p.m. now. God, the esophagus butterflies are going so wild, she could barf.

"You two can go," she says to Beatrice and Jamal. "Go play some games. Have fun. I'm fine."

Beatrice raises an eyebrow. "You don't look fine to me. You look like a nervous wreck." She turns to Jamal. "He *is* coming tonight, right?"

Jamal bites his lip and shrugs. "I don't know. When I asked him last night, he told me he hadn't decided yet." He pauses. "I shouldn't have shared that with you. I'm breaking bro code."

Zyla gulps. Kai hasn't decided if he's coming? Should she even be surprised? He didn't respond to the text she sent a few days ago. She'd naively hoped he'd show up. That maybe he wanted to work this out as much as she did. What if he's decided it's not worth the trouble anymore?

"Seriously, I'm okay," she says, ushering Beatrice and Jamal away. "I'll text you and let you know what happens."

Beatrice is reluctant to leave, but she squeezes Zyla in a tight, quick hug.

"No matter what happens, I think you're brave," she whispers in Zyla's ear.

"Good luck, Matthews," Jamal says. "Or maybe I should start calling you Lovergirl."

He winks and Zyla smiles. She watches her best friend and her new boyfriend walk away, hand in hand. She's happy they finally admitted their feelings for each other. She just hopes she and Kai will get the same chance.

She checks the time on her phone. Seven o'clock. She stands

on tiptoe, searching the crowd. Kai is rarely late. If he is com-ing, he should be very close.

The minutes pass, and there is no sign of him.

She stares down at the red heart she's drawn around her. At the literal hearts on her sleeves.

With a sinking feeling, it becomes startlingly clear that Kai might not be coming after all.

———

Red lights. They are going to be the death of Kai.

He seems to catch every single one as he rushes to Sailor Joe's. This is partially his fault. He wouldn't be rushing if he hadn't lingered at home, wondering if going to meet Zyla was the right decision. A few days ago, when he got her text about meeting where they started, he didn't reply. He didn't want to jump in head over heels again. He thought about it and thought about it and thought about it. And as he sat on his bed, staring up at his ceiling, thinking about meeting her at Sailor Joe's, thinking about the memories they had from last summer, he thought about history, his favorite subject. What would the history books have to say about him and Zyla hundreds of years from now? That they fell in love hard but gave up? What a dis-appointing ending.

Then he thought back to their first conversation about love. How she'd told him she avoided love because of her parents. And what had Kai said to her? That love is a beautiful thing to witness when it's real. When it's right, it makes all the differ-ence in someone's life.

And hadn't being in love with Zyla done that for him?

Yes, so what the hell was he doing lying on his bed when he should be meeting her in less than twenty minutes? He hopped up with the quickness.

And, of course, now he is stuck in traffic. He watches the clock on the dash board inch closer and closer to 7:00 p.m., and he fantasizes about getting out of his car and running there, because honestly, he's fast enough for it. But he can't leave his Jeep running in the middle of the road . . . can he?

When he does get to Sailor Joe's, he parks haphazardly and runs out of the parking lot. Thank God he spends so much time running, because he zooms through the amusement park, occasionally knocking into a kid or two, but they'll be fine. Heart pumping, breathing hard, he makes it the Balloon Darts booth and . . . she's not here. There's only the Games attendant, fixing one of the balloons on the board.

What?

Where is Zyla? Kai looks down at his phone. Shit. It's 7:06.

Did she assume he wasn't coming and leave?

"Yo," Kai calls to the attendant. "Was there a girl here a few minutes ago? She's short, Black, wears red glasses. Really beautiful, like really—"

He pauses when the attendant turns around. Because it's not an attendant, it's Antonio.

"Hezekiah, your first shift isn't until next week, I thought," he says.

"It's not . . ." Kai stares at him. He's literally never seen Antonio *behind* the Balloon Darts booth before. "What are you doing?"

"Adding some balloons that will pop, I am," he says. "I thought hard about what Zyla pointed out to me last summer. Thought I'd make it a bit easier this year."

"Have you seen her?" Kai asks desperately. "Zyla, I mean. I'm looking for her."

"Yeah, she came by my office earlier, asking me if she could write on the ground with chalk. She promised me she'd clean it up, though. Check on that for me, will you?"

"Chalk?" Kai repeats. Why would she be writing on the ground with chalk? And sure, he'd go deliver Antonio's message if he knew where she was.

This right here is the spot where they started. Is there something he's missing? Is this some kind of weird riddle he doesn't understand?

He turns in a circle, looking for her, just like he did at the homecoming dance. But this time, she's nowhere to be found. He should probably call her, because that's the most logical thing to do here. He pulls out his phone, turning in one more circle, because maybe this time he'll spot her, but he doesn't see Zyla. Instead, he sees the Ferris wheel in the distance. Then it clicks.

Oh.

He starts running again.

It's 7:11 now. He's not coming.

Zyla looks down at her feet, surrounded by the loopy heart she drew. It was kind of a silly idea, wasn't it? Maybe she took the idea of living out her own rom-com too far. At least she can say she tried. But right now, that doesn't bring much comfort. Right now, she feels kind of pathetic. Maybe she'll feel better tomorrow. Or, like, in a month or something. Maybe five.

She backs out of the heart and pulls the folded piece of paper out of her pocket, taking a deep breath. She sniffles and feels her eyes begin to well up. She'd better get out of here before the crying starts. Should she find Beatrice? Call her mom to pick her up? She turns in a circle, frazzled and overwhelmed, choosing a random direction to walk in.

"Wait, I'm here! I'm here!"

She whips around, and Kai is running toward her. She freezes. The esophagus butterflies take flight, forgetting that their wings ever felt clipped. She stares at Kai as he reaches her. He bends over, hands on his knees, catching his breath.

"Don't leave," he says, winded. He stands upright. "I'm here."

She is so happy to see him, the only thing she can do is stand there and blink. He is here. He *came*.

You have a plan, remember?!

Right.

She immediately hands Kai the folded piece of paper, hoping that this wasn't only a good idea in her head.

Kai looks at her, then takes the paper. He unfolds it and stares at what he sees. Zyla steps closer to explain.

"It's you and me," she says, pointing at the sketch she drew Saturday night. She and Kai are standing side by side. In the sketch, she is wearing the same shirt she wears now, a plain white long-sleeve tee with red hearts. The only difference is that in the sketch, she's wearing a black beret, the most obviously Parisian thing she could think of. And Kai is wearing the Morehouse sweater she knitted him for Christmas. Drawn around them is a red heart. "You and me in the future, I mean. When we're both in college, and we visit each other." She takes in his serious expression, then adds, "Possibly."

Kai continues to stare quietly at the sketch, and Zyla begins to wonder why she ever thought this plan was a good idea. Then he looks up.

"Your shirt," he says, then flashes a small grin. "You're wearing your heart on your sleeve."

She nods, emboldened. "You were right," she says. "About me comparing us to my parents. I think this whole time I just wanted to be proved wrong, to know that love *does* exist, and that's what you've shown me. I didn't give us a fair chance, and I'm sorry, Kai."

He flattens the sketch and holds it to his chest. "You were right about me too. The perfection thing, wanting someone to be with me always. I'm working on it, and I don't want to be that person anymore."

Zyla takes a step forward. They aren't touching. Not yet. But they are very close.

"I *love* you, Kai," she says.

He also steps forward. Now they are nearly touching. "I love you too."

Zyla smiles. The smile is wobbly, so she bites her lip, holding back happy tears. "I'd really like it if we could start over."

Softly, he says, "I'd like that too."

She takes a deep breath and sticks out her hand.

"Hi, Kai Johnson," she says.

"Hi, Zyla Matthews."

He takes her hand in a firm shake, then pulls her closer. He leans down, pressing his forehead against hers. He closes his eyes, takes her in.

"Do you want to ride the Ferris wheel with me?" she whispers.

"Yes," Kai says. "I do."

They entwine their hands and walk toward the bright lights of the Ferris wheel. Together.

And this is where their story ~~ends~~.

Begins.